Portrait of a

LOST BOY

Portrait of a LOST BOY

Michael
BARTRAM

Alliance Publishing Press

Published by Alliance Publishing Press Ltd
This paperback edition published 2014

ISBN: 978-0-9569992-9-0
Typeset in Times New Roman
Book & Cover Design by Mark James James

Biography

Michael Bartram was born in Australia of English parents, and came to the UK at an early age. He has first-hand experience of the Middle East, having spent a year on an Israeli kibbutz and travelled widely in Turkey, Syria, Jordan and Egypt. He worked for some years as a language teacher and has a doctorate in English literature. His other passions include classical music, German and Jewish history, and the work of Carl Jung.

Michael lives in London, and is married with three children and one grandchild.

To Pamela

1898

Chapter 1

The couplings clanked. The creaking wheels slowed. The Jaffa-Jerusalem train hissed, shuddered and expired in the midday heat.

Stefan sighed. The scalp under his blond mane itched. His cravat chafed. He was sweating in his groin. Why do it? Why travel? He looked out, away from the stifling compartment with its five cramped travellers.

No relief there. The terrain was flat. It made him feel even hotter. Rock and scrub patched the red earth. Ahead, the start of the climb to Jerusalem, olive trees dotted a slope. With the air sucked dry by sun, far objects were whipped into dreamlike nearness. A white dome beside a cluster of cypresses blinded him.

Tying a bush, an Arab farmer looked up at the train. Is he wondering why it has stopped? Does he care? In this heat, does anyone care about anything?

Stefan's friend, the stocky, short-haired Hugo Fischer snored gently. Sweat had eased his glasses down his snub nose.

Stefan caught a glance of the small boy opposite. He was handsome, this little fellow, beautiful even, with huge eyes of deep blue, dark lashes and a tumble of thick, nordic hair. As a portraitist Stefan was always on the lookout. He had gazed outside partly to avoid fixing on such a perfect subject.

The boy's father and mother, also perspiring in their formal travel clothes, sat by the other window. The man's book seemed tiny in his big hands. The woman, heavily pregnant, shifted, trying to find a more comfortable position.

'Johannes.'

'*Ja Papa?*'

'It's a long journey. Wouldn't you like to read?'

'I haven't got a book.'

'We'll all die of heat,' gasped the boy's mother.

'Magda,' murmured her husband. 'Close your eyes. Lydda... Ramla... Sejed... Names to conjure with...They will pass quickly – like a dream. Then, there it will be! The greatest name of all. Jerusalem! As the Jews say, *shel zahav*, the City of Gold.'

'What do the Jews know, Anton? Camel dung, beggars by the thousand. And that's our home, God help us!'

The boy smiled shyly at Stefan, who was pretending not to listen.

'I hope they've tidied the city up for our Kaiser while we've been away,' Magda added briskly.

Anton winked at his son. 'Johannes, what faith your mother has in her Kaiser. Our crusader emperor! Our great saviour! He'll ride into Jerusalem, touch the dung with his spear. It'll sparkle and vanish. The streets will be made straight. Lutherans and Catholics will embrace each other, Jews and the Arabs will swear undying love. Germany will take her place among the nations. The Kaiser! What he can't do!'

'Don't fill his head with your ideas, Anton,' sighed Magda. 'Go back to your book. That's where all your nonsense comes from.'

Anton pulled a serious face. 'Magda! Don't say that. Books impart wisdom.'

The engine hissed. The train moved. Hugo shook himself awake and looked blearily at Stefan.

'*Wann kommt das Zug in Jerusalem an?*' he mumbled.

Stefan and Hugo talked briefly. Anton leaned across. 'You're from Dresden from your accent.'

'Y... Yes,' stuttered Stefan.

'A beautiful city,' continued Anton.

'Actually, I... I've settled in Venice,'

'Indeed...'

Silence fell. The wheels rolled on.

'And what do you do in Venice, sir?'

'I... I'm a painter.'

'Aha! And what is your name, sir? Are you famous?'

'Um... well no. I'm Stefan Lehmann... No, I'm not famous.'

'He will be,' Hugo beamed loyally.

'That's interesting! And you've come to paint our Palestine?'

Stefan waved towards the passing landscape dismissively. 'Oh no, I couldn't paint this.'

'So what do you paint?'

'Portraits mainly. Sometimes allegory – you might say dreams.'

'I see... That's very interesting.'

Anton turned to Hugo. 'And you, sir?'

Caught unprepared, Hugo pushed his glasses back up his nose and scratched his head. 'I'm... well, I'm in the agricultural business... We make equipment, up-to-date farming machines.'

'You hope to sell some here?'

'Yes... er... yes... and... well, how about you...and your family here?'

'We were originally from Württemberg,' Magda chipped in.

Hugo sat bolt upright, bleariness vanished. 'Then you must be Hoffmanites!'

'We are, yes.'

To Stefan's astonishment Hugo leaned across and grasped both the strangers by their hands. 'I'm honoured. I never expected to meet you so soon... like this. Which Templer community do you belong to?'

'We're from the Colony in Jerusalem. We're returning after a visit to another Colony near Jaffa. I am Anton Gustavus. This is my wife Magda and son Johannes.'

The introductions were complete.

'It's a long time since I met cultured men like yourselves,' said Anton, appraising the travellers' linen suits. 'You remind me of the young professors I used to see in the old streets of Tübingen. I once wanted to study myself.'

'But you came here instead,' enthused Hugo.

'It's a backwater!' exclaimed Magda.

'Magda, don't say that!'

'What you're doing is important,' urged Hugo. 'It's a beacon.'

'Beacon?' interrupted Stefan. 'I must say… I'm in the dark here. Who are Hoffmannites? What are Templers?'

'Same thing,' explained Anton. 'Herr Hoffmann was our founder.'

'Yes,' added Hugo, 'and he believed that Jesus Christ will only return for the Second Coming when the Jews have converted to Christianity. He led a movement to establish Christian colonies in the Holy Land: *ein kleines Reich Gottes,* he called it, isn't that right? A little kingdom of heaven on earth from where the work of conversion could begin.'

'Just a fantasy,' said Anton.

Hugo raised an eyebrow. 'Really? You think so?'

'Few of us hold with that any more. It was an inspiring idea at the time. Now we cultivate the land and run our communities on egalitarian principles. That's what attracted me, as well as the respect granted to things of the spirit in a materialist age.'

Inwardly Stefan winced. Socialism and religion. What a ghastly mixture. He fingered the silk of his cravat as if to affirm his belief in things beautiful and useless.

Hugo on the other hand was bubbling over. 'I've heard you Templers described as the first "Zionists". You may not be Jews but you love Palestine, you want to transform the land, you're after new social arrangements. There are parallels.'

'Compared with Jews?' expostulated Magda. 'What next?'

'Very interesting,' murmured Anton. 'Personally I'm flattered to be compared with the Hebrews.'

Magda shook her head. 'No one knows what we've been through.'

'What have you been through?' asked Stefan.

'Where to start!' she replied. 'The first settlers came here in '67.

There were twelve of them, they settled near Nazareth, and all twelve died of fever within the year. It's been hard ever since. Backbreaking. Our Colony is just by Jerusalem on the southwest side. Herr Hardegg, one of the first Templers, has broken with us and runs a hostelry in Jaffa. There are always rows with the Lutherans. You can be sure it's hard.'

'Whatever my wife says about Jerusalem,' countered Anton, 'it's booming at the moment. We've got everybody at the German Colony – teachers, builders, engineers, vintners, wagoners, butchers, everything. I myself keep busy as a carpenter and printer. The problem lies in another direction. We've become lazy in our thinking. People have lost their ideals.'

'We are good Germans,' said Magda. 'That's enough.'

Anton sniffed.

'It's true,' she insisted. 'And now His Majesty is coming. It's wonderful support for us.'

Stefan was aware that there was little entertainment for the boy.

'And Johannes, how do you spend your time in Jerusalem?'

The boy shifted. He looked first at his father then his mother for help.

'He studies,' said Magda. 'Don't you Johannes?'

'Studies…what?'

'He likes history and scripture,' said Anton. 'Tell the gentlemen who your heroes are, Johannes.'

The boy was speechless. When at last he found his voice it could hardly be heard above the noise of the train. 'I like David…Saladin... and William Tell.'

'A fine trio,' said Stefan encouragingly. 'And how old are you?'

'Eight.'

'Ah... good boy.'

'So…' said Anton. 'Do you two gentlemen have somewhere to stay?'

'I have a contact,' said Hugo, 'but not as yet…'

‘Only I’ve had a thought,’ said Anton. ‘Our friend Eva lost her husband in a building accident last year. Since then she’s put guests up in her house at the Colony. ’

‘Well, er…’ stuttered Stefan, ‘if there’s someone you can recommend…’

‘Lots of our Colonists offer accommodation. They charge a pittance compared with the pilgrim hotels. Eva is respectable… she keeps a clean home… a Berliner by the way. She came out here a few years ago to marry poor Niklaus.’

Magda frowned, leading Stefan to a moment of doubt; but Hugo was already persuaded.

‘A good idea, don’t you think, Stefan? Thank you. Then I shall be well placed.’

‘To sell the Colonists your new-fangled machines?’ enquired Anton jovially. ‘Don’t be too hopeful. There’s not much money to spare.’

‘We can but try.’

‘Good, come with us then. We shall be honoured and you will have no regrets. I promise you.’

Johannes fixed his father with a worried expression. ‘Papa, is the Kaiser king of Jerusalem?’

‘Oh no, Johannes. That’s the Turkish Sultan sitting far away in Constantinople. But Jerusalem should belong to everybody – Arab and Jew, Christians, Russians, even we Germans. However, the Kaiser is against sharing. He is aiming for Germany to be the dominant power in these parts, at least that’s what I think.’

‘That’s enough, Anton. Johannes doesn’t need all that.’

‘Very well, my dear. We’ll talk about it later, Johannes.’

Conversation flagged. The chugging train carried them up and away from the plain. Anton went back to his book. Hugo and Magda slept.

Stefan gazed at the rugged hills and fierce blue sky, waiting for the fabled city on the horizon. He was aware of the boy, who watched him at intervals and seemed to know his thoughts.

~

'Home at last,' exclaimed Anton, gazing out of the carriage window.

The sun was setting, creating a fiery panorama. The red sky, pierced with arcs of silver and gold, burned the boundless soft-curved hills. Running the length of a rocky escarpment, the city walls glowed.

'Hunks of golden gingerbread!' the big man bellowed, though everybody ignored him as they struggled with their boxes. 'Look at those walls. I could eat them!'

Rosy light flooded the compartment. The travellers' faces shone. To the east, opposite the sinking sun, dark mountains rolled into the embrace of advancing night.

They made their way out of the station. With the burden of luggage and Magda's condition, progress across the valley and up to the German Colony, a line of buildings on the horizon, was slow.

'Nothing like it in the world,' enthused Anton. 'Not even your Venice – not that I've been there. Here, this very spot, the Valley of Rephaim. Tell our friends what happened here, Johannes.'

'David killed Goliath.' The little voice was hardly more than the whispering of the breeze.

'What an event! Just here! One of these very stones, maybe. Excellent. And now look! Light's fading, but coming into view over there, to the right of the city walls, the Mount of Olives, and to the south, the Hill of Evil Counsel. Can you see the crooked tree on the top? The one from which Judas hanged himself. People say so. Personally I doubt it.'

'The twisted shape certainly reminds me of someone tortured by guilt,' said Stefan.

'That's it, it's just an association. Still I love it all. I must take you to Hezekiah's tunnel by the way. Now that's got a bit of historical truth about it. Johannes, shall we take our friends to the tunnel tomorrow?'

'He's too young,' cut in Magda. 'Besides, you may be busy tomorrow, Anton. The baby might come.'

'That's women's business.'

'I'll still want you around, not off on one of your escapades.'

'We'll see. Anyway, Hezekiah's tunnel is terrific. Not like the mythical Hanging Tree. Along with the Wailing Wall of the Herodian temple, a factual link with the distant Jewish past. Only for the discerning visitor – and the adventurous one.'

'Well, at eight years old Johannes shouldn't go anywhere near it.'

'Please, Mother! I want to go.'

Magda shook her head. 'I said no.'

'I never imagined the land quite so arid,' observed Hugo.

'Jerusalem, I can hardly believe it,' added Stefan. 'So dry, tumble-down and rubbish-strewn. So much *merde* to wade through. This whole place has a hopeless air about it.'

'You're just looking at the surface of things, my friends,' riposted Anton. 'Scratch the earth, put in seedlings, and see what you get! Cauliflowers bigger than footballs, clusters of grapes as long as your arm. If the Zionists come here and Jews start farming, they won't find it all hard-going. It's a practical possibility.'

'You think so?'

'It's the centre of the Earth as far as I'm concerned, for all of us, Jews – anybody who sees it that way. Look there! These people streaming up the valley.' Anton gestured towards a Bedouin camel train followed in the twilight by an excited group of Arab boys. 'And there, coming down the slope. Ringletted Jews, a moustachioed Ottoman – probably a government official all the way from Constantinople. Where else but Jerusalem can you see Arabs, Turks, Persians, Jews, Armenians, French nuns, Greek monks, Italian priests, not to mention European artists and scholars?'

'It's cooler back here than down at Jaffa, I'll say that,' said Magda.

'Yes, where we were staying they still sweat at 6 o'clock.'

'It's still making me puff.'

Anton touched Stefan's arm. 'What do you think?' he whispered. 'The reconciliation of Jew and Christian. A melting of differences. You're an artist, a thinking man. In sight of Zion's holy hill. Do you think it can be done?'

Stefan recoiled from such earnestness. 'It seems a tall order...' he stuttered. '... And what about the poor Mohammedans? Where would they fit in?'

'Them too of course.'

'Mm...'

Leaving barren terrain, they entered the German Colony, a settlement neater and greener than anything the travellers had so far come across in Palestine. A row of identical houses set among young Aleppo pines and cypresses were lined up on either side of a paved road. Street lights showed the newness of everything: bright stone and red roofs of the houses, freshly laid out gardens. Tags from scripture were carved in Gothic script above each doorway.

Stefan moved over to Hugo. 'What do you think of this little corner?' he murmured.

'I'm keeping an open mind,' replied Hugo.

Stefan read out the inscription from the doorway they were passing. '"Arise and shine for the light is come and the glory of the Lord is risen upon thee." God help us, Hugo, I didn't come all this way to meet a set of holy Germans living in a suburb!'

'Sh, Stefan. These people could be useful to me. We'll give it a try and it will save us money. They do mean well, our Gustavus friends.'

Anton came over. 'You see, we have it all here. The Meeting House. Up there the *Bierstube* – big drinkers this lot. And a school house of course.'

'It's dark now but there's a lot going on.'

'For his Majesty!' said Magda. 'The preparations have to be fitted in after the working day.'

Men were hammering, sawing and tying up bunting. One called to Anton. '*Grüss Gott!* How were our comrades in Jaffa?'

'Boiling to death, Dieter.'

'Worse than here?'

'It was, believe me.'

'Ah well… And who are your fine friends?'

Dieter rested his mallet as Anton introduced Hugo and Stefan.

'You seem very busy,' said Stefan politely.

'I'm doing the path here. After that, heaving beer. I will be having a drink for His Majesty since he's good enough to pay us a visit. But I'm not sure our socialist friend Anton will be joining us.'

'You don't understand, Dieter, never will. Go back to tidying your path.'

'So busy!' said Dieter's wife emerging from the front door. 'Sesame cake, date bread, the finishing touches to the white dresses we're wearing for His Majesty, I haven't stopped.'

Dieter looked shrewdly at Stefan and Hugo. 'Believe you me, we're grateful for His Majesty's visit. We're hoping he's going to do something about the Jews.'

Hugo held Dieter's gaze. 'The Jews?'

'Unfair competition, lenders charging extortionate interest. They throttle us. Mind you, the Arabs are just as bad. The neighbourhood over there is expanding. We get their smells and the call-to-prayer every hour of the day.'

'Every *four* hours, Dieter,' corrected Anton.

'It's all the same. It keeps us awake. You're on the other side. You don't hear it.'

'But we must be tolerant, mustn't we, Dieter? We're all God's children.'

Dieter picked up his mallet and strolled off.

'Your time is nearly here,' said his wife, turning to Magda.

'Another week maybe.'

'A nice present for His Majesty.'

'It's not the best timing.'

'And you're already blessed with such a pretty child!' She turned to Johannes. 'Even more gorgeous than you were last week. How's my lovely angel?'

The boy backed away.

Stefan turned to Anton and spoke in private. 'This lady is right, you know, he's a fine-looking boy. I was wondering... Do you think he's old enough to sit a few times for his portrait?'

'You want to paint Johannes?' Anton was beaming.

'I'd try to be quick. Oil on canvas. I was hoping to do a few interesting faces while I was here. Absolute innocence... fine looks... what can I say? He's the pure type of German child.'

'He's just a young boy, but if it helps the cause of art! Here, Johannes. Would you like your portrait painted by Herr Lehmann? He's a real artist.'

Johannes was now playing across the street with other children from the Colony. He looked shyly at Stefan and shrugged.

'I wouldn't like to paint your son if he wasn't willing,' said Stefan.

'Nonsense. The perfect German boy. I can't wait to see it. I'll tell him that if he'll do it, he can come with us on our expedition.'

'Expedition?'

'The tunnel we talked about. It's as dark as Hades. A thrill. Something to remember all his life. He's already said he doesn't want to miss it. He'll allow his portrait in return for an outing to Hezekiah's tunnel. I'll persuade Magda. She'll be proud to have a real portrait of our son.'

Dieter's wife went indoors, Johannes said good-bye to his friends and the party moved on.

Soon Stefan and Hugo were shown to their accommodation and introduced to the widow Eva who turned out to be younger and prettier than either had imagined.

There followed a three-day programme.

Hugo, assisted with introductions by the charming Eva,

interviewed the Colonists about their lives and the agriculture of Palestine.

Stefan painted the portrait.

During the long sittings Johannes, in white smock and black breeches, was remarkably tolerant and did not fidget. He seemed to accept that this was the price that must be paid for the visit to the tunnel, not that he talked about the coming expedition. In fact, neither spoke much at all.

The silence was intense. Stefan, brush in hand, stared at Johannes. Sitting with his hands between his knees, Johannes persistently stared straight into the artist's eyes. Stefan felt as he had on the train. The boy seemed alive to what was going on in his mind.

Unnerved, Stefan kept to his purpose. The portrait was finished in good time and presented to the delighted parents. With pride and ceremony Anton hung it on the parlour wall.

Chapter 2

On the fourth day, shaded by the canopy of a hired cart, Anton, Johannes and Stefan rested on the summit of the Mount of Olives. Johannes leant against his father munching a seed cake. As usual the boy hadn't said much, but then the two men were absorbed, Stefan with viewing the spectacular surroundings, Anton with slaking his thirst for discussion.

Now he was at the top Stefan was happy. For days he had been distracted from Jerusalem itself. The numbing train journey, the German Colony oddballs, the portrait of Johannes. He hadn't really taken in where he was. Here he could finally appreciate the city he had travelled so far to see. The vaulted sky, great hills arching to the horizon. And down across the valley, a honeycomb of ancient dwellings, minarets and domes, the city. Jerusalem!

He breathed in deeply.

It wasn't exactly quiet. Cicadas rasped and cocks crowed. There was the tinkle of goats bells and shepherd calls. Nevertheless the entire panorama conveyed an impression of immense silence, of profound inactivity. It seemed to Stefan that the litter of tombs this side of the city walls said everything.

'What's the biblical phrase?' he murmured to Anton. '"The abomination of desolation." It's beautiful but very... dead.'

Anton didn't argue with that. He wanted to ask about Hugo. He was already at ease with Stefan, whom he counted a friend. About the other visitor he was less sure.

'Your friend, Hugo Fischer, Stefan... Many of our Colonists have talked with him. Herr Fischer made no mention of machines. He just asked questions. The best land here in Palestine, the climate, soil, crops. It seems he wanted a geography lesson!'

'Background...' said Stefan, still distracted by the vista. 'Hugo wants background.'

'He doesn't seem like a salesman. More like a professor.'

Stefan was only half-listening. 'An open map at your feet. Everything, it's staggering... What's that by the way?' He pointed at a domed octagonal building on a stone platform raised above the warren of the city's buildings.

'The Dome of the Rock,' replied Anton. 'On top of the Temple Mount. And to the left the Al Aqsa mosque.'

'Ah, I remember from Baedecker. Two mosques on the site of the old Jewish temple...'

'Yes, that sums up Jerusalem. One thing piled on another, everyone squabbling over who owns what – Al Aqsa was once a church. I don't know about "dead", but this is the least spiritual place on earth. The different communities are at each other's throats.'

They sat in silence, Johannes eating his cake.

'Father, when do we get to the tunnel?'

Before Anton could answer Stefan cut in. 'Let me be frank with you... if we're to be friends... I can't take this... I don't even like the word "spiritual."'

Anton was taken aback. 'Ah! So you're a materialist. A very clever man who misses the essential.'

'Maybe I'm clever, who's to say. But religion, God, no... I admire a good sceptical intelligence. I'm with Spinoza, Heinrich Heine, Karl Marx...'

'Clever fools!' exclaimed Anton.

'How can you say that? They broke shackles – above all the shackles of religion.'

'They knew nothing.'

'Nothing?'

Anton pointed to the left. 'Do you see that? Those flat-topped tombs, thousands of them, many broken and vandalised, falling down into the valley. The ancient Jewish cemetery. Stefan, my friend, in the vicinity of this holiest of Jewish sites you dare to breathe the names of Spinoza, Heine and Marx, anti-religious Jews so clever they denied their spiritual heritage?'

'Anton, I despair of you!'

Johannes hopped down from the cart and stroked the pony with his head pressed against its scrawny side. He looked up. 'Father, who is that man?'

'What man, son?'

Both men peered up the hill along a line of buildings to where the boy was pointing.

'Nobody, son. There's nobody.'

'He was there. He was staring at us.'

Stefan, guilty that he had taken so little notice of the boy, jumped down, walked up the hill, looked around and returned. 'I couldn't see anybody, Johannes,' he said reassuringly.

Johannes remained unconvinced. He looked up at his father. 'Can we go to the tunnel now?'

'Of course, little fellow. Climb back on, both of you. It *is* getting late.' Anton took the reins and they broke into a brisk trot down the hill. Once on his way Anton was keen to resume the discussion.

'Stefan!' he called above the rumble of the cart. 'We must infuse every minute with the spirit. God in all our thoughts and actions, waking, eating, loving… That is what the Jews, *real* Jews, the great rabbis and holy men – not your Jewish atheists – know, and tell the world. God is everywhere, Stefan. Feel that glorious presence! Lose that cleverness. Look at the world! Holy Zion! God's world!' Anton threw his arm out as if to embrace the sky itself.

'Stop!' Stefan cried.

'What?'

'I insist, Anton! Stop the cart. Stop.'

Anton reined in the pony. The cart came to a halt. 'What, my friend?'

They turned and faced each other. The bruising afternoon heat and pounding rhythm of the cicadas heightened the sense of discord. Both felt it.

Johannes sighed. 'Father... please...'

But neither heard the quiet, plaintive voice.

'Listen to me, Anton, once and for all and then we can forget about it. There's something I must tell you. I... I don't want to hear this. I don't want to hear about religion. I have an extreme aversion to religion!'

'I feel sorry for you,' Anton sniffed. 'Your vehemence is itself revealing. You fight off what you dread succumbing to because if you were to believe, you would lose your puny human omnipotence.'

The argument carried on noisily as Anton drove the cart on down the bumpy track.

'Father...' Johannes was close to tears. The raised voices had frightened him.

'Listen,' exclaimed Stefan. 'Why do you think I live in Venice?'

'Because you can do what you like there? I heard from a Franciscan here that in Venice married people take lovers at the drop of a hat and men openly love other men.'

'Not that, I assure you.'

'So you could paint then?'

'Venice *is* good for painting. Think of the Old Masters who painted there. But for me, it's the water! Water is flux, water is freedom. Living surrounded by water you are inspired by the most benign and liberal of the elements. Freedom from fixed ideas, dogma, in short, from religion. We get nowhere by creeping around in fear of priests and holy writ.'

'You completely misunderstand me if you think I blindly follow religious doctrine.'

'But there is something else I need to tell you, Anton.'

'What else?'

'Something even more important.'

'Yes?'

Stefan grasped his arm. 'I don't want to hear any more from you about Jews.'

'My dear fellow…'

Once again Anton drew the cart to a halt. Stefan fixed him with a warning, defiant look. Anton drew away instinctively.

'You… are a Jew.'

Stefan nodded slowly. 'Yes.'

'You don't look…'

'Yes. I am a Jew and I don't look like a Jew. Many of us don't!'

Anton held out his hand. 'Let me apologise. No wonder you were offended.'

Stefan ignored the proffered hand. 'I'm not offended, Anton. I just wanted to clear the matter up before you lectured me more about "real" Jews, for goodness sake!'

'I'm embarrassed.'

'Well... You weren't to know. I am not Orthodox by upbinging. My parents are liberal Jews. They are Germans first. They will always be Germans. Germany values them. They value Germany as the most civilised of nations. I have taken it further. I am a sceptic, *materialist*. Since I was a child, being a Jew has meant very little…' He motioned to the city opposite. 'Perhaps now, seeing this, it means something at last. I am moved by a sense of connection, I can't deny it. Simply to think my ancestors came from here...'

'Please, father…'

Now at last both men looked uneasily at the child they had been ignoring so long.

'All right Johannes, we're on our way. Herr Lehmann is explaining something important to me…'

Anton touched the pony with his whip. Stefan turned to Johannes.

'I'm sorry, young man. We'll stop talking now. How far is it to the tunnel, Anton?'

'It's not far. Five minutes.'

They drove on but Anton had not stopped talking.

'Herr Fischer – is he Jewish, and a Zionist by any chance?'

'Both. One reason I didn't mention that I am a Jew was Hugo. He said it would lead you to this conclusion.'

'What would be wrong with that?'

Stefan put his finger to his lips. 'He's on a secret mission. On your oath, Anton, please keep this to yourself.'

'Of course.'

'About a year ago he visited me in Venice. He'd undergone a conversion. He was inspired. Would I go with him to Palestine? I don't agree with Zionism. Jews as colonisers? It'll only lead to trouble. This disagreement causes tension between Hugo and me. But I was happy to keep him company. I wanted to get away. I like travel.'

'So… you two fair young fellows. Both Jews. You, an artist and sceptic, Herr Fischer afire to build a Hebrew nation here in Palestine.'

Anton tailed off, glancing down at Johannes, who had finally fallen asleep on his lap.

'Anton, we've finally bored Johannes to sleep.'

'Poor boy. We have ignored him.'

Anton stroked his son's head for a moment, then turned and confided. 'You know, Stefan, I long for intelligent people like you. You have no idea. Even if you are an atheist! Can I let you into a secret?'

'Certainly.'

'I adore Jewish women!'

'Really?'

'The Hebrew women here,' murmured Anton, 'with their dark eyes, their pale skins! The emancipated ones, the Zionists from Vilna and Odessa, they stir my loins. They seem so clever. I want to give them children!'

'I say!'

'Not a hope. They want Jewish men. But it doesn't stop me dreaming. For goodness sake, my friend, Stefan! Not a word to anyone about my secret passions, especially not to Magda. Now with the baby coming.'

'You must be a trial to her, dear fellow.'

Stefan was wondering whether to ask about his connection to Eva, but they had finally arrived at their destination.

~

'What is the tunnel anyway, Anton?'

'It's living history! There, at the bottom of the steps is the spring of Gihon. You can hear the running water.' Anton pointed above to a craggy escarpment gilded by later-afternoon light. 'And there is the Hill of Ophel. It's outside the city now, but three thousand years ago this Hill of Ophel was *inside* Jerusalem. When the Assyrians were besieging the city the Jewish king, Hezekiah, blocked off the spring so the Assyrians couldn't get to it. Then he had a tunnel cut through the rock to bring the water from the spring into the city at the Pool of Siloam – or Pool of Shiloah to the Jews. What we're going to do is walk the length of the tunnel right through to Siloam.'

'Father, it's dark down there!'

'Hold my hand as we go down the steps.'

As they descended a white-bearded monk emerged from the gloom.

'*Bon giorno.*'

'*Bon giorno,*' replied Stefan. 'Ah,' he muttered to Anton, 'an Italian. I can talk to him.'

The monk explained that a guide would take them the length of the tunnel, holding a light, warning them of eddies and narrow stretches. Another man would take their shoes and the cart round to the other end and would wait for them to emerge.

The monk gave each of them a candle and flint lighter. They rolled their trousers to their knees and gave their shoes and socks to the man who was taking the cart. Lighting their candles, the group passed through the arch and stepped into the water. The guide led them into the darkened tunnel in single file, Anton first followed by Johannes, with Stefan bringing up the rear.

'It's cold, father.'

'It's cool, son. It might make your bones ache.'

A musty tang invaded Stefan's nostrils. Shadows loomed on the pitted rock. The sound of splashes filled the tunnel. Was it only a moment ago they had stood in the sunshine?

'The bottom's smooth at least,' boomed Anton. 'Comfortable on the feet. Worn away by the water. All right, Stefan?'

'I'm fine.'

'The guide is moving ahead too quickly,' Anton murmured to himself. 'He should stay nearer. When he goes round a corner, I can hardly see.'

Johannes moved ahead steadily, his blond hair eerily illuminated by the flickering candlelight.

'How's your candle doing, Johannes?' asked Stefan.

'All right.'

They waded on. A short time later Johannes stopped.

'What is it?'

'Father's gone on. I can't see him.'

Stefan called out. 'Anton! Wait!' The voice reverberated. 'Wait! Johannes needs you.'

'I want to go back,' said Johannes, who was now shivering.

Stefan glanced back. Nothing but darkness.

'We can't, Johannes. We're half way.' This was a lie. Stefan knew there was much further to go. 'It makes more sense to carry on. Keep going, eh, young fellow? Let's catch your father up. He can't have got that far ahead.'

Later, much later, Stefan and Johannes at last became aware of candlelight ahead.

The guide was waiting.

'Where did you get to? Where's my friend?' asked Stefan.

The man didn't understand. He pointed to the wall. He mimed the banging of a hammer and writing. Meanwhile Anton waded back towards them from the tunnel exit.

'Ah, there you both are! I've just been to look outside. We're all but there. But Stefan look, look what he's showing us. This is where the famous inscription was.'

'Inscription?' said Stefan wearily. 'I'm done in, so is Johannes.'

'Some years ago,' Anton said, 'there was a chance discovery just here. It turned out to be Hebrew lettering.'

Stefan looked at the rock. 'I can't see any inscription.'

Unnoticed by the two friends peering at the wall, the guide slowly raised an arm and beckoned to Johannes.

'There's nothing there *now*', declared Anton expansively. 'It was stolen not long after. It recorded the moment when Hezekiah's tunnellers met, having started at different ends. They heard each other's pickaxes and then they were through. "Pick-axe knocked against pick-axe," said the inscription. And then the water gushed out into the waiting reservoir – just out there.' Anton jerked his thumb towards the exit. 'Living history! What did I tell you? Thousands of years.'

'It's a pity the inscription's gone,' said Stefan testily.

'It found its way to a museum in Constantinople,' replied Anton. He looked round. 'Where's Johannes by the way?'

'The guide must have taken him out. He could tell the boy had had enough. Me too!'

'Then they'll be waiting at the pool, that's all right.'

With Stefan forging impatiently ahead they moved towards daylight. Emerging, Stefan found himself in a sunken hollow edged by tightly packed stones. Water trickled gently from the tunnel into a rectangular reservoir, the Pool of Siloam.

A minute later Anton lumbered out and looked round.

'Do you have Johannes?'

Stefan shook his head.

'Johannes!' shouted Anton.

Silence.

Stefan's pulse quickened. 'Anton, you go that way,' he said pointing at the path leading out of the hollow. 'I think I should check back in the tunnel.' He pushed past his companion and waded back.

'Stefan!' Anton called after him, 'What's the point! He must be out here.'

But Stefan was gripped by the idea Johannes had not moved past them out towards the exit. More likely he had fallen in the dark and even at this very moment could be lying in the shallow water, enveloped by dark, drowning even.

'God save him,' he muttered, gripping his candle, his steps lengthening. Back and back he went. Careering round bends, now stooping, now bumping into the wall of rock.

'No!'

At last he knew he was wrong. By no stretch of thought could the boy be this far back into the tunnel. Rapidly he re-traced his steps.

'Anton! Anton!' he shouted almost exultantly as he drew once more towards the exit. 'He isn't here, you're right. Everything's fine, he must be outside.'

Anton was silhouetted against the oval glow of the exit.

'Stefan, have you got him?'

'No! Didn't you hear me! Isn't he there, outside?'

'No!'

'Where's the guide, and the other one with the cart?'

'They've both gone – and the cart.'

'What?'

Stefan plunged towards Anton. He, Stefan, had been looking after the boy. *He* must find him. He hurtled forward. A few steps on his head collided with a rock.

His legs trembled. He felt the blood with his fingertips.

'That hurt!'

Closing his eyes, he fell.

The pool in the late afternoon light… stones packed vertically… ferns growing out of the cracks… the boy, hair bright, bending down, his fingers playing in the water… He looks up… An arm outstretched… His hand is taken… He goes, apparently without a thought…

In time Stefan forgot that this was a dream that came to him as he lay unconscious by the side of the pool where Anton had laid him.

He believed that was what he had seen. Also, that it would have been simple for him to prevent it.

~

They staggered through the cavernous lanes of the city. Battered pomegranates, figs, prickly pear, cauliflower, turnips littered their path. The air smelled of rotting meat tinged with spices and coffee. They barged through the crowd, leaping over bloody butchers' carcasses.

'The monk said they'd gone towards the city… He swore it…'

They ran on. Past an archway overgrown with cactus and henbane, they came to the busiest and most enclosed part of the bazaar. Shouts of tailors and embroiderers, hammerings of shoemakers and tinsmiths, filled the air.

'Oh God!' Anton cried out.

They darted in different directions, rushed back.

'We need a plan,' gasped Stefan. 'The police… the authorities…'

'Of course… soon… but let's look first, that makes sense…'

'But why would they bring him here?' queried Stefan as they hurled themselves along another passageway. 'We can't even be sure he came into the city.'

'It's my only lead. My best chance.'

'But why would you trust that monk?'

'It's all I've got. What else can I do?'

'Stop!' said Stefan. 'Look, we'll separate. Meet back here in, say, ten minutes.'

'Fine.'

Stefan hurried further into the maze of lanes. A shopkeeper eyed him from a recess hung with muslin veils, silks, prints and calicoes.

'Have you seen a boy?'

'There are many boys,' replied the man in passable German. He pointed up the alley.

Stefan turned and walked forward. He was blinded. The sun was reflected off a glass pane above the passageway and formed a pool of light in a recess. Somebody – somebody small, a child it must be – was sitting bathed in the light. Heart pounding, Stefan ran forward.

'Be careful!' someone said, in English.

With narrowed eyes, Stefan tried to puzzle the little shape out, a pale ghost merged with the light, an angel.

He stepped forward. His foot kicked over a tin. Coins ran out. He bent to pick them up. The figure leant towards him. A stump edged out from under a dirty blanket. For a nose, two holes below gluey, half-closed eyes. The mouth a lopsided slit. A little man, how old it was impossible to say.

The leper grunted and flapped his arms. Stefan found his wallet and pulled out a note.

'This Ottoman money,' he muttered, trying to work out its value. He was sure it was a large amount. Having nothing smaller and no coins, he put the note back in his wallet.

'I'm sorry… I'll come back…'

He spotted a drink vendor and realised he was thirsty. A gleaming silver jug was attached to the vendor's back. Joining the queue of customers, Stefan forgot the knot in his stomach, mesmerised by the way the man dispensed drink to his customers.

Removing a cup from a hook attached to the long spout, the

vendor tilted his trunk low to one side with delicate skill so that the fruit juice just trickled into it.

'Never seen anything so strange…'

When it came to his turn, Stefan paid the man with the note whose value he had possibly overestimated. He downed the juice and hurried off.

In the recess the little man with no face rocked and keened, banging his can against the ground.

~

That same afternoon, Magda was on her knees, naked on the stone floor.

'Would you like to get on the bed?' asked Eva.

Magda shook her head. 'Cold, Eva, cold. The floor's cold.'

'You like that?'

Sweat coursed down Magda's face. Eva mopped her fleshy neck and shoulders with a towel.

'Cushions maybe, just for my knees.'

'Can you push?' asked Bette, the midwife.

'He's coming. I'm pushing the swine. He's a fat swine, a monster.'

Magda closed her eyes, shaking her head in crazy rhythm. She glanced at the windowsill. She saw a chimpanzee, with hat and woodland tunic, cross-legged and whistling.

'Stop whistling…'

'What Magda?'

'On the windowsill…'

The chimp grinned at Magda.

The sharper the pain, the wider he grinned. He laughed a lot. He pointed. He thought she was a right fat-arse.

'Go away!'

'Come on, Magda,' soothed Bette, 'you can't want us away. We're here till your new one comes.'

'Not you! Him! *Scheisse!* Hell! Where's Anton!'

'He's taken Johannes for the day with the visitor…'

'God help me with the pain. I'm shitting this creature.'

'There, there. Hold her Eva.'

The monkey stuck out his tongue.

'GO AWAY! *SCHEISSE!*'

Magda opened her eyes wide.

'*Ja! Ja! Es kommt!*'

'*Ja!*'

Still on her knees, panting faster.

'Easy. Breathe more slowly. Here it is. The head. We can see the head, Magda. Everything will be all right now.'

Magda slowed down as she had been told. Outside a neighbour chatted, people walked past. Eva sponged Magda's head. Bette waited. 'Ah, here we are…' Bette held the head and allowed the trunk to ease out.

It was all over. The baby slid to its conclusion, its beginning in the world. Bette cupped its blood-smeared trunk in her hands.

'A boy,' said Eva.

The blue cord pulsed. When it had been cut and tied, Magda sank down onto the floor.

'Magda,' said Bette, 'you've got another little boy. Let me show you.'

Magda sniffed hard. She lifted herself on to the couch and put on the robe offered by Eva. She looked at the baby. Overcoming exhaustion, she took him to her arms and began to nurse him.

Chapter 3

'*A deputation of the sons of Israel approaches the German Kaiser with the deepest reverence*,' read out Theodor Herzl. The heat and murk of the tent's silk and mother-of-pearl interior swallowed up the declamation.

Herzl paused to gather his strength and belief. Sweat ran down his forehead and soaked his beard. Like the other members of the Zionist delegation, he was enduring full evening dress in the midday heat. It was his doing. He'd argued for it. To be taken seriously by the lounging man in helmet and gleaming boots, the five must dress up. Each was now immersed in his own personal lake of perspiration.

'*We are bound to this sacred soil by no valid title of possession...*'

The helmet, a romantic veiled affair, twitched. Herzl missed it. His lieutenant, the zealous Wolffsohn, saw, and feared the worst. The Kaiser's nod endorsed the disclaimer. *Jawohl!* the nod said, the Jews had indeed no 'valid title to the land'.

Herzl pressed on. '*Many generations have come and gone since this land was Jewish. If we speak of it now it is only a dream of ancient days. But the dream still lives in the hearts of many hundreds and thousands; it was and still is a wondrous consolation in many an hour of pain for our people...*'

Prince von Bülow ran his finger over the Zionists' script. The wily foreign minister had already made cuts. He didn't want the exclusions creeping back in again. Out had gone Jewish suffering and a right of redress. Out, also, a request for a German protectorate over Jewish settlements in Palestine and Syria. The suzerain, the Ottoman

Sultan, with whom the Kaiser hoped for good relations, would have torn his hair. German policy of thwarting Britain by cultivating the Turks would have come to nothing.

Herzl reminded himself that the next sentence was the heart of the matter. But the Kaiser was restless. He tapped the side of his boot with his riding whip. His imagination was outside the tent, caught not by the idea of a nation reborn but by his own dream of the orient conjured from the faint sounds that met his ear: the muezzin, the cicadas, the braying of camels and donkeys.

Herzl raised his voice. *'The land of our fathers! It cries out for people to build it up!'*

The Kaiser came to himself. As agreed with Bülow beforehand, he must prevaricate so as not to provoke the Sultan. In any case he felt distaste for these Jews and their political presumptions. On both counts a mask was necessary. He frowned, contriving at the same time to smile innocently.

It was not only the Jews, continued Herzl from the declaration, but the Turks and indeed 'countless human beings' who would benefit from Zionism. Desolate areas would be 'reconstructed' to the benefit of everyone.

With his ordeal coming to an end, the Zionist leader ended on a rousing note. '*An emperor of peace is making his great entry into the Eternal City. We Jews greet your Majesty in this high moment and wish with all our hearts that an age of peace and justice may dawn for all humanity.*'

Silence fell like an axe. Bülow cleared his throat and rustled his papers. Herzl, bold now he was free of the script, looked into the Kaiser's eyes. The Kaiser stared back.

'I thank you for your communication. It interests me very much. The matter in any case still requires careful study and further discussions.'

Herzl now knew what Wolffsohn and the others had already guessed. The Kaiser, inexplicably given his earlier enthusiasm, was indeed prevaricating.

'Let me tell you, water's the thing here,' he pronounced.

'Yes, your Majesty.'

'Water and shade. That's the basis of it.'

With amateur zeal the Kaiser held forth for a minute or two on the subject of irrigation, then broke off. '*Mein Gott!* The heat, even in this tent.' His discomfort did not lead him to consider his five supplicants, on their feet, sweating in their serge evening suits. Instead he recalled the day a week before when Herzl and he had coincidentally met at the gates of Mikveh Israel, the Jewish agricultural school near Jaffa.

'That day we met at Mikveh Israel was the hottest... thirty-one in the shade, forty-one in the sun.'

'As His Majesty the Kaiser was gracious enough to say,' commented Bülow, 'water is the main thing. Herr Herzl will know what the Greek poet says: *Ariston men udos*.'

The Kaiser frowned.

'"Water is best,"' mumbled Bülow, to help the Kaiser in his ignorance of the ancient saying.

'We can bring the country water,' said Herzl. 'It will cost billions but will yield billions.'

The Kaiser rapped his boot. 'Well, money you have got plenty of! More than any of us!'

'Yes,' chimed in Bülow. 'The money which gives *us* so much trouble, your people have plenty of it!'

Barring further brief exchanges, that was it. The interview was over. The delegation filed out of the tent.

'*So soon?*' said the aide-de-camp stationed outside the tent, adding sarcasm to his earlier condescension.

Out of earshot the delegation all spoke at once.

'He said neither yes or no.'

'What on earth...'

'What next?'

Herzl exploded. 'Whatever he said, he meant no! Obviously. He's exchanged the Zionist hobbyhorse for others.'

'Come now Theodor, don't be discouraged.'

'His earlier enthusiasm was hardly flattering to us anyway. For him the Jews are a damn nuisance in Europe and it would be good to get rid of us – especially if we hand over millions for the privilege. The idea's dead. The Sultan has done for us. No more Jews in Palestine. No charter, no return, no protectorate. He's told the Kaiser and now the Kaiser's told us – in so many words.'

'We don't know that yet!'

'*I* know it.'

They reached the compound gate. It had taken months of planning to get into the imperial presence. Now the Turkish guards refused to let them out. The Jews were at a loss. An unlikely saviour appeared out of the shadows – the Ottoman police spy who had been tailing them since they had landed in Jaffa persuaded the guards and the gate swung open. The delegation headed down the Street of the Prophets towards the hotel while the spy resumed his watch from the shadows.

'What would that fellow do without us?' said Bodenheimer, aiming at a lighter mood.

Herzl moved grimly forward, staring at the ground. His head ached. He was back at the beginning. The key figure, the ruler of the glorious Second Reich, had turned out to be a fraud. He looked up. Blinding light. Dust. Flies. A tethered goat munching dry leaves. What a place. Was this wilderness worth returning to?

'We never had the millionaires behind us. The Rothschilds scorned us, so did the rabbinical establishment. But at least we had the Germans…'

Herzl barely noticed four Europeans hurrying in their direction but Wolffsohn and Schnirer, recognising one of them, were happy to stop and find a distraction from their woes.

'Herr Fischer. What's up?'

'Something terrible.'

'What is it?'

'Herr Gustavus here. His son.'

Trembling, Anton stared at the fluttering pennants of the Kaiser's encampment. 'My son…'

'Our friend's son was abducted three days ago,' continued Hugo. 'Just a lad of eight. The family are from the German Colony here. The gendarmerie were told at once but they haven't been helpful. They seem to be doing nothing. Nothing at all.'

'What do they care!' exclaimed Stefan. 'All they care about is the Kaiser's visit.'

'Can *you* help?' cried Eva.

Wolfssohn was prepared to put himself out for such a good-looking woman. 'Yes, I'm sure… but what should we do?'

Eva clasped his arm. 'We need to see the Kaiser in person. You've just come from there, haven't you?'

'My dear lady,' replied Wolfssohn, 'Yes, yes, absolutely, yes… We would like… but I fear that we would weaken your case.' He glanced over his shoulder. 'The gentleman back there in his brocade tent has no high regard for us.'

Eva looked anxiously at Anton. His head fell on hers. They held hands briefly.

'Where did it happen?' asked Schnirer.

'The boy was last seen at the Pool of Siloam,' replied Hugo. 'We think he was being followed before that. There was someone on the Mount of Olives – possibly. Johannes himself saw someone. We've been to everybody. Consuls, bishops, everybody. Lots of sympathy, but they have no influence on the authorities. Nothing to offend the Turk, delicate moment in the relationship of the two empires, pressure would imply criticism and so on. So we're going to try His Majesty. Our last attempt.'

'But you have no appointment?' asked Schnirer.

They shook their heads.

'My fellow Templers have not been helpful,' said Anton bitterly. 'The Kaiser is visiting the Colony. They're all ready with beer and brass bands. They don't want anything to mar the occasion.'

'Ignorant,' spat the fierce-eyed Eva.

Stefan put his hand on Anton's big shoulder.

'Anton's wife has just had another child. It's a terrible coincidence.'

Wolfssohn and Schnirer shook their heads in sympathy.

'Herr Wolfssohn,' said Hugo, gathering his courage. 'I know I have asked you favours before...'

'No, you have done *us* a favour with your paper on Levantine farming methods. I have perused it with utmost interest. I am only sorry we couldn't invite you to come with us today but in the event...'

Wolfssohn glossed over the main reason for Hugo's exclusion from the delegation: his lack of a tail-coat.

'Well, was it a success?' continued Hugo. 'I frankly cannot believe that Herr Herzl and yourselves failed to impress His Majesty. You were so well prepared. I'm sure he's thinking about it. Did the agricultural question come up by the way? Be that as it may, I dare to ask you one last favour.'

'Yes?'

'Well, just this. Can you come back with us and explain this catastrophe to the guards or whoever it might be. I know it is asking a lot.'

Wolfssohn faltered. 'I...'

'Look, David,' said Schnirer. 'You go on back to the hotel. Theodor needs your support in this black hour.' He turned to the others. 'I'll willingly come back up to the camp and do what I can.'

'Ah, thank you,' said Hugo. 'So much appreciated.'

Schnirer sighed. 'But I have to say... the Turkish guards, an insolent aide-de-camp, an *oily* foreign minister. It's no small barrier before you meet the man himself. And when you get to *him*, well... let's say he seems... just an actor – a bad actor – playing at being a powerful man...' He broke off. 'Look, I'll do my best. At least I may be able to get a note through to the aide-de-camp and perhaps when the Kaiser comes to your German Colony... Who knows?

Let's hope.'

The four murmured their appreciation. Wolffsohn, saved by Schirer's offer, shook Anton's hand. 'A boy of eight… Your poor wife and baby… I'm so sorry…' He turned on his heel and sped after the retreating Herzl.

Chapter 4

It was dark but Stefan hadn't lit the lamp. He sat alone in the darkness of Eva's parlour cursing the singing that had started a few doors up. As Eva had said, they were already at the beer.

'How can they do that?' she had said. Her tone was so bitter that Stefan wondered how she managed to live among the Colonists. 'A boy lost and they celebrate. It's disgusting. But I'm not surprised. Herr Gustavus is too clever for them. They love things to go wrong for him. But this…'

She'd gone early to her bedroom. The moon was high above the garden. Warm air, heavy with honeysuckle, wafted through the window. Stefan sensed someone come in.

'Hugo?'

He turned. No, not behind him. There, outside. He peered through the window. The singing had stopped. Was it a sigh, or a whisper?

Surely he was imagining it. He stood up and leant out. The wind from the hills tugged the trees. Was it just dry leaves?

Was someone weaving between the pines? Who was sighing? Heart pounding, he hurried out to the garden.

'Johannes!'

Silence. Only the wind in the trees. Then the revellers' singing started again.

'Hey! You! Who are you?'

What should he do? Chase the voice? Follow it across the hills to the desert, then to the sea and beyond?

'Eva. I'll tell Eva.'

He raced back inside and approached Eva's bedroom door. He lifted his hand to knock, then heard the sigh. It came from inside the room. His eye fell to the keyhole and he bent down.

Moonlight bathed two figures on the bed. Anton and Eva. They were still, side by side on their backs, looking up, like sculptures on a medieval tomb.

'So here it is. It is... unbelievable. Magda. Her child kidnapped. A new baby. A husband in bed with a neighbour.'

Across the gardens, they were banging tables as Stefan tiptoed to the front door.

He made his way to the Gustavus house and knocked. Magda opened the door holding the baby.

'I...'

'What is it?'

Stefan was at a loss. 'I wondered if there had been any developments.'

'Come in. Anton won't be long. He's just gone for a walk.'

'Thank you.'

She showed him into the parlour and lit the oil lamp.

'Would you like you some mint tea?'

'If it's not too much trouble.'

'I'll put him down.'

Unsmiling, she laid the baby in a wicker basket and went to the kitchen.

Stefan sat down, his attention going immediately to his portrait of Johannes hanging opposite, illuminated by the glow of the lamp. With all that had happened he had not given much thought to it. The colours gleamed and gave him pleasure. The baby was waking, starting to cry, but he didn't notice.

How alive Johannes was here. A pensive boy, staring – enigmatically as Stefan had intended. Stefan's pleasure in his work – as the baby's cry grew louder – merged into an old idea that had gone out of the window recently: that he, Stefan Lehmann, was after all quite an artist.

It was a good likeness. The golden mop, full lips, those extraordinary eyes, burnished skin. Then there were the incidentals: the wall hanging in sunlight, the landscape through the window (a Venetian touch, that), the folds on the shirt, the foot resting lifelike on the bar of the chair, the texturing of the stone floor. Skilful in certain details, yet more vague than not.

'Detail and vagueness: each has its own poetry. Blended with skill they express a paradox. Here is a real boy, yet here too is a dream of what a boy might be…'

Stefan was separated from his own distress, from Magda's, from everything around him apart from the portrait, in which he saw with joy proof of his own skill. Still the baby cried.

Magda came in, shot him a look, picked up the baby and settled him quickly.

'You don't know about babies then, Herr Lehmann…'

'I'm sorry… I… I was thinking about Johannes.'

'You were thinking about him. I don't stop thinking about him.'

'Perhaps,' said Stefan, 'he'll come back soon. I thought I heard something outside. That's why I came round…'

'Heard something?'

'I hoped…'

Magda shook her head, engulfed in grief. 'You think he's hanging round the bushes here? No, my poor dear boy, he's gone. We have to get used to the idea.'

'But that's terrible.'

Magda rocked the baby, struggling to hold back her tears. 'There's your mint tea. You're welcome to enjoy it here till Anton returns from his wanderings. I need to try and get some sleep.'

~

Two bodies lying bathed in moonlight. She held his head to her breasts, stroking his scalp under the thick curls. A whisp of her own fair hair fell across her wet cheek. She brushed it away and with it tried to brush away fear.

'Calm, my love, calm,' she whispered.

His sobs knocked against her.

'Anton, my love, we will find him.'

'No,' he moaned. 'He's lost. The world's gone dark. Everything is lost...'

'Don't give up.'

More singing came through the trees

'I hate them,' she murmured.

'Don't hate, I don't want you to hate...'

They lapsed into deep silence.

'Lost...lost... it's all lost.'

'Anton! No! Don't... You'll drive yourself crazy this way. You must have hope...'

He came to himself, pulling the sheet over them both, clinging to her more strongly.

'Us too, you know, Eva... we're lost... Magda... we can't... *I* can't...'

And now Eva too was crying because she knew it was true.

~

Autumn sun bathed the villas, warming the Jerusalem stone, brightening the paintwork. In laundered tunics and spotless white dresses they came out to greet the famous day, to slap each other on the back, crack jokes, guffaw.

The imperial carriage trundled up towards the Colony. Spotting the crowd waiting under banners the Kaiserin nudged her husband. Willi was looking the other way, over to the purple mountains of Edom. A desire to possess had taken hold of him. He loved this land. He wanted to hold it to his bosom, cherish it. He lifted his right arm and clenched his fist, as if plucking fruit.

It was a typical gesture, bold yet forlorn. As in all the portraits and newspaper illustrations, his other arm, that poor shrivelled thing, rested useless on his sword, trying not to be noticed. The right arm made up for its deficient twin by over-exertion.

He screwed up his face. 'Now we're going to meet this strange lot.'

'Don't dismiss them so readily, Willi.'

'I'm told they never use surnames, never eat meat and always talk nonsense – democratic, millennarian bilge. However, there are reports that they have become more patriotic of late.'

'Let's take them as we find them.'

The flag-decked entrance came nearer. The Kaiserin murmured placatingly. 'Willi, so far on our journey we've been surrounded by strangers. But look at these people. Look at the children. Here we're with our own. Germans. In such a far off backwater – but look how they love you. You and they have the same dream. You *are* the German people.'

The Kaiser glanced down at his uniform, the pristine cloth, medals, braided cuffs, boot tops.

'*Ja, ja…*'

It was not easy for him to be convinced.

In the Gustavus parlour Magda sat upright, tight-lipped. Anton had laid his olivewood carvings out on a table outside, to the disapproval of his neighbours. He was expecting to sell a few to the Kaiser's party. Hoping they wouldn't mistake the carvings for tourist knick-knacks, he was polishing them one by one. He came inside. The baby woke up.

'He's hungry,' said Magda, 'but he can wait. He chews me to pieces.'

They fell to separate thoughts. The baby went quiet; perhaps he was dropping off at last.

Across the road, their neighbour opened the front door, raised a stein and gulped the beer down. He shouted and ran to the Colony entrance.

'The idiots' parade is just beginning.' Eva passed the window in white dress and scarlet sash. She glanced over. He raised his fingers to his lips.

'Time to go,' he said. 'Let's see what the great man has to say.'

In ten minutes the Kaiser's party was ushered into the simple stone Meeting House. Everyone strained their necks, more intent on getting a view than contributing to a dignified atmosphere.

Anton and Magda sat near the back at the end of a row. Anton could leave with the baby if he woke up. Magda would stay. She was determined. She would smother the little creature rather than allow him to ruin this for her.

With everyone settled at last she could see the Kaiser.

'What a fine figure,' she thought. 'How nobly he carries his poor arm.'

The Kaiser began his speech resoundingly.

'Jerusalem, the respected city in which you worthy people have chosen to settle calls to memory the redemptive activity of our Lord and Saviour...'

'...And what a fine voice!'

'The world-renewing power of the gospel that went out from here pulls us to follow it...'

Magda wiped away a tear. 'At the tunnel exit. Why?'

She caught sight of Eva. '*Her.* The "tragic widow". She's a whore. People talked even when her husband was alive.' She stared fiercely. She was no longer listening to the Kaiser. She was gripped by hatred towards Eva.

The Kaiser was coming to the end. 'What the German people have become,' he boomed, 'they have become under the banner of the cross of Golgotha, the true sign of sacrificing love. As for almost two millennia, so also today the cry rings out from here unto all the world... Peace on earth!'

'What fine words. I should have listened more carefully.'

All eyes were trained on the Kaiser. The Colonists shuffled to their feet. The procession made its way towards the door. The imperial couple smiled, inclined their heads, came nearer.

She quivered. Her throat was tight. Her face turned puce.

'Johannes, Johannes. Where is he? My boy, my boy.'

The baby howled. She thrust him into Anton's arms and leaping into the aisle and threw herself down.

'Magda!'

Two guards grabbed her but the amazed Kaiser ordered them to leave her. She lay prone on the floor. He gazed down, spreading his healthy right arm.

'What is it?'

'Help us, help us, Your Majesty! My son was kidnapped.'

Anton came forward with the screaming baby. 'It's true. Forgive my wife's impetuosity. She is grief-stricken. Don't let her detain you just now. Later perhaps we…'

'Why not!' screamed Magda. 'Why shouldn't my grief detain His Majesty?'

'Magda…' hissed Anton.

The congregation were craning their necks and muttering. Guards were trying to usher the Kaiser out. The Kaiserin was willing to listen but her husband had moved from instinctive sympathy to a detachment dictated by caution.

'We'll look into it,' he said. 'You have another child?'

'Yes, another boy,' replied Anton. 'He's noisy. My apologies.'

'Whatever has happened,' said the Kaiser affably, 'you still have one son. Be sure to make him a good German'.

With that the imperial party moved on.

'What did he say?' moaned Magda from the floor.

Anton repeated the Kaiser's words.

'A good German! Never! He'll never be that! Listen to him! Look at him!'

'Magda! No! You must…'

She remained spread-eagled on the floor, the baby still howling in Anton's arms. A few of the Colonists gathered round, some outraged, some sympathetic. Someone lifted Magda to her feet. Eva sought Anton's eye, held it for a few seconds, then left the building.

~

'Hugo, you're embarrassed.'

'No…'

'Yes, and you're hiding something behind your back.'

'Not embarrassed exactly…' Hugo brought his arm round. He was holding a letter. 'This came and I had to think what to do about it.'

'News from home?'

Hugo threw himself onto the chaise and sighed. 'I've been told – *ordered* – to come home. Father makes out I'm needed in the business. Someone's fallen ill…'

'Yes?' queried Stefan.

'It's too damned early! There's work to be done here.'

'But the Kaiser's departed. And hasn't Herzl gone too? What's left for you to do?'

'There is so much I can do! I could spend a year – at least a year – travelling and surveying the terrain. We Zionists have to buy whatever land comes up, that's clear, but if we have some idea of which tracts are suitable for farming… I'm an expert on these things. I've studied it. It can affect the price we offer. Help us choose well, avoid mistakes. Look at the German Colonists in the north who all died of malaria… that kind of thing…'

'So tell your father to jump in the lake.'

'You don't know my father! Well…you do know him.'

'He terrified me! The Jewish patriarch. I was scared of him in those days. Very different from my father. My father could never decide anything.'

'Stefan, listen, there's more to it than this.' Hugo waved the letter.

'What?'

'Miriam.'

'Miriam?'

'Miriam Levy, I told you about her. Father drops it in just at the end. He says he has it on good authority that the Levy family is on the point of receiving another offer. The suitor is a lawyer. Rich. If I don't declare my hand…'

Stefan was intrigued. 'How is it with you and this Miriam? Have you been writing to her?'

'We're childhood sweethearts. It's always been understood…'

'Do you *want* to marry her?'

'She's… yes, she's Miriam. Everybody thinks she's just the right sort, a Jewish girl from a suitable family. Sheltered life but well-educated. She's my dark striking beauty, a passionate girl. Mind you, her passions are artistic where mine are political. She has no interest in Zionism but maybe that can change… Anyway, Stefan it's all academic. I've decided… and…'

Stefan's eyes opened wide. 'Yes?'

'What I want to know is, if I leave, will you stay? My going is earlier than you and I planned. It's only December. But really I have no choice. I am not prepared to lose Miriam to a lawyer when all is said and done. But… but… all this terrible business with Johannes. I just feel bad about it. And I suppose I would feel reassured if you were willing to stay on. I know I shouldn't ask. The understanding was that we would travel back together.'

Stefan waved magnanimously. 'No Hugo, have no fear. I will stay as long as I'm needed. I will paint of course....'

Hugo paused before dropping his bombshell.

'By... By the way,' he stuttered, 'I'm taking Eva with me.'

'Eva? What do you mean?'

'We... we have developed a certain understanding…'

'Hugo, you amaze me. All these women in your life suddenly!'

‘No, don’t get me wrong. Eva and I have spent a lot of time talking. We have a certain amount in common. She’s a thinking, modern woman.’

‘She’s an *attractive* woman…’

‘Oh, Stefan really! You’ve got love on the brain. It’s those harlots you waste your money on in Venice...’

Stefan punched his friend playfully on the arm. ‘Not harlots! Women of the world.’

‘Well, let’s call them women who make a profession of love. I’m sure you miss them.’

‘I wish I hadn’t confided in you. It was only the boredom of travel that made me. And no, I don’t miss them. I left a cloud of amorous complications behind, let me tell you. A relief. Besides, I am pursuing my calling. I am becoming serious! And if I wasn’t, this dreadful event would make me so. I feel responsible. I can’t help it. I go over and over it in my mind. The tunnel, the pool, my carelessness...’

The two friends had talked about this many times and Hugo had run out of things to say.

‘Yes, but anyway... As you know, Stefan, Eva teaches the youngest children at the school here. The mothers don’t really want her because of her “misconduct”. She’s sick of the life here, she’s lost her husband, has no children, no friends and now no lover. She told me all this in the most uncomplaining fashion with no idea that I might be able to help.’

‘And how can you help her?’

‘It just came to me a couple of days ago.’

‘Yes?’

‘I’ll offer Miriam a gentile helper or companion – in time, I would hope, a highly proficient governess. Miriam will be delighted, I know it. I’ve suggested it to Eva and she’s thinking about it.’

‘I’m astonished, Hugo. What does Anton think?’

‘I don’t know. He’s cut off communication with her. He’s been avoiding me as well since I started talking to her. He has no right to expect anything of Eva of course... '

'So first he loses his son, then his woman! I fear for his sanity.'

'His woman!' exclaimed Hugo. 'What about Magda? Does anybody think of her!'

Stefan sighed. 'I will try to comfort her as much as I can.'

'It is now only a matter of comfort, Stefan, and I'm grateful to you for staying on when I'm leaving early. In practical terms we've done all we can. We've badgered officials, bribed all and sundry. We contacted Herzl's party and tried to get a message through to the Kaiser himself. I don't know what else is left. As for Anton, he is his own worst enemy. Believe me, Stefan, it will be better if Eva leaves the Colony.'

JOHANNES 1

I know how they travel. I've travelled with them since. They go by paths only they know, following a star, or homing on a landmark at first hardly seen: a ruined khan, a tree, a rock with a name older than their tribe.

The slow tread, hour after hour, broken by bumps and lurches as the train clambers into a wadi or mounts a cliff.

I was trussed to an animal, folded into a scratchy blanket. I sobbed and rubbed my eyes, covering my face with sticky hands. The insects which shared my putrid nest sucked my sores.

The animal stank.

And the thirst. Now and again, a hand would enter and shove a can against my teeth. I longed for the sour liquid but feared the gnarled hand. It had a will of its own. It was going to grab me by the throat and throttle me.

When they took me out of my blanket, they blindfolded me. I circled round, tearing at the cloth, crying out, '*Wo ist meine Mutter?* I want my mother! Help me please! Help me!' – before a crust or nut or fig was pushed between my lips, or hands pulled my trousers down and buckled my knees so that the waste from my body could fall pitifully to the sand.

In the evenings I crouched in the corner of a black tent, twisting the tasselled ends of the carpet. The rasping voices of fierce-eyed women tore my heart.

No one spoke to me. If the women were moved by me, they didn't show it. No tucking of chin or ruffling of hair. They sat apart as I lay crying under the black tents.

After a long journey, something different. Shouts and commotion – tinkers and traders, hawkers and street musicians. And smells. Pungent food and spices.

Someone shouted from above. There was discussion and haggling. The word *jamila* kept on cropping up – 'pretty' as I learnt later. I followed a man up a narrow stairway. From the dingy lobby I saw through to the salon, with cushions, hangings and spangled lamps. A labyrinth of corridors led to the fountain in the tiled courtyard. I was dumped in the 'dormitory'.

'I am Johannes,' I said, 'I am from Zion.'

They gathered round me staring uncomprehendingly. I was sick that day, sick to my guts, like a drunk who holds himself straight but feels the world rocking. The blood in my ears pounded. It was raw agony, worse than in my desert blanket, which had become a kind of home.

That first night they pointed and stared, and seemed to talk about nothing else but me. One girl stood out. She had beautiful eyes and smooth olive skin. My suffering was lifted – at least that's how I remember it. She was my age and the same height. When she touched my fair hair – still tumbling in waves before the barber got to it – she repeated a word over and over again – *Amir.* I was to be her prince. 'I shall call you Prince Ali.'

Zoraya was allowed to get away with anything in that place. She was laying claim to me. I accepted it but never forgot that I was Johannes from Zion.

I was pitched into lessons. The teacher was hideously strict. He had hairs coming out of his nose and breath that reeked like a latrine. He cracked a whip across the top of your head at the slightest fault or sign of inattention.

At nights I wept into my bolster, remembering my mother's love, my father's laughter and fond teasing.

We were kept busy with a furious regime of cleaning and kitchen preparation. Recreations were simple. Tag, or football or pitch and toss in the narrow yard. By the fountain we read and played board games like snakes and ladders and backgammon. On rare occasions there were excursions to an oasis or a mosque. Later I remember boat trips on the Nile. I learnt to swim. We camped in the desert.

I was forgetting my German and took to Arabic. In time I could write the language.

Visitors paid for boys and girls to sit on their laps in the salon. Later it changed. The children grew older and past fourteen or so gave favours for money (which they handed straight to the establishment) in the cell-like rooms off the labyrinthine corridors. The clientele varied from Europeanised young bloods to fat merchants, anxious clerks, visiting Cairenes, foreigners.

Through Zoraya I came to the flute, the Persian *ney*, end-blown with six holes and one at the back.

The early morning sun streamed through the skylight of the inner court and sparkled the fountain drops. Zoraya was practising. She was no good at it. It was a pain to listen to.

I watched her through the lattice that surrounded the courtyard. She knew it was me. 'Ali,' she called, 'stop spying on me.' I didn't yet know much Arabic but I understood since I was already a willing slave hanging on her every word.

I edged from my hiding place. She removed the instrument from her lips. 'You take it.'

I put it to my lips and blew. One note, then another, a semitone higher, softly, then more up the scale and down.

She opened her eyes wide. 'Again.'

I repeated my performance. I varied it. It came naturally to me. I felt myself speak through the instrument. Stepping towards me, she made me lower the *ney*, then slowly rested her lips on mine. We stood, lips pressed together, warmed by the sun's rays. I breathed in and felt her breath in my mouth.

'Play more for your princess. I *am* a princess, you know.'

Zoraya stopped her *ney* lessons and I took them instead.

My teacher kept snakes and used to charm them. As a matter of fact I loved animals. I made a fuss of any cats and dogs around and in time kept insects, caterpillars, a lizard, the odd small rodent and a caged canary. As my flute playing progressed I learnt to charm snakes. I had my own basket where my viper slept only to emerge and sinuously elevate himself when I played.

Zoraya watched over me. She loved stories from children's history books.

'Ali and I will be the Ferdinand and Isabella of the Muslims. We will drive the infidel British from here in Omdurman right up to the Nile Delta and away for ever.'

I loved the look in her eye which said, you and I, we laugh together against all misery. We held hands shyly and sometimes kissed each other on the lips, standing stock-still like statues.

But when I was about eleven, a great shadow fell.

A European in a black suit, with a cross on his chest, hovered in the cushioned salon. He spoke to me in German. I said nothing but I understood. For the second time in my short life, it became clear, everything was to change.

'Ali,' he said, placing his hand on my shoulder, 'I am going to take you with me to Cairo. Do you know of Cairo? It is a great city where, as throughout this Dark Continent, the Lord's work must needs be done. I have paid some money to these Unbelievers to save you for the Lord. They didn't want to lose you but I persuaded them. I hear you work hard at your lessons. You play the flute too.' He scowled. 'Yes, music... Music is mischief. Your flute will remain here. Come, get your things, Ali – we will give you a Christian, German name in due course – and we will depart forthwith.'

I froze at these words. I would never go with this man. I would never leave Zoraya. I turned and ran down the stairs followed by the shouts of the owner, who saw his dinars slipping from his hands. I burst between the market stalls and made it to the corner of the square. Fatally I paused, working out where to go next. I felt an arm around my neck. I was grabbed by both legs and upended.

The visitor was waiting at the top of the steps with an unctuous smile. Zoraya pushed past him down the steps arms outstretched.

'Ali, don't go! Don't let them!'

The Christian, tumbling down the stairs past Zoraya, grabbed my arm and wrenched me away. There was no getting my 'things' now. He frogmarched me to a waiting carriage.

'Ali, I will wait!' I saw her dark eyes, wet with tears, for the last time.

'Come back, I will wait!'

My captor dug his nails into my arm. The carriage moved off. He did not let go of me till we had crossed the Nile into Khartoum.

Later I learned that Zoraya drowned my lizard and rodents. She asphyxiated the canary and buried it. No one was allowed to mention me or she would slap them. She said, 'Ali is my *amir*. He will come back to marry me.'

Heart-sore, I learnt on the endless Khartoum-Cairo train journey what was in store for me. Fixing on the desert horizon, Pastor Hartmann listened to that which soothed him against all trials and doubts: his own voice.

'Master Johannes – I had told him my pre-Ali name – we have a great opportunity. The key is education. Hitherto our enterprise has depended on our missionaries from the Fatherland, learned and pious in the faith but without much Arabic. They have tried to learn the language but have resorted, when spreading the Word, to English, which is more often spoken in Cairo. Of course, we have local converts who can preach but their education is minimal and theology crude. You are an intelligent boy mired through no fault of your own in error and filth. We have rescued you for the Lord. Nobody knows your origins. I was told you were a foundling.'

'I... come...' – my German was halting – 'from Zion...'

His eyes opened wide. This thrilled him. 'Ah! I don't doubt it!

Here, have another of these.' He handed me a sticky date as a reward for assisting his line of argument. 'We are not to take this as a literal statement. This notion of Zion that has arisen in you is a breath of the Holy Spirit, an inner template if you will, not betokening origins, but Destiny. Surely you are chosen. You are not *from* Zion, but *of* Zion. Master John Calvin...' and he proceeded to lecture me incomprehensibly on pre-destination. He had quickly decided that I was 'elected'. This would determine my future on this earth.

If I understood little of what he was saying in the railway carriage, I was to learn soon enough when I reached Cairo and took up residence with him and his wife.

A new life began. Five mornings of the week I received education in German. Arabic lessons took place in the afternoon. German included a heavy dose of theology, Arabic of mathematics. I was bored and not a very good student. Saturdays were spent accompanying the Hartmanns on 'missions' – meetings with potential converts in modest homes or slum shacks. On Sundays I was all day in chapel, singing hymns and listening to sermons, very long ones, which might be in German, Arabic or English.

Frau Hartmann was a plain woman denied motherhood since her Destiny was to serve her husband and the mission. She had an instinct to mother *me*. She slipped me cakes and choice fruits from the market. But she was under her husband's thumb and awed by my 'elect' status. She hardly spoke to me, still less put an arm round me. Evenings were spent with the couple in prayer and the reading of theological tracts.

Both my German and my Arabic teachers were kindly, but the lessons suffocated me. There was an exception. I loved the stories from the Old Testament, David and Jonathan, Samson, above all the saga of Joseph. I worshipped Joseph. Reader of dreams, man of influence, finally ruler of Egypt. He too had been taken from all that he had known – and yes, to Egypt where I had ended up.

I believed I was special like him. I would triumph in the end. Would I too rule Egypt? Zoraya had said so.

When it came to Joseph's reconciliation with his family at the end of the story, a mist shrouded my mind. I could not imagine such a thing. My parents were fading. A hand, a look, a feeling or atmosphere was all that remained. Much clearer were my memories of my life at Omdurman. Above all Zoraya.

The Hartmanns couldn't see the child in me. They thought about little other than sin but they could not imagine that their chosen one would ever be tempted by the thieving ways of souk urchins. How wrong they were.

Since I contributed nothing to the Saturday 'missions', in fact spoiled them with my restlessness, I was allowed a day of freedom so long as I undertook to stay at home and read the Word of the Lord. I promised but did no such thing.

Passing through Bab Zuweila, I noticed a middle-aged European man, an orchid in his buttonhole, talking in Arabic to the handsome policeman, a friend of mine, who patrolled the ancient gate.

'And who is this young denizen of the streets, fair as Endymion?' asked the stranger, eyeing me roguishly.

'This is young Ali,' replied the policeman. 'He is studying to convert us all to your Jesus.'

'*My* Jesus! Heavens above, I would think not... Mm... intriguing.'

The policeman smiled encouragingly. 'Ali, tell my English friend, Mr Rose, about your weird life.'

'I live with some Germans who pray all day long.'

'Really,' responded the Englishman with a wave of the hand. 'Clearly, my dear, you need a diversion from *that*.'

I was about to move on.

'Wait, young man,' said Mr Rose, 'I have an idea. If you have a while – and who does not have a while in this city where nothing gets done? – come with me to my favourite coffee house. I will introduce you to my charming young friends. They are sure to adore you.'

My friend gave me a nod as if to say, he's all right despite appearances.

This is how I came to know Ismail the pickpocket, Khalifa the shoe black, a lame boy whose name I forget, Mussa the Jew and many others. I quickly became a once-a-week member of the group and happily joined them loitering and pilfering in the souk.

Mr Rose gave us food and drink in return for our company. His interest in children was unhealthy but to us he was just a slightly absurd 'uncle' who drew interesting gadgets or tricks from his pockets, which he always ended up by giving away.

However, if one of us let him down by rudeness or disloyalty, that one was cast into outer darkness. Rose would bribe us to shun the traitor.

On the other hand he had favourites he drooled over in an unpleasing way. I was chief among them. But this is to run ahead.

On Sunday evenings Herr Hartmann brought home the money from the collection box and put it in a drawer. I'd known where the key was from my first days there. When I was alone in the house I would open the drawer and stare. The money would accumulate week by week and eventually be removed – I assumed to a bank – after which the process would start from scratch again.

The day came when, having learnt to thieve in the souk with my friends, I took a note from the drawer and stuffed it in my pocket. A few weeks later I did it again. I didn't steal too often as I knew they'd get suspicious. It became a habit and went unnoticed since Herr Hartmann only counted the money when he finally removed it from the drawer. I didn't spend the money, I saved it.

In the souk I noticed a coat I fancied. Winter was coming on and an extra layer would be welcome. It was to be my 'Joseph' coat. It was of 'many colours', gorgeous and bright and full of contrasts. The velvet was light and soft to the touch, the lining of smooth, luxurious satin. I longed to own the coat but calculated that by the time but I had stolen enough to pay for it the short winter would be over. I wanted it then and there.

When the owner wasn't looking I whipped it off its hanger and was beating it down the alley when I bumped straight into Rose.

'Ah, so you have noticed this delectable garment too, Ali, even to the point of scarpering without payment. I just saw what you did. I really should turn you in, you scamp.'

He walked away from the shop.

'Come back to my house, Ali, and persuade me with your sweet tongue not to behave as a good citizen ought.'

At his house he sat me on the sofa and took my hand.

'Ali, of all the friends you are the most congenial to me. You have a quality about you. You are a petty criminal but beneath the rough surface you are true, you are deep. I see your suffering which I daresay mirrors my own… This coat… I will keep quiet, heaven forgive me. However, I'll kill you if you mention it to anyone. If I ask one thing of you in return, it is to come here to my home as part of your Saturday routine – just an hour or so will do – and again not to say a word to anyone. We will read together. I have a Victrola…'

'What's a Victrola?'

'A phonograph. Look, over there on the sideboard. We shall have music! What music do you like, Ali?'

From then on my life included a new element, an hour a week being pampered by Rose. It was only unpleasant when he stroked my hand. Eventually I put a stop to that. I ate the best cuts of meat prepared by his discreet servant. Sometimes I smoked hashish, which made me giggle. I heard the works of Mozart, Schubert and Tchaikovsky, though I can't say they made much impression on me.

Above all I had the coat. It wasn't much use as I couldn't wear it outside for fear of being caught. In any case I put it away when the weather warmed up. The following winter out it came, though I was careful to hide it from the Hartmanns.

All the while I missed Zoraya and when I was thirteen I plotted my escape back to Omdurman. More ambitiously I planned our future life together. The key was money. With or without Zoraya, I knew, young though I was, that without money I would be trapped for ever. And in a corner of my mind – always – I knew I must eventually find a way back home to Jerusalem.

Luck was on my side. I found I'd been wrong to think that the money from the chapel collection box disappeared off to a bank. One day I discovered Hartmann removing it to a strongbox in the cellar. It only remained to locate the keys – to the cellar itself and to the strongbox. I bided my time but since no suspicion surrounded me it wasn't difficult.

One Saturday with both keys to hand when the house was deserted, I found my way to the box. I opened the lid. The sight took my breath away. Layer on layer of bank notes tied in neat bundles. This was far more than could have been collected at the chapel. Perhaps it had been sent from Germany in preparation for the 'great leap' Hartmann was always talking about.

I needed to think quickly. I was a dab hand with a needle. Sewing was one of the skills they had taught us in Omdurman. I ran to fetch my coat. I snipped open parts of the lining and began to load the bundles of notes in, finally to create what was in effect a padded coat once I had sewed it back up. The coat was only strange to look at if one knew how it looked before.

There was so much money in the box that even when I had taken as much as I could, a lot was left. I wrapped my coat into a cloth which I attached to a stick. Quickly I threw in a few things I'd found in the souk. I left the house and headed for the river. Stick on my shoulder, strolling along the banks of the Nile, I had not a care in the world. Now I was truly free.

The quickest way to undertake this thousand-mile journey was by train but I thought this would risk detection. I decided to travel by river, working my passage. I was soon taken on as cabin boy on a Nile steamer. This took me as far as Aswan. After the Cataracts I picked up another job on a barge heading for Khartoum.

After weeks of travel I crossed to Omdurman. I was given a hero's welcome and Zoraya fell on my shoulder weeping. I didn't tell them I was only intending to stay a few months. Did they think I was about to surrender my freedom for the privilege of getting fondled, or worse, by inverts?

I returned to my chores and lessons. I was still a poor student. Most of my spare time was spent playing the *ney* and charming snakes in the courtyard while Zoraya looked on, hugging to herself the secret we now shared of the coat and future we planned together.

If any customers tried to talk to me through the lattice screen, I played mute. Afraid that the police would come after me, I followed a rule of silence with strangers.

Never talk to them, I said to myself. Don't even listen to their rubbish. Just play your flute and get the snake going. That'll give them something else to think about. They revolted me anyway with their fingers wiggling through the screen.

1904

Chapter 5

On the terrace of Shepheard's Hotel, Cairo, Stefan Lehmann sipped his breakfast coffee in the winter sunshine. He smiled to himself. What pleasure to take time over the newspaper, to plan an excursion with the whole day ahead, simply to take things in. How entertaining, how ludicrous, this temple of idleness and colonial domination.

Against a backdrop of Italianate décor and potted palms, waiters delivered sumptuous treats along tracks of crimson carpet. At the next table an elderly milord complained about the tea. The head waiter theatrically reprimanded an underling. Outside, down below, a band with a red-coated officer riding in front bore down on the noisy crowd of vendors, tour guides and beggars.

It reminded Stefan of attending an operetta. Relaxed and well-fed, one enjoyed the exotic setting, buffoonery and pretty women without feeling deeply involved.

Meanwhile the daughters of haughty British memsahibs fluttered their eyelids at him. Some were pretty enough. Maybe there would be a chance encounter. Perhaps he would even find a wife.

'Mr Lehmann.'

Stefan jumped. A thin man with a mop of grey hair, monocle and an orchid in his buttonhole beamed down at him.

Stefan stood up. 'Ah, *ja*, Mr Rose. I was not expecting you so early.'

'Well, here I am. How do you do, Mr Lehmann. The manager pointed you out.'

'Ah, the manager, *ja*...'

'Puffed up fellow,' confided Rose, holding out thin fingers. 'Thinks he's got the ear of Lord Cromer and the British high-ups.'

'I am sorry, Mr Rose. My English is not so good. Can you speak slowly, please? Thank you for coming here. Will you have some coffee?'

Stefan motioned to the waiter and they sat down.

After a few pleasantries, Rose declared, 'I am at your service, Mr Lehmann. Our mutual friend, the noble baron, wrote to me to welcome you. I'm happy to be of help. Time hangs heavily here, I can tell you.' Sweeping the terrace with a pained gaze, he whispered, 'My countrymen are such regular stuffed-shirts.'

'Stuffed-shirts?'

'Too... formal, too conservative.'

'I see.'

'Everything has become so spruced up and regulated since the British had things their own way. Only on the surface, mind. Here as everywhere the Muslim holds the infidel in silent contempt. And beneath that there is another layer, so to speak: the old Egyptian gods, of burial, of death...'

'Interesting... I also have been thinking about this since I arrived in Cairo.'

'You are a perceptive man, I can see it, Mr Lehmann.' Rose looked Stefan up and down. 'Tell me, what is your profession?'

'I am a painter.'

Rose's monocle dropped. 'I might have guessed! For I can see you are a man of style, of visual sense. How exciting. And what are you painting here? Are you *seduced* – by the light, the colours of people's clothes, the desert – like Delacroix in Algiers?'

'I cannot compare myself to Delacroix but I find exciting scenes and paint many things.'

'Admirable.' Rose sipped his coffee with pleasure. 'I say,' he said, flapping his hand at a waiter passing with a tray of honey cakes, 'could I have one of those?' When the pastry was brought he set about it in a manner both dainty and rapacious.

'But I gather you have another reason for being here,' Rose said at last, laying his napkin on the table.

'Yes.'

'A boy?'

'As the baron has told you, I am looking for a boy who was taken in Jerusalem six years ago. Johannes. He was a son of my friends. The Turkish authorities said he was dead but they did not prove it. The baron told me in Venice that you knew a German boy who was the right age.'

'Well, he was the right age, about twelve when I knew him.'

'Can you describe him?'

Rose rolled his eyes to the ceiling. 'He was striking, beautiful…. Words fail me. Brown skin, blue eyes, fair – so strangely fair for these parts. Mind you, the Mamluks were fair and sometimes the blood of Norse pirates or Teuton crusaders finds its way hereabouts.'

'What language did he speak?'

'Arabic with me, but he also spoke German. I bought him a few meals and trinkets and then a few months ago he disappeared.' Rose sighed. 'Just the smile…'

'The smile?'

Rose leant across to Stefan. He was no longer the poseur. Unhappiness was on his sleeve. 'Unforgettable, sad, timeless. Knowledge like that of *La Gioconda* herself was in that smile. He had courage that boy, I know. Also, a certain refinement of spirit, the fruit of suffering. He was like one who came to me in a dream, a dream I can neither forget nor summon again.'

'You liked him very much.'

'I am desolate. I was like a father to him. I planned to educate him, give him another life. In doing that I would have rescued myself too.'

'How?'

'It would have given me a purpose. Without Ali…'

'Ali?'

'That was his name. Without him I… ' Rose's eyes moistened. He looked away.

Stefan reached into his pocket and pulled out a notebook with a drawing folded inside.

'Did he look like this?'

Pulling himself together, Rose looked at the picture. 'Older than this, but not unlike.'

'Do you know where he went?'

'On a river steamer south, I learned.'

'Why?'

'He never said. He just left. I found out by simple detective work. I heard that he had been in Khartoum before. The Sudan may have been his birthplace.'

'He has gone by river back to Khartoum?'

'That's not possible in the precise sense because of the Nile Cataracts. At Aswan you have to get out of the boat. But people and trade go back and forth all the time. There's even a railway now. Who knows how far he's gone? Perhaps he'll be back in Cairo after a jaunt. Perhaps he went home to Khartoum. But I have reason to believe it was the latter.'

'What reason is that?'

'A diplomat friend of mine has just returned by rail from there on government business. He makes local friends wherever he goes and unwisely visits certain establishments.'

'Establishments?'

'Places of diversion… of entertainment.'

'Ah, I see. He is not a "stuffed shirt."'

Rose grinned. 'Indeed not! I have to tell him to be careful in his profession! I was talking about Ali only two days ago and he was amazed. He said, "There's a boy just like that in a place in Khartoum. Fair, blue-eyed, exquisite." Well! Can there be more than one such boy in Egypt and the Sudan? There could, I suppose but… it set me back. On the one hand, it is good to hear something of him – if it is he. On the other, I do not like to think of him as a boy…' Rose bit his lip.

'Working in such a place,' said Stefan helpfully.

'Precisely. Anyway I have the address of the establishment. Lord knows I could never contemplate Khartoum at my time of life. It's in Omdurman – the other side of the river from Khartoum proper.'

'Anton Gustavus, the father of Johannes, wrote to me about the slave trade. He said the Bedouin still take people from Palestine, usually young village girls, not boys. Do you know anything about this?'

Rose's eyes lit up. 'Indeed I do know about such things.'

'Do you think it might be important in this case?'

'It was certainly common in pre-British days. To tell the truth I once made a study of it. I was intrigued. I wanted to write a book about this very subject. I had a picture of myself as a great righter of wrongs. Unfortunately it was just another unfinished project.'

'What did you learn?'

'Many things. In the Sudan, for example, Abyssinian traders sold girls they'd captured from tribes to the south. They were bought by the Turks, either for distribution throughout the Ottoman empire or for the garrison in Khartoum. This force was continually diminished by malaria and plague and was replenished by more slaves, negro men, again from the south – another profitable line. In turn they were allowed to own slave girls. You had slaves owning slaves.'

'I see.'

'Do you know who were the most brutal among the Ottomans in Khartoum?'

Stefan shook his head.

'Balkan officers – and those most inclined to inversion, the Albanians. They would lock a prisoner in a cell for several days to be repeatedly… I hesitate to use the correct word, but we are talking about a certain biblical city of the plain… by a squad of Albanian soldiers.'

'I am shocked. Does this still happen?'

'Who knows? The British have stamped on it to some degree – after Kitchener did for the Mahdi at the Battle of Omdurman. But maybe the Mahdi's own fanatical puritanism had previously had some effect too... Perhaps such things are more...voluntary these days... By the way Mr Lehmann, what were you doing in Palestine at the time?'

'I was with a friend, a Zionist.'

'A Jew who believes in recreating the Jewish homeland?'

'Indeed. We met the Gustavus family by chance in on the Jaffa-Jerusalem train. They were friendly to us. I painted the boy's picture, partly to thank them – though I was also influenced by his fine appearance, I have to admit.'

'And what has happened to this poor couple who have lost their son?'

'They have suffered of course. However, they have another son. His name is Werner. Strangely he was born on the day that Johannes was kidnapped. Maybe he comforts them but I do not know. His father does not talk about him in his letters to me, only about Johannes. The father is a craftsman and does many jobs. Maybe he keeps busy. But now he has written to me again. He wants me to look for Johannes. I have to try.'

'Are you free to travel where you wish?'

Stefan looked guardedly at Rose. 'You think I should go to Khartoum?'

Rose shrugged. 'I have the address...'

~

He hired a felucca and was enchanted by his vessel gliding across the Nile like a majestic swan. A servant came with him. Hamdi looked after everything: sailing the boat, searching for supplies, discouraging the naked men who climbed aboard asking for *baksheesh.*

The days were lazy and soon stretched into weeks. Stefan hardly spoke to a soul. Hamdi had no German, just a few words of English. Nor could Stefan paint though this had been as much a pretext for the trip as the search for Johannes. The sweep of placid grey water and the banks dotted with palms were soon monotonous. Instead, he read, slept in the afternoon and at sunset raided the crate of whisky he had surprised himself by buying just before his departure.

With that trickle of fire in the throat, the crying cormorants and creaking boat spoke of magic. Every evening he saw the Nile bank and the palms as if for the first time. Bottle in one hand, glass in the other, he stared west. The luminous sky was red with truth. Then darkness closed in. Only just able to stand, lost in the stars, he called out coarsely for Hamdi to bring his dinner.

'Dammit,' he muttered. 'Why am I drinking? Nobody in my family drinks. Jews are never drinkers. Hamdi, a teetotal Muslim, feels disdain – which he hides. Anyway, I'll stop soon. There's only one more bottle left.'

At Korosko they left the boat and Stefan hired camels. They took the overland route across the desert to avoid the Cataracts and the great curve of the Nile. Passing from oasis to oasis they shot gazelles to eat. Discomfort was extreme, they couldn't eat without swallowing flies, the monotony of sand replaced that of the river and the whisky had gone.

Stefan was calmer. Perhaps the desert soothed inner desolation by mirroring it. The animals in this vast creature-kingdom, their number, variety and oddness, caught his attention as the ruins of ancient Egypt had not: giraffes, hippos, lions, buffaloes, hyenas, baboons, antelopes and the mighty elephants. Perhaps they too echoed something inside him. He would crouch behind a rock or meagre bush, mesmerised by a sleeping creature, a kill or mating performance. What separated him from them? He was aware of nothing significant.

He didn't have the will to paint the animals.

'I can't lift a pencil,' he would sigh to Hamdi, who seemed to understand. 'Where is everything? Where is everybody? Why am I doing this?'

'The boy,' said Hamdi, gesturing south to Khartoum. 'Find the boy.'

From early on Hamdi had made enquiries. Usually he had drawn a blank, but some people weren't so sure. Yes, maybe a fair boy had passed this way. Some weeks ago, or was it months? A boat boy, part of a camel train, or maybe it was that young theology student with Koran and prayer mat.

At one oasis Stefan was ill. He was put in a mud hut. Feverish, he slept for an hour or two at a time. The stench from his sick bucket woke him up.

'Hamdi,' he croaked, leaning on one elbow, pulling at his servant's sleeve. 'I can't go on. We have to go back. I have to get to Venice.'

'Sir! The boy.'

'No, there is no boy. He is dead.'

'Sir!'

Stefan sank back on to the pillow. 'Oh God. What madness is this? Why am I here?'

Chapter 6

It was a relief to reach Khartoum with its cooling green water's edge: a dusty shanty town in the process of transformation into an imperial capital, with boulevards, 'Roman' governmental buildings, neat residential areas. At his hotel Stefan had a balcony overlooking a garden with palms and fruit trees. Beyond, and to add to his consolations, lay picturesque minarets and the three domes of the Coptic church.

He was too depleted to consider making overtures to the small British community. He preferred the rougher European element – traders, adventurers, ex-criminals – holed up at his hotel. Not that he talked to them much, but they helped him to feel anonymous. Before he himself ventured there he heard from them about his ultimate destination, Omdurman. In seedy huts on this other, 'native' side of the river, they whiled away their time drinking absinthe and getting into fights.

Hamdi was no longer useful. Stefan bought him a train ticket back to Cairo and paid him generous *baksheesh*. Early one morning the two men bid an emotional farewell at the station. Whatever divided them, the human bond was there.

'Without you, not possible, my friend,' said Stefan, holding Hamdi's gaze as a lump formed in his throat.

'Thank you, sir. May Allah bring you everything you wish for. Perhaps you see me again in Cairo.'

Stefan went back to his hotel. He was alone. He opened the door to his room and surveyed the narrow bed and rickety chair. He hovered, as if even to lie down or sit would be to acknowledge that he suited this place: he had become a hermit and this was his cell. He closed his eyes and leant against the peeling wall.

He ordered whisky and moved to the balcony as the sun was setting. Without Hamdi's surveillance he was free. He could drink, oh, how he could now drink. The first glass was like the embrace of a long lost friend. He drank more, much more, watching the red-gold sky, his old habit from weeks on the Nile.

Everything from Palestine in '98 came back to him. The Gustavus family, Eva, Hugo, the portrait. The wretched irony that this work had been his best to date, the one in which he had at last fully expressed himself. He recalled his rapport with Anton, the quick growth of friendship, their consuming discussions. And then the day of the kidnap. His dreadful feeling of responsibility, the sense that it had been his carelessness alone that allowed the tragedy to happen. Agonising days after the disappearance.

As he drank he kept thinking back to his first impression of Johannes in the railway carriage. Besides his arresting looks, the boy seemed uncannily knowing. Had he some premonition of the disaster?

The whisky revealed these questions and made them seem romantic. As the sun set over the desert, alcohol took the edge off the tragedy by placing the drinker in the role of heroic saviour. Stefan could and would save the day! He was about to find the boy. No question! He would deliver him safe and sound. The rescue would be a great page in the history of the German Colony. There would be a triumphant entry into Jerusalem to match the Kaiser's.

A knock at the door. Stefan shouted 'Come in' and staggered to his feet in an effort to sober up. Herr Gross, a fellow guest, entered.

'*Lehmann, alte. Ich habe mich erinnert*. That address you were asking about. It's off the souk over there across the river. It's a refuge for beggar boys and girls, orphans, runaways.'

'I see,' said Stefan stiffly. 'Well, thank you, Herr Gross.'

Gross handed Stefan a crude map.

'Would you like a drink?' asked Stefan. 'I'm just finishing a bottle.'

They went out to the balcony and sat down.

'What sort of refuge?' asked Stefan blearily.

'It's the system here. There are places where a starving child will end up. The janitor looks him up and down. If there are no signs of scurvy, leprosy or contagious skin diseases, he'll be taken in. He'll get a mat and food. In return he sweeps, scrubs privies, works in the kitchen. If he's pretty, he'll deliver teas and sweetmeats on silver trays to the clientele.'

'I see.'

Another bottled was fetched.

'I'll find this boy,' Stefan slurred. 'Rescue him.'

Gross was now getting drunk as well. 'What is with you and this boy?' He grabbed Stefan's arm and breathed unpleasantly into his face.

Stefan shook him off. 'No, it's not what you think. It was all my fault you see.'

'Why? What have you done? You can tell me, old chap.'

'I've got to get him back... even if I go the ends of the earth, which... as a matter of fact... is where I am!'

'What?' hiccupped Gross.

'It's where I am!'

'Where?'

'Khartoum.'

'Khartoum? What of it?'

'You're drunk, Gross!'

'You're drunk too, Lehmann!'

'I'm drunk too!'

They gave up, collapsing in giggles, two lost souls under a silent tropical moon.

~

The street was dark and deserted. Only one building was lit up. Stefan went towards it, glancing behind him. Voices and the whiff of hashish drifted down from the balconies. At ground level there were high barred windows and a narrow door. He fingered his cravat before pulling the rope. The bell sounded inside.

The grilled spy hole was pulled back.

'Yes?'

'I am looking for a young boy.' Stefan gave Gross's name by way of introduction. 'He comes here, he says. You can trust me. Can you let me in?'

'You are a friend of Mr Gross? Very good man. Friendly man. You want a boy?'

Stefan shook his head. 'I am *looking* for a boy.'

The door opened. The entrance was at the bottom of steep stone steps. The young man – he wore a striped robe – peered at Stefan, turned and climbed the steps with sandals flapping.

At the top the youth entered a large crowded room and beckoned to Stefan. 'Come,' he called above the voices.

Stefan hesitated. 'I…'

'Come!'

'I don't want to stay,' said Stefan, hovering at the door. 'I am just asking a question.'

The young man looked disappointed. 'Come. Sir. You like to drink? We have very good absinthe, whisky, gin, Russian vodka. We have every drink.'

'No thank you.'

'You like hashish? We have the best quality. A hookah?'

The young man pointed to a chair, which had just been vacated by a man leaving the room with a girl.

'Yes. Very good. Whisky please. Then perhaps you will help me.'

While waiting for his drink Stefan glanced round. It was a den reeking of drink and hashish, with wall hangings, carved tables, brass lamps, sofas and rugs. Half-naked young girls and boys lolled everywhere, giggling and tickling each other. Some sat on the laps of European men, pulling their beards or playfully resisting their kisses. Other guests just ogled, or were oblivious, more interested in backgammon or a conversation.

There were no Europeans amongst the boys. Stefan was both wasting his time and humiliating himself. Why had he agreed to the drink? He was stuck now.

The young man returned with the drink and sat down. Stefan drank slowly. He was keen to keep his head clear.

'This boy is not here,' he said. 'They look too young and they are not European.'

'We have very nice boys and girls from every country. Arab, negro, Abyssinian, Berber.'

'But no European.'

The young man eyed Stefan. 'How much you pay?'

'Pay? Of course I will pay for my whisky but...'

'I will show you. How much you pay?'

The whisky fired Stefan's indignation. 'This is very stupid. Why am I paying you?'

'You give me three sterling.'

'Three sterling!'

'I take you to a boy and you pay me three sterling.'

Some of the people nearby were starting to notice. Stefan lowered his voice. 'Maybe I pay you if you find the boy I am looking for but that is after.'

The man got up and walked out of the room. Stefan finished his drink and left too. The man was now sitting gloomily in a cubicle at the top of the stairs.

'How much for the whisky?'

The man gave a figure three times what Stefan was used to paying. Stefan handed over the money and started down the steps. He got to the bottom.

'Ridiculous,' he muttered. He climbed quickly back up and rapped on the cubicle.

'This boy is called Johannes or Ali. He is about fourteen. He is fair. Do you have him here, yes or no?'

'Three pounds sterling.'

Stefan paused. 'One.'

The young man shook his head.

'Two,' said Stefan.

'I am not a stupid man. This is special information. It is dangerous. The police. I could be in big trouble.'

Stefan ground his teeth. 'All right. Three.'

'You have three now? You can give me? You show me?'

Stefan felt for his wallet and thrust the notes down on the counter.

'OK. Three sterling. Good. Now you follow me.'

Another flight of steps led down to an airless corridor lit by a row of flickering oil lamps. His guide moved quickly and Stefan had trouble keeping up. The noise from the room above had receded.

'Wait.'

The guide stopped. 'You hear it?'

It came from along the passage.

'A flute.'

'Come.'

Out of the darkness came another sound, the splash of water. A faint panel of light appeared. Stefan strode forward. The light came from beyond a lattice screen. The music and fountain were the other side.

'Sir, please look. You will be a very happy man.'

Stefan pressed his eye against the screen. The beauty and strangeness of what he saw took his breath away.

The moon shone down on a blue-tiled courtyard dotted with shrubs, palms and lamps. A fountain dropped soft rain into a shallow pool. Dressed in veils or scraps of cloth, children dangled their feet in the water, leant against the walls, lay on divans or piles of cushions.

Stefan noted their vacant eyes, how lazily they moved. They had none of the normal energy of children.

Cross-legged, with his drum by his side was the flute-player, a blond European boy naked to the waist with his back to Stefan. He lifted the flute and his playing coaxed the viper from its basket. As the flute trilled the snake darted higher and seemed to threaten the boy's face with its flickering tongue.

All round the courtyard were other lattices. Whites of eyes behind, even a protruding finger, told Stefan that he was not alone in staring through the lattice at the enchanted scene.

'These are children…'

'They are children.'

'Who are they?'

'We look after them. They have everything they need.'

'I need to speak to the European boy.'

Stefan felt his guide's hand on his arm. 'Sir.'

'What?'

'Leave him.'

Stefan turned to look at his companion. Striped shadows from the lattice fell across his face.

'What is his name?'

The guide shook his head. 'We have special name for him. It is Arabic name. He came to us from far away. He was *very* unhappy. Now he has friends, even an education.'

'But I know his father, his mother. They want him back.'

'I don't think so, sir. He has no mother or father. He is an orphan boy.'

'How do you know?'

'He says so. He was *very* happy to come here.'

'What language does he speak?'

'Wait, you see.'

Through the lattice the guide whistled and called in Arabic. Several of the children looked round but the blond snake charmer carried on with his work with his back turned. The snake was now wound around his naked torso. Heart beating, Stefan continued to peer through the slats. At last another child tapped the fair boy on the shoulder and pointed.

With the snake still coiled round him the boy turned and came towards the screen. He looked though the slats into Stefan's eyes. He was near enough to touch.

'Johannes, I am your father's friend,' stuttered Stefan in German, 'the artist who painted your picture.'

The boy frowned. A terrible doubt seized Stefan. Was this Johannes? He was fair and blue eyed, but he was grave, cold, unfamiliar. Or was it just that he was older now?

'I know you can't see me but can you confirm that you are Johannes Gustavus?'

The boy looked away. There was no glimmer of recognition or interest.

'Your father… Anton… your mother Magda at Jerusalem.'

Stefan turned to the young man by his side. 'This is stupid,' he said, reverting to English. 'Can I please meet him. He can't even see me.'

The guide spoke Arabic to the boy, who replied briefly.

'Sir, he doesn't know you. He doesn't speak German. He speaks only Arabic.'

'I want to see him. What did I pay you for?'

'Sir… he is a happy boy. Do not disturb him.'

Already the boy had turned his back.

'Johannes!' Stefan called through the screen.

Stefan's guide touched his sleeve again. 'If you are not happy, I give you back the money.'

Stefan closed his eyes. 'I don't want the money…'

'Maybe, sir, this boy is from the south, not Jerusalem.'

'South?'

'There are Germans in Uganda.'

'Uganda?'

'I don't know... There are many rumours... But his home is here now. He has been here many years. No German language.'

Stefan peered out again at the courtyard, the blue tiles, the listless children, the blond snake charmer. He heard the flute and the splash of water.

'I am tired,' he murmured. 'Do you have a room where I can sleep?'

'Are you a Christian?'

'No, not a Christian, a Jew. Is that important?'

'We have every religion here.'

The guide took him to a room with a mat. Stefan lay down and tried to sleep. A Jew? Ancient arguments clattered into his brain like bones shaken in a can. Spinoza, Maimonedes, Hume, the ontological proof, Descartes, Aquinas, Renan... He remembered his arguments over religion with Anton.

'*Nicht christlich... Jude.* I am a Jew. How strange. I am a Jew.'

He remembered Johannes as he had been six years before in Jerusalem. The intensity of the portrait sittings. His impatience and boredom on the Mount of Olives.

'No... I don't think it's him...' Yet he could not be sure.

Later he woke with a start.

'Sir!'

The young guide, reverting to his earlier rudeness, ordered him up and bundled him out into the dark corridor. Where was the fountain now, where the flute? All was quiet. A door was opened. Stefan stepped out into the dawn.

'I am not finished here. I will come back...'

'Yes sir, come back. We will always welcome you. We have nice boys and girls.'

Stefan hobbled between mud houses towards the river, the sky lightening to the east behind his back.

~

Years later he had forgotten how many times he returned to Omdurman. What might have been days or weeks, or even months, was distilled into a single memory.

Certainly he had been back a few times and drunkenly he had slept with one or two of the young girls – probably more than once.

The guide had continued to toy with him. His main game was to find ever more ingenious ways to get money out of this unusual client by holding out the hope of a meeting with the young snake charmer.

'Tomorrow, tomorrow,' he would whisper, laying a hand on Stefan's arm.

Stefan paid a deposit without which nothing apparently could be guaranteed, arriving full of anticipation the next day only to be told that the boy was indisposed or 'at his lessons till late'. There would then follow a long argument about the deposit, ending in a laughable 'compromise' – for the young guide never ceased to remind Stefan of his power to ban him from the establishment or even involve the police.

Perhaps the guide had offered Stefan his own body. Certainly, if so, he looked both baffled and contemptuous when Stefan said he was not interested.

When the boy was present, a bar to communication descended against which there was no appeal.

It should have been simple. There was the boy, a few steps away through the lattice. Where was the entrance? Could one not just step through?

No one else fared any better. Stefan never saw the other clients enter that court where the fountains plashed and the palms cast huge shadows on the blue tiles. He only saw fingers poking through the lattice, and the whites of eyes.

He was just one of them, no different. He must have grown used to the treatment and by the end expected nothing else.

Finally, after many years, his memory came down to this: a blue court, leaf shadows, the fingers and eyes of his companions; a blond flute-playing boy, a stranger with indifferent eyes, a snake curling round his waist.

JOHANNES 2

Zoraya at sixteen was no longer a child. She had blossomed into a beautiful young woman. Her figure had filled out. Her lips and cheeks glowed. Her glance captivated visitors as she passed them on the steps or brought a tray. Enquiries were made. One day she grabbed me in the corridor.

'Ali! Come in here.' She pulled me into one of the fetid rooms and locked the door. Her dark eyes flashed with defiance. 'We have to go!'

'What?'

'Tonight.'

'Tonight?'

'A merchant has seen me and offered thousands.'

I struggled to take this in.

'He wants a virgin. Men always want virgins, they will pay a fortune. If I don't go with him tonight, they will force me.'

'I thought…'

'There's no time for thinking. Tonight Ali. Where's the coat?'

'Where it always is.'

'Get it. There's a five minute gap when Nasr leaves his post to check that everything's OK in the kitchen. When you see him go past you towards the kitchen, that's your moment. I'll meet you at the corner past the abattoir.'

'Where are we going?'

She was breathing fast but brimming with determination.

'To Uncle Massoud's.'

'I didn't know you had an uncle.'

'He's my cousin actually. It's a long way from here, on Elephantine Island at Aswan. He has a hot-air balloon.'

'How do we get there?'

'By train. First class. You're paying, my clever thief. Don't come without your coat! I will wear *burqa*. You will cover your hair and darken your skin with *mehnd*. You will travel as the son of a deaf-and-dumb woman. You'll tell a good story to anyone who asks.'

'Won't we need papers on the train?'

'Ali! You are forgetting you are rich. You will pay anyone who needs encouragement to do our bidding.'

It turned out as she planned it. By the next day we were on the train to Aswan. All I had with me was my *ney* and the coat stuffed with bank notes.

Massoud lived in a villa set amongst the trees on Elephantine Island on the Nile, across from Aswan.

He was friendly and welcoming but asked no questions: neither where Zoraya had been in recent years nor why she was travelling with a European boy. It was enough that she was family. Family to him meant respect for privacy and everyone being allowed to do what they want.

Apparently he had himself benefited from this laissez-faire attitude. A bachelor approaching middle age, he had been left alone in life to indulge his every whim. He had a range of interests and his domestic needs were catered to by devoted servants.

He told us that he had been drawn to the island by the archaeological riches littering the island despite Ottoman vandalism. His interests extended beyond Egyptology, however – to entomology, botany, meteorology, astronomy, photography. Every room was cluttered with the tools and troves of these various passions. He had an extensive library where Zoraya would often bury herself while I pottered with Massoud. Through his academic interests he was fluent in German and out of kindness to me he would speak the language to me. This way I remained fluent.

Obscured from view with enough space between the trees for lift-off was tethered Massoud's pride and joy, the balloon.

'My dears, shall we go up today?' he would say with a twinkle.

We headed for the clearing where the precious object, in its collapsed state, was berthed. Preparations were an elaborate ritual. The servants acted like devoted acolytes, with much fetching and carrying. The main task was lighting and controlling the rate of burn on the fuel. Tension mounted. Would the whole thing go up in smoke? Tempers could become frayed.

At last we would clamber in. The basket was furnished like a miniature salon, with a little sofa, cushions and a small table for refreshments.

Slowly, as if by magic, we rose. I breathed in sharply. How strange, how alarming this sudden lift. We passed the leaves and branches. Soon we were looking down on treetops.

The Nile with its spattering of felucca sails, Elephantine Island itself and Massoud's house, all slowly, slowly sank. Aswan was already a little toy village. The Cataracts lay to the south. The other way the river curved smoothly towards invisible Luxor. All around the limitless desert.

Now we saw a map, a distant representation of that place we knew, the world. No colours, smells, hard and soft edges. We were only a part of the sky, the arch of blue, the soft breeze.

We became very intimate in this little home in the sky. Zoraya and Massoud debated the great questions: whether there is a God, spiritualism, re-incarnation. I listened and said the odd stupid thing while pretending not to be fixated on Zoraya's body, mentally roving over every contour hidden beneath her light summer robes.

Zoraya was turning into a fierce atheist and loathed all superstition. Massoud on the other hand believed, though in his own way. 'I see God in the microbes,' he said. I didn't know what I thought. Sometimes we fell silent. We were overawed. Our words had seemed like nothing, specks in one great immensity.

Massoud's balloon was not of the most advanced kind. It could not be guided untethered. We were connected to the ground by a rope of limitless length which, when the balloon was berthed, lay in a large coil in the launching area.

At last we would have to leave our home in the sky and return to earth. We doused the fuel – if it had not run out – and the balloon started to fall. We hung out a large red flag to let the servants know we were on our way down. They would pull us in, coiling the rope so that all was neat and shipshape when we arrived.

When our feet touched the ground and we walked the short distance to the villa, we had to steady ourselves. Ah, so this is the place we must live in. Up there, emptiness, pure light, clear mind. Down here, mess, mud, complication, the heavy foot, the anxious brow.

Time moved on further. We were perhaps around eighteen. Massoud was to visit Cairo for a meeting on some obscure 'business'. He would be gone a month. We were to have the run of the place.

'You can take the balloon up,' he said. 'Just follow the procedures and don't do anything stupid.'

We made a plan. Much as we enjoyed Massoud's company, it would be something to go up without him. We would make a special trip, just for us, exactly as we wanted it. We would take a fancy picnic, even a bottle of cognac from Massoud's regular if not-much-drunk supply, which he was always offering us in any case.

High above the world's woes, the balloon swaying gently, we sat on the little sofa gazing at the sky, full up from the savouries, fruits and seeded cakes we had brought.

Wobbly from the cognac I got up and gazed out at the level horizon. Zoraya's fingertips brushed my bare arm.

'What?'

'I'm worried you'll tip over the edge. That would be a fine ending wouldn't it?'

'Ending to what?'

She smiled knowingly. 'The thing we never talk about.'

I sat down and bold with drink put my arm round her. She rested her head on my shoulder. I heard the breeze, felt the hot sun on my cheek. She put her lips against my ear.

'Ali,' she whispered: '*What you seek is seeking you.*'

There was a long, deep pause. Our lips met. I tasted her tongue, the inside of her mouth. I breathed her breath. Our hearts began to race.

We laid the red flag on the floor, took off our clothes and lay down. Her skin was warm and soft. I could not take in the wonder of it. I could only reach again for her mouth with mine and drink as if from a holy vessel.

We were skylarks. We were angels. We were man and woman at last, no longer children.

Later, much later, we dressed. Waving the flag, which had invisibly absorbed Zoraya's virginal blood, we signalled we were ready to come down.

Thus we became lovers and remained so for the two or three years that remained to us on Elephantine Island.

Massoud surely guessed the situation but never spoke of it. He was shy about personal matters and always distracted by his interests. Out of respect for him we were discreet but like all young lovers we found ways of being together.

We were especially free during his further trips to Cairo. Asking the servants not to trouble us, we would lock ourselves away for days on end. Our passion knew no limit. On warm nights we swam naked in the river and lay out under the stars until dawn brought our caresses to an end.

It was from one of these trips that Massoud returned in pensive mood.

'Let me speak to both of you,' he said gravely, as we sat outside in the cool of the evening drinking the Twinings tea he had brought back. 'On second thoughts, Ali, why don't you get your *ney* and play for us delightfully as you always do – but a little in the background. I have family matters to discuss with Zoraya.'

I fetched the flute and was silently – I must say resentfully – passing to take up my place a little way off under a tree, when I caught Massoud's words.

'In Cairo I met quite by chance your father.'

I looked at Zoraya in astonishment. She too was shocked and when she turned and saw me was in no state to begin offering explanations. I wanted to interrupt, 'But you said you had no father!'

Instead I drew back. I strained to listen. When they both fell silent, I would play. They were so taken up that they hardly noticed whether I was playing or not.

I only knew the full story when Zoraya and I were left alone. Bidding us good night Massoud cast me an apologetic look which filled me with foreboding.

'What is this!' I hissed.

She threw herself sobbing into my arms.

'Oh, Ali.'

'What?'

'I have to leave you.'

'What! Where are you going?'

'To my father.'

'But...'

Still crying she led me inside to a divan.

'I have to go to Germany. To somewhere called Leipzig.'

I was speechless. 'To Leipzig? Why Leipzig?'

'My father is a professor in the university.'

'I thought you were a Persian princess!'

'Oh Ali...' She looked at me imploringly. 'Where do I start?'

I was getting more and more angry and upset. 'What have you been keeping from me?'

'I didn't want to tell you I had a father because I was trying to forget him. I wanted to pretend he didn't exist. It was my stupid pride.'

She told me the facts. Zoraya had been born in Cairo from the union of a married German archaeology professor and the daughter of a wealthy Cairo couple, a high-class Egyptian and a minor princess of the Persian royal family. Zoraya herself, though Arabic-speaking, was barely Arab, in fact one quarter Egyptian, one quarter Persian and half-German.

Following the scandalous affair with the archaeologist, Zoraya's mother had died in childbirth. The grandparents would have nothing to do with Zoraya and so her father paid a woman of his acquaintance, an educated Nubian, to take her.

Before long this woman returned from Cairo to her home in Khartoum. She was the nearest thing that Zoraya had to a mother. Besides loving and caring for her she read her stories and taught her to read and write. Zoraya still retained fond memories of her substitute mother.

When he was in Egypt on an archaeological dig, Zoraya's father would travel down to Khartoum. Zoraya grew fond of him. He took her to visit his friend, her cousin, 'Uncle Massoud', in Aswan.

But then Zoraya's Nubian 'mother' died of dysentery. Her father visited briefly to sort the matter out. He found what he believed was a good home for her, an institution across the Nile in Omdurman.

Zoraya's father told her that that the orphanage would remain her home and provide for her every need until adulthood.

'He paid – perhaps he's still paying – the institution to take me. At first he wrote to me but he gave me no address to reply to. Eventually the notes stopped coming and I decided to forget him, forget he had ever lived. Then my respectable home became a whorehouse! But for you I would be a whore now. Ali, you saved me. When you came back from Cairo with money, I knew I was right to believe in you.'

She clutched my arm but I shook her off angrily. 'I came back because of you but apparently it means nothing now.'

'No!'

'Then why?'

'Because I have no choice! I can't depend on Massoud for ever. Listen. My father told Massoud he is a widower now. He is lonely. He wants me to go and live with him in Leipzig. He will educate me properly in the modern, European way. I will learn German of course, and maybe English or French. I will be sent to a finishing school in Switzerland and taught all the graces befitting a westernised Persian princess. My past as a near-slum whore will be forgotten for ever.'

My world was falling away under my feet. I cannot describe the pit of desolation into which I felt myself tumbling, further and deeper with every word that she uttered.

'But Zoraya,' I cried desperately. 'What do you owe that man! Nothing. Never mind how much *I* love *you. You* love *me*. We belong to each other. I am your prince. *You* said it. We will marry each other. We are one. We...What started in the balloon... How can you forget?'

'I can't forget!' she howled. 'I will never forget!' She broke off and ran to the other side of the room. 'Ali, I have an idea. You must wait. We will be together again. We will find each other. At the moment I have no choice but in time...'

'You had no choice in Omdurman,' I shot back, 'but still you chose. Me and freedom, instead of slavery and whoring. Once you've been educated like a proper little German and "finished"...' I broke off in despair.

I knew I would never persuade her. She was aware that her father needed her and wanted to respond. Poisonously I began to believe that she was feeling the pull of a European life with money, culture, opportunity.

'You *want* to go!'

'No, Ali!'

'Then at least let me come with you.'

She shook her head. 'I suggested that to Massoud. He had already put it to my father – he had told him about you. My father said no.'

'Why can't I? I'm going to. What's to stop me?'

She put her hand on my arm. 'Ali.'

I sighed bitterly. 'It makes me sick. I'm going to bed.'

On the station platform we stood awkwardly facing one another. Massoud busied himself to give us our last moments together. The engine chuffed towards us, a thing of dread to me, dark, noisy carrion feasting on death.

We looked into each other's eyes. I bit my lip not to cry. She began to sob. Massoud took her hand and helped her onto the train. I handed her bag up.

The engine groaned and hissed. Zoraya stood at the open window. I looked up at her. 'Come back, Zoraya.'

'I will, Ali. It's just an interlude. We'll be together again.'

We looked into each other's eyes with great tenderness. The last few days had brought us closer together than ever. For a moment I believed that there was nothing to stop us meeting again.

Only as the train moved further away and her fluttering handkerchief vanished did doubt fall on me like an avalanche. Crashing to my knees, I sobbed and beat the parched ground with my fist.

Massoud helped me to my feet. 'Come, my boy, we have plenty to do. Let's go back and develop those delightful photographs we took at Philae. And then there are those specimens of *Adenium obesum* to attend to...'

I stayed two more years with Massoud, helping him with his projects and improving my German. At last I became a reader, devouring from Massoud's library Tolstoy, Dickens, Zola and others.

Zoraya sometimes wrote but didn't tell me much about her new life, perhaps to spare my feelings. I was still so angry I hardly knew how to reply.

One night, missing Zoraya unbearably, unable to sleep, staring up at the ceiling, I realised that something had to change.

A plan came to me. Using the considerable sum of money I

still had even after paying Massoud my keep, I would return to Jerusalem, bring about a reunion with my all but forgotten parents, then travel to Leipzig. There I would find work and live. I would be with Zoraya once and for all.

At breakfast I told Massoud I would be leaving in a week.

The seven days soon passed. Once more I stood on the station platform at Aswan. Massoud's handkerchief came out. He dabbed his cheek. 'My dear boy, I shall miss you.'

'I can never thank you enough, Massoud. I will come back.'

'But when? And why should you? You have your life to lead now. I have just provided a resting post before you get on with the proper thing.'

'Much more than a resting post, Massoud. Without you where would I be? Through you I seem to have become an educated man. I speak my own native language to a high level. I read literature. I understand science. I can never forget what you have done for me.'

He shook his head, containing his sorrow. 'I will survive, my dear Ali. But now you see: this is why I avoid people and stick to microscopes and specimen cases.'

It was time for me to climb aboard. We embraced and then like Zoraya before me I waved from the moving train and was gone.

1912-15

Chapter 7

'Heaven knows where he picked that thing up from,' his mother had said. 'But I want it out.'

The creature's home, a glass tank, was too deep for the shelf and stuck over the side. It was weighted by earth and stones but it could still fall off. The creature could escape. It could kill somebody.

The boy knew it was only a matter of time before he would be ordered to kill it. Meanwhile he must enjoy his captive – and feed it lest it sting itself to death rather than starve.

He dug a hole in the garden and covered it with a stone. He removed scraps from the dinner table and asked his friends to do the same. Inside the earthen hole, the pile grew. Gristle, bone, gizzards, swarmed on from all side by ticks, mites, flies, flees, spiders. Daily he put on protective gloves, lifted the stone and scooped a portion of this putrid mess out of the hole and into a bucket.

The dangerous part came next, back indoors. He had to check that the creature was well down in the tank before he took the lid off. If it were lurking behind one of the stones high at the back, it could be out in no time.

Always check. Never open the lid before checking.

'There you are, fine fellow.'

Today especially, the boy smiled.

'Wake up. Time for dinner. Prepare your pedipalps. Today's the day. You must eat well.'

He lifted the lid from the tank and poured in the dinner. The creature launched itself. Insects scurried to the corners but it found them one by one. Pincers seized, crushed and tore, then lifted morsels to the jaws.

He watched through his magnifying glass. The creature was a banqueting lady lifting sweetmeats to her lips.

'Why do you keep a scorpion,' a girl had asked him, 'especially a deadly yellow one?'

'For duelling.'

'Duelling?'

'He challenges other arachnids.'

'Arachnids?'

'Spiders, to the uninitiated.'

Hunter, ambusher, killer. How the creature could move. The armour plating. What protection. And the sting, the twin poison glands. Death to his enemies.

The next minutes were taken up with coaxing the scorpion into a jar. With the lid safely on, the boy made a dash for the front door.

'Where are you going, Werner?' called Magda from the kitchen. 'Are you getting rid of that scorpion?'

'Soon, Mother.'

'If you haven't got rid of it by tomorrow, I'll do away with it myself.'

'You need to consider. Since it's one of God's creatures, it would be immoral to kill it – other than in self-defence.'

Over her sink, Magda breathed her habitual sigh.

Werner shut the door quietly, squinting at the neat rows of the Colony leading out on to the track to Abu Tor. Sunday bells tolled peacefully from the city. He hummed to himself as he walked along. He heard voices and looked up. 'There they are.'

A group of men and boys were gathered at the edge of the Arab village. Jabr came towards Werner, shook hands and pointed to another boy, who smiled shyly.

'Galeodes,' said Jabr.

Jabr worked in the Colony and spoke a few words of German.

He explained to Werner that the challenger was a Galeodes spider owned by the other boy. The Galeodes was well known for fighting prowess. Werner's scorpion was as good as done for, Jabr seemed to say.

'We'll see,' said Werner.

Jabr laughed, grabbed the jar and held it up. Everyone shouted at once. Jabr pulled Werner by the hand. The noisy procession passed the older villagers who watched from their doorways. One or two got up and followed. After clambering over a rubbish tip between two derelict houses the crowd emerged on to a flat dusty space.

At the edge, in the shade of an oleander, lay a large box. Beside it a circle of stones had been assembled.

The younger boys rushed ahead, shouting.

'Galeodes! Galeodes!'

'Is this where they fight?' asked Werner. 'In this circle? Is the wall high enough? Are there any holes?'

'It's a perfect fighting ring.'

'The spider's fought here before?'

'Many times.'

'It's not neutral territory.'

Jabr translated for the owner, then turned to Werner. 'The fight has to be here.'

Werner tried to stay calm. For everything he knew his scorpion could get the spider with one lash of his tail. There was no backing down. He took the jar back from Jabr, glanced at the immobile creature inside and held it up proudly. 'My scorpion is ready.'

There was a pause. Everyone had a good look inside the jar and in the box. Odds were discussed. Bets were laid. Gradually silence fell as the crowd assembled round the stone circle, craning forward.

Jabr and the spider's owner picked up the box and placed it in the ring. They slid the lid back and tipped the box. The spider scuttled out and sought the shade of the wall where it settled ominously.

Now it was Werner's turn. Kneeling, he held the jar over the ring, turned it upside-down and unscrewed the lid. The scorpion fell and landed on his back.

Disaster.

'Give me a stick! Quick! A stick!'

With a twig, Werner helped the scorpion to its feet. To gasps from the crowd the Galeodes spider shot forward. It circled and came in from the back, the direction it might have feared, given that the scorpion's sting was in its tail.

The scorpion's tail went up and wavered as if it had an eye on the end and was looking where to strike. The spider stood where it was.

'Go on,' whispered Werner. 'Strike now.'

But the scorpion had mis-judged. The crowd murmured. They could see what was going on, so could Werner. Scorpions sting by bending the tail. If the adversary stays directly behind he is safe. Now the scorpion was turning, the spider following him. Round and round they went. The dance continued. The crowd was hushed. What would happen next?

'No!' breathed Werner.

The scorpion was in flight! The Galeodes was chasing. The scorpion reached the wall, scuttled along the edge, tried to make for the centre again but was cut off and retreated to the wall again.

Now the enemy moved in. The scorpion cowered. Possibly it knew the end had come – or did it have something up its sleeve?

Yes! He leapt forward. He faced his foe. He quivered. His tail was up.

Werner's heart beat hard. The crowd fell quiet.

Timing. It was all timing. Could the spider get its teeth into the tail before the scorpion had whipped round and delivered its poison to the hairy abdomen?

Werner closed his eyes. He prayed as he had taught himself never to do. He dared to look. The scorpion's tail was up. An eternal silence. The spider lunged. The tail was trapped. Into the tail sank the infinitesimal teeth.

The scorpion sank, quivered and died. The Galeodes watched with mean slits of eyes.

After a collective sigh came shouts, back slaps, counting out of money; and, more quietly, the practised cajoling of the spider by its owner, back into its box.

Jabr touched Werner on the shoulder. The bespectacled German boy, a native in a foreign land, shrugged and turned away. He had come to Abu Tor with a friend. He was going home alone.

Near the Colony he met his father on his way into town.

'What have you been up to?' Anton asked, his eyes already wandering to the horizon. Werner had long learnt that he was wasting his breath answering his father's questions for all the interest he took in his replies.

'Nothing.'

'Listen, take care of that damned scorpion. Mother will kill you if it gets out.'

Anton moved off.

'Father was in a hurry,' Werner said to Magda when he got in.

'He has to work – even though it's the Lord's day.'

'If work's what you call it.'

'What do *you* call it?' retorted Magda as her raw fingers fiercely pushed the darning needle in and out of the sock.

Werner shrugged and looked away.

'You and your father, you don't know the meaning of work. But you'd better knuckle down, young man. Stop wasting your time drawing. You must learn a trade, live in the Colony, and be a good Christian. I don't want your head filled with strange ideas like your father.'

'Some people might find the ideas of the Colonists strange, Mother.'

'There's nothing wrong with fearing the Lord,' continued Magda, still darning.

'I could be an entomologist. I'm doing well at school – better than Hans next door, better than Helmut Kappel who's supposed to be the star pupil even if he is full of himself.'

'He a good, polite boy.'

'That won't be enough to get him to university in Germany.'

'Is that your idea?'

'When he gets round to noticing my existence, Father sometimes talks about a scheme or a scholarship. He says he's going to look into it. Perhaps he will. Or I could become an artist,' Werner continued coolly. 'Father doesn't think I'm much good but others have a different opinion.'

'What others?'

'Friends I show my drawings to.'

'What do they know?'

She looked up. A tear welled in the corner of her eye.

'What, mother?'

'Sometimes...'

'Yes?'

'Just sometimes...' she repeated. 'I just have to come out and say it. Otherwise I think I'm going to burst.'

'Say it then.'

'I might as well have gone and hung myself from wretched Judas's tree for all the life I've had since your brother was taken. I'm just hanging. For ever, till I die.'

She put down her darning and turned to the bare wall. Pale rectangular marks smudged the whitewash where the portrait of Johannes had hung until recently.

Werner also looked at the wall, remembering the picture. It had been there all his life, as familiar to him as the kitchen sink. The little boy with his blond hair and smock. His brother had always been a mystery to him and now even this memorial was gone.

'I know, Mother,' he said with a pretence of calm. 'You'd have had a perfect son, your perfect Johannes, and that would have been wonderful for you and Father.'

Magda silently bowed her head.

He went to his bedroom. Only when he was in the room did he believe the best thing to do with the door was slam it as hard as he could. The explosion shook the walls. In the after-shock, the little house was quieter and emptier than ever.

Werner opened the cupboard, took three books off the top shelf and reached in. He pulled out a glass jar and tipped a yellow scorpion into the recently vacated tank.

'There,' he murmured to the creature. 'Your brother's gone, but there's still you.'

Chapter 8

'And this year, with the snow, it'll look so lovely!'

'What?'

'The Christmas tree.'

'Ah.'

'Will you come with us, Father?'

The old man sat hunched in his pantaloons and slippers. 'What next, Miriam?' he expostulated. 'At Chanukah, a Jew should take his daughter-in-law and grandchild to gawp at a Christmas tree?'

'We go every year, Father. We pick up a few things at the Striezel market. This year with the snow… Anna can't wait. Eva's keen too.'

'Let Eva go. She's a Christian.'

Miriam narrowed her eyes against the bright winter sun. Across the river the snowy pinnacles of the Schloss pointed into the blue sky. The Hofkirche was an ice palace. Dresden, the Altstadt. Would it melt away? Was it a dream?

'Do come and see. You haven't stirred from that chair all day. We'll get there as it's getting dark. Anna adores the lights on the tree.'

'What Jew needs Christian lights? We have our own lights here! Anna has her own *shamash* to light her own *chanukiah.* And by the way, Miriam, don't knock the *chanukiah* over while you're mooning about by the window.'

Miriam glanced at the eight-branch candlestick. 'I'm nowhere near it, Father. Anna will light it when we get back. She'll enjoy that too. We can be *ecumenical.*'

'The Almighty One knows our failings,' muttered the old man. 'I'm not as observant as I should be, not since I was widowed.'

'You're a good Jew, Father.'

Miriam rang the bell and soon the maid came in.

'Can you ask Eva to get Anna ready, Doris. She should wrap up warmly. Eva may come with us if she wishes.'

'Yes, ma'am.'

'And Doris...'

'Ma'am?'

'Do you know where the master is.'

'I believe he's asleep on the couch in his study, ma'am.'

Miriam bit her lip.

'Should I let a man who sleeps all day take over my business?' muttered the old man.

'The factory's closed today, Father. Hugo can sleep.'

'That I should have given him so much money when he was a young man and pay him so well now. May the Lord forgive me.'

Back safely turned, Miriam rolled her eyes. She recalled that it was her family money, not Hugo's, that had diluted any commercial ambitions he might have had. Ironic, but there it was.

As Doris left, the man in question shuffled in, yawning. 'I've had an idea.'

'Heaven save us,' came from the chair. 'My son has had an idea! It must be all that sleep.'

Hugo ignored his father. 'Why don't we walk over the river and go and look at the Christmas tree in the old tilting yard? Get some Christmas presents in the Striezel.'

'Oy! So Christmas *presents* is it next?'

'Don't you want a Christmas box, Father?' asked Miriam.

'Don't waste your money.'

'I thought you might come with us,' said Hugo.

The old man waved his hand.

'Hugo dearest,' said Miriam, 'great minds think alike. I'm glad your sleep brought you this inspiration. Come on, let's not waste time.'

In ten minutes, together with Eva and the eleven-year-old Anna, they were striding across the bridge towards the mournful pleasure steamers moored for the winter. The cold air, their boots crunching the dry snow, invigorated them. Anna hurled snowballs. Soon they were all joining in.

'Hugo, that's not fair. Poor Eva was looking the other way.'

Miriam brushed the snow off Eva's back while Anna and Hugo ran ahead. The two women looked at each other, smiled and held hands briefly. Over the bridge Anna was bubbling with excitement, calling to Hugo and pointing at the statue of Augustus the Strong on his horse.

Miriam breathed steam into the cold air and surveyed the Altstadt, the ancient stone, the Hofkirche nearby, the statues, the pinnacles and domes of the Schloss.

'Oh Eva, who needs to leave Dresden – ever? What a wonder it is. And in the snow…'

'Well, Miriam, I've lived in two famous cities – Jerusalem and Dresden.'

'Of course, so you have. And which do you like best?'

'In Jerusalem I was first widowed, then deceived in love. Besides that, the city seemed hardly more than rubble. So all in all…'

'You like Dresden best!'

Eva smiled. 'Dresden is perfect, and you and Hugo saved my life. I shall never forget your kindness. Certainly I love Dresden. And I love Anna as if she were my own.'

Eva glanced fondly over at the young girl, with her mother's handsome features and her father's fair, wavy hair.

'Mother, Eva, what are you talking about?'

'About Dresden, dearest.'

Eva and Anna strolled off, arm in arm.

'Beautiful,' breathed Miriam. 'Celestial, a man-built paradise…'

Hugo grunted. His wife's artistic passions normally didn't bother him. Indeed he appreciated them and benefited from them. As a young wife she had persuaded him to Paris and the Loire valley; later to Rome, Naples and beyond. While he couldn't match her fervour, he was happy to broaden his knowledge. How many pictures and buildings had he seen all because of her craving for art? It could never be counted.

But just now this side of Miriam was a threat. It might get in the way of more pressing ends. A man with a difficult subject to raise, he must time it right, approaching crabwise.

'Fine if you ignore all the smokestacks over there. Forget the poverty created by unfettered capitalism.'

She smiled affectionately. 'Hugo, I'm glad you pay your men a good wage.'

'Not even Father went into business to make people starve. Mind you, if I had my way there wouldn't be any distinctions between managers and workers. To each according to his need. Why should we be paid any more? They work harder than us.'

'But then,' said Miriam, 'there would be nothing to stop the workers coming and planting themselves next door to us.'

'Why shouldn't they?'

'There should be – always will be – certain distinctions.'

Hugo glanced over at Eva. 'But you want no distinction between Eva and us, you said.'

'Oh Hugo, that's different.'

'Why?'

'It's personal.'

He shrugged. 'It's all political, Miriam. The decision to allow Eva to call us by our first names had a political implication. It marks us out… we are different from others in this society, which by the way is something I want to talk you about. I had a letter last week.'

'Who from?'

'Do you remember Simon Gold in Vienna?'

'The Zionist?'

'Yes, he arranged that assignment for me in '98.'

'When you met the Kaiser in Palestine?'

'Well, nearly met is more accurate.' He cleared his throat nervously. 'He's written to offer me a job.'

'In Vienna?'

Miriam imagined Hugo travelling every week on the train to the Austrian capital while she and Anna stayed put in her beloved Dresden. The picture wasn't too alarming.

'No.'

'Where then?'

'He wrote to me from Tel Aviv.'

'Where is that?'

Miriam's ignorance was both a surprise and a warning.

'It's the Jewish town that has sprung up next to Jaffa in Palestine.'

'He wants you to go there?'

'No, to Jerusalem.'

She closed her eyes and took a deep breath. 'Well, we can't do that, can we?'

'Can't we?'

She reddened. Her hands went to her cheeks. 'Anna's education… everything… it's our life here… we…'

A horseman trotted past. The trail of the animal's breath evaporated like the happiness of the day.

'Hugo, it's the ends of the earth.'

'You've never been there.'

'No, but Eva says it's rubble…' Strategically, she switched to a tone of neutral enquiry. 'So, what's the job?'

'Gold is one of those trying to set up a Jewish trade union federation in Palestine.'

'A trade union? You, a trade unionist? You're an employer.'

'That's it. They want someone who knows it from the other side. Gold thought of me. There are other candidates but they're already out there. Gold has given me first refusal because what they really want is more immigrants, more Jews to come into the country, more families especially. He's always tried to persuade me. Now he has some leverage because he's found a job for me.'

Miriam closed her eyes. Her stomach heaved. How could this have been going on without her knowing?

'I have to tell him by the end of January.'

Miriam hardly noticed as Anna ran up and whispered, 'She's annoying me, she's so bossy. She says I should stop the snowballs now.'

'Run along, Anna, and do as Eva says. Daddy and I are talking about something. We'll join you in just a minute.'

Anna shrugged and went off.

'Hugo, have you thought?' Miriam lowered her voice. 'Eva... and that religious crank she was involved with out there.'

'Anton Gustavus.'

'She's still in love with him.'

'What of it?'

'There you are, we can't go. We can't set all that off again. He's still married.'

'It was fourteen years ago!'

'In such matters, Hugo, years, decades, are nothing.'

'She's forty.'

'Don't you know the way the world spins? She's kept her looks. He won't turn up his nose at her.'

'She doesn't have to come with us.'

Miriam stopped and put her hands firmly on her hips. 'If – and it's the biggest "if" you can imagine – I were remotely to consider what you are suggesting, she would have to come with me. She's my confidante. My best friend. Besides, we are all she has in the world.'

Hugo scratched his head, hiding his satisfaction. He had a long way to go but she had not refused outright. Round One to him.

'Come, *liebchen.* The Christmas tree. Other things can wait.'

At the Striezel Miriam found distraction from the horrible idea of Jerusalem. The yard was packed with stalls piled high with midwinter bounty: sausages – curved and bowed, fat and thin – big round cheeses, vegetables, fruits, spices, Christmas strudel, sweets, teas and coffees. All was bustle and colour. Decorations hung between the arches of the arms gallery. Stars twinkled between the snowy turrets.

Wandering between the stalls, she stopped and looked around. 'How can he want to leave all this?' She wouldn't let it happen. Her father-in-law would be an ally. He adored Anna. He'd never see her again if they went to Jerusalem. And the firm. Whatever the old man's opinion of Hugo's business abilities he would hate to think of the family connection going.

'Mama!' Anna pulled Miriam across the snow.

'Careful, darling, it's slippery.'

Anna pointed to a stall selling Christmas decorations. It was a model mountain whose slopes were covered with snow, trees and carved figures, from shepherds and Wise Men to goblins and fairies. Carriages and wagons wound up a stony track between clinging firs. Above, hung on invisible wires, angels blew tiny trumpets and cherubs puffed out their cheeks.

'Oh, Mama, can we buy something, please.'

'Um...'

She stared at the blond infant Jesus, surrounded by Nordic worshippers at the foot of the mountain? Could Jews allow themselves to buy here? What would it mean?

She caught Hugo's eye.

'Come on,' he hissed. 'Let's get away.'

'What? Why?'

She bent down and looked where he was pointing, a cave cut into the model mountain.

Her heart skipped a beat. 'Oh no,' she breathed.

Above the small entrance, daubed in blood-red, were the words,

'Hell of the Christ killers.' Inside, lit by flickering oil lamps, this miniature 'Hell' was full of tiny Jews. There was a rabbi with a Torah scroll, a banker in morning coat, a tailor with a murderous pair of scissors, and many more characters, all with large noses and thick lips. They held up their hands in terror. The roof pressed in on their heads. Miriam peered further inside. Devils with forked tails herded victims into a flickering furnace.

'Come along, Anna, not here, we'll buy somewhere else.'

'Mama! Why? I love it.'

'You don't love it! You didn't see...'

Moving away she muttered to Hugo, 'It's a disgrace. We must complain. What about the Chamber of Trade? Father-in-law is a member.'

'*Was* a member, Miriam. What do we expect anyway? Every week the anti-Semitic papers publish a new lie. Some Jews even support the right wing and the nationalists, but what do they get? Nothing but kicks. When will they learn? When will *you* learn? Anti-Jewish feeling is all around us, even here in your precious Dresden. There is only one solution.'

'Jerusalem I suppose!'

'Well...'

The model cave in the miniature mountain was a second victory for Hugo.

They came to the Christmas tree. Eva joined them. Though she'd longed for it, Anna was indifferent, absently kicking the snow which had been swept into piles under the tree. More snow was starting to drift from above.

Miriam looked up into the night sky.

So? What was 'anti-Jewish feeling'? Some people loathed Russians, English or the French. Some couldn't abide Catholics, some couldn't stick Lutherans. And some hated Jews. Why make such a fuss?

A snowflake fell in her eye. She blinked.

The snow. The slow tumble to the earth. Soon, all around, Upper Saxony under a cover deeper by the minute. The thickening silence.

What would happen to them all? Where was life taking them?

The cave in the wooden mountain had disturbed her. She wanted to go home and crawl into bed. Pull the blankets over her head until the Jew-haters had left town.

Flakes were settling on the great sparkling tree. Down, down, thicker and thicker. She couldn't think why, or what it meant – though she would remember it for many years to come.

A brief waking dream. Magical Christmas trees twinkling so beautifully in the sky. Suspended, glowing in space, floating down, bringing peace on earth.

~

A few days later, Eva went Christmas shopping. On her way home with two full baskets, she turned down a side street and struggled along a narrow pavement. Snowflakes tickled her cheeks and brushed her eyebrows. Exhausted, she hardly glanced at the shop windows.

Another woman came towards her and Eva turned towards a shop window allowing her to pass.

'*Entschuldigen!*'

'*Macht nichts.*'

Glancing in, Eva gasped and stood transfixed. The window display was dominated by a solitary gilt-framed picture on a stand. Eva lowered her baskets and put her hand to her mouth.

'It can't be!'

An elderly man came up. 'Here, shall I help you move your baskets into the doorway? They are blocking the pavement.'

'Oh, I'm so sorry. No it's all right thank you, I...'

'I stop and look at it every day,' said the old man. 'Gorgeous. Like the Giovanni Bellinis in Venice. The window behind; the little trees and faraway hills. And what a pretty fellow. Why is he looking at us like that? Impossible to date, too. A Nazarine work of the 1840s? Even older?'

'I can tell you that. It was painted fifteen years ago, in 1898.'

'Really?'

'I knew the boy. I just didn't expect to see the picture here.'

'You knew him?'

Eva smiled ruefully. 'It's a long story.'

'And who is the artist? I've had half an idea to ask in the gallery but you can tell me.'

'Stefan Lehmann. A local man... he was born here anyway. Perhaps he's come back home.'

'Stefan Lehmann! Well, well...' The old man was already moving on waving his cane. 'Well, at least I know who painted the picture now. You've saved me having to go inside. A fine work. Well, good luck, my dear, and a Merry Christmas to you.'

The snow was settling on Eva's shoulders. She tried the handle of the gallery door. It was locked. She peered inside. The lights were on but no one was there.

On her walk home Eva's thoughts raced. What was the picture doing here? Could this mean that something had happened to Anton and Magda? Was Stefan back in Dresden? Did Hugo know anything about this? Then again, perhaps the Fischers would want to buy the picture. Johannes was a part of Hugo's history almost as much as he was of hers. What should she do? Tell the Fischers first of course, then what? Write to Anton?

Her thoughts turned, as often, to her former lover. It still hurt. Occasionally she received news of Jerusalem through Colony contacts: the expansion of the Jewish part of the city and everything that went with it – parks, newspapers, even a theatre; visit of the German Prince Eitel and his wife in 1910. Last she heard, Anton and Magda were still at the Colony. Their son Werner was studying at the German Evangelical secondary school.

'But just now,' she sighed, approaching the Fischer residence, 'the main thing is the portrait. It's unbelievable.' Glancing at the familiar *mezuzah* on the doorpost, she turned the gleaming brass doorknob.

In the hall she was met by an excited Miriam. 'Eva, I've something to tell you.'

'Miriam, I have something to tell *you*. That boy, the one who disappeared when Hugo... Anyway, can I just take my things off?'

She hurried to her room then returned downstairs. Miriam had moved to the drawing room. They sat on the sofa.

'I've agreed,' said Miriam, brimming over, unable to let Eva speak first. 'I am going to Jerusalem.'

Eva's eyelids flickered. 'You've come round?'

'Yes!'

'Why? How?'

'Hugo has persuaded me of the beauty of the orient, and of Jerusalem in particular. I am ready to expand my cultural horizons. The sights and sounds will bring fresh inspiration to my verse.'

'Well, that's that,' said Eva brusquely. 'Congratulations. As for me, I can probably get a post here somewhere if you can give me a reference.'

'Eva, you don't understand!'

Eva frowned. 'What?'

'We want you to come with us.'

'Now wait a minute, Miriam. I've lived there. Life in Jerusalem wouldn't suit me at all.'

'But Eva, Anna wants you to as well.'

'I'm settled here now!'

'Anyway,' Miriam threw out. 'I've told Hugo I refuse to go unless you come with me.'

Eva paced the room, came to rest at the window and looked out at the bare winter garden, her back to Miriam. For the first time she was noticing a hint of selfishness in Miriam. Did she not care that Eva had no wish to return to Palestine?

‘That,’ said Eva, ‘puts a power in my hands I am not sure I want. You both have to decide what you want. Don’t bring me into it.’

‘Oh, Eva,’ replied Miriam, ‘I believe you must come round, you know. You’ll find that things have quite moved on there. Hugo has been telling me.’

‘Well, that aside,’ said Eva turning briskly, ‘I’d better tell you what I’ve just seen...’

~

Eva passed the gallery many times in the days to come. She would linger and gaze at the little fellow whose fate had been so unhappily linked to her own, cursing the gallery remained closed and that she couldn’t find out more.

She felt quite alone with the matter, the Fischers being far too absorbed with their departure plans. Hugo was thinking only of a future far from Dresden and had no thought of buying the picture, muttering absently that he ‘must go and have a look at it before I leave’. He had heard nothing from Stefan for years. He assumed he was still in Venice.

Miriam went to see the picture, told Eva she was impressed and touched, then went back to her packing and round of farewells.

The impact of the portrait on Eva on each return visit was increasingly powerful and poignant. The little boy, staring out, lonely and vulnerable, pierced her heart. His mute appeal mingled with a sense of her own tragedy of love lost. Standing motionless on the pavement, the snow whitening her shoulders, she felt tears freeze on her cheek.

It was excruciating not to be able to find out more. Why, oh why, was the gallery closed before Christmas of all times?

At last, one day in the new year, she saw with relief that someone was moving about inside. Without delay she opened the door. A woman costumed in maroon velvet and an extravagantly feathered hat advanced towards her. 'We're closed!' she called out imperiously. 'I meant to lock it.'

'I... I'm sorry.'

'All is under preparation for our opening in two weeks. We are new, you see. In the Year of Our Lord 1913, we plan to take the city by storm.'

Eva was taken aback but wasn't going to be put off. 'I'm interested in the picture in the window.'

The woman placed her hand together as if about to offer up a prayer. 'Ah, Stefan Lehmann... Some people call him reactionary but I say he will be praised when moderns like the *Die Brücke* group here in Dresden have had their day – much as I champion them too by the way. I am not against experimentation. I have handled Messrs Kirchner and Schmidt-Rottluff myself.' The feathers on her hat trembled. 'Anyway, Lehmann's picture is a masterpiece – but you'll have to come back in February.'

'Can the picture be bought before the exhibition,' asked Eva, 'and how much is it? I am sure my employer will want to know when I tell him about it, and since he is leaving the country soon he would need to make an immediate purchase.'

Despite her firm line, the woman's curiosity was piqued. 'Might I ask...'

'Herr Fischer of Fischers, the agricultural products firm. He is an old friend of Herr Lehmann. They have lost touch but I'm certain the picture would be of interest.'

'It will be *somewhat* expensive.'

'Herr Fischer is *somewhat* wealthy!'

The woman glanced heavenward.

'Darius!' she called.

A man clutching a hammer pottered, wheezing, from the back of the gallery.

'This lady is in service with a friend of Stefan Lehmann, Herr Fischer of the Fischer agricultural company.

'You work for Jews? You're a fair German woman yourself, not one of the Chosen.'

The woman affected pious disavowal. 'Do excuse him. Darius is a race-purist. It is bad for business. There is no place for exclusive thinking in my profession. Some of my best customers are Jews, some of my best *artists* are Jews. Heine was a Jew. Felix Mendelssohn-Bartholdy was a Jew. Darius, you should stick to what you do best, hanging pictures and checking the accounts.'

'I'm not saying they're all bad. There are just too many of them, in this city anyway.'

'You can't complain. Look at the painting in the window. Look at the stir it's caused. A Jewish artist...'

'A drunk who keeps writing to us for money.'

'... And maybe a Jewish buyer.'

'Ah well, you handle it, will you? I'm busy. Perhaps when we've fought a war and gained some territory we can offer some of it to the Jews.'

Darius wandered back to his tasks.

'I knew the boy in the picture,' said Eva.

'Ah... Are you still in touch with him?'

'Oh no, he's... gone.'

'I ask because as a matter of fact he was here the other day, or at least...'

Eva's jaw fell. Staggering back, she clutched her forehead.

'Really?' she managed at last.

'What is it? Is it so surprising?'

Eva was struggling for breath. 'It's astonishing. He's supposed to be dead. Who... What happened?'

'I noticed this young man standing outside staring at the picture. He was there for an age. Curiosity overcame me and I went out. He said the picture was of himself as a boy. I asked him if he knew Stefan Lehmann. He shrugged. The conversation became rather difficult. He was an intelligent young man but he was rather... yes, withdrawn. I can't describe it. I felt quite uncomfortable and I am afraid I retreated.'

Eva's heart was pounding. 'So he just... went off?'

'Yes,' said the woman, losing interest suddenly in this interloper. 'Now, if you'll excuse me...'

Eva was passionate in her appeal. 'Please, madam, please, if he comes back will you be absolutely sure to find out where he can be contacted.' Hurriedly she wrote out the Fischers' telephone number. 'In any case,' she added judiciously, 'they might be in touch to buy the portrait.'

'Here,' said the woman handing Eva an envelope with fierce finality. 'Inside is a card inviting them to the opening of the gallery. Let them come – early mind you – and compete with the connoisseurs for that wonderful portrait... and many other fine works.'

'Y... yes,' stuttered Eva turning towards the door, 'of course, the portrait is one thing but it's the boy himself... If he comes, please, I beg of you. It really is most important... a matter of life and death.'

'Just tell them to come to the opening.'

'But... but... yes... of course,' Eva concluded helplessly, not mentioning as she closed the door that they would all have already left for Palestine.

Chapter 9

'What a rigmarole at the port in Jaffa, Hugo. And now this train is so uncomfortable. I'm exhausted.' Miriam leant her head against the carriage window and closed her eyes.

'But wasn't it interesting to see Jaffa, dearest?' enthused Hugo. 'What a hive of activity. And now, look out of the window. Orchards, corn, every sign of a thriving land.'

Miriam opened her eyes briefly. 'It's raining.'

Hugo breathed in heartily. 'Ah, those earthy smells the rain wafts into the carriage!'

'I was going to suggest we close the window. It's cold. I thought Palestine was hot.'

'I can't believe you're cold, Miriam. It's much warmer than a Dresden spring.'

The train rumbled on. Eventually Miriam stirred herself to break the silence. 'The branches of those trees are so bent and gnarled... Like witches fingers... misbegotten... misshapen.' Stimulated by travel and ever the poet, Miriam tended more and more to pepper her speech with striking comparisons.

'You mean those olive trees?' queried Hugo.

'What your father said about growing things here is right, Anna,' said Eva. 'It's especially easy down here on the plain. Up where we're going it's rockier. Ahead you can see the Judean hills. Beyond is Jerusalem.'

Anna was grumpy. 'This famous Jerusalem! Father's built it up so much I'm bound to be disappointed.'

‘Oh look!’ exclaimed Eva. ‘The sun’s come out. What a surprise.’

Brilliance suddenly shone on a hillside dense with clusters of scarlet, white and mauve-pink flowers.

‘They’re the biblical “lilies of the field,”’ said Eva. ‘They “toil not neither do they spin” yet “surpass Solomon in all his glory”. Spring was always the best time.’

‘Nothing surpasses Palestine for flowers,’ Hugo beamed, keen to banish pessimism once and for all. ‘Eva, can you teach Anna their names? Young Zionists should know every aspect of the Land. In time it will strengthen our claim.’

‘Does everything have to be a lesson, Father?’

‘Come on, Anna’ said Eva. ‘I’ll teach you the names as I taught you the constellations and the Periodic Table. We can work out a mnemonic. It won’t be boring. Let me see, there are so many. Thrift, hyssop, orchid, speedwell, acanthus, vetch... Hyacinth, ranunculus, cistus, broom, mandrake, asphodel… And the trees. Terebrinth, tamarisk, juniper, Persian lilac, acacia, oleander…’

The sunshine briefly cheered Miriam up. ‘Beautiful names,’ she breathed. ‘Tamarisk… asphodel… Like something from *The Arabian Nights*.’

‘Yes, it’s as I told you, Miriam. But it’s not just a romanticised past, you know. We’re in Palestine to build a new nation.’

‘You said yourself the names were important. You want Eva to teach them to Anna.’

Hugo leant across and squeezed his wife’s hand. ‘Feeling better now, dearest?’

Miriam shrugged. Back in Dresden she became excited about coming to Palestine but the journey had been hard and her enthusiasm tempered. ‘Hugo, is Gaza near here?’

‘Not too far. Down the coast.’

Miriam took her poet’s notebook out of her bag. She whiled away the next part of the journey composing a stanza.

‘Yes,’ she said when she had finished. ‘A poem about Samson

and Delilah. 'Do you want to see my efforts, Eva?'

She handed her the notebook. Eva read.

With dire intent
Delilah holds the scissors
Fingers bent,
Crook'd like Gaza trees.
Samson, through foul ruse,
With his hair doth lose
His manhood 'spite his pleas.
He cries,
My love, my asphodel.'

'Very good,' Eva said loyally. 'But why was she an asphodel?'

'That's for you to tell me, Eva. I just love the word!'

~

Thus in the spring of 1913 they settled into their new home in west Jerusalem. This was a large, cool house built by a wealthy Arab who like many had decamped to the east of the city as a response to Jewish immigration.

Life in their first summer was full of pleasant surprises. Outside their retreat all was noise and smells, dust and ruin, but Miriam found her new home perfect.

She left off her corsets and stays and wore the loose cotton robes of the Arab women. In their leafy courtyard, she would ask Eva to pour a bucket of water over her head. The shock of cold was pure sensation. Then the sun warmed her again until she headed for the tree shade. Glancing up at the points of blue between the leaves she breathed aloud some line of Persian verse or the Song of Solomon. Sometimes she might go indoors and feel the winter coolness preserved for their comfort and delight.

She was often alone. Hugo was out pioneering and politicking. Eva was busy, first finding private pupils then teaching them in their homes – if she hadn't believed herself an outcast from the German Colony, she would have looked for a kindergarten position there. Anna was already enrolled at a German school.

Miriam looked forward to the days off when they could all be together and explore. Away from the crumbling city lay a bounteous land, of corn, wine and honey. The country was so full of vines that when they visited the growers, they were offered as much as they wanted in return for small gifts.

Anna took to the outdoor life, riding camels and horses, chasing lizards. To Miriam the animals of this country seemed benevolent. Camels, sheep, goats and mules were uncomplaining servants. Others were touched with a remote, solemn beauty. On an evening amble, they could glimpse the gazelle, the eagle, the fire-braving salamander, storks winging to the south, flamingos passing in a pink cloud.

The household kept a chameleon. Lifting it from its box, they watched the slow change in colour. Miriam saw it as the image of her own self. The light and the colour acted upon her. She wrote a poem about this and sent it, together with her Samson and Delilah lyric, to a magazine in Leipzig. They liked the poems and wrote asking for more.

But there was another side to their life more consistent with Miriam's original doubts.

One day, while Miriam was queuing in the bank, an elderly German-speaking Jew, turned to her. 'Just arrived? You like it here?'

'So far, yes.'

'I'm a neighbour. I saw you move in.'

'Oh.'

His side-locks quivered. 'Wait till high summer.'

'It gets hot?'

'Burning. Take care with your little girl. Watch out for sunstroke.

And after a hot day, the cool can be bad. Of course you know about malaria, typhus…'

'We'll take care.'

'And the Chamsin – you know, the Sirocco. That'll blow from the desert like a hot oven. The longer you live here, the more you suffer. The Arabs hate it more than anybody. The shade in your yard won't help.'

'I don't think I want to know any more!'

But this High Street Cassandra wouldn't stop. 'The winters! What misery. You've only a few months to find out. Snow, rain. The little heaters here can't warm up a large room. Of course people here are foolish. They cover their heads but leave their legs bare. Then they die from the fumes of the *kanoon*.'

'*Kanoon*?'

'Charcoal brazier. They leave it burning all night in a sealed room.'

'Well, we won't do that.'

The queue in the bank was so long more talk was inevitable.

'What was the Most High doing that he should give us this land?'

Miriam hoped her frosty manner might discourage him but he carried on.

'Just look at the creatures here. They're a test in themselves. Boars, hyenas, jackals, wild cats, centipedes, scorpions, spiders, rats, locusts, vultures. I've seen snakes locked together swallowing each other. Trap a scorpion under glass and it stings itself to death. Not only scorpions. Humans kill themselves – Jews even. What a crime!'

'Then, sir, why do you live here?'

He responded with the millennial Jewish shrug. 'You want a rabbi who's come to die in Zion to tell you his life story?'

She shook her head graciously. As they waited he told her anyway.

She mentioned the conversation to Hugo. He was defensive. Her criticisms were fewer than he had feared but they made him anxious.

'Well, a little bit of the *shtetl* is bound to follow us here before we create a new kind of Jew. But look at the new Jewish quarters going up everywhere here in the west. They deliver the right message. The twentieth century. Wide, paved streets, lit at night. Functional dwellings, easy to keep clean. Where else can Jews live like this?'

'I don't find the Jewish areas attractive.'

Miriam's romantic expectations were disappointed by this modern Jerusalem. There was nothing 'oriental' about these neat rows of Jewish dwellings. She preferred evocative Arab flat roofs, domes, minarets. Among the modern buildings, the Christian hospices and schools made a more varied contribution to the skyline.

She also objected to the civic pomposity in the modern suburbs. 'You say those are Herod the Great's towers. Then why put a clock tower and a municipal fountain in front of them?'

Hugo always had an answer. 'It's the Jaffa-Jerusalem carriage-line terminus. What do people want after a long journey? A drink and to know the time! Eminently practical! I hear by the way a tram service is to start soon...'

What was Miriam to do with her time? Hugo asked his colleague Gold, who'd come over from Tel Aviv, if he had any ideas.

'You should have no concerns, Hugo. A new, Zionist Jerusalem is taking shape. Modern Jews, the *maskilim*, are gaining strength. The Bezalel Academy of Art, the Hebrew *Gymnasium*, kindergartens, the National Library... There's the Teacher Training College too. Has she thought of training as a teacher? If she has the inclination she can fit in anywhere. She should certainly join the Beit Ha'am.'

'Beit Ha'am?'

'The community centre. A fine nest of the *maskilim*.'

It turned out Miriam had already dropped in on the centre but had not felt at home.

'Hugo, it's like a student club. They're too young and eager for me.'

'You're thirty-two! That's not old. What about a profession? What about teaching?'

'Like Eva! That would hardly be suitable. Hugo, dearest, I'm all right. It's enough for me just helping us to survive day by day.' (In truth she did little of that. It was Eva who, as well as teaching, shopped, found tradespeople and dealt with crises.)

'What do you mean?'

'Just to live here,' she said vaguely. 'You know, the primitive sanitation in this house and crumbling buildings in the old city. I do miss Father and all our friends. Letters seem to take for ever... '

'Don't go to the old city,' said Hugo, sticking with the here and now and ignoring anything that touched on regret.

'I like to go there. It has the true poetic note. But the lepers with their open sores – I have to drag Anna past. If she were ever infected! And the begging *shtetl* Jews. How do they survive? The bedouin and the fellaheen, they seem so dispirited.'

'I agree. A cholera epidemic recently, malaria a constant threat. The Ottomans are a curse on the country. High taxes, bribery, and since 1908, military conscription. That's why everyone looks so miserable, that and the recession since '09. But we Jews must turn these disadvantages around. There's plenty for a Jewish trade union to do I can tell you. Modern medicine is helping... Would you prefer Tel Aviv? The sanitation is better. Or we could be radical and join a kibbutz.'

She was aghast. 'Hugo, I'm no pioneer. No, if it has to be Palestine, I prefer Jerusalem even if life is hard.'

Hugo had manoeuvred her into saying she wanted to stay where they were. As for returning 'home', even she knew she had to give it more time before the idea was even breathed.

'But sometimes, Hugo, I just feel afraid. It's Anna. What if war comes?'

'If there's war,' he concluded irritably, 'Anna's in the safest place. As I've said many times, Palestine is safer than Germany.'

Over the next year Hugo heard rumours which he kept from Miriam. The German government had smuggled weapons into

Jerusalem. It had withdrawn gold from circulation. The Kaiser sent a scientific expedition ostensibly to study malaria, in fact to gather information useful to the military.

'Now they know the depth and capacity of every cistern in Jerusalem,' Gold said.

'The problem is that the military and the Right in Germany dominate everything,' commented Hugo gloomily. 'Their plans extend as far as here. I've told Miriam we'll be safe from war out here but the Germans keep provoking the whole world.'

'Try not to worry, old fellow.'

'You don't know the cost to me of bringing my wife and child out here.'

'Try to relax, Hugo. Perhaps you need a break. Take Miriam away. I know a good quiet place, the German Lazarist hostel at Amwas. You can rest, eat good food, read the books in their excellent library.'

'We could leave Anna with Eva, I suppose.'

But it was around a year before Hugo acted on Gold's suggestion. Finally, with tears from Anna, they went to Amwas. It was the beginning of August 1914.

The hostel was indeed charming and restful, but late on the second night, as they tried to sleep, they heard shouts and cheers. It went on for too long.

'We came here to get away from noise,' moaned Hugo from his bed. 'I didn't realise they were a lot of drunkards.'

Next morning, wandering in the garden to the buzz of insects, Miriam met one of the brothers.

'Was it a festival last night?' she asked, trying to avoid a note of complaint since by and large they were enjoying themselves.

'No, no. Haven't you heard? Of course, you wouldn't have.'

'What?'

'Our consul at Jerusalem sent us news that England and Germany are at war.'

'Really?'

'Indeed.'

'But... but you sounded as if you were rejoicing. Surely not over that.'

The man of God grinned. 'Madam, for years we have gone on making our army and navy larger and larger, and the country has been taxed to keep them up. If we don't use them, what excuse have we for keeping them so large? And if our people at home are taxed like this, and still the army and navy are not used, they will rise. War in Germany itself. Revolution. German against German. It wouldn't be the first time, look at the Thirty Years War. We would take two centuries to recover.'

'But is not war a terrible thing and quite against your religion?'

'It will be war, either at home or abroad. Therefore we rejoice because it's war abroad.'

'But Turkey will declare for Germany. Palestine is a fief of Turkey. "War abroad" will mean war here.'

'That is better than revolution in Germany. We must endure the clash of war for the sake of the Fatherland.'

He bowed serenely. 'As a Jewess, you may not feel the same.'

~

There was no 'clash of war'. On the contrary Jerusalem quietened, reverted, became the backwater it had been in the mid-1800s. The consulates of enemy countries closed; their educational establishments emptied. The Greek and Armenian Patriarchs were sent away. Unlike the Fischers, most Jewish immigrants were of enemy, Russian nationality and earmarked for deportation.

Grain was scarce. Every day meant a fresh search for food: trekking, queuing, paying over the odds. Miriam undertook some of this. She became ill. Anna went hungry and grew thin instead of growing.

'Oh Hugo, can't we go home?' pleaded Miriam. 'This war is the last straw.'

'Wait my dear. It will be over soon. For Zionists it's our great chance. Now of all times we need to be here. By the end of it the English may have marched in and be in a position to give us what we want.'

That first winter there was a plague of locusts. Turkish soldiers dug pits, beating the creatures in and setting fire to them. A locust settled on the face of a neighbour's baby and almost ate it away. One night Miriam woke to Anna's shrieks. She rushed to her bedroom. Eva was already there. A locust had been burrowing in the poor girl's ear.

'It was bad for Anna,' said Hugo the next day, 'but that was nothing to do with the war. Do you think things are any better in Germany? There they suffer more.'

Eva had left it very late but she had at last visited Anton – at his shop in the heart of the old city, the new business he had set up (as she was now to learn) with the money Stefan had given him for the portrait of Johannes.

The shop opened on to a narrow alley. Eva peered in. Carvings were ranged on shelves. A printing press stood against one wall. There he was bent over a bench, Anton Gustavus, her one-time lover, sixteen years older.

Surrounded by planks and hammers, inks and dyes, he was more imposing now than back in 1898. With his spectacles and greying beard, he conveyed a weary concentration and – she immediately felt – the sense of a strong arm and deft hand wasted on producing tourist souvenirs.

'I won't be a moment,' he said gruffly, without looking up. 'Please look round.' He straightened up. 'Eva!'

'Yes, it's me. I'm surprised you recognise an old schoolmarm.'

He smiled mischievously. 'Rumours of your return have circulated in the Colony.'

'But you didn't come looking for me.' She tried to say it with light mockery but old feeling gave it more weight than intended.

'I don't know what to say, Eva… How are you?'

'Anton, I've come to tell you something. Don't expect to see me again after this.'

The story of a young man transfixed by the portrait at the Dresden gallery was quickly told.

Anton sat down trembling, head in hands.

At length he said, 'I almost wish you hadn't told me. If you'd come earlier… but now there's a war. Normal life has stopped. Private things are at a standstill till it's over. As for travel… Any idea of going to look for him…'

'You are annoyed that I didn't tell you before…'

'No… I... '

'I've been busy. I work from morning to night.'

'Of course.'

'Besides, the Fischers need constant nannying.'

'It doesn't matter, Eva. None of it makes any difference.'

'I'm sorry… I should have come before. You had a right to know at the earliest opportunity. Hugo wants to meet up with you, by the way. I think he feels guilty that he didn't buy the portrait before we left. It was very expensive and there was so much going on at the time.'

'No matter. Stefan came here, a drunk offering gold. I needed the money but I was sick of looking at the cursed portrait to tell the truth. Magda misses it, says I took away her only comfort. Anyway Hugo can drop by here any time. Tell him not to feel guilty.'

'Will you give Magda this new information?'

'This… rumour. I don't think so at the moment. It won't help her to think Johannes might be alive and living in Germany. It would be worse for her. After the war who knows?'

JOHANNES 3

Twenty years of age, gazing across the Egyptian desert from the Aswan-Cairo train, I reflected on my happy years with Massoud. What a great man he was. How much I owed to him. Without knowing it himself, he was a natural teacher. He had given me all I needed for what lay ahead, then allowed me to go.

I had left him a substantial amount of money for all the years of keep. The rest remained stitched into the lining of my small brightly coloured coat. I had packed it carefully in my travelling bag. My plan to join Zoraya in Leipzig after seeking out my family in Jerusalem depended on money and luck. My coat was two things, a secret purse and a lucky charm. I kept it close to me at all times.

From Cairo I took the train to Alexandria intending to sail for Jaffa by working my passage. I was worried about money. If I was to go about with Zoraya in Leipzig it was the one thing I would need. I had to hold on to what I had, for sure, but add to it when I could.

After plying the docks for some time I found work in the galley of a primitive steamer, the *Apollonia*, a freight ship heading for Haifa via Cyprus. It was a roundabout way to get to Palestine but the captain paid more than others. Dockers told me the *Apollonia* was a rust-bucket and a sieve. The extra pay was danger money. I glanced at the calm sea. The pay was good. What could go wrong?

The *Apollonia* set sail on a perfect Mediterranean day. Egypt, and all the pains and joys of my life, lay behind me. I peered ahead at the horizon dividing the still, dark sea from the brilliant sky above. I was at peace. Perhaps Zoraya's departure had not been such a bad thing. Otherwise, would I ever have left Aswan? Now I knew where I was going. I would re-connect with my past, then build a future with Zoraya.

I went down to the sweaty galley. As cook's boy, my job was to check the lowered nets, haul in the fish and prepare them along with the vegetables. Exhausted after a few hours of this I was ready to sleep. My bunk lay alongside sacks of rice and lentils. The cook handed me a club as I bedded down.

'When they wake you up, bash'em.'

'What?'

'Rats. That's your job too.'

'Then how do I sleep?'

'Don't worry, you'll get some shut-eye. We'll be resting up in Limassol for a day. We can go ashore for some Greek jiggy-jiggy. I'll show you a place.'

There was one job worse than mine on the *Apollonia.* A grey-bearded oriental fellow in a loin cloth worked the buckets in the hold. He scooped the sea water that leaked permanently into the hull into buckets, hauled them on to a ledge, clambered up a wooden platform and emptied the water through a porthole. He never took a break. If he didn't keep up, the water level rose, everyone cursed him and he had to go even faster.

'Akira is paying for his grandson to receive his sight,' I was told.

In the middle of the night the wind got up and the boat began to heave. I tried to ignore it and go back to sleep. The wind roared, the waves crashed against the hull. Suddenly in one violent movement I was hurled from my bunk. The rats scattered, careering from side to side with no interest now in the sacks of food, only in saving their lives.

A single light came from an oil lamp strung from a beam. The flame was somehow surviving the mayhem. Men shouted and pushed to get up to the deck. Shadows loomed as in the caverns of hell. When someone got to the top of the stairway the boat would plunge.

The hapless crewman would tumble and find himself back where he had started. Fights were breaking out.

How would I succeed where others were failing? And my money! The coat! Heart beating, I reached under the bunk for my bag. Where is it! Where is it! The lurching of the ship must have sent it flying. I looked around helplessly. At that moment I saw, rolling the length of the hull, engulfing everything in its path, a huge wave.

The hull had been breached and the ship was going down. I launched myself into the water, praying to Massoud's god of the microbes to save me. I was not ready to leave this earth. I was not ready to lose Zoraya. I *had* to live.

At first I swam with bold strokes. Now everything was dark. Kegs, wooden rails, nautical flotsam passed me. I never saw a face or heard a human cry. It was as if I had been on a ghost ship.

I must have swum through the hole in the hull or perhaps I was saved by the boat breaking up. Now I was floating in open sea. I turned exhausted on my back and looked up at the stars.

I rested for a few minutes, then searched for something to attach myself to, some bit of wood or floating wreckage. In the moonless night I saw nothing. How empty was the world now. How alone I was. Despair gripped me. A feeling I knew from long ago.

'All drowned? All gone? So soon?'

How long could I keep afloat? Hours? A day or two at most. What chance was there of rescue in that dark empty sea? And if I should by some remote chance be rescued, what of my plans? My money had gone for ever.

'I'm a thief. It's my punishment.'

I trod water veering between numbness and despair.

Slowly dawn lightened to the east. I squinted towards the sun as it slipped its mooring in the blue darkness and rose majestically. To one side of the bright orb – I could have missed it against the rosy sky – I saw a pinpoint of brighter red. I narrowed my eyes. Was I dreaming? No, there it was, a bright red spot and below, something pale and hard to make out. I swam urgently towards it. I must catch it. I gained slowly, then I began to see that it was some kind of craft. I guessed that the red was a signal or flag. I came closer. Yes, there was somebody there. A person was sitting on a raft waving a flag, or perhaps the flag was attached to a mast.

'Stop! Stop!' I roared, splashing frantically. 'Stop! Don't go away!'

I was near enough now that the person must have noticed me, but so far there was no sign from him. He seemed to be all but naked, and as I looked more closely I could see him properly at last. He was white-haired and bearded. He did not wave but was now clearly following my progress.

I realised who it was. 'Akira!'

There was no reply. The old man kept looking over towards me. Finally as I drew near he lifted an arm in grave salutation and said something.

'I'm sorry, I don't speak your language,' I spluttered.

'Then we shall speak the language of the Prophet,' he replied in perfect Arabic.

He helped me on board. I fell back panting heavily.

He reached into a leather bag and pulled out a flask. 'Have some – but only a little. We need to conserve it.'

I took a swig of the water.

'Thank you, Akira,' I panted.

I wanted to ask him how on earth he had managed this impressive escape but he seemed distracted, and rummaged in his bag.

I lay back and gazed up at the red cloth he had tied between two poles. It was an identical shade to the cloth waved from Massoud's balloon. With a stab I thought of our times in the balloon, of Zoraya's virgin blood.

When I turned to look at Akira, he was holding my coat of many colours.

'What!'

'I observed you and that bag. You had your nose in it. I knew there must be something important there. Lo and behold, it went floating past me. I picked it out of the sea and looked through it. The only thing of any possible value was this coat. So I took it out in case I should see you and threw the bag back into the sea. Fate works in mysterious ways.'

'But Akira, how did you escape?'

'I was always prepared,' he said, nodding pensively. 'I knew the *Apollonia*. It was only a matter of time. I tried to tell the captain but he was greedy. He would never put his profits back into repairs. I tied barrels underneath the platform I worked on. The masts and red cloth, basic provisions – my own personal lifeboat. When the ship was doomed I unhooked the platform, attached myself with a rope, fought my way up to the deck, threw it in and jumped. Now I'm waiting for a passing boat. If none comes...' He smiled.

I spent days with Akira astride our tiny craft, kept alive by the food and water he had prepared and which he had no hesitation in sharing. I discovered that this man was the wisest of philosophers.

'Now,' he said at the beginning, 'with death very likely ahead of us, we will divide our time as follows. To keep mentally active, each will teach the other the language that he knows and the other doesn't. I will teach you Japanese and – since you tell me you know the language – you will instruct me in German. Another section of the day will be spent in recounting the story of our lives, taking turns. No detail need be spared. This too will energise us. The talker will gain a sense of the uniqueness of his path and the listener – who may interject at times with his own thoughts or questions – an awakened capacity in himself for empathy. And the third part – I leave aside the time for sleeping and eating – will be spent in a shared spiritual practice. This will prepare us for death whether that should come sooner, as I suspect, or later. We will sit cross-legged in the oriental manner facing out towards the sea and allow our thoughts to pass before us as though they were phantoms distracting us from a deeper reality. Our very fear of death will become no longer a thing fully felt, as it were, but something watched with a certain detachment. Here, I still have my pocket watch. The activities will change by the hour. During the heat of the day we will cool ourselves by dipping in the sea for five minutes as we change activities. Are you agreed?'

And that was how it was. After the storm, the sea had returned to its natural calm. Sustained equally by Akira's provisions and his schedule, we became the closest of companions. At night we took it in turns to sleep. I have never slept better than I did at that time. Nor did I experience boredom.

I learnt much of Akira's life. He was a Japanese born in Alexandria – there was some connection with the building of the Suez canal – and his grandson suffered from congenital blindness which was, however, curable by an expensive operation. Akira had been working on the *Apollonia* for a while but he was still some time away from accumulating the amount needed. When in the days to follow he fell into despair it was not on his own account but on his grandson's. 'I would die happy if only I knew he could see.'

The language learning was not a great success. Neither of us had a motive for learning the language on offer although it worked well enough to keep us awake. Even to this day I can say, 'Can you direct me to the municipal baths' in Japanese.

The life-story business was another matter. I was astonished to find when gently pressed by Akira how much I was able to remember about my early life.

'It was rocky everywhere. The earth was red. There were thistles and lizards which sat in the sun and then darted away. Father wore dusty boots. Mother's hands were rough from washing and cleaning. Hymns and sermons in a stone chapel. I remember a ruined village, a train ride. Not much else. How bright the sun was. I had to shield my eyes to stop it blinding me.'

I found myself staring out across the sea speaking as if to my parents.

'Mother, you were a loving woman and I'm sure you did everything a mother should. Father, your eyes twinkled when you looked at me. You loved to hug me in your big arms. You took me everywhere with you right up to that last trip. Where are you both now?'

I wept to recall the desolation I felt on my desert journey away from everything I knew and loved. Remembering how Zoraya had saved me in Omdurman I cried more. Then there was my life in Cairo, which I recalled more fondly since I had made friends in the souk and learnt to survive on my wits. This story entertained Akira as too my return to Omdurman and the long idyll at Aswan with Massoud and Zoraya. I was not too shy to tell him I had lost my virginity at a height of five hundred metres. He laughed so heartily he nearly fell back into the water.

Would I ever see Zoraya again? I stared out, searching as ever for a ship. (Sometimes we did see them but always so far away that there was no chance of them spotting us though we shouted and waved frantically.) Was it all to end here in the immensity of the lonely sea, Akira and me floating skeletons picked clean by passing carrion?

It healed me to talk about these things and to feel the deep attention of so wise and modest a man as Akira, who had himself had his own share of suffering.

As the sun set, perhaps for the third or fourth time that day we began our spiritual practice. We faced away from the sun so as not to be distracted by the beauty of the world as shown at that moment by the red orb dropping through space.

With the raft gently rocking I half-closed my eyes and watched my thoughts come and go. Zoraya, ravishing, sensual, funny, sweet. Let her pass. See her go. My fear of starvation and death, a knot in my stomach, rising and ready to choke me. Allow it, feel it, see it go. Memory, desire, fear. An endless procession but passing, a show, riding moment by moment away. Death too will be such a moment. Death too will pass.

Treat them all the same. Watch them, let them go.

I learnt from Akira the habit of sitting with my thoughts that has never left me.

The food and water was all but gone. We were hungry, thirsty, weak, close to despair. I saw it first, a large passenger ship heading straight towards us in the gleam of the dawn.

I stared in exhausted disbelief.

'It's homing on us,' I murmured. 'It's as if it knew we were here.'

The boat slowed. Someone shouted down first in French, then in German, also in English.

I replied in German. A ladder was lowered and our ordeal was over.

The ship was on its way through Suez from the German East African colonies to Hamburg. The next stop was Tangier. The captain and crew were welcoming enough but as soon as we had recovered we were politely asked to work our passage.

Akira planned to get off at Tangier and find his way back to Alexandria. Unlike me he had no money and his plan to pay for his grandson's operation was, with the loss of the *Apollonia*, more or less in ruins.

I was in a dilemma. I could go back with Akira and then on as planned to Jerusalem. On the other hand the arrival of a German ship seemed like fate. The problem of how to get to Leipzig from Palestine was solved at a stroke. In ten days I would be in Hamburg, a mere step from Zoraya. Could I pass up this chance? I asked Akira's advice.

'Do what is fitting.'

'It is fitting to return home to my parents but I will lose Zoraya.'

'Well, there you are.'

What kind of advice was that? He had simply returned my dilemma to me. I wrestled with my conscience and deceived myself that I would write to my parents from Germany telling them I was alive and that I would soon visit them with my new bride. In reality

I always had the option to write to them but had put it off for reasons I could not explain to myself.

As we drew near to Tangier, the parting of the ways with Akira loomed. I knew this would be hard for both of us. We were swabbing the deck together on the last morning.

'Akira, I am not going back with you. I am going on to Germany.'

'I know,' he said.

During the break from our work I spoke to one of the German cabin crew.

'How much will a train ticket from Hamburg to Leipzig and a week's board and lodging cost me?' He gave me a rough calculation.

Armed with this knowledge I returned to my cabin. I retrieved my coat, cut open the seam and took out my money. Taking account of rates of exchange, I removed the sum the German had mentioned and put it in my pocket. I put the rest back into the lining of the coat and sewed it back up.

The ship berthed at Tangier. Akira and I stood at the top of the gangplank ready to say good-bye. He seemed impassive but I could tell he was suffering. We both knew we would never meet again.

'Akira, you saved my life. I can never thank you enough. Besides that, I have learnt a great deal from you. I fear you disapprove of my choice but I am driven to go on, rather than back. Forgive me.'

His lined face crinkled into a smile.

I took my coat from my bag. I looked at the colours, as bright as on the day I stole it.

'I have a gift for your grandson, the very coat that you saved from the sea and which has been so precious to me. It's a child's coat. It's time for me to pass it on. Inside the lining you will find enough money to pay for your grandson's operation. Maybe the colours of the coat will be among the first things he sees. If there's any money left over please give it to the German Christian Brothers on Shariah Ramses in Cairo. They are good people and looked after me as you know.' I wasn't going to tell Akira that I stole the money from them as I knew he would take it all straight back to them.

'There is some trickery in here,' said Akira, 'but I will do as you say.'

He looked me firmly in the eye and bowed. He walked down the gangplank. I waited for him to turn and wave but of course he did not. That day in the year 1912 was the last I saw of my shipmate and saviour.

Everything went more or less according to plan. True, I found myself in utterly unfamiliar terrain once the ship docked at Hamburg. How cold and inhospitable was this land of my fathers. I spoke the language but in a way that seemed to arouse suspicion. Perhaps too it was the way I looked. I spent money on a haircut and clothes to help me fit in but this ate into my funds. All the same, I quickly travelled to Leipzig by train and headed straight for the university.

Here I was told by the bursar that the professor had left. He had taken up a post in Dresden. Was his daughter with him?

'Ah, the beautiful princess from Persia?'

'That's the one.'

'Yes, the invalid.'

'Invalid?'

'She broke all hearts here but now she's gone.'

'What was wrong with her?'

The bursar tapped the side of his head.

'Her mind?'

'She was all over the place.'

'Did she go with her father to Dresden?'

'As far as I know.'

How my heart sank. Zoraya ill, and I didn't have enough money for the train to Dresden.

'How far is Dresden? Can I walk it?'

'It will take you three days.'

Three days later I crossed the Elbe towards the Altstadt. I was not so tired that I couldn't see that the city was a miracle, something far surpassing Hamburg or Leipzig, a fairy-tale of towers and domes, pinnacles, countless graceful statues. I had never seen such a man-built wonder unless it was the pyramids at Giza.

I rested by a fountain, eating an apple, and then set off into the heart of the city. I turned down a small street off one of the wider thoroughfares. I was in a dream and had quite forgotten where I was.

'This won't do,' I said to myself. 'I need a plan. I must find work first. Anything. I can't present myself to my princess Zoraya as a vagabond.'

I came to a halt on the narrow pavement and stared down, scratching my head. Where was I to start? When I looked up, I was facing a small shop, or rather a gallery. In the window, strikingly displayed, was a painting.

A portrait of a boy.

He sat on a plain wooden chair. Behind him a window opened onto a dry landscape. A rich hanging fell on the other side. The boy stared intently at me as if he knew my very mind.

My scalp tingled. My heart began to race.

1917-20

Chapter 10

'Be careful of what you say,' said Magda.

'I can't promise.' Anton slammed the front door and walked head down towards the Colony meeting house. Inside, the Colonists packed the benches.

'Good morning brother Anton. Something biting you today?'

'Could be.'

Hans, one of the elder Colonists, called for silence and began his oration. In weighty tones, he reminded everyone why they were there. They were three years into the war and things had reached a crucial point.

'This Year of Our Lord, 1917. How much we have suffered, but now we are at a crossroads. The English and Australians might march into the Holy Land any day.'

'Defeatism!' shouted one or two hotheads.

Hans raised his hands. 'I don't say it will happen. But we have to agree on what to do if it does. How much to co-operate, how much to resist? What if we are asked to billet English soldiers? Should we destroy our stores before they get them? We have to be clear where we stand on all these things. It's only prudent.'

'Prudent?' sneered the young Helmut Kappel. 'You're pulling our legs, venerable Hans.'

'What would you have us do then, Helmut?' countered Hans.

'Get guns from the Turks to defend the Colony!'

'Since when were we fighters?' asked Hans mildly.

'From today! We must fight to the death! Give way to the English who've had their own way for too long? Never!'

Support for Helmut rippled through the hall. 'Hear, hear!'

'It's good the young are talking sense,' someone said.

Anton stared at the floor. He seemed to be in a trance. More people spoke. At last he rose. 'Friends…'

Groans.

'Here we go!'

'The voice of reason!'

Sweat trickled from under Anton's greying mop. The barracking threatened to silence him. Hans called for hush. 'Brethren, remember your principles.'

'I'm grateful to you, Hans. Yes, principles, exactly. We Templers came here with ideals – free speech included. In a moment I'll remind you of more of those ideals, but first, to show I've thought about it properly...'

'Stop rambling!'

Anton pressed on. 'Who for instance now believes we Templers can act as a magnet for Jews who will come to Palestine and convert to Christianity? Now, with Zionism, the Jews have their own reasons for coming here and don't need a push from us…'

'Shame!'

'Jews do convert still – and Arabs. It's still our aim.'

'Christ, will damn you, I say, Anton!'

'Maybe, Paul!' Anton shot back at his accuser. 'But we're not here to talk about my sins. I leave such things to my Maker. Meanwhile you, brother Paul, might like to consider the plank in your own eye.'

Paul shifted uneasily.

'Everybody strikes his own bargain with his Maker, Paul. We're Protestants. That's what it means. We don't rely on the authority of pope or priest. In our religion tolerance is the watchword.'

'Hypocrite,' sniffed Paul. He wasn't giving up. Long ago his wife was rumoured to have been one of Anton's conquests.

Other protests were threatening once more to drown out the

speaker. Hans tried to quell the racket. Finally he declared that if Anton was not allowed to finish he would close the meeting to allow time for tempers to subside. This worked. Silence fell. Anton leant forward.

'Look, I was born a Templer. Our beliefs are in my bones. Freedom-loving, tyrant-hating, that's what brought the Templers here. My friends, we *must* see what follows. This great conflict engulfs the world. Accident has put us in territory belonging to the Turks, allies of Germany and Austria. Palestine is now in effect a fief of the German Reich. So we feel at home here. And certainly we should do nothing to provoke the Turks who are nominally in charge. "Render unto Caesar..." But in our hearts...' Anton struck his chest. ' – the heart, that is where it counts – we must, as internationalists, remain...' He paused. The dread word was about to escape his lips. '...neutral.'

There was a shocked pause, then mayhem.

'Neutral? Disgrace!'

'Lock him up!'

'We are Germans. How can we be neutral?'

'Traitor!'

'Christ will damn you, Anton Gustavus.'

But the dissident hadn't finished. 'It follows,' he called above the noise, 'that if – I should say when, since the English will soon increase the pressure at Gaza – their army arrives, we offer them every hospitality, as well as the co-operation we've always given the present authorities.'

Anton sat down, folded his arms and stared at the floor.

'We,' shrieked Helmut, 'who welcomed the Kaiser in '98, Prince Eitel Fritz in 1910! We'd never live it down!'

Even Hans was indignant. 'I said we were here to consider all possibilities, brother Anton. But we're Germans. Surely we know which side we're on.'

Anton did not move. As the uproar continued he spoke, arms

folded still, bemused, murmuring, 'Wasn't Christ a man of peace? The Arab Maronite, the Jewish convert, they are more Christian than our Templer colony. Puffed up patriotism, smug unanimity... materialism... bogus religion.'

Helmut was on his feet pointing accusingly at the pariah. 'I say to you, Anton. If you can't stand it, get out! Join us in our oath to the Kaiser or clear out! Long live the Kaiser!'

The Colonists rose to their feet and broke into the national anthem. It was ragged at first but rose to a unified chorus. The young men, Helmut and the others, eyed each other triumphantly.

Anton sat down and buried his head in his hands.

A tall, good-looking young man with neat hair and glasses stood apart. Leaning against the back wall with his hands in his pockets, he'd been watching the row. After the anthem he waited till there was a space and sat next to his father.

'Well, *I* agree with you, Father...'

Anton turned. 'Oh, it's you.'

'Yes. Your lone supporter...' His father's indifference was so familiar that Werner didn't react.

The meeting continued with discussion of less contentious matters. Father and son sat on side by side, each in his private world. Werner's mind began to wander to a plan far from war and politics.

He had recently met a girl...

~

'"A housemaid on her way to the shops needs to buy three-quarters of a kilo of mutton, three cabbages, one-and-a-half kilos of potatoes, and a quarter-kilo of lard. Mutton is twenty-seven and a half pfennigs a kilo, cabbages are four-and-a-half pfennigs each, potatoes are eleven pfennigs a kilo, lard seventeen pfennigs a kilo. How much change will the housemaid get out of one hundred pfennigs?"'

Anna read again. '"A housemaid on her way..."'

It was no good.

'I remember doing this kind of thing back in Dresden when I was eleven. I couldn't do it then and...'

She closed the book and gave it a hearty sniff.

'Musty! At least father is right about one thing. My German school is fifty years behind the times.'

She reached for another battered book. '"Parse the following sentences."'

The word 'parse' made her groan, along with 'pluperfect', 'subjunctive' and the rest. She could never get the hang of any of them. Still...

She looked out of the window. No, today was not the day. After weeks of grey sky, snow and biting winds, spring had arrived. The sun bleached the wall and cooked the windowsill. The airy smells teased her.

But then...

She clutched her stomach.

Hunger...

What emptiness. No, it went beyond hunger. A light-headedness, an ache of deprivation as much emotional as physical.

Oh, to eat something nourishing, filling, delicious. Roast meat, or the *cholent* they used to have in Dresden – fat brisket of beef swimming in a huge pot with haricot and butter beans, potatoes, onion, prunes, syrup, with dumplings floating on the top.

She sighed heavily.

She would go for a walk in the street. Maybe she'd track down some bread or a street peddler with almonds or pistachios. Did she have enough money? She shook her savings jar and hurried downstairs, tying her braids as she went.

It was against the rules set by her parents for these dangerous times but what harm could she come to? Just a walk.

She stepped from the courtyard into the street. What a din! That too made her feel faint. Hagglers, street kids, Jews, fellaheen, shouting and cursing. A group of bored Turkish soldiers calling after her as she went. Wounded servicemen with outstretched bandaged hands.

'*Guten Morgen, Fräulein Fischer.*'

She shielded her eyes from the sun. A young man held his panama aloft.

'Oh, Werner...'

'I was on my way to see you and here you are in the street. What a stroke of luck.'

'But... why aren't you up at your Colony?'

'There's a meeting.'

'What do they meet about?'

'Everything! We are very democratic!'

He held up a wicker bag. 'Feel inside.'

She put her hand in and felt around. 'What is it? It's warm.'

'Guess.'

She shook her head. She had an idea but couldn't bear to be wrong.

He grinned. 'A cooked chicken.'

'Werner! How did you get it!'

'From Emile, who barters from his cave at Aceldama. He offered it to me.'

'What did you give him in return?'

Werner ignored the question. 'Want to share it with me?'

She blinked. 'I...'

'I know just the place. We can make a picnic of it.'

'I can't be out too long, Werner.'

'Thirty minutes there, thirty minutes for the picnic, thirty minutes back. Ninety minutes altogether.'

She'd rather have just torn into the chicken there and then. 'All right. I'll just go back and leave a note. But I mustn't be late.'

'Come on, Anna. Look at your unchaperoned Jewish girls, the Zionist ones. Out at all hours. Some of them even live with men without being married to them.'

'How do you know?'

'My father has Zionist friends.'

'Oh.'

After she'd returned home to leave the note, they set off on the excursion.

'What's that?' she asked as they passed the Jaffa Gate. Soldiers guarded a line of large wooden frames.

'Gibbets.'

'Gibbets?'

'To hang people. See the ropes?'

'It gives me a horrible feeling.'

'The Turks are trying to put the fear of God into all of us. It's because they're desperate. They know they haven't got much longer here.'

'Who will they hang?'

'Anyone who supports the English. Spies, turncoats, traitors. Arabs or Jews who want the English to win, to further their own aims.'

'Like my father,' she murmured.

'And mine. Perhaps our fathers will end up swinging side by side.'

'Werner! That's not funny!'

'Seriously, this war has to end soon. You should see the country once you get out of Jerusalem. There's no village life left. The fellaheen have all been conscripted by the Turks. Food and animals have been commandeered. Trees have been cut down for fuel. The improvements of recent years have come to nothing. Hunger and poverty are everywhere, not to mention typhus and malaria.'

'You seem to know a lot about what's going on, Werner.'

'I like to keep informed.'

Past Herod's Gate they rounded the north-east corner of the city. A panorama opened out, the ground falling sharply away and rising again to a height. Everything was fresh and crisp in the spring light: the snaking paths, the new grass and flowers beneath the black trunked olives.

'The world famous Mount of Olives,' he said. 'Not bad.'

She laughed. *'Not bad?'*

'I speak as a painter. I am blind to the place's associations. I judge the Mount of Olives visually – as a subject. Look at these hills. They are hard but have been shaped over millennia into the softest curves, like a lute. Hard… and soft. An intriguing contradiction.'

She leant her head against the city wall. 'It's very peaceful. The war seems far away… No cruel world.'

'I think, Anna, the world is cruel everywhere.'

'Why, Werner?'

'The fauna in this paradise, this Eden, are all killing to survive. Everything kills or is killed. It's one great system of murder. The fittest survive. You've studied Darwin?'

'Is that what Darwin says?'

'Yes. The Survival of the Fittest.'

She eyed him from under the brim of her hat. 'Well, Darwin's'wrong. He's a big fool if he can't see there's more to it than that. I don't *want* to study such a brute.'

He strode away, down the boulder-strewn valley. 'The Survival of the Fittest, Anna! Catch me if you can! Beat me to the bottom of the valley!'

He was far ahead before she limped after him. Scratched by thistles, she finally reached a low wall beyond.

'You didn't give me a chance!' she puffed.

'Are you hungry now?'

'You're really making me suffer for my bite of chicken.'

'Nonsense. You're the picture of health. Look at your glowing cheeks.'

He pointed up the hill. 'To the tower!'

~

High above the battered door was a window.

'It's a Rapunzel tower, Werner, a fairy-tale. Is there a witch in there, or a handsome prince?'

'Witches and princes? For me it's an observation point.'

Werner retrieved the key from under a stone and they went in. The ground floor consisted of a kitchen with a sink, cupboards and cast iron burner. There were knives and a chopping block but no sign of food. Werner led the way up to the first floor. The faded hangings and Persian rugs were charmingly picturesque. Anna collapsed onto the chaise.

'Let's get some air in here,' he said.

Werner opened the shutters. Instead of getting the chicken out he fixed his eye to the telescope on the sill.

'There it is.'

Anna could hardly control herself.

'What?' she said wearily.

'The Dome of the Rock. What a view of it from here on the Mount of Olives. When I look at the coloured brickwork it seems close enough to touch.'

Anna forced herself to her feet and peered at the city opposite, along the horizon of minarets and towers until she came to the softly gleaming dome.

'Have a look,' he said.

'I am…'

'Of course, you're hungry.'

'Aren't *you*!' she burst out.

'I just want to record something for a painting I'm doing. I keep materials here. You help yourself. There's bread in there as well, and a flask of water.'

'Can't your sketch wait? Can't we eat together?'

He held up his hands. 'Anna, you're quite right. How ungentlemanly of me. I'll draw afterwards.' He removed the bird and unwrapped it on the table. 'A leg?' he asked.

She nodded.

Werner sat on the sill while Anna sat cross-legged on the floor.

'Shall we start?'

'Oh, Werner.'

She ripped her leg into chunks and crammed the flesh in. Then she remembered it was a bad idea to rush if you were underfed. You could sick it all up. What a waste that would be.

'You're hungry, Anna?'

'Who isn't nowadays? It's good.'

'Emile can be relied on.'

'Did he cook it too?'

'In his cave.'

They munched silently and then shared some more.

'Werner, who does this tower belong to?'

'A friend of father's. Father rents it for a pittance. He brings his women here.'

'Werner!'

'The old dog doesn't know I come here too. I discovered where the key is kept. When I know he's busy elsewhere I come and paint here and hide my materials in a box upstairs. It's my secret studio.'

They ate on.

'You don't *look* Jewish, Anna.'

'No. I've inherited Papa's light hair mixed with a touch of red. Our ancestors were probably that Polish tribe. Their king ordered them to convert to Judaism. But why do you say that?'

He shrugged.

'Are you an anti-Semite?'

He rose, collected the scraps and threw them into a rubbish basket.

She found an answer to her question on the way back – the one she hoped for. They passed by a synagogue and heard the sound of music.

'Can you hear it?' he asked.

'What?'

He cocked an ear above the street racket. 'Fiddles and drums, Anna. It's Shulamit Goldman's wedding. Her father, Nathan, is a friend of my father's. Come on, there's time.'

He strode forward, turning and waving her on.

'Oh Werner, I'm supposed to be home!'

He grabbed her hand as they were swept in a throng towards the doorway. Gaunt, undernourished Jews swarmed round a door, clinging to the rail, packing the steps. Inside, the guests were ranged along a table clapping furiously to the band.

She pulled him aside. 'Werner, it's barbaric! Look at their matted hair and filthy gabardines. Father can't bear this. I'm forbidden. Listen to that gypsy music!'

'They aren't gypsies, Anna, they're Jews! *Your* people. Look that's a cimbalom, like a dulcimer. This is real Jewish music.'

'That's all very well. I bet at your Germany Colony weddings they have smart accordionists with white shirts and leather shorts.'

'They do – and it's so tedious!'

The cimbalom player beat on his strings like a madman. The violins jumped and wailed like cats. Werner and Anna edged their way in.

The music stopped. Shulamit's father, Nathan Goldman, stood up and called for hush.

'My friends, forgive me. Heaven would wish I could have provided more!'

'Can you follow Yiddish, Anna?' whispered Werner.

'More or less.'

'Me too.'

'Many Jews here in Jerusalem,' continued the proud Nathan, 'were nationals of the enemy powers – Russia, Romania and so on. They have been expelled, a new Exodus. Our community is depleted. Those of us remaining, what misery. Some of us, God forbid, are ill. We have plagues, we scavenge. At my daughter's wedding we have had no wine! You, the guests, are still hungry. A wedding where guests must go hungry! My fathers would be ashamed. They were poor but they knew how to provide. Friends, I have done my best, may I burn in Gehenna if I have not. Only if this crazy war would end!'

He signalled to the musicians. 'But we have music. Without our musicians what would our wedding have been?'

Nathan searched for his handkerchief, wiped his lenses, then his face. 'These men of music express the sorrow and the joy of our faith. They affirm life. With them, even without wine, we can offer the time-honoured toast. To Life. *L'chaim!*'

'*L'chaim! L'chaim!*'

'Come on, musicians, lead us into the dance. Lead Dov into the dance with my dear daughter Shulamit. Let them separate and find new partners until we are all dancing. Let everyone be included...'

He broke off, pointing at Werner. 'Yes, everyone, especially our German guest, the handsome, clever fellow over there, young Werner. Werner, is your father here? He was ever a friend to us.'

'Here he is,' someone called and sure enough Anton had appeared and stood tall in the doorway. He waved cheerfully.

'For is it not written, that we shall welcome the stranger within our gates?' Nathan concluded.

'Now, my daughter...'

A slow tango rhythm began. Dov took his bride in his arms and led her across the floor. After a few turns, Nathan and his wife joined them. The floor filled with couples.

Slowly the music became louder. The pulsing rhythms accelerated. The musicians swayed wildly, transmitting the fever to the guests who shouted out and threw themselves into the dance with ever more abandon. Out of this joyous mayhem a young man emerged and whisked Anna on to the floor. She whirled past Werner, eyes wide, as if to say, 'Help! Rescue me.'

Anton came up to Werner. 'You should be careful, son. Hugo and Miriam Fischer will want Anna to save herself for a Jewish boy.'

Werner had to shout above the merriment. 'I'm not thinking about marriage to a Jewess or anybody else. Anyway Father, you won't have to worry about that much longer. I'm going away.'

'Where?'

'To our precious Fatherland...'

Now Anton knew his son was dreaming. 'In wartime?'

'I'll get there.'

Anton saw the resolve in Werner's eyes.

'The world is in turmoil, Werner. It's not the time. Stay here. Finish your studies.'

The music had stopped. Werner could see Anna looking for him.

'Excuse me, Father.'

Anton's opinion was clear but years of paternal impulses thwarted by loss held him back. He shied away from further expressing his feelings in the matter and with a shrug allowed Werner to walk away.

'You're popular here,' Anna said, 'you and your father.'

'Yes, more than at the Colony.'

The music began again and this time it was Werner who swept her away.

~

Just as Werner set off to take Anna home a storm blew up. The wind whipped through the streets, loosening tiles and slamming shutters. Rain lashed the walls and filled the potholes. Water dripped off their chins.

'What a night!'

He draped his coat over her head.

'Oh, thank you Werner!'

After her initial resistance Anna had adored the wedding. She'd loved the dancing. It had a different flavour from the wholesome, socialistic kind of dancing she knew but the steps were much the same after all. Anton had been jovial, and kind to her. He'd asked her all about her schooling and talked about her father as his old friend.

'Eva will be waiting up for me,' she said to Werner.

'What about your mother and father?'

'Father's forever out being a good Zionist somewhere. Mother's always got some complaint or other – backache, dyspepsia. At the moment it's migraine.'

Rounding the corner to the Fischer house with its big door and handsome balcony, they were nearly blown over by the wind.

'Oh dear!'

He seized her hand. 'Anna...'

'Come under the balcony, Werner. You're dripping. Let me give you your coat back.'

'Anna, your hair...'

'What?'

'It's very beautiful. I watched you today as we walked along.'

She blushed and put her hand over her mouth.

'...Thick, shiny gold...'

'Sh, Werner! Be quiet!' She laughed.

'And your jaw, I like that. It comes down to a charming point. I notice such things. I'm an artist, remember?'

Eyes sparkling, she clamped her fingers over his mouth. He lifted them away.

'Will you kiss me, Anna?'

'Here? In the pouring rain?'

He closed towards her. His arms went round her. His lips touched hers. They were surprisingly cold to her and since she hadn't kissed before she didn't know what to do. She felt stuck to him as if by a part that didn't belong to her. At last she moved her tongue forward. It met his. A jolt, a warm wave, the beginning of pleasure.

The bolt behind them was drawn back. They sprang apart just before the door opened.

'Here I am, Eva!' Anna blurted. 'Werner's just walking me home.'

The eyes of the handsome woman standing in the doorway met those of the dripping, bedraggled boy. Neither spoke. Anna looked from one to the other.

'Well, good-bye, Werner. Thank you for the chicken and for introducing me to your Jewish friends – and your father.'

'Good-bye, Anna. Let's meet again.'

Eva shut the door. Werner hurried down the wet street without looking back.

'You met Anton?' asked Eva warily.

'Yes! He was so kind to me!'

Eva remained steady. 'He is part of this family's history even though we never see him. He is basically a good man and he never stops suffering. What do you think of his son by the way?'

Anna took Eva's arm and squeezed it. 'Oh, Eva. Werner is wonderful.'

~

'I've brought you this,' said Eva. 'It's a honey drink with a little cognac in it. It will make you feel better.' Placing the drink on Miriam's table, Eva sat on the bed. 'Are you warm enough? You look pale.'

Miriam smiled weakly, sat up and pulled her shawl round her shoulders.

'Here,' said Eva, 'take a sip.'

Miriam peered distractedly at the play of light on the surface of the pale liquid.

'You must eat,' said Eva.

'I eat enough.'

'Really? None of us do. We're all trying to survive on barley and goat's milk and you even push that aside.'

'I'm a fat Jewish hausfrau. Look at my spreading middle. Ever since I had Anna...'

'You're too thin. Dr Hamar said so.'

'Mm...'

Eva looked towards the window. How quiet they were, these wartime evenings. To manage her impatience, she got up and peeped through the shutters. How dark too. Just one street light on the corner, a few lighted windows. No moon tonight.

'Where's Hugo?' came from the bed.

'He took Herr Hussein with him.'

'What's going on?'

'If Jews and Arabs are spending time together,' Eva surmised, 'it'll be to plot against the Turks, and to aid the English.'

Nowadays Miriam had little time for politics and the war. With her husband at home less than ever she had retreated into books, memories, poetry composition and mild hypochondria. It was left to Eva to worry about the risks of Hugo's activities.

Eva peered at the stars, a spangled curtain over silhouetted buildings and distant hills, wondering where Hugo was.

'He told me that there was no risk in sheltering Hussein,' she said, 'even though he's a notorious Arab nationalist.'

'I can imagine the scene,' said Miriam. 'Hugo supping on sweetmeats in some sumptuous Arab villa. Perhaps the Zionist women will be there. Crop-haired teachers, librarians, plotting away with him. They love Hugo. But Hugo won't be thinking about the food or the women...'

'No, just the politics!'

'For Hugo the cause is all that matters.'

'I suspect,' Eva added as an afterthought, 'when it comes to guns – or plotting with Arabs – the Zionist men keep the women away.'

Miriam shrugged.

'Do you miss Dresden, Eva?'

'No. They're hungry there too.'

They fell into silence. Eva stayed by the window.

'I'm worried about Anna,' Miriam said at last. 'She's stopped studying. She hides in her room.'

'You've noticed that.'

'Eva, I'm not that bad!' Miriam said waspishly. 'Sometimes I think you consider me a neglectful mother. Anyway,' she said changing the subject, 'have you seen Anton again?'

Eva looked at Miriam calmly. 'No, only the once, to tell him about the young man – the possible Johannes – staring at the portrait in Dresden.'

'I wonder what his wife thought when he told her.'

'He said he wouldn't tell her. Who knows? I never go near the Colony, never speak to any of them. The people who spat at me in '98 are still there. The children who threw stones at me have grown up. If I see any of them down in these parts I cross the street. They know I'm here. And now…'

She hadn't meant it to come out at this point.

Miriam looked up. 'What?'

'There's another connection to vex everybody if they hear about it.'

'Yes?'

'His son, Werner.'

'Mm?'

Eva was looking at Miriam with an awful intentness. 'There's no mystery about Anna's current misery, Miriam. She's in love.'

Miriam's jaw fell. 'What!'

'With this boy, Anton's son, Werner.'

'No!'

'I hoped it would cool down and then you wouldn't need to know.'

Miriam's expression darkened.

'Yes,' said Eva, 'he's a gentile. Nice enough, perhaps, but not Jewish.'

'Oh, good lord,' exclaimed Miriam, 'we can't have this happen. Marrying out, it's just not on.'

'Steady on, Miriam. There's no thought of marriage yet.'

'Yes, all right, but… What's this boy like anyway?'

'He's tall and fair. His spectacles make him look rather serious. He reads books, wants to be a painter. I've heard his father doesn't have much time for him, which is sad but perhaps unsurprising. That's about as much as I know.'

With an effort Miriam rose from her bed. This was a crisis. She paced the room. 'Hugo already blames me for sending Anna to a German school. And now a German boyfriend! Anna's children are supposed to have pure Jewish blood. That's what she's here for as far as Hugo is concerned.'

'They'd still be Jewish through Anna.'

'Of course I know that, Eva, but Hugo's credibility with the movement would be compromised. You must speak to the boy's father. Get him to forbid it.'

Eva folded her arms. '*You* can forbid it. Miriam, you can forbid *her* to see *him*.'

'No, I don't want to upset her. I don't want her to know that I even know. Organise it, Eva. I beg you.'

Eva felt this was asking too much of her. To see Anton would do her no good at all. She looked at Miriam defiantly. 'No.'

'Please!'

'No. *You* go and see him, Miriam. It's your affair, not mine.'

'Oh Eva!'

'See how it looks in the morning.'

With a curt goodnight Eva left the room. She tiptoed along the corridor past Anna's room. The door was ajar.

'Are you all right, darling?'

'Yes,' Anna sniffed.

'You can't sleep?'

Eva sat on the bed and stroked Anna's hair. 'Try not to worry. Everything will work out for the best.'

Anna buried her head in the pillow, squeezing Eva's hand. There were many complications in her situation but tonight it was simply that Werner was not with her. He was across a hard terrain among enemies, a fine, bespectacled Romeo to her lonely, suffering Juliet.

~

Anna's love for a German boy fired Miriam up as nothing had for some time. She couldn't bear the idea of giving Hugo something else to worry about on top of his clandestine activities and their constant hunger.

In the morning she headed for the old city and found the shop. She went in. Anton – she supposed it was him – was hovering in a back room.

She looked around the shop. At first glance it was the usual fare of the pilgrim shops: Virgins, angels, crucifixes, the infant Christ. On inspection it was more interesting. A group of animals, including a tiger and a gazelle, in a darker wood, were full of life. And here was a striking 'Jewish' shelf. A craggy Moses, Delilah shearing a muscle-bound Samson, a David with sling in hand.

The carvings reminded Miriam of her days as an art-lover, a familiar of the Dresden and Munich galleries, an excited tourist in Italy and France.

Other objects added to a picture of a varied and purposeful artistic life: prints, etchings, lithographs, poster designs, letterheads, bills covered the walls. Miriam wondered if Eva, whom she secretly scorned a little for her pragmatism, appreciated that her old lover was – to judge from the evidence – an artist.

'Can I help?'

He came forward, towering over her in the confined space.

'I… I think your work is marvellous. Quite out of the ordinary.'

He bowed stiffly. He seemed indifferent, suggesting he knew the value of his work better than anybody.

'Is business bad, with the war and everything?'

'There are no tourists.'

'No.'

'But your military men will sometimes buy. Officers of the Habsburg forces like Virgins...'

'Oh.'

Was this a rude joke?

'... being Catholics.'

'Yes.'

'And there are Jewish soldiers here from Austria and Germany. They'll buy a Moses or two.'

She looked away. It was awkward this mention of Jews since he would certainly have guessed she was Jewish.

'Soldiers generally want a souvenir of the place they were posted to, however godforsaken.'

'But this isn't a souvenir shop, it's an art gallery.'

'Thank you.'

She cleared her throat. 'However, that isn't why I came to see you, Herr Gustavus.'

He stepped back in surprise. 'You know me?'

'I am Miriam Fischer. You know of me through Eva. You knew my husband Hugo a long time ago.'

His face lit up. There was something in his expression warm and wise, mixed with humour, that she found attractive.

'I never forgot Hugo,' he said. 'It always seems strange to me that we live in the same city yet never meet. Something stops it. It was a difficult time. Perhaps it is too painful for us... all of us involved. And then the war... And to think we all met in a railway carriage... Stefan came back a few years ago but...'

'One way and another', she said, 'I know quite a lot of the story. I'm sorry...' She shook her head. 'I... well, anyway. The reason I came...'

'Yes, do tell me! I suspect it's about my son Werner!'

'Correct!'

'Do you want me to horsewhip him!'

She smiled but there was steel in her voice. 'I blame Anna, not Werner. She should have conveyed to him that certain things were not possible.'

'Why didn't you send her to a Jewish school? Wasn't she bound to make such connections?'

'Well, there's a story behind the choice of school.'

'What is it?'

'I wanted a German education for her. It was a condition of my agreeing to come here. It all seems such a long time ago,' she added.

'Indeed.'

'This connection with your son is not... good for her. The situation needs clarifying before her heart engages further.'

'Clarifying?'

'He must tell her that he cannot see her again. I would rather he stopped than we should simply forbid her.'

'Why?'

'So many in this city die from illness and famine. A confrontation with her might carry her off.'

'But the same thing could happen if he tells her. It might even be worse. However, I understand your request. The "confronting" must be done by me.'

She gripped the ivory handle of her parasol. 'I would be so grateful.'

He returned her gaze. It was not clear that he had agreed.

'Would you like some mint tea?'

'Oh dear. My nerves need steadying. Perhaps I would.'

'Please sit down. It won't take long.' He moved to the back and lit a burner. She sat on a divan and waited in silence.

'Can I ask you something?' he said, returning with the tea.

She nodded.

'Are you still a believing Jewess?'

She sipped the tea, pondering.

'We observe the festivals even though Hugo is not religious. Hugo sees them as national folklore and therefore to be fostered as part of his Zionism.'

'That's not what I asked. I'm interested in whether you *believe*.'

'Do *you* believe?' she parried.

'I'll prevaricate by saying that I'm not a Jew. Besides, just at this moment I'm more interested in *you*.'

'If you must know, Herr Gustavus, I do try to speak to God…'

She paused.

'Yes?'

She blushed, suddenly aware of the heat and the confined space. He held her gaze like the practised womaniser he was.

'I'm sorry. I shouldn't be so inquisitive. Let me confess. I like Jewish women, especially the pretty ones. I want to know all about them. Let's change the subject. How do you spend your time here in Jerusalem?'

'Is that being "not so inquisitive?"'

His amused, intent look charmed her further.

'Well…' she said, softening her tone.

'Go on, tell me. Do you have any hobbies?'

She couldn't resist. 'Just one.'

'Yes?'

'I write verse.'

'Frau Fischer! How interesting. Have you been published?'

'Once or twice in poetry magazines.'

'Would you let me see some? Maybe comment on your drafts?'

'Well, I don't know…'

'I have an idea.'

'Yes?'

'If you were to agree to visit me again with a sheaf of poems, well, that just might persuade me to speak to Werner.'

'You're bargaining with me! I thought you'd agreed. You're being inconsistent, Herr Gustavus.'

'No actually, Frau Fischer, presumptuous!'

They laughed together.

'Well, how about it? You bring the poems and I'll talk to my son. Tomorrow. Make it tomorrow. I'm sure you don't want a delay before ensuring the insulation of your daughter from German contamination.'

'That's a horrid way to put it, Herr Gustavus! I protest. You'll see what an admirer of everything German I am.'

'When I read your poems?'

'Of course, Herr Gustavus. Of course. Wife of a Palestine Jew that I am, practically stateless, I am more German than the Germans. Ask my poor husband!'

She smiled, rose from the divan, moved through the shop and with a wave disappeared into the thronged alley.

~

Miriam returned with her sheaf of poems and took tea again. Anton was attentive. She couldn't remember such entertaining talk. Though he teased her in his amusing way, her opinion seemed to carry weight with him. She who had never made anyone take her seriously, felt important.

Convention might frown at such meetings but the Fischers' Zionist milieu had thrown off convention in the matter of the relations between the sexes. War itself had turned custom upside-down. The problem lay in how Miriam began to feel. As she stepped into the shop for the third time – to hear his opinion of her poems – her heart raced, nothing else now seemed important.

'A little like Heine,' he commented genially. 'My favourite poet, by the way.'

Her eyes sparkled. 'I am so pleased you say that. I was trying to bring Heine up to date – and show things from a woman's point of view.'

'Mm... interesting. I thought it was particularly successful in that one, what was it called – "Harlequin's Muse."'

'Ah yes.'

'We hear the muse's view. Very good! As if Effi Briest had put her frustrations into verse.'

Miriam was disconcerted by Anton's reference to the heroine of Theodor Fontane's notorious novel of adultery. It was like savouring a fine view, then noticing your feet are on a precipice.

'Do you like Wedekind?' he asked, puffing at his Turkish cigarette.

Heine, Fontane, Wedekind: the mention of these names in these intimate surroundings, the atmosphere intensified by his soft tones and direct looks, captivated her. She was not naïve. She knew she was being 'worked on', but began to feel that this was a true meeting of minds.

Her fourth visit was fatal. The pretext was to buy chicory in the old city.

As she entered, he raised an eyebrow. His implicit mockery of them both made her heart stop.

'Ah... It's you...'

'Yes, I... just thought... I was passing by...'

'You could have gone by another route.'

'Yes, I could have.'

'Frau Fischer...'

It was perhaps the last moment when refuge, peace of mind, was possible.

'It was a mistake to drop in, Herr Gustavus. Let's talk another time, or perhaps...'

'We should stop talking altogether?'

'Well, I've been thinking, for Anna's sake... I don't suppose Hugo would care. He doesn't have a lot of interest in how I spend my time. You haven't spoken to Werner, by the way.' She knew from Eva that Werner and Anna were still meeting.

He shook his head wryly. 'Let the young have their fun, Frau Fischer! As for us, well, definitely, yes, perhaps we should stop having our discussions.'

She hid her dismay. Did he mean it?

Stepping forward he held her arms firmly in his big hands. He looked deeply into her eyes. 'Let me tell you something, Frau Fischer. I can't sleep. I toss and turn. I hit the bolster. If we are to avoid complications, you mustn't come here anymore. It's as simple as that.'

'I...'

'In other words,' he said softly, 'for me, love is coming into the picture.'

'Don't you mean infatuation?' she said, lowering her eyes.

'Perhaps.'

'I wouldn't find it easy...not to see you.'

'You too then,' he murmured.

Her breath came uncertainly. Her lips quivered. 'Eva must never know.'

'Nor Magda.'

'Nor Anna, nor Hugo, nor Werner, Herr Gustavus!'

He took her trembling hand, led her into the back room and put his arms round her. They kissed tenderly, with relief and joy.

She broke away. 'I must go!'

'But come back!'

'I don't know!'

Heart beating, she fled up the alley past the pedlars and lounging shopkeepers.

'They can see it. They know I'm a fallen woman!'

~

Thirty-seven years old and what a fool!

In coming to Palestine, had she after all been colluding with her secret wishes? Had she been looking for a way out all along? Were her 'daring' poems a prelude? For sure, if she'd stayed in Dresden, encouraged by her doting father and immersed in a Jewish middle-class life of Sabbath and festival observance, and good works, she'd never have contemplated violating the seventh commandment.

It was Palestine that had seduced her!

'Oh, if I'd never known this terrible, beautiful land! Never watched spring sunshine spatter a thousand colours across the hillsides. Never drawn into my pores the heat that, growing fiercer by the day, withers the flowers and parches the grasses to straw. Without this scorching Levantine sun, would my soul ever have been so kindled? Would there have been such a conflagration? Miriam, how could you let this happen?'

She'd read about it in books but nothing could have prepared her for the reality. Longing and guilt wrestling inside her, a pair of irrepressible demons.

On the days she couldn't contrive a meeting with Anton, she spent hours in her bedroom. Staring up at the ceiling she would run through the cinematograph of her previous life. She remembered arriving in Palestine wife and mother. She saw a corseted *Hausfrau* with tightly coiffed hair, tiptoeing primly.

Who was that person? That stranger? How old she'd looked even at thirty-two. How... finished.

Had love recovered Miriam's youth? Was that it?

She would sigh and stretch out, her legs clammy against her cotton robe.

No, it wasn't quite that. Now she was... beyond age. Nature itself had taken possession of her. Mind, reason, God, had absconded.

'I'm not young, or old. I'm one breath of eternity.'

She shook herself. 'How exaggerated, how like a young girl. Anna must talk to herself like this. Absurd, but... how else to put it?'

Oh, this heat. Even indoors. It was one suffocating breath with her besotted state. 'Oh, Anton. You're what I've waited for. How terrible! How stupid I've been. Nothing will be the same anymore.'

His twinkling eye, his tousled grey hair. How serious he was about all the things that mattered. How incurably, beautifully sad.

Their talk was what she loved best. Her longing for this was almost a physical desire. From the first whispered 'How are you, dearest?' to their tender good-byes, they never stopped. Now calm, now turbulent, their conversation was a symphony, a duet, with expositions, developments, recapitulations – and plenty of solo cadenzas, one expatiating under the admiring gaze of the other. History, poetry, art, religion, Palestine and the war... As if neither of them had ever talked in their lives before.

There was another motive here. If they talked in the open air, in cafes, it was easier to promote the fiction that they were just good friends.

Oddly, her condition made her better at housekeeping. Half-dazed, relying on instinct and advice from old hand Anton, avoiding discussion with a jumpy, distracted Hugo and a newly suspicious Eva, she was remarkably successful in tracking down supplies that had previously eluded them.

'How did you get those?' Anna would exclaim, gazing open-mouthed at sweet potatoes, oranges, honey-cakes.

Whatever the tensions, every day was a blessing. Air as pure as an angel's kiss blew down from the hills, caressed her wet forehead and lifted her shiny black curls – among which were woven (she tried not to notice) the first strands of grey – flattening the furrows ploughed by guilt and worry.

And she knew.

Miriam Fischer was fully, ecstatically in love for the first time in her life.

~

One morning in the height of summer they stood hidden from view on the walls above the Zion gate. He put his arm around her.

'Oh dear,' he said wearily, 'to think that not so long ago I was so nearly grown up, so nearly wise.'

'What do you mean, dearest?'

'Once I was all over the place, a dreamer, bookworm, would-be artist. In religion I was an endless questioner, driven hither and thither. Eventually, I calmed myself. My religious faith settled. I learnt to put self aside. I led an ordered, practical life, working to support myself, my wife and son, spending more time on furniture and printing than art. Of course, I was still considered a rebel by my fellow settlers over there...' He pointed to a low ridge on the right crowned by the red roofs of the German Colony. 'But until *you* came I was, as I say, so nearly... a grown man, let's put it like that.'

'You are wise! You are good!'

'No, Miriam. I'm neither wise nor good. You've changed everything. I'm back to where I was, simply following what I want. The only difference is that this time my desires come from the deepest part of me. They spread out, take all of me. What now? Simply, you are the woman, dare I say, the Jewess, I've been waiting for. Rachel to my Jacob. Ruth to my Boaz. The "Beloved" of the writer of the Song of Songs.'

He gazed down. '"My beloved is unto me as a cluster of camphire in the vineyards of En Gedi. Behold, thou art fair, my love; behold thou art fair... Thou hast doves' eyes."'

'Maybe,' she said lightly, in response to his husky declamation in which she had detected irony.

'Dearest, it's a dream, I know. Whatever we're feeling we must face hard truths.'

'Yes... But what truths?'

'I can't promise anything to you. I will never leave Magda. And you're tied too.'

She leant gratefully against him. So nothing had to get out of hand, that was a relief.

'We're mad, dearest Anton. We have no future. But in the meantime I just feel desperate to see you, that's all I want. For that I'm a tigress. And if that's sinful, well, I'll take the consequences. You move my soul. Before you I was a sleepwalker. I don't care what society says.'

'There's no society here to *have* an opinion. Everything's in pieces. Anyway we have to wait and see.'

'Anton, perhaps the war offers us hope. Sometimes I imagine the English marching in here and somehow after that everything will be changed. A new life. Changed utterly.'

He squeezed her hand. 'I've had the same idea.'

They stood silently looking over the Valley of Hinnom. The blue waves of hills to the south – through which the invading army must march – offering a promise of this new dispensation.

'Now,' he said. 'Have you noticed *that*?' He pointed to a tethered mule and cart. 'I've commandeered that poor scrawny beast for the day. He's taking us on a journey.'

'Oh Anton. How delightful!'

'"Rise up my love, my fair one, and come away. For lo winter is past, the rain is over and gone. The fig tree putteth forth her green figs; the time of the singing of birds is come, and the voice of the turtle is heard in our land..."'

He chuckled. 'Beautiful eh? Now there's poetry.'

'I'm your "bird" and "green fig," am I? But Anton, should we?'

'Hush, my love. The sunshade will hide us from prying eyes. See this bag? In here's water, bread and, yes, figs, ripe ones, not too green. *Yalla!* Let's go.'

~

Miriam stood at the end of the tunnel where the stream trickled into the pool. The high, dense walls were part-covered with moss, fern and trailing maidenhair. She felt suffocated by the seclusion, the suspense.

Anton paced round the pool, squinting at the sluggish water.

'Is this where…'

'Yes, the Upper Pool of Siloam.'

She had a bad moment, a miserable suspicion. Did Anton bring all his women here? Was it a morbid and perverse ritual, a test?

'Just as it was nineteen years ago. The world's changed but nothing's changed here. These stones, the last thing he saw...'

'The water isn't very clean.' She meant 'not clean enough for such a precious shrine.' She hoped he took it the right way.

'It's basically healthy. The water passes over a slimy deposit which covers the bottom of the tunnel. People bathe and wash their clothes here. And then they draw water for drinking. Like that woman is just about to do.'

A woman with belt and loose head dress was dipping a pot in the pool. She lifted it nimbly to her shoulder and ambled away.

'Do you think he could be still alive?'

'He'd be twenty-seven. I used not to think so. I thought they must have killed him. But since hearing Eva's story everything seems up in the air.'

'Do you bring all your women here?' she asked out of a long silence.

'No.'

She knew he was lying.

'Let's take the cart round to the other end of the tunnel. That'll be it. Then I've got something else to show you.'

She touched his arm. 'I want to ask you something.'

'Yes?'

'What was my husband like then, in '98, when you knew him?'

'Hugo? Let me think. Distracted, the absent-minded professor type. But a good chap. He was very conscientious when Johannes was taken. He put himself out no end though he hardly knew us. He tried to get the Kaiser and Theodor Herzl to help.'

‘To think we were married a few months later,’ she murmured.

Why had she mentioned Hugo? The thought of him exacerbated her guilt just when she was – not enjoying the moment, it was too sad for that – but experiencing the day’s quality, its fineness. The picture of young Hugo with all his life and hopes before him was so agonising that for a moment she heard another voice.

Yes, now, go on, hurry back home to normal life. Just go. Leave him. He would survive. This whole thing never happened. Life is safe again. Do it. Now…

She could have. But Anton took her hand and led her back to the cart. He cracked the whip and the mule set off. That moment had gone.

The mule hauled them up to the tower in the heat of the midday. Like Anna before her, Miriam was enchanted by the coolness inside, the faded rugs and hangings, the cushion-strewn chaise and divans, the brass telescope on the lintel, above all the view over the city.

‘Anton, it’s wonderful, but how…who…’

The explanation was given. Like their offspring, they relaxed, eating the picnic, sitting on the sill facing the city.

Drawing her over to one of the divans, he took her firmly in his arms.

‘Miriam, we’ve known each other some time.’

She fell trembling against his chest. He stroked her hair, loosened her combs and began fumblingly to unbutton her chemise.

‘I’ll do that,’ she said. ‘You lie down. That’ll be easier.’

Naked from the waist up, they lay side by side stroking each other, kissing gently. There was no frenzy.

‘Maybe,’ she whispered, ‘we can do this only once and then…’

‘We have to wait to see what happens.’

‘Yes, dearest, we’ll have to take things as they come.’

She glimpsed blue sky through the shutter; cocks crowed, cicadas rattled.

The call to prayer broke out from across the valley: a plaintive wail familiar to her from all her years in Jerusalem, yet still with its haunting power. She held her breath.

The sense of a final mystery held for a few seconds – then passion rose up and overcame her.

She plunged, could only devour him with her kisses. Explosive, famished, unrecognisable to herself, Miriam Fischer fell. Now they were in a fever. They cried, they groaned. Her skirt and her loosened drawers were round her ankles. He moved on top of her.

Her eyes were tight shut. Need, need, she only felt need. She was going down, down, down, away from everything she'd ever known, coasting away from home and friends, husband, daughter, family. Even at the last she heard them calling.

Come back Miriam, don't leave us. It's not too late. We want you.

She closed her ears. She wanted to go, she must.

MIRIAM. DON'T. IT ISN'T WORTH IT. BELIEVE US.

Too late. A whirlpool drew the vessel into itself, sucked it down. She heard the voices no more, only a great rushing in the ears, the wrench into the currents of the deep.

~

Darkness was falling. A lamp flickered on the table. The city was a gather of twinkling lights in a dark sea. Half-naked, they lay together, dozing.

He jolted awake.

'What is it, Anton?'

'There's somebody downstairs,' he hissed.

He sat up. A light was coming up the stairs. His eyes bulged with horror. He grabbed his shirt. Miriam hid her face under the cushion. Peeping out she saw a young man with neatly combed hair and glasses. She hid her face again.

'*Guten Abend, Papa.*'

'Werner! What are you doing here?'

'I've come to fetch my materials.'

'What materials?'

'I've been using the tower to paint the view. I didn't think you would mind. They're in a box upstairs. I'll fetch them and soon be away. I'm sorry to have bothered you.'

'Go on then. Get them and leave.'

After Werner had fetched his canvas and paint box, Anton followed him downstairs to the kitchen.

'How do you know about this place?'

'Have you forgotten you brought me here a long time ago?'

'Did I? Well, next time tell me when you're coming here.'

Upstairs Miriam's head was buried in her hands. Utter disaster. Worse than her worst imaginings. She wished she were dead. Hurriedly she put her skirt on.

'Has he gone? What are we going to do?'

He was maddeningly calm. 'Nothing, dearest. He didn't see it was you. It could have been anybody. All he saw was a naked foot.'

Chapter 11

High above, lanterns gleamed from the city walls. Paths leading out from the gates, circling round to the Mount of Olives, the Valley of Hinnom and towards Silwan, were pale ribbons in the moonlight. Werner avoided these ancient tracks, wary of trigger-happy patrols. He stumbled on uneven ground between jagged rocks and twisted olives trees. He sighed with the effort of protecting his canvas. Thorns scratched his ankles.

His painting was buffeted. Bits of paint flaked off. He was sure passages he'd pored over for hours were damaged.

'This is impossible. Why did I do it? All because I wanted to show Anna the finished painting tomorrow. It could have waited.'

As for the embarrassment of catching his father in bed with a woman… It was an old story, not worth dwelling on.

He hobbled on and finally came to an ancient building with a large pointed arch, set in a rock. This was Aceldama, home to Emile.

Emile: supplier of anything he had ever needed, from scorpions all those years ago to painting materials and cooked chicken.

Emile was a mystery. Though he lived in a cave he wore stylish European clothes. He spoke languages from his education in a mission school. Some people said he was a Jew, others an Arab. Or was he the son by a Coptic priest of an aristocratic German nun, as Werner had once heard? Certainly he spoke perfect German.

He was smoking a hookah and reading by the light of his terra cotta oil lamp. Werner told him about Anna.

Emile was surprisingly hostile on the matter. 'Why do you want a Jewess? Listen, they stick to their own kind. She'll dump you in the end and settle down with a Jew.' Emile picked up his book. 'And it's funny you should be telling me about this now. I've just finished this book that'll tell you all you need to know about Jews. The *Protocols*.'

'Protocols?' asked Werner.

'*The Protocols of the Elders of Zion*. Everybody has it here. I got it from an Austrian officer.'

'What does it say?'

'The Jews have a conspiracy to take over the world.'

'Really?'

'The tentacles go out from Russia and spread all over the Earth like an octopus. American money to fight the war is all from Jews. The revolutionaries in Russia are Jews. So, there you have it: Jews run capital and Jews run labour, with Jewish intellectuals egging them both on. And to cap it all, look at Palestine. The English will hand the country over to the Jews if it falls to them. What'll happen here then? There'll be no work for the rest of us, you can be sure, except as cooks and bottle-washers.'

Unemployment had never stopped Emile living well as far as Werner knew.

Emile's eyes bulged. 'It's too much. Somebody must stop it, strangle it.' He was sweating, rubbing his hands together. Werner had never seen him so worked up. It was like a fit of madness. Had all this come from a book? What was Emile frightened of?

Emile touched Werner's arm. 'Look around this cave.'

Red rock flickered in the lamplight. The cave was silent and musty.

'This is where it all began. A Jew betrays the saviour of mankind for silver. With the silver the rabbis buy this, the potter's field, the field of blood, for the burial of foreigners. Everything is in that story. Jewish craftiness, dishonesty, greed, the Jews setting themselves apart.'

'Judas was a long time ago.'

'You read the book! I'll lend it to you. It's no myth.'

Werner was sceptical. He had grown up in a melting pot of a country. Jews were just one of a group of competing nationalities and religions. If they were dishonest and stand-offish that went for everybody else as far as he was concerned. No one group – Armenians, Arabs, Druze, Turks, the others – stood out for their virtue. Europeans were supposedly more civilised but you didn't have to look hard to see lies and greed amongst them.

'I bet she gives you what you want,' said Emile shaking his head sagely. 'They work through the women. They're like a contagious disease. Even strong men become addicted to them. They are... complicated, not like your Arab or European women. She could do you down this Jewess, destroy your manhood.' He leant over and whispered a familiar Arabic obscenity.

'I doubt it, Emile. My problem is that I love her.'

'Huh! There you are! They suck you in, those Jewish whores, like those black widow spiders. Pull you in then eat you alive. It's part of the Chosen People's plan to weaken other races.'

Werner was hard put to connect Anna's vulnerability and innocence with a master plan for world domination. If anything she was too passive, too trusting for her own good. There was no doubting Emile's experience – with women and with most other things – but sometimes he talked the plainest nonsense.

Nevertheless, the conversation kindled Werner's interest in the book. He read it through the night while Emile slept. In the cool of dawn he handed it back.

'Well, it could be true as far as the basic idea is concerned. There might be a Jewish conspiracy. But I'm not sure. It doesn't seem to fit with the people I know, certainly not Anna who is all innocence. Anyway, my father wouldn't agree with you. He admires Jews above everybody.'

Emile yawned and sat up. He seemed scarcely interested now.

'Werner, before you go, that plan of ours.'

Here was Emile with his pipe-dream again. Emile had made Werner all keen at first but time had dragged on and Werner had begun to doubt it.

'There's been a development. My Turkish friend at the Post Office is going back to Istanbul. He says he can get passes for us. I have to do a favour for him in return but that's all right. We go overland on the caravan route. From there we can get to Germany. My relative there will take us in for a while till we get settled.'

'How would we travel?'

'Passes, we get passes. And once we're there, the war hasn't changed the fact that my relative feels guilty about me living in a cave. He's dying to rescue me. Of course I'll have to reassure him that I can make my own way and not just leech off him. But he knows that I can look after myself. I'm no sponger. I never came anywhere near him for money, though I had every right.'

It dawned on Werner. 'He's your father?'

Emile nodded coolly. Werner gestured as if it was nothing to have the mystery of Emile's paternity revealed after all this time.

'There we are,' continued Emile, 'we've got a plan.'

'When?'

'About a month. What do you think?'

'I doubt it, Emile. Not while Anna and I…'

'We'll see about that. You'll see the light, I bet. Maybe in a month… I won't give up on you.'

'I don't know…'

'By the way,' Emile said, as Werner picked up his canvas to leave. 'Aceldama is the potter's field all right. Clay from round here is still used by Jerusalem potters. No myth about the Jews, you see. Facts.'

~

'Hugo, I believe you are up to dangerous things.'

Hugo looked at Miriam innocently.

'You are plotting with Arabs. This is what I hear. You'll get us all thrown into gaol even though we're German.'

'I am a Jew – and so are you.'

'Then why plot with Arabs?'

'Let me tell you how I see it as 1918 approaches.'

'I'm not interested. I just...'

'You never *were* interested.'

'I never pretended to be.'

'Look, the Zionists' situation...'

The Zionists' situation, there it was. It was Hugo's passion. Always had been. It cut her out.

'Everything is poised,' Hugo continued. 'On the one hand, things are bad for the Allies. They are suffering big shipping losses from the German U-boats. There are air raids on London. The Russians will give in after their revolution. On the other hand, the Americans have joined in and could change everything. Germany is close to exhaustion. This theatre here in the Near East is crucial. It could tip the balance. Here there *must* be an Allied victory. We Zionists will join with anyone who is working to that end. The English are on the doorstep. We are working to persuade them. Most Arabs want to be rid of the Turks. They have suffered from hunger, typhus and malaria just as badly as the remaining Jews here, with the added burden for them of conscription. That is the background situation.'

Miriam waved her hand impatiently. 'I'm not interested in the background, Hugo, I want to know what have you have been doing?'

'I can't tell you.'

'Oh, Hugo...'

He lowered his voice. 'Very well. Look, a few acts of sabotage are planned. They won't be traced to us. The English will be here before the Turks even think about trying to find out who carried them out. Don't worry, my dear!'

~

The shutter was closed, muffling footsteps and shouts from the alley. Candlelight played patterns of light and shade on their scattered clothes. Tools and carvings lay strewn on the table.

Normally they made love in the tower but sometimes Miriam – who now lived for her time with Anton – would come to the shop in the old city. Of course, she had to make sure Eva was busy in another part of town. Today she had only sought relief by seeing him, but one thing had led to another.

Once she would have thought of this opportunistic love as sordid but now she didn't care. She was alive, that was what she told herself. She had no scruples. She couldn't think of others. To lie on the floor in her lover's arms was not sordid. It was… beautiful.

'Oh Anton…'

He too was in thrall though he'd lain on this same floor with his trousers off more times than he could think.

'My dear fine Jewish mistress, my Bathsheba, my Salome… Bind me with your dark tresses… Speak to me of the pain, the passions and deep questionings of your race… '

She laughed fondly. 'You and us Jews!' She sighed. 'I want this… for ever.'

They kissed slowly, murmuring more endearments. Suddenly she felt him tense. He sat up and reached for his trousers.

'What?'

'Get dressed!'

Someone was banging on the shutter.

'In heaven's name who's that!'

'Miriam!' came from outside. 'Miriam!'

'It's Eva!' he whispered. 'Go out the back. I'll stall her.'

She grabbed her clothes and pushed past the curtain at the back of the shop. Anton waited a moment and opened the shutter.

Eva eyed him with icy calm. 'Is she there?'

'Eva…'

'Don't try to explain. The important thing just now is, is she there?'

'She… I…'

'Anton, there's no time.'

'What is it?'

'It's Hugo. He's been taken.'

'Taken?'

'Arrested by Turkish soldiers.'

Miriam opened the curtain and rushed forward. 'What!'

'Ah, so you *are* here. Anna was right. I hardly dared to believe her. Only desperation led me here. You weren't anywhere else. It was the only place left.'

'Eva…'

'You are a deceiver, Miriam. I shall not forgive you though I know how this man operates.'

Miriam stretched out her arm. 'Eva…I have my reasons…'

'I've come to tell you that Hugo's been arrested, not to hear your pitiful excuses.'

A rush of indignation eclipsed Miriam's interest in Hugo's fate. 'Is this how you repay our hospitality?'

'Your hospitality? I've slaved for you ever since the day I entered your home. I've held you all together, Miriam. I've brought up your daughter. Without me you'd never have come here. Without me you'd never have survived – till the moment you set your cap at this… this Don Juan.'

Miriam laid a protective hand on Anton's arm. 'He's an *artist*. You no more appreciate him than his wife does.'

'He's a rutting goat.'

'Eva, you betray your farmyard origins.'

'Farmyard? I'm a Berliner.'

'Be that as it may,' Miriam continued calmly, 'what is this about Hugo?'

Anna burst into the shop, panting, her cheeks wet with tears.

'Mama! Eva! Come quickly! They're at the Jaffa Gate!'

Now there was nothing for it. Everyone knew what happened at the Jaffa Gate.

'Go, go, I'll follow you!' shouted Anton but the three were already out of sight as he slammed the shutter and scrambled after them. He caught up as they emerged from the crowded alleys out on to the open ground.

'Stop! Stop!' they all shouted, pushing their way through the gathering crowd.

'Let us through. Stop! We have to see the officer.'

Pulleys were attached to each of the frames with a rope threaded through. Under each frame a prisoner stood on a stool, with a rope round his neck.

They were barred. Soldiers stared impassively.

'You have to let us through!' they shouted. 'In God's name!'

Hugo did not see them. He looked like a man in a dream, strangely unprotesting. Was he content for his life to end like this?

A shout rang out. The stools were kicked away. The crowd sighed. The bodies of Hugo and the others hung in a line from the ropes, about a dozen in all. The hangman walked the line to check that all were dead.

Anna held her head in her hands sobbing. Eva pulled her into her arms.

Miriam fell to the ground. Anton leant down to lift her but she was beyond comfort, no longer an Effie Briest, a Madame Karenin – a 'modern' adulteress – but a keening Hebrew widow banging her head against the rock of Zion.

~

A few days later, Werner's belongings, a few books and artist's materials together with clothes, were loaded onto a handcart along with Emile's.

They were to meet the other travellers at the Damascus Gate but first Werner, who had been staying with Emile at Aceldama, had to return to the Colony to say good-bye to his parents.

Magda was curt with him. She supposed he knew what he was doing. Doubtless he'd turn up again if it didn't work out. Even at a parting as momentous as this she was unable to find words of love.

'I won't ask you to say you'll miss me, Mother.'

'Get along with you! You've always gone your own way, you and your father.'

'Well, I'll be off your hands now. Where is Father by the way?'

'How would I know?'

'Well, say good-bye to him for me.'

Magda shrugged. Sorrow and bitterness were written deep in the lines of her face. 'They'll make you join the army when you get to Germany.'

'That's not the idea, but I won't shirk it if I have to.'

'You won't have any choice.'

'The war will be over by then.'

'Maybe,' said Magda. 'We'll win yet. It's all the talk among the Colonists. Our German Asien Corps is on the way. The Yelderim troop are already here – Turks with German officers under Falkenhayn's command. We Germans will carry the day.'

'Palestine is a sideshow, Mother. The trenches in France and Belgium are where it will be won or lost.'

'Just like your father. You want Germany to lose.'

'I want it to end. I want to get on with my career. I need a studio, a good teacher. I want peace. Peace favours the pursuit of art.'

'And where will your money come from?'

'I am very determined, Mother. I will find a way.'

Magda put her hand on his arm. 'I hope so, son.'

She sniffed and wiped a tear away. Without embracing her, he turned and was gone. No one looked as he passed the shuttered windows and neat gardens.

In the Valley of Rephaim between the Colony and the old city

Anna ran towards him calling out. Her hair was dishevelled and her face showed anguish.

'Werner! I had to see you. Where have you been?'

They hugged briefly.

'My mother is in a bad way. She's taken to her bed. Eva tries to comfort me but it's you I need to see.'

'I was on my way to see you.'

He stared down at the stony road and then away at the city walls, massive in the morning light.

'Anna… I'm going away.'

Her jaw fell. 'What! Now of all times! With my father just murdered! How could you? Where? Why didn't you tell me?'

'I've been staying with Emile… and then what with your father... I didn't want to bother you in the middle of your loss…'

'Bother me! I needed you.'

'Anna, I'm leaving Palestine.'

'You're leaving the country! Worse and worse. I'll never see you again. Shouldn't you have told me?'

'I did mention it in the early days … don't you remember?.. and then… what with everything. I didn't want to leave and then just recently, I did, it seemed right. It's my only chance. I have to get out of here. I'll die if I stay.'

'But what about me!'

'Anna…'

Her tears welled. Angrily she brushed them from her cheek. 'You're a coward, Werner. You didn't dare tell me. And now you're leaving me. Where are you going?'

'To Germany.'

His eyes fixed on the dusty hem of her skirt. He had run out of explanations.

'I'll never see you again! You promised that we would be together for ever. How could you do this to me, especially?'

'I *will* see you again. I promise. I will write to you when the war's over.'

Behind a tree, he held her and they kissed. She felt like a dying bird in his arms.

~

In the cold and drizzle of 8th December 1917, the British 53rd Division, on its way into Jerusalem, passed near the German Colony. An orderly, sent off to find a billet for his commander, came across a burly man at the entrance.

'Good *hevening*,' said the desert-worn cockney tommy.

'Good evening, sir,' replied Anton smiling. He was pleased at the chance to practise his English.

'Have you a place for my *hofficer*?'

'Certainly.' Anton pointed towards his house. 'He can stay with us.'

The orderly looked Anton up and down. 'What nationality are you?'

'German…'

The orderly glared.

'…but as an individual I like the English and your officer is welcome.'

'No!'

Anton was taken aback. 'I…'

'No, not in a German house.'

'But we are not soldiers. We do not fight.'

'Yes, you do, every German man, woman, child, dog, cat and chicken are soldiers, and you all fight.'

The soldier turned on his heel and tramped back down to the Bethlehem road. Anton went inside to tell Magda about the curious exchange.

'Like it or not,' she said, 'we'll have to do what they tell us now. And isn't that what you wanted?'

'Well, I'm not impressed by their manners.'

~

The prison train stopped at dusty Gaza where they choked into their handkerchiefs and argued about whether the carriage window should be open. After a long wait the whistle blew and the train trundled out into the Sinai desert.

For Miriam the journey was torture. The prisoners, Jerusalem Germans, most members of the Templer community, were all crammed tight. The Colonists eyed Miriam and Anna with suspicion. They were Jewesses, the widow and daughter of a Zionist traitor who supported England. Why were they here? Weren't they on the English side?

Miriam noted that Eva fared no better with the Colonists. Clearly they had never forgotten her affair with Anton or ceased regarding her as a whore. Magda in particular glared at Eva – though her husband was now indifferent to his former mistress since he was in love with Miriam. Meanwhile Eva herself was of course still angry with Miriam on account of her liaison with Anton.

Here they all were herded cheek by jowl in a railway carriage heading for a desert prison camp. It would be a farce if it wasn't a tragedy. And what about Werner? Would anyone ever see that strange young man again? He must also take some blame for Anna's misery. At times his absence seemed to upset Anna more than the loss of her father.

The stupidest thing was that Miriam and Anna didn't have to be here. If Miriam had pleaded her husband's work for the Allied cause she might have avoided captivity. Instead, she had kept quiet because, vulnerable as she was, she had wanted to go where Anton was going. How can she have been so short-sighted?

Miriam avoided looking at anyone and gazed out at the level sands. Patches of scrub were strewn across the desert like skeletons from an ancient battlefield. She closed her eyes.

What had their life come to? However often her thoughts returned to her situation, she couldn't get used to it. What a catastrophe. Hugo, husband and father, dead. Whatever her remaining feelings for Anton, the end of their idyll. Nothing was as important as that she was now a widow and mother who had lost her husband in the most brutal of circumstances.

After a long time the flat roofs and palms came into view. Miriam glimpsed blue through the line of trees.

'Is that the sea?' she asked disbelievingly.

'Yes,' said someone. 'El Arish.'

'Oh, how I'd love to fling myself right into it.'

As night fell, they were herded into trucks. Children cried. But as the bumps set into a rhythm and the stars shone, they slept in their parents' arms. At last the lights of the perimeter fence danced towards them. Soldiers, desert-hardened Australians and New Zealanders, helped them down.

'Anyone speak English?'

Anton raised a weary hand.

'Okay, explain to the others.'

'I will try.'

'The British Occupied Enemy Territory Administration,' declared the soldier, 'have decided in their infinite wisdom to pack you Palestine Germans up and send you to us, plum in the middle of the desert. They reckon you might have started stirring up the natives over there in Palestine.'

He looked at them shrewdly as Anton translated.

'Well, my first impression is you don't look up to too much stirring up. That's good. The men here are Aussies and Kiwis. They're a dinkum lot of bastards. Not stuck up like the British. All I want to say is fair play and we'll do the same.'

The prisoners were too worn down to ask any questions. Anton gave Miriam a meaningful stare. Miriam, her arm round Anna, avoided his gaze.

The soldiers led the Germans off to their tented compound.

Life at the camp began. The regime was by no means irksome. The guards were easygoing and had little prejudice against Germans. Food was adequate. Civilians could always look across at the adjoining compound for prisoners-of-war, mainly Turks and a few Germans, and see that they were better off.

As the days turned into weeks, the main problem was boredom. They were allowed activities: school for the children, organised by the ever-competent Eva; literature and bible reading; football and singing. Not that much could compensate for the cramped tents, the shame of captivity, rumours of imminent German defeat.

Miriam managed to talk to Anton occasionally but the practical difficulty in maintaining their liaison was insurmountable. The affair was over and in time Miriam realised it was a relief to her.

She saw Anton at a distance, grey-haired, saturnine, face as blotchy in the sun as when she would illicitly stroke it some months before. He pottered, mended, expounded to anyone who would listen. What an upheaval her love had been. But it had been eclipsed by something far larger. She loved Anton for who he was and what he had given her but her future could never lie with him now.

As for Eva, she still spent time with the unhappy Anna but was so estranged from the Gustavuses and Miriam that when she witnessed something beyond the perimeter fence that reminded her of the event of 1898, she kept it to herself.

A fair European man, a prisoner-of-war, presumably German, was in conversation with some Bedouin tribesmen in fluent Arabic. It struck her that he was around the age Johannes would have been. She was determined to find a way to speak to him but that very night she heard that 'the Arab', as he was inevitably nicknamed, had taken off with the Bedouin, making good his escape under the noses of the easy-going Australians.

Eva became the custodian of a haunting image: that of a fair young man, a hero as it seemed to her. He could take off, free himself from what bound everyone else; a German in Arab dress, accepted by Arabs, carried by camel across the desert.

Eva kept the notion to herself that Johannes Gustavus was with the Bedouin. In this bizarre captivity and her alienation, it was a curious comfort to her, if it was to be believed. One day, when she had forgiven Anton, she might tell him.

Chapter 12

Later they staggered giggling from Paulo's. She clung to his arm. In a deserted alley they came to a house with peeling paint and rubbish piled at the entrance.

'Do you want to come up?' She lent against him and whispered. 'Snow? Cocaine! Do you like cocaine?'

He hiccupped.

'Come on. You can try some. A friend bought it for me.'

They clambered up the narrow stairs.

'Just a little. We don't want you passing out.'

Neck bent, hands across his stomach, he fell asleep straight away on the chaise in the middle of the dingy room. When he woke up she was sitting by him, her rump pressed against his thigh. The moles and pimples on her bare back struck him as intensely beautiful. He ran his fingers over them.

'*Aspetta, caro mio*. I'm just fixing this. But that's nice, that stroking. Don't stop.'

He glimpsed her life in rooms through the doorway: cramped bathroom, under-used kitchen.

'Do you live alone?'

'Yes. We're alone. We can relax.'

They took the cocaine.

Slowly his brain unfurled like a rosebud under summer sun. Lolling back, he ran his hand over her back again. He was an explorer on this female planet. She was rich with seams of gold. She gave him an amused look, as if to say: 'You'll do for what I have in mind.'

Curling the hairs on her temple round his fingers, he began a speech on 'the irrationality of modern times'. It lasted five minutes and was filled with euphoria and conviction.

'No, dear Rosina, there's no mystique... One must be rational... We are human beings... Fancy you being on the vaporetto just then... Do you have any whisky by the way?'

'*Certo.* I'm well supplied.'

He poured himself a tumbler from the bottle she brought him and quaffed it down. Rosina drank some too. At last they were properly fuelled.

She pulled at his collar and studs. 'You...'

'Yes?' he murmured, lifting her skirt. 'You liked me on the vaporetto, eh?'

'And you liked me, too, eh? You naughty man!'

'Ah Rosina. If only you knew...'

'Come on.'

They stumbled through into the bedroom. She kicked off her shoes. Stockings, suspenders, pants flew through the air. Naked under the coverlet, he kissed her neck, stroking her hair, caressing her buttocks, her thighs.

At the same time he was involved in ferocious mental effort. He must banish from his mind an image which, as she reached to turn out the light, flashed on to his retina. A scar, an inflamed bulbous ridge, stretching diagonally from under her breasts to her hip.

Afterwards, it seemed to Stefan that the scar stood between them like a devil with hideous powers. He tried to talk of this and that but the conversation would go nowhere. Eventually he said, 'I'm tired. I'd better go now.'

'If you want to.'

'Probably for the best.'

'There's more scotch in that bottle. We can have a little drink. Later I'll make you breakfast. Do you like eggs? I make a good breakfast.'

'I never have breakfast.'

'You should have breakfast, you know. It sets you up for the day.'

He fumbled with his buttons and studs. Dressing seemed to take for ever. Checking in the mirror he saw an old man with a grubby shirt, patchy red face and grey hair falling in a mess to his shoulders.

'Christ...'

'Here,' she said, 'take the bottle. A present. Come and see me again. You know where I am. Or you can look me up at the hat shop. I told you where it is.'

'Behind the Miracoli…yes… yes… *Ciao.*'

He bent and kissed her hand.

'You're very formal,' she said. 'Just like a German!'

He staggered down the stairs out into the night. Perching on a wall over the water, he drank deeply from Rosina's bottle. He saw the canal-side lanterns as beads, the stars as diamonds laid across dark velvet. In the palace across from where he sat – years ago he'd known the place well – nymphs and turbaned men with flashing eyes decked the walls and ceilings.

'See! Through the window! The gods are illumined by the moon. The pastel pinks and blues, green and pale orange, are silvered. All colours, all deities dwell in the moon's bright favour. Magical moon! You frescoes… the pinnacle of grace and art… a gold tooth in the mouth of a cadaver, Venice…'

The empty bottle crashed against the wall. His head fell. 'God, I drink too much and that's God's truth. I'll die and… Rosina… poor Rosina with that scar… dreadful… I'll visit the hat shop… one must be kind… Could I love her?'

Later he headed for a doorway and slept.

He woke to sunlight and the smell of newly baked bread. He felt as bad as he did every morning, but no worse. At the nearest café he avoided looking at himself in the mirror. Settled with coffee and brandy he pulled the letter out. He had promised himself he would look at it again before sending it. His fingers were trembling too much to hold it. He laid it flat on the table and read with fierce concentration.

Venice, May 1920.
My dear Anton
A man I met here recently, a German tourist, could be a lead. I started to converse with him, mentioned my travels, and when I spoke of the disappearance of Johannes, a penny seemed to drop. This tourist had briefly known a young man early in the war who had a near-eastern background. He remembered this fellow because they'd met at the recruiting office and had a beer afterwards. He had told him some unusual things. He'd been born in the near east. He knew the pyramids, the Nile. He had come to Germany before the war. Unfortunately the tourist didn't remember his name.

Despite this gap of years, I am writing to tell you what I intend to do. I will visit Berlin and several provincial capitals. Systematically I will approach the headquarters of local regiments and provincial government offices. I will examine lists: recruits, conscripts, dead and wounded, electoral rolls, householders. I will put advertisements in the 'missing persons' columns.

It was wrong of me to wheedle the painting out of you with money. I will restore it to you when I can.

I float along in Venice, this city of water. I'm not making the best of my opportunities at the moment but perhaps things will improve when I have returned from my search in Germany. I live in hope of success there.

To you, my dear friend, and to Magda, I send all the affection of a lifetime.

Stefan

The walk to the post office took him past the synagogue. Standing apart, he waited for everybody to go in for the Sabbath service and then on a whim slipped in. He took a prayer book and sat at the back. He settled his gaze on the sea of black suits, prayer shawls and beards in front. He opened the prayer book and ran his finger over the text just as when he was a child. The cantor's voice rose and filled the space. A wail, hovering, swooping, rising again. Pharaoh's curse, the tears by Babylon's water, Jerusalem sacked, vodka-soaked Cossacks eyeing the *shtetl* from the forest. Rape, fire, murder.

At the end of the service he stepped out into the sunlight hoping to escape the chattering throng unnoticed.

'*Bon giorno, signor Lehmann.* Sabbath greetings.'

'Greetings to you Signor Amato.'

'We are pleased to see you, but when will you start to attend regularly?'

'When I start to believe in your religion. In my opinion, the Jews have no real religion, no *Kultur*, only a primitive herd instinct. The Talmud is no guide to immortality, just a set of rules for the present world, and to keep Jewish blood pure.'

There was an awkward silence.

'Some of my friends would say you are a Jewish anti-semite, Stefan Lehmann.'

Signora Amato, frowning at her husband's side, exploded. 'You're a disgrace. We don't *want* you at the synagogue. And now my husband encourages you!'

'That's not a charitable attitude, my dearest,' remonstrated Signor Amato.

'Signor Lehmann is a drunk, an atheist and scoffer, and now insults us by turning up at *shul*.'

'So, we should welcome him. Where is it written…'

'Look at him! He ambles about the city, with an array of lady-friends, an ageing gigolo. Jews are not drunks. Anything like that gives Jews a bad name. If he turns up here he attracts insults to our community.'

Removing his hat, Stefan bowed with a flourish. 'I'm just off for a drink, my dears, but I leave you with a parting thought. I am the Wandering Jew of Venice. Heir to Shylock. An outcast. I am used to insults. But if I start to get them from Jews…' He walked away muttering. 'Think about it, my friends... Think about it... Now, where's that letter?'

JOHANNES 4

I stood dumbstruck in front of the gallery window. How had I forgotten about the portrait? Now suddenly the memory was quite clear.

Hours wriggling on a hard chair while a man with long hair and darting eyes brushed and dabbed and scraped.

Here in front of me. Myself, aged eight.

'And how are you, my Boyhood Self?'

'Not so bad. And you, my Grown-up Extension? You look in a bit of a state.'

'I'm broke and desperate about a woman but look, that's nothing compared to the coincidence of running into you of all people. And you're still as pretty as... a picture.'

'I have kept my looks, I'll admit. But I've paid for it, believe me.'

'How? You look... perfect.'

'Don't you start! Everybody coos over for my "perfections". I am a "miraculous distillation", "a sublime enigma", an "angel", the "Soul of Loss". I'd rather have been *you* even if you are a mess. I'd prefer to have got straight off this chair and carried on, wherever it took me. At least you've had a life.'

'But right now I'm in a fix.'

'So it seems. By the way, don't you think it's about time you got in touch with Mother and Father? They got rid of me because I reminded them of you. It's you they want. They're still grieving about it.'

'I will, I will... when I've sorted this thing out.'

'The woman?'

'Yes, the woman.'

'Surely duty to your parents comes first.'

'It's not that simple.'

'I've had plenty of time to work out what's important.'

'Me, I have to follow my heart. Duty isn't everything.'

This imaginary discussion was soon followed by a real one, with the owner of the gallery. She resented my curiosity and was unimpressed with my scruffy appearance. Nor did she want to believe me. She admitted she knew the picture had been painted in Jerusalem. The artist, apparently a drunkard and penny-pincher, was holed up in Venice. He had never told her who the boy was or if he had, she'd forgotten.

'It was me, Madam.'

'If you say so. However,' she added haughtily, 'the identity of the subject is of mere documentary importance. It has no bearing on art. The painting will sell because of what the artist has *done* with the subject, not through any qualities inherent in the subject himself.'

She was talking as if 'the subject' was a stranger, not the person standing in front of her. I was wasting my time and decided to leave. Outside, I glanced briefly at the portrait and went on my way.

I decided to be patient and to get myself established before seeking Zoraya out at her father's. I found labouring work and settled into a working men's hostel.

The day eventually came when, heart pounding at the prospect of at last seeing Zoraya, I knocked on the professor's door. My hopes were immediately dashed. Zoraya, I was told, was not living there. No, it was not possible to say where she was, but she was not with her father. He was away on a field trip and would be back later in the year.

More months of uncertainty and misery passed while I waited for the professor's return. I remember little of that time other than hard work, the hostel, and occasional pilgrimages to the portrait in the gallery window. I took care not to be noticed by the owner and found an odd comfort in this image of myself as I once had been. One day the picture was gone. I felt strangely bereft.

Eventually Zoraya's father returned to Dresden. He welcomed me being a decent man so far as I could tell. I was connected to his friend Massoud, above all to Zoraya herself.

Leading me into his book-lined study, he told me straight away what had happened to Zoraya.

'I should have known better,' he said ruefully. 'It was the radical change in her environment. At first she was merely excited but then it turned into a kind of crazy *over*-excitement. She lost interest in her studies. There were parties, unsuitable entanglements. Finally, breakdown, when she was found wandering in the streets in her night dress. They wonder if there are genetic factors, and it is true that some of my forebears were… mad, not to put too fine a point on it. They say that if she had stayed in Africa she might have been fine. What could I do? It wasn't right for her to go back there. She is an invalid now.'

'Where is she?'

'At a renowned institution in Switzerland. Certainly not cheap. It's her best hope.'

The next day I wrote Zoraya a letter telling her I was in Germany and that as soon as I was better established I would visit her. I would find work nearby and be by her side daily until her recovery.

The letter I received back from her, written in Arabic, tore my heart. I still have it.

My Darling
Come quickly but you will find me not as I would like you to see me. I am thin and distempered. I do not know what I can have done to deserve this horrible fate.

Once I was happy despite my early troubles. You came to me, pale Teutonic prince, with your own sorrows. I never lost faith in us – until now, but that is because I have lost faith in life itself. How bitter I am. How angry with my father for persuading me to this gloomy continent, with myself for agreeing. How I long for Africa.

You were right. At Aswan we had everything. We should have thanked our luck and stayed. We could have married and begun a family. I thought life was pushing me on, demanding something of me that I could rise to even though I must sacrifice you in the short term. I was wrong. Life was cheating me and leading me untimely to the exit.

I am talking to a doctor about my dreams.

I want to see you. I am ever yours

Zoraya

I was more desperate than ever to see her. I wrote to say I would indeed be coming soon. However, it was taking longer than I had expected to save the money I needed to have a spare suit of clothes, to travel in reasonable style and present myself to Zoraya as a solid citizen.

A few months later the war began. The momentous event all but passed me by. It was summer. I started out for Switzerland by rail. When the train passed through towns and villages I glimpsed flags in the streets, marching recruits, waving crowds. Hearing that the border was closed due to the war, I crossed on foot by night and picked up a local train to my destination in the mountains.

I found an inn in the village below the hospital and asked where I might find work.

'Here, as matter of fact,' said the cheery innkeeper. 'You look like you need a bath, but I like the cut of your jib. Are you handy?'

I said I was and blessed my luck. And that was how I met Liesl.

Liesl, the innkeeper's niece, was surely the prettiest girl in Switzerland. She had long brown hair, smooth cheeks, a cupid-bow lip and lithe limbs which swung gracefully as she walked between the tables carrying mugs of beer. Most beguiling, so that I had to look away when speaking to her, were her large hazel eyes circled with long curling lashes. Those ever-fluttering lashes delivered a message as if by semaphore.

The effect of those deep pools on my peace of mind when she called me to help, or stopped to chat when I was unloading casks or mending a chair! I wasn't in love with Liesl but as soon as she fixed those eyes on me, I trembled. I wanted to dive through the lashes, into those pools.

'What is this?' I asked myself. I wasn't used to thinking about girls other than Zoraya. I no longer seemed to know myself. What was more, Liesl's spell was delaying my first visit to Zoraya. I had not even sent her a note to say I had arrived.

My excuse was that I wanted to present myself not as a rootless drifter but as well-established locally: strong, mentally and physically. It might take a short while but in this way I would really surprise, delight, and – dare I believe it? – cure her.

One night there was a tap at the door. It was Liesl.

With alarming boldness she stepped into the room, shut the door, leant against it and fixed those eyes on me. I sat up sharply. She was breathing heavily. Her lips were half-open. A slight flush was visible above her bodice.

'Johannes. Uncle is asleep.'

She came forward. Without a moment's thought, I reached for her hand and held it to my cheek. Zoraya did not exist. Liesl's large eyes came ever closer, beckoning me, willing me on. Now I could dive. She wanted me to. Our lips touched. I moved as if drugged. There was no going back.

My first encounter with Zoraya had been as a boy taking his first faltering steps into manhood. With Liesl I was there already, a passionate man. Whether from previous experience or innate confidence, Liesl responded with what I can only call dedication. Our love-making that night was uninhibited.

Once I had possessed her I could not get her out of my mind.

Whenever we could we seized our opportunities: on my bed, on straw in a barn, up against a wooden pillar, on a table, under a bush. We were in a capsule released from Earth, so full of each other that the world and words meant nothing. Would you *speak* if you awoke in Eden or Samarkand, in the Hanging Gardens of Babylon or in a space rocket? Gaze around dumbstruck, more like, and pray for the dream not to fade.

Her uncle surely knew – and didn't mind. He was getting on. It would suit his plan well if Liesl got pregnant, we married and together took over the running of the inn.

One night I woke up screaming. Liesl came rushing in.

'What is it?'

'Nothing… a dream.'

Zoraya had come to me barefoot, shivering with cold. All around, hideous black birds flew from their nests in caves set in looming cliffs. The predators circulated. From a great height one of the birds, with a wicked beak and fierce eyes, flew down. It paused to regard me with contempt and, wings flapping, swooped and drove its beak into my left eye.

Liesl put down her lamp and took my hand. I was in shock, holding my hand to my eye, trembling.

'I have to visit the hospital. I have a sick friend there. That's why I came here.'

A shadow passed over her. She withdrew her hand and looked away briefly. She had guessed she had a rival.

The newspaper that morning was full of the early battles of war. I looked at the headlines with indifference. There in the mountains, the first snows were arriving.

I set off for the hospital staggering up the track buffeted by an icy wind. Thick flakes splattered my frozen face. By the time I came near the mansion the curving road was covered over and I walked to the entrance in a straight line across the fresh carpet of snow.

My request to visit Zoraya was greeted with a resistance that alarmed me.

'I am not sure that today would be a good idea. Let me speak to someone.' The receptionist disappeared behind a curtain and came out shaking her head.

'Look, I've come a long way.'

'You should have telephoned. Are you a relative?'

'No but…'

Eventually a man behind the curtain, who must have been listening, appeared and signalled a change of heart with an ominous summary.

'She has turned right in on herself. Entertain her, make her laugh. Sometimes, you know, it works.'

My heart beat hard as I walked down the corridor towards Zoraya's room. Guilt had robbed me of faith and strength. I was a cheat. I was bringing her nothing. I would be no help at all.

I opened the door.

She was sitting at the window gazing out at the falling snow. She turned. I was shocked at her changed appearance. Her face was thinner and drawn. There were shadows under her eyes. She didn't smile.

'Ali…'

'Zoraya. I took too long… I…'

My feelings for Liesl fell away. I experienced the force of my love for Zoraya, our history, the misery of separation. I went forward and tenderly reached down to kiss her.

Weakly she pointed to a chair which I pulled up beside her. The snow pelted the window pane. I took her hand. How soft it was, yet thinner than I remembered. Fragile and pulsing like a dying bird.

'It's true, Ali dearest, I've been waiting for you for a long time. Maybe you weren't in such a rush to get here after all. Did something detain you?'

'I came as soon as I could,' I lied.

'Ah well,' she sighed ruefully, 'at least you're here before the funeral bell.'

'Zoraya, don't say that!'

Withdrawing her hand she turned her gaze away from the whirling snowflakes and looked at me with narrowed eyes. 'Ali, everything must die, you, me, everything and everyone. If I don't die now, I'll be dying sometime soon enough. Let's say I die at seventy. That's seems a long way off but in the eye of eternity it's nothing, a second. Might as well go now and not prolong it. That's how I reason it.'

'Reason!'

'Yes, reason. For a long time – do you remember our discussions in Massoud's balloon? – reason, not religion, has been my salvation. With reason I can conquer my fear of death.'

I reached for her hand again, too fiercely perhaps.

'But Zoraya,' I urged, 'it is love, not reason that is stronger than death.'

She grimaced, then said something I was unprepared for.

'Oh Ali. What is love? Not some idol, carved in stone for eternity. You can love other women – perhaps you already have done. Look at me, starving wretch that I am – I've grown up too. I'll let you into a secret. I'm attracted to my doctor. He's clever and sympathetic and rather handsome. He has interesting ideas about my dreams. I always used to think that dreams were nothing but nonsense but he thinks that if only we can decipher them they are the key. It's not a serious attraction – don't be jealous! It's just…' I didn't know what she was trying to tell me.

'Really?' I murmured miserably.

Why did her words hurt me so much? Why should I object to what she was saying? Didn't I of all people know she was right about love?

Not entirely, I thought. Our love was something different. If I had allowed myself to fall into the arms of Liesl, this was loneliness and lust. It didn't detract from Zoraya's and my love. I had no use for this 'rational' downplaying. It was just Zoraya's way of coping.

'We were in fairyland before, Ali.'

'No! Nothing, not even my own stupidity, will stop me loving you.' The words rang hollow.

Again she took her hand away and stared silently at the snow outside. She had changed since she had written to me. This detachment, this slightly cynical humour. Perhaps I had made her wait too long.

The remainder of the visit was taken up with my trying to get her back by 'entertaining' her with stories of my adventures, my shipwreck, Akira and so on. When she looked at me she seemed to be saying 'Try as you might, you can't reach me. That's how much use I am to you and how little your "love" can help.'

My spirits sank further. A doctor appeared – presumably the 'handsome' one – all soft words and bedside manner. He irritated me. Besides, it was getting late and I did not want to be going down the mountain in the dark.

'Now I must go.'

'Yes, Ali.'

We said our good-byes.

'Zoraya,' I murmured finally as I stood by the door, 'I'll be back soon.'

'Yes, Ali, good. Yes, do try.' She gave me a tender, mournful glance. 'Ali, I didn't really mean what I said.'

'I know… I understand….'

In the snow I tried for a shortcut and lost my way in the woods. Darkness fell. Finally I sank down beneath a tree sheltered from the wind. I knew that I must move or get frostbite, even die of the cold. I found myself slipping into sleep.

Half-dreaming, I came to with a jolt and sat up. I saw everything clearly.

'She knew! She saw my deception. She spun the stuff about the handsome doctor out of compassion for me. She didn't want me to suffer from guilt, to think I was the only one who had strayed.'

I slumped down again. The fitful moon shone down through the buffeted branches. Now I wasn't so sure. A sense of defeat and helplessness took away my clarity.

'Or maybe she does love him. Either way it is horrible to think about. Let the doctor step in and take my place. He is no doubt worthy of her and can probably cure her too!'

My thoughts went to Liesl. Even before the visit to the hospital I had been aware that I was beginning to tire of her.

'She is a good girl but I don't even know her. Still less does she know me.'

I leaned heavily against the tree trunk, staring straight ahead with the wind howling round me.

'I must leave Switzerland. I must go and join the army to fight in the war. Zoraya has no use for me. Liesl is a treasure but I was never born to be a Swiss innkeeper.'

That was how I came to abandon two women at once.

Back at the inn I convinced Liesl with lies about my duty to the Fatherland. Truthfully I had no feeling for the country of my ancestors and derived my arguments from newspaper editorials. As we kissed goodbye at the local railway station, I said, as I had to Zoraya, that I would be back soon. Like everybody else I thought the war would soon be over so it may have sounded convincing. However, there was no truth in my promise. She cried and hid from me her suspicion that my departure was linked to my visit to the hospital.

I have no memory of whether I wrote a letter of explanation to Zoraya. God forgive me if I didn't.

At the recruiting office in Munich, the officer was very interested in the fact that I spoke Arabic.

'This is unexpected. Let me just make a phone-call.'

While he waited to get through, he explained to me, 'We have officers seconded to the Turks but most of the Ottoman soldiery are Arab. A German soldier who speaks Arabic. Now that's something! How many of you are there? A handful. You are a useful commodity, young man. After a week's training you'll be on your way to aid the Turk, in Mosul or Sinai.'

It turned out to be Sinai, which, following basic training, I reached by a tortuous journey on the Baghdad railway. As I passed through Jerusalem, the ancient city of my birth, my thoughts inevitably turned to my parents. Were they still at the Colony? Indeed, were they still alive?

No sooner had I arrived than I was sent up to the front. From their base in Palestine the Turks had pushed the British back across Sinai to within a few miles of the Suez Canal. My job was to fight alongside the Arab troops and interpret orders. Pretty soon I was involved in raids into the British-held area.

On one of these I was captured and taken to a desert POW camp. This was the beginning of a completely different life.

Marooned in the desert I said very little to anyone, kept my thoughts to myself and just lived in the moment. My past receded – my kidnap, Omdurman, Cairo, Zoraya, Massoud, Akira, Liesl.

Severed from the past, making no new connections, I was as if re-born on another plane of existence. I stared through the fence at the level desert stretching to the distant horizon. The empty expanse reminded me of my time on the raft with Akira. I missed him. He would have understood.

'Nothing… no one… only the mind, always agitating, caught in the wheel of eternity…'

I was a prisoner for almost three years. Sometimes I chatted to the Bedouin who were allowed to barter with our captors at the perimeter fence. I didn't mind talking to them because they always left.

By 1918 the war was about to end but no one foresaw it. If I myself had known I would simply have stayed put. As it was I had no plans to escape but on the other hand I could see that the laxity of the guards and my contacts with the Bedouin would make it easy. Even so, I doubt I would have gone if another factor had not come into play.

I heard people talking about a new batch of prisoners who had just arrived, German civilians, men, women and children, from Jerusalem. The city had just been taken by the English in their sweep north and the Jerusalem Germans had been rounded up and sent there.

I made it my business to find out where the new prisoners were billeted.

I stood a little way off and peered at the desultory but not unpleasant scene. An accordionist sat on a crate playing a Viennese medley. The women hung out washing as if they had all the time in the world, which of course they did. Some of the men and boys were lazily kicking a ball about.

There was more than one candidate for my father – middle-aged bearded men, with skin like parchment, and several too for my mother, aging and careworn souls. I just could not remember my parents well enough. Besides, except with the Bedouin, I had become silent and socially awkward. I could not go forward and announce myself. I was rooted to the spot.

Perhaps anyway, I said to myself, Mother and Father have left the Colony or died. I continued to stare from behind a cluster of bushes, somewhere between angry, repelled and indifferent.

The staring episode impelled me. I had to get away. I went through the fence the following day.

I spent my first night of freedom under the black tents of my Bedouin friends. I felt no elation, just numbness. The tents reminded me of my kidnapping. I couldn't think about my parents as they might be now, or the possibility that I had left them in that camp.

1923-28

Chapter 13

Werner put his brush down and peered from his garret. Hyper-inflation had been going on for weeks. Everyone in the street below was running. With suitcases of bank notes the citizens of the republic crashed into each other liked demented ants.

'Hurry, hurry, get out of my way. At one o'clock the baker puts his prices up!'

'The world's gone mad,' he murmured.

After contemplating the scene for a minute, he moved away from the window and turned his attention back to the canvas.

The line beneath the eye: he must soften it away. The thumb would do it. He leant forward, made the smudge, stood back and sighed.

Better.

It was a good likeness, this self-portrait. His landlady said as much. Her opinions on art weren't worth much but even an ignoramus could recognise a likeness.

He frowned. The problem was that his teacher told him that his skill at drawing was worthless. In art as in everything else, things were changing so fast.

'But you took me on because you said I could draw!'

'If you want your work to live, to express the modern age, you must release something else. It's twenty years since Picasso painted *Les Démoiselles D'Avignon,* since the *Die Brücke* group here in Dresden followed the primitive African example to reach to deeper levels. Do you know these works?'

'Of course.'

'But you are working as if those landmarks had never been attained. Loosen the line, "uncivilise" your colour.'

Werner's lips tightened. Why didn't the man see what he was aiming at? He was no mere mimic of what he saw. His line was there to express something. It was a synthesis of his own subjectivity and the object. This was what art *was*.

'Imagine you are child with his first box of paints,' the teacher droned on. 'You *can* draw, it's true. This skill will re-emerge once you have kindled the fire within. Look at Paul Klee. His draughtsmanship is as refined as that of Dürer himself. It is not forfeited because he no longer draws – as surely he did when he was a lad of fourteen discovering that he was an artist – what the eye sees. His sublime line has emerged attuned to a different reality... Forget everything you ever knew, Werner. Become a child. Daub, paint with your eyes closed. Anything... '

Didn't the man know how much paint cost? Werner couldn't afford to splash it around for fun. Every squeeze of the tube counted.

He'd acquired some cheap powder paint and experimented with slabs of colour, but his heart wasn't in it. His passion was this portrait. It was a culmination of his careful studies of the plants and insects, the landscape buildings and exotic costume of pre-war Jerusalem. Here, in his poverty, he himself must be the subject. But the same question tormented him. Detail was his passion. Didn't the attention that he lavished on his hair, his skin, the weave of his jacket communicate the desire to see and know? Wasn't this timeless? Wasn't the rest just fashion?

The arguments milled constantly in his head. Meanwhile his teacher conveyed the boredom of a man who to make a living is wasting time with mediocrity.

Werner sank on to his bed and stared up at the grubby ceiling.

Could he really go on like this?

His restaurant job, how it degraded him. He peeled mountains of potatoes and spent hours with his elbows in washing up water. The chef kicked the assistants. They in turn kicked the skivvies like Werner. Everyone called him a yokel.

'Your accent,' said a waiter, flicking dust from his starched cuff. 'Where did you get it from? Jerusalem? Since when were there Germans there? Are you a Jew?'

'No... for the hundredth time...'

Apart from Werner's origins, for which he was endlessly picked on, the main topic of conversation was women. Women were to be tricked, taken advantage of, and prevented from being a nuisance. There could be no admission of romantic thoughts. He told no one about his deep yearning for Anna.

Then politics.

Here it was Red Dresden all right. These kitchen Dantons dreamt of revolution. But their idea of this was crude, though oddly innocuous. After the 'deluge' they'd be eating cutlets under the chandeliers while the bourgeoisie would be condemned to the hell of the kitchen.

Meanwhile they urinated into the soup and, in the privacy of the latrine, masturbated into oven-warm loaves.

The bad air and grease in the kitchen gave Werner spots. At twenty-five! Spots! Anna Fischer used to say that without his glasses he was as handsome as a god. Now he looked in the mirror and saw only hollow-eyed desperation.

Yet he had to admit his life suited him. Working in a restaurant meant food. When he started at five in the evening, there was a meal. He could nibble scraps all evening. For lunch he would bring an onion and a few cabbage leaves from the kitchen the night before. That made a soup. Half a loaf on lucky days. Moreover he was calm and clear. His ambition was fierce. What true artist had not suffered? He stood by his choice. There was plenty of time...

How had he ended up in Dresden, the city of the Fischers?

From Palestine it had taken longer to reach Germany than Emile had predicted. They were waylaid at borders and indulged in time off when they came to a pleasant beach or friendly village. To save money they would walk for days on end instead of taking the train.

By the time the young men arrived in Germany it was the late summer of 1918. The army was in retreat on the Western Front. Surrender soon followed and the country slid into chaos. Emile wanted to press on. Werner chose to stay where he was, just over the Upper Saxon border. He said good-bye to his friend, lay low and considered his options.

He thought of going to Württemberg. It was where his mother and father came from, and family connections might be to put to good use, but he concluded he wanted to succeed without family help. He liked the idea of Berlin. It was the capital after all, but he'd heard about inhospitable Berliners. You could get swallowed up in such a sprawl. The city lacked both the beauty and long history that appealed to him.

Then there was Munich. He soon heard by letter from Emile that he and another friend who had arrived from Palestine, the Colony hothead, Helmut Kappel, had gone to the Bavarian capital to join the 'patriotic' forces hostile to the red revolution in the city. Emile urged Werner to join them.

But what did Werner believe when it came to politics? In those tumultuous days everyone talked about democracy but democratic politicians were all out for themselves. The revolutionaries – of Left or Right – who wanted to destroy them were worse. They'd bring the house down with their appetite for violence.

Werner disdained this worldly chaos and dreamt of art and the spirit, and indeed later events in Munich had confirmed his fears. Emile and Helmut joined the National Socialist Workers' Party which caused a stir by staging a coup. Like their leader, Adolf Hitler, they were now behind bars.

Back in 1919, still waiting near the border, Werner thought of the nearest large city, Dresden, city of art and sublime architecture.

Besides convenience, at the back of his mind was the thought that Miriam and Anna might have returned there, with Hugo Fischer no longer alive to plead for Zionism and a life in Palestine.

Dresden it would be.

Once in the city, settled in a small room, he slowly assembled a life. His job paid enough money for rent, food and art lessons. He had one or two friends. He was free to paint all day. But even after four years much was still lacking. There was no sense of belonging, of real social connection.

Despite the inflation the restaurant was surviving. The food and the décor had improved. The Marxist municipal health inspectors issued a glowing report. Werner was vaguely aware that the restaurant was becoming fashionable.

Back on his bed, he stared gloomily at the ceiling. How would that help him?

He rose and returned to his canvas.

~

The very next evening he glanced through a doorway in the restaurant and saw Miriam Fischer.

He all but dropped the pan he was carrying. She had always had a certain style but here was something new. Jewels, make-up, modish hairstyle. Opposite her was a fat fellow with a gold watch chain.

He worked on in a daze, feeling a curious warmth. Here was a chink in his anonymity. There she was, just through the wall. He would never signal to her here of all places, but he was known to this woman. A chance of proper social existence to add to his private sense of mission.

It had been impossible to search out Anna before, not literally impossible, because intelligent enquiries can be fruitful, but psychologically impossible. Being anonymous, he could not initiate. Perhaps too he had feared devoting energy to a quest that might have been hopeless. In the chaos of war and post-war, anything *could* have happened to Miriam and Anna.

Now Anna – or at least her mother – was flesh, here in Dresden.

He could act. He would pay a call. He would find out – however different their circumstances – whether there was still hope with Anna.

Did she still love him as he loved her – even though he'd run away from her? That was all he needed to know, because love could conquer all.

Through discreet enquiries to the head waiter he eventually secured the Fischers' address.

One autumn day, full of resolve, he threw on his moth-eaten jacket and headed down the stairs, fists clenched, lips tight. He walked through the city towards the Elbe. Hope fought dread as he crossed the river.

Finally he came to a mansion in a leafy corner of Neustadt. The door was opened by a servant girl.

'Good morning, kind young lady,' said Werner raising his hat. 'Please excuse me for bothering you but is this the Fischer residence?'

'Y...es.'

'And a further question. Is it the abode of Miss Anna Fischer?'

The girl couldn't hide her interest in this poor but handsome visitor. 'What do you want?'

'I wish to see her. She's an old friend.'

'Name please?'

Werner told her and she went inside. He kicked his heel against the step, whistling a snatch from *Lohengrin* and glancing at the freshly-painted façade.

'They're not short of money, that's for sure.'

He recalled the levelling effect of war in Jerusalem. Everyone was hungry. There you wouldn't separate the Fischers from anybody else. Here, in his garret, he was as far from this gleaming mansion as from the summit of an alp.

The door opened again.

'Come in,' said the girl, with a warning in her eyes.

'Where's Anna?'

There was no reply. Werner entered and went cautiously towards the woman who stood waiting for him at the bottom of the stairs. His steps echoed round the large hall. Miriam wore a dress in the new, short style. Geometric earrings added a final touch.

'Frau Fischer, how nice to see you again.'

'Good morning, Werner. It is nice to see you too. However, before we go any further I have something to say.'

'What is that?'

'No one in this family wants to be reminded of the past. I don't know how you came to be in Dresden but I am asking you not to renew the friendship.'

'But Frau Fischer, I must insist. I recall that the fates of our families were once intertwined. My father…'

She held her hand up. 'Stop, Werner. I cannot hear another word. I must ask you to desist.'

Miriam was unnerved. She lit a cigarette with shaking hand, bracelet jangling.

'I came here to see Anna,' he said politely but firmly. 'I wonder if she should be allowed to speak for herself. Might I ask where she is?'

'I'm afraid that will not do. I cannot tell you and now I would ask you to please leave.'

'Forgive me, Frau Fischer, but if she's in Dresden, then I will find her. Once I have seen her you cannot influence her feelings.'

Miriam drew nervously on her cigarette. He pressed his advantage. 'Are you still in touch with my father by the way? And Eva? Is she still with you? Another time for such questions perhaps.'

Miriam reached for brass bell on the side table to call the servant.

'Listen to me, Werner. I have shaken the dust of Palestine from my feet. I am building a new life. Anna and I don't need you here as a reminder of the past. Your father was a friend of mine but you must know there is no future in your relationship with Anna since you are not Jewish. I wish you well but I must insist.'

'I am an old friend of the family,' he protested.

Miriam ignored this and gestured to the servant to show Werner to the door.

He sank into gloom as he returned past the other grand mansions. Was that it? The hopes on which he'd built a future – a girl, a family to whose affairs, however tenuously, he could attach himself, a place in the city other than as an industrial statistic; the promise of a decent social life: was it all to vanish? Was there to be no end to the imprisoning monotony of his life, so different from his old dreams of freedom and artistic success?

~

Over the next few days he couldn't get Anna out of his mind. For sure she was in Dresden, and it was likely she was living with her mother. He took to waiting around where better-off young people congregated, certain bars, cinemas, even shops. There were plenty of pretty girls who seemed unreachable enough, but none as elusive as Anna in those hopeless days.

With time on his hands he became newly mesmerised by the city that had become his home. He was struck by the contrasts: poverty and riches; factory chimneys and soaring spires; pin-striped profiteers and painted women mingling with tramps and desperadoes. Disabled veterans sold matches in the doorways of jewellers and parfumiers. Every second door was a club: clubs for cards, for beer, for boxing, for heaven knows what.

The theatres and opera houses in this part of town made his heart sink. They were forbidden temples – he could never afford them. Cinema though – the people's art – was different. Searching for Anna, he passed the cinema where he'd sat bewitched by the sinister *Nosferatu*, by *Dr Mabuse, The Gambler* and just recently the second part of the *Niebelungen.* Film to him was enthralling. In the anonymity of darkness, magic soothed a mind fraught by this modern Babylon: its choking chaos of buses, trams, cycles and cars interweaving on a mindless journey.

He passed the headquarters of the Social Democratic Party. The building made him smile. How hard it was in this republic to transfer one's idealism to current politics. Shallowness was expressed in the very buildings of trades unions, municipal departments and political parties. Pretentious facades echoed feebly the Baroque glories of the Zwinger palace, great Dresden churches and Altstadt mansions. These fake edifices merely created suspicion: human betterment was a Marxist-liberal fallacy.

Despite all that he saw and absorbed that week, he was getting nowhere. His vigil was hopelessly random. He realised he must narrow it down. There was nothing for it but to return to the Fischer residence, hide nearby and hope to catch Anna on her way out or in.

More days passed in this way with no result.

He was on his way back from one of these forays when the miracle happened. Ahead, unmistakeably, was a girl dancing with familiar natural grace along the pavement towards him. Slim, her red-blonde hair now bobbed, in a brown short coat and cloche hat, she was instantly recognisable.

With beating heart he strode towards her. Their eyes met. She put her hand to her mouth. 'Werner!'

'Yes,' he said, trying to quell his nerves. 'It's me.'

'Why are you here?'

'I live here,' he replied with studied casualness.

'Do you?... How come?'

Her tone was guarded. The hurt he had left her with a few years ago in the Valley of Rephaim made her look away. Was she also shocked that he looked so pale and down-at-heel?

'Well, that would be telling.'

She faced him, narrowing her eyes. 'Werner, tell me why you're living in Dresden. You don't look that good, to tell the truth.'

'Walk with me, then I'll tell you.'

She glanced in the direction of home.

He touched her arm. 'Anna... a walk, for old time's sake.'

Her anguished gaze settled on the rippling surface of the river below. 'Well, I suppose Mother isn't expecting me,' she said at last. 'We got a surprise afternoon off. There's a strike.'

'A strike? You're a worker?'

'No, studying. It's the professors who are striking.'

'What next? What are you studying anyway?'

'Now I'm on to further studies. Architecture.'

His eyes lit up. 'Ah, then you can give me a learned tour of one of the city's landmarks. What about the Marienkirche? It's not far.'

At last she smiled. 'It so happens I have to write an essay on it.'

'Then you agree?'

'It would be useful...'

They strolled on, Anna careful to keep some space between them.

'Did you know I was here, Werner?'

'I thought you might be... I didn't know.'

Their footsteps echoed from the pavement, beating out the rhythm of Werner's joy and hope. Impulsively he reached for her hand.

'Werner! We're in the street!'

'Very well, Anna, but times have changed, you know. Respectable mothers sell their daughters and themselves to Americans for bread. There are orgies and cocaine behind the curtains in your very street, I'll bet! In the circumstances, if I take a pretty lady's hand...'

She remained firm in her refusal. At the Marienkirche they passed through the hushed interior, climbed and emerged panting from the stairway. The sun shone hard down on the ramparts of the Schloss nearby. Far below, tiny vehicles glided like clockwork models. People were pins etched against the ground.

Everywhere at this height there were statues. Around the rim of the church roof, across the square on the opera house. On the Zwinger too, on the Kronentor, the Wall Pavilion. An incongruous army of saints and sages, graces and tritons, dwarves and demiurges, signalling, beating their breasts, on tip-toe as if about to leap.

'Superb,' murmured Werner. 'From above I see the city afresh. I'm a bird... or a balloonist. I see how perfect it is for the very first time. The statues are keeping us company up here… surveying it. They see it's perfect. Perhaps they are… protecting it. The courtyards, the galleries, the fountains, coffee shops. All they want is for it to be preserved – for ever.'

'You *are* still the artist.'

He contemplated the remark as someone might roll fine wine around their tongue. 'Mm… maybe. That's what I'm aiming for anyway.'

Turning away from the view, she looked him hard in the eye.

'Werner Gustavus, you are a horrible man! You deserted me in Jerusalem, left me, abandoned me to the Egyptian desert. Then it turns out you've been here all along. What's going on?'

'Stop it, Anna. Isn't it obvious you're the reason I came to Dresden?'

'You deserve to be punished! I am going to chain you up and kick you like a dog every time I pass.'

He took her hand. This time she let him.

'Anna, I'm no dog. I'm a man in paradise with an angel who has been restored to me. I'm poor now but with you...'

He put his arm around her and pulled her to him, whispering gently. 'Now let me take the angel to my elegant abode. My landlady is an excellent woman. Unfortunately she mustn't meet the angel because if she did that might be the end of that. I will smuggle you in! I'll boil the kettle and we can eat strudel.'

She broke away. 'Werner, I am not ready for this. I'm going home now.'

'Anna!'

'I don't know! I must go.'

This was a setback. He felt suddenly intimidated by the statues. Their impassive stares mocked him. Descending from the roof in gloom he walked along with her in silence. Before he left her he persuaded her at least to meet him again in a few days' time.

The wait was intolerable. He couldn't settle. He was certain: life without Anna would remain squalid and hopeless.

Their second meeting, at a well-known student rendezvous, was a strain. She seemed nervous with him but happy to swap greetings and banter with others. He saw her in a new light. She was confident in this setting, had a purpose and a place. It made him jealous.

He did not entirely lose heart. Once they were out walking she did not discourage his sweet-talk, or his ardent kisses when they parted. She agreed to a third meeting.

This proved a turnaround. She appeared to have resolved her doubts, signified by a gift of various items of new clothing to 'smarten him up'. Werner was too grateful to feel humiliated.

'Next time,' she whispered as they said good-bye, 'you can meet me in your new clothes and take me to your room for tea.'

The next time came and they went to his lodgings. Once there she seemed to relax despite the subterfuge resulting from his landlady's rules.

Clandestine encounters became a habit with them over a number of weeks.

On one of these he was reaching to the back of his cupboard and discovered half a bottle of schnapps that he had forgotten about. They had that with their tea. By now after so many meetings they were fully restored to their habit from Jerusalem days of lively, combative talk. Led on by the schnapps, they fell from disputation to more than usually passionate kissing, thence to feverish undressing.

Just as they once had among the rocks and darting lizards near the German Colony, though more comfortably, they at last made love.

'For a while I'll carry on visiting you secretly,' she said as they lay peacefully together, 'while we work out our future. We must be careful not to have babies. That would ruin everything. I'm going to be an architect and design proper workers' flats, decent places with plenty of light and air. You're going to be a famous painter. Us. Young people. The future. Not like mother, a middle-aged poetess turned a little bitter I'm afraid, with no ideals. We are going to be an artistic couple, cultural ornaments, pillars of a modern republican Dresden.' She squeezed his hand beneath the cover. 'But not yet! It will take time...'

'My once-shy Anna has become a confident, modern woman,' Werner thought as he stared at the dim-lit ceiling. 'This is a new world at last.'

Chapter 14

In the poverty, debt and runaway inflation of post-war Dresden, undreamt-of prosperity had come to a woman with a taste for startling hats.

The owner of the art gallery where in 1912 Eva had seen Stefan Lehmann's portrait of Johannes was now rich. It had come about in spite of the advice given to her by her companion, Darius Vogel.

As her accountant, he had doubted her wisdom in spending her inheritance on pictures. But if she had gone into railways or government bonds as Darius had recommended, she would by 1923 have been on her uppers like most Germans. She had gone into the art business at the right moment and been confident in her artistic judgment. She was shrewd in business and, though she couldn't talk about art beyond vapid superlatives, had an uncommon eye for quality.

Before the war she had bought cheaply the works of precisely those 'outrageous', 'decadent', 'Jewish-bolshevist' artists who had emerged from obscurity to world-prominence by the Weimar period. While buying and selling she also, like many dealers, pursued another project, the building of a collection. These were her 'untouchables'.

In time she and Darius (whom she had charitably married) were sitting on a fortune. They had the two things necessary to survive inflation: property (already before the war she had bought an elegant mansion in the Altstadt) and foreign currency. Just after the war foreigners could buy everything desirable that Germany in its post-Versailles Treaty poverty had to offer: symphony orchestras for an evening, Rhine castles, whole streets in picturesque towns. Not a week went past without foreign dealers offering Frau Vogel dollars for this Vlaminck, or that Kirchner, Nolde or Kandinsky.

Sometimes she allowed an 'untouchable' to be touched. A sale could mean high-living for six months. Darius had counselled high-living for three months only, and the other half invested in bricks-and-mortar. This made sense to his wife. The Vogels' holdings in Dresden property grew. Income started to flow from rents. They could imagine a time when they would not be tempted to sell any more pictures. Truly the Vogels were in clover.

And the hats. Gone were the florid inventions of the pre-war years. A new generation of jazz-age creations arose, crafted from richer materials – turbans draped with amethyst, cloches of rare animal skin stuck with sequins and jewelled geometry, satin helmets, velvet pillboxes, and in the evenings – for Frau Vogel now made a bid to become a salon-mistress – a tiara bought from an exiled Russian countess.

~

'Come with a handful of sketches or cabinet pieces,' she had replied to Werner's letter. 'To show the essence. I shall expect you at 2.30. At 3pm I am to receive His Excellency the Spanish ambassador, but talent can be recognised at a glance, so we shall have enough time.'

Werner's teacher had mentioned that the famous Frau Vogel had once given money to a young artist he knew. The student had simply written her a letter and asked to show her his work. A loan or a small allowance – the man couldn't remember which – had followed. Later she'd bought his work and helped him set up an exhibition in Leipzig.

Distracted by his afternoons of love with Anna, Werner delayed. Eventually he'd written tactfully. Frau Vogel did not rush to reply but in time an invitation came.

He dared hope that his luck had changed. Or rather that love was the catalyst to a new form of life summed up by one word: success. This became Anna's faith. She saw his Vogel initiative as a miracle wrought by their reunion, to be followed inevitably by others in an ascending arc. With the impossibility of presenting a gentile and penniless artist to her mother as future consort, she trusted fate. This clandestine love-making must end. She needed Werner to scale the heights, so, simply, he would. But she was an architecture student – of a socio-political more than aesthetic bent – not an art connoisseur. She lacked the knowledge to rate his chances. Her faith in his talent was blind.

He longed to share her confidence, but could he? He needed to know what others thought. Did he have it: not just talent and skill but that indefinable other quality? Now, since Anna's re-entry into his life, he couldn't afford to tie himself to a doomed project. Faith must be backed by sense. He was obsessed with the practice of art and had no idea how he might survive the loss of his dream. But that was a risk he now had to take. Asking Frau Vogel for funds, advantageous practically, was also a way of obtaining a verdict.

Directed to a small sitting-room hung with Italian Futurists, Werner waited, heart in his mouth. Frau Vogel floated forward in a silk gown and a cap with two pheasant feathers diamond pinned in a fierce V.

'Show me,' she commanded. 'I always have a flutter of excitement seeing new work.'

She pointed to an empty easel. Werner produced a drawing. Frau Vogel nodded, the feather V waved. He took out another. She humphed enigmatically. Agonisingly it went on. Occasionally Werner added an explanation. It was the positive, waving V or the ambiguous humph. Only when it was done did she pronounce.

'You have applied yourself to the art of drawing, Herr Gustavus, that's clear. I like the still life and one or two of the pastels, the figure studies.'

Werner nodded respectfully.

'However, I'm not sure... I need to think about it.' More prevarication followed. It was hard for Werner to work out what Frau Vogel was getting at. It seemed to boil down to 'carry on' and she would have another look in due course. Meanwhile the hands of the mantel clock moved dangerously towards three o'clock.

'But to sum up, Frau Vogel,' Werner managed to say, 'do you believe I have the gift?'

She put her hand on his arm. 'Come, let me show you something. We have a minute or two still. I have a roomful of works which are – how shall I say? – hard to place. Neither modern nor old-fashioned. They might interest you, suggest something to you.' She continued speaking as she led him out of the room and rose like a stately air balloon up the staircase. 'You need examples. Not to imitate, that would be death but I sense you are working in a void.'

They came to a corridor hung with pictures of blond gods in thigh guards and Teuton helmets.

'Not these, Herr Gustavus! This is my "patriotic" corner. My husband likes them and I buy them as a hedge in case fashion turns that way again. *Loge and Siegfried at the Forge*. Very good! *Heinrich the First with his Vassals*.' With a flourish of gold bangles she indicated the door to the next room. 'But *this* is the room I want you to see. Lose yourself in there.' She looked at her watch. 'Look, it's three o'clock. I'll send a servant up to keep you company. Wait for me till His Excellency departs.'

Werner settled on a bench, hardly looking at the pictures. However Frau Vogel expressed it he felt put in his place, a beginner, a talentless misfit. He stared sullenly at the floor.

The servant appeared, picking his nails with a fork. 'She's with the ambassador. I'm to keep an eye on you in case you steal anything.'

Werner hardly heard. Eventually he stood up and moved from picture to picture, distracted, indifferent to the unspectacular works that passed before his eyes.

The servant clicked his tongue. Werner moved silently on.

His heart missed a beat. He stepped back, steadied himself then stared, open-mouthed.

'Do you know...' He didn't finish his sentence. The servant shook his head. He knew nothing about the pictures – obviously.

Retreating to another seat Werner gazed at the painting, as awed and rapt as those visitors to great art collections who have crossed continents to view a particular work in the flesh for the first time in their lives.

He was back in Jerusalem. The suffocation of a Sunday at home. Drawing, reading Schiller or Shakespeare, dreaming of girls, of escape. The muezzin calling from the valley, the Colonists gossiping in the street, his mother and father bickering. This picture was a part of his childhood. It was an utter mystery how it came to be here in this bourgeois salon in Dresden, hidden away as a treasure.

Coming to himself slowly, he began to appraise the work with an artist's eye.

How interesting... What a success... The defenceless little figure, alone, vulnerable... the face and hands, the golden hair. Behind, the oriental hanging, the scrubby landscape glimpsed through the window. Nothing was laboured. Details were individually eloquent, yet fused within an overall scheme. There were hints too of distortion, of the bizarre, which merely added to the work's originality and power. The tools on the table suggested instruments of torture. Why was the clock sitting, suspended as it were, on nothing? And his brother's direct gaze. How to decipher it?

The picture was a dream. To call it an image of perfect German youth would be both to deny its strangeness and to succumb to the same crude classifying impulse which had led Frau Vogel to hang it with others which it supposedly resembled. It was an icon, rich and unfathomable. It would surely not be long before it was reproduced and hung on a million parlour walls.

Werner stayed seated while the servant remained on guard. Frau Vogel eventually returned.

'Herr Gustavus, how are you getting on? His Excellency is admiring a work by Picabia. I have excused myself for a moment.' She sat down next to him. 'Ah, this portrait of a boy. You admire it? It's a fine work isn't it? It caused a stir before the war, I can tell you, when we had it in the window of our little gallery. This was one I wanted to hang on to.'

'Frau Vogel, you may be surprised to learn that the subject of this wonderful portrait is my very own brother.'

Frau Vogel was not interested. 'With Stefan Lehmann everything is conjecture.'

'Frau Vogel, this is no rumour. Not only is this my brother but this very work used to hang in my childhood home.'

'Really? I bought it from Lehmann himself. Yet, come to think of it, yes, there was something I recall when we first acquired the work. A young man at that time claimed to be the sitter…'

'My brother? Are you sure?' Since his father had kept Eva's story of the portrait and the mysterious young man to himself, this was astonishing news to Werner.

'I am sure... Yet perhaps after all I don't remember so well. He was just an ordinary young man. His hair was fair. I don't think he was so striking as when he was a boy. I think I should have remembered otherwise.'

'I am telling you this boy is my brother, Frau Vogel, and it is of the greatest interest to know that you met him as a young man, since most people believe that he is dead.'

'Oh yes, I think I remember something about that. Heavens! In which case, I wish I could tell you more. Oh dear… It was such a troubled time with the war and everything…'

'Frau Vogel, I would be very much obliged if you could let me know if anything comes back to you more clearly. But if you have met Johannes himself, well… My mother and father, who are still in Jerusalem, would give anything to know more.'

'I am certain I met him for a few minutes, also that I told someone at the time, now who was that? A woman I think. I can't be certain of anything else. What I *am* certain of is that Lehmann is back painting again. There are new masterpieces. Unfortunately nobody can get at them.'

Frau Vogel's eyes widened. She'd had a brainwave. 'You have a family connection!'

'I met Stefan Lehmann before the war when he came to Palestine to buy the picture from my parents.'

She smiled ingratiatingly. 'Herr Gustavus...'

'Yes?'

'Would you be prepared to go to Venice for me?'

Werner was surprised. 'What do you want me to do?'

'Stefan Lehmann is said to be hoarding a great number of wonderful canvases. Given his condition when I last saw him, it's hard to credit. He had evidently fallen into every kind of vice. He was practically dead from drink and desperate for money. Not a pleasant person to deal with. The story is that he finally entered an asylum in Venice and was put under the care of a doctor who brought about a miraculous transformation. Hey presto, Herr Lehmann, who now lives permanently on the asylum island, is painting once more. He has, in secret as it were, become a modern master. A veritable monk of art, he refuses all visitors and will not show or sell his work. But the asylum staff, some of whom understand painting, have not hidden the truth from their fellow citizens. It is believed in Venice that there is a genius living on the island like Fra Angelico in his monastery. A man rescued from hell, freed into sublime creation.'

'What are his paintings like?'

'Some are like certain Picassos, I'm told, others have a hint of Chagall with his floating goats and angels. But all great art is unique. We cannot imagine the paintings, we have to see them – but we can't.' She gave Werner a gruesome smile. 'However...'

'You think I might be able to contact him?'

She clutched his arm. 'Write to him stressing your family ties.

Tell him you yourself are an artist. You need his advice...'

'But I couldn't afford...'

'We will fund your trip. The train fare and a week in a modest pension. All I ask is that you report back whether he will consider releasing some of his work for the market. If he will show you some, all the better.'

Werner was thinking on his feet. 'I will do this, Frau Vogel, but I have a condition.'

'Yes?'

'I need a small allowance to enable me to continue my painting. If you will agree to support me modestly for two years I will not only do what you ask, I will do it with diligence. I am certain that your plan will require a lot of ingenuity to carry out. I may have to persist till I achieve your wishes. I need payment. That will make a difference, you can be sure.'

Frau Vogel did not like this. But she was a businesswoman and she knew what she wanted.

'Very well, young man. Not an allowance, but I will give you a lump sum on top of expenses.'

The amount she mentioned surprised Werner by its generosity and helped him overcome his reservations. The arrangement was quickly concluded, details to be worked out later.

Frau Vogel rose. 'Max, show the gentleman down, please.'

Shaking hands with Frau Vogel, Werner took a last glance at the gleaming portrait of the brother he had never known, and followed Max down the passage past the Teutonic maidens and tin-clad gods.

Chapter 15

Snow drifted from a sullen sky, coating the roofs and lawns of San Lazzaro down to the dark sea.

Out of the white silence, a piano. Thrilling notes met the ear from a high window. What finger-work – from the man who had once played the Schumann concerto (Gabriele d'Annuncio and King Victor Emanuel in the audience) with Toscanini on the rostrum.

Rolling arpeggios. Sweep up the keyboard, tumble to the bass, over and over. Roll it out. Roll it back. Declare nothing more. Life is in D minor. Grief is the key.

At last the piano stopped. White silence fell again. Hungry birds batted their wings against ebony branches. A man who hadn't spoken for years, a tomato enthusiast with spade, scraped the earth beneath the window.

A gondola homed to its mark. Disembarking, a visitor, a tall man carrying a large black folder, walked up the jetty.

'So that's Werner,' murmured the dottoressa. Clara Lehmann was five months pregnant and resented having to give her time to him.

Soon the maid, Valentina, showed the guest in.

'My husband is busy painting just at the moment,' said the dottoressa in perfect German, strongly accented. 'His routine is strict. No interruptions till midday. Will you be happy to wait?'

The visitor was all politeness. 'That's fine. I'm obliged to him in any case. By the way, I saw some pictures in a room off the hall. Was that Herr Lehmann's work?'

'Yes. All his recent work is here.'

'Since I'm waiting anyway I'd be interested to take a closer look.'

'I'll show you. Valentina can bring us some coffee.'

~

Werner stood back, chin in hand, surveying a dark landscape crossed with luminescent squiggles. The main motifs, crudely represented, were a river, a hut and trees with bare roots. He turned to his hostess for elucidation.

The effort of small talk over coffee about Frau Vogel and Stefan's recent history had tired Clara. Nevertheless, she responded to the young man's curiosity with passion.

'The work is a re-working of Tintoretto's "Flight into Egypt" from the lower chamber of the Scuola di San Rocco in Venice. At one time Stefan practically lived in that building, setting up camp among the Tintorettos. The landscape here is empty or at first seems to be. Those trees, the ground underneath, the roots: the mind is lost, cut off from nature. The task is endless. It's a labyrinth.'

Werner peered yet more intently.

'Stefan studied the Cabbala. In the Cabbala the image of the labyrinth can express many things: the divine name, God's plan for the universe, things to do with his unknowable nature. Here in Stefan's work the labyrinth conveys an individual predicament, the final unknowability of the psyche. We move from religion to psychology – or perhaps we discover that religion was psychology all along. The picture suggests perhaps Stefan's own "flight."'

'Flight?'

'From his illness, to something… safer, happier for him.'

'His present life?'

'I dare to say so.'

'He's a lucky man,' said Werner graciously.

'Maybe luck was involved, Herr Gustavus, who knows. He has

avoided destroying himself but he still struggles mightily. He lost many years. He will always bear the burden of that. Besides which he is an artist. Artists can never be quite at peace. I have my own ambitions and preoccupations which are nothing to do with him. I am a busy woman here at the hospital. I am far from being the ever-comforting wife. But yes, Stefan is no longer unwell, he is happier... and we have a child coming.' She patted her midriff.

'Are you a Jewess?'

'No,' she replied, a little awkwardly. Since he had walked through her door Werner appeared apprehensive beneath his polished exterior. He disconcerted her but she felt sorry for him.

'If I might ask, how exactly did you come to be together?'

'As I told you, he was committed here a few years ago. He was the patient of my colleague. This man did wonders with Stefan. They talked, over many, many hours. As he recovered, Stefan was always to be seen about the place. He became less of a patient, more of a... an interesting fixture on the island. We just started chatting – on a bench, in corridors. Before long we fell in love and married. Now it's our life: he a painter with the best of conditions for work, I a psychiatrist.'

'But now he will not show or sell?' queried Werner.

'In time he will. At present he doesn't want the contamination of the gallery world. He has no great need for money.'

'Frau Vogel is keen to make overtures...'

'Tell her to be patient. He doesn't want to lose all he has gained. We are not entirely out of the woods.'

Werner's eye went back to the painting. 'I... I'm just...'

'Ah,' said Clara, 'you've noticed. The silhouette.'

'A human form – in the roots. What does it represent?'

'Hope perhaps – and maybe Stefan himself. Stefan depicts himself emerging from the shadow that has been his life. From his isolation, his subterranean silence. His condition is outside him now, objectified in this painting, and being outside, may at long last stop dominating internally. Perhaps the figure is Stefan's self reborn – though he gives the silhouette another name.'

'What name?'

'Johannes.'

Werner started. 'My brother?'

'He has been haunted all his life by that boy. He believes he was responsible for his disappearance. Then there was another development which added to his guilt. Have you not heard through your family?'

'I have lost touch with my parents.'

'I see. I am sorry but I am not altogether surprised. Families where such tragedies occur often fall apart.'

'I suppose so... You would know in your profession... What happened anyway?'

'Before Stefan came to the island a few years ago, he met a German tourist in Venice who seems to have known your brother briefly during the war.'

Werner turned pale and his heart thumped. 'Really?'

Clara touched his arm. 'Are you all right?'

'Yes... please tell me more.'

'Well, that's what the man said. Stefan wasn't in a very good state at the time so there has to be some doubt. The point is that Stefan was convinced. He wrote to your father promising to go to Germany and investigate. Of course he was in no fit state. He should never have promised such a thing. He never went – and to this day has not been able to bring himself to write again to your father confessing this. It might be better not to mention it to Stefan, not initially anyway. It's a sore point.'

It was easier to turn back to the pictures than go further into this. Werner looked some more at the canvases while the dottoressa sat down nearby.

'Herr Lehmann *works* now,' he murmured. 'My god, he does.'

'You admire what you've seen?'

'Yes, but if I'm frank, he presents a problem to me.'

'A problem?'

Werner flopped on the chair beside her, sitting a little too close for comfort, waving and clutching his hands in his passion to put across his meaning.

'He's aligned himself with the moderns… There is no form as such... I should be repelled… Yet the rumours I heard in Dresden are correct. Herr Lehmann is a genius. His portrait of my brother – I grew up with it, left it, then had an unexpected reunion with it a while ago – *announces* him as a great artist. After that, to judge by what I've seen here, he develops what he was born with, he does not stay still.'

'You are agitated, Herr Gustavus.'

'I am! I am frantic to know whether I too "was born with it." And *he* will be able to tell from my work. Yes, he will. By the way, I've taken the liberty of bringing some of my work for him to judge. To be frank, my desire to know his verdict goes beyond my mission for Frau Vogel, though of course I will entreat Herr Lehmann on her behalf as I said I would.'

'Listen, Herr Gustavus. *Everyone* is born with the potential to make a unique contribution. Whatever Stefan's "verdict."'

'No! I will die *not* to be born with it… with the *thing*… Some milk-and-water "unique contribution" will not do! I will give up. What would be the point? Others may be happy to be second rate… To sum up, Mozart was *born* Mozart, Raphael, Raphael. For all the rest, why bother?'

The dottoressa breathed in slowly. As it happened this question was close to her interests professionally (through her work with certain patients) and – since she had married an artist – personally. After a pause during which Werner stared at her in tortured anticipation, she said, 'I take your point, but it's not so simple.'

'Isn't it? I think it is.'

'Listen Herr Gustavus, even among the greatest, there is a

struggle. There is above all a psychological battle. They work to release something. The phrase "born genius" does not cover the complexities. Look, I don't know what my husband was born with. But I do know what has healed him as a person. His painting was a part of the process and that painting itself improved as a consequence. Whether his work was an essential part of his healing, I don't know. I've a feeling there was something else that was more important.'

'What?'

'His connection with his doctor here, a wise, listening man; his connection with me, with his unborn child. Connection,' Clara concluded. 'That's it. *There* is something which is more important than art. Though as an Italian I personally love art, I reject the idolatry of art. I believe Stefan does too. Anyway…' She broke off. 'Here he is; he can tell you himself.'

Stefan ambled in, humming distractedly to himself. Werner had not seen him since his visit to Jerusalem before the war and was astonished. It wasn't just that Stefan had aged since 1910. He was a different person altogether. His flowing fair hair was grey and had been cropped brutally short. Instead of expensive tailoring and fine linen he wore an artisan's blue smock. Flamboyant neckwear was gone. The stylish libertine had turned ascetic. He was a desert hermit, monk in a cell, no creature of the corrupt and sensual world.

Werner hid his surprise. 'I'm obliged to you for this, Herr Lehmann.'

Stefan looked keenly at the young man and shook his hand. 'So… Werner! We last met in Jerusalem. I fear I did not cover myself in glory. I did a wicked thing taking that portrait back for which I will never forgive myself. However, I am a reformed character – in the main. I will try not to let my shame about that cloud our meeting. Welcome to San Lazzaro, my good fellow.'

'As I wrote, I am here to speak to you on behalf of Frau Vogel.'

'Yes indeed...'

For the next few minutes Werner earnestly delivered his message.

It was not entirely unsuccessful. Stefan would indeed respond to the Dresden dealer. Things were improving in Germany at last and it would be useful to have someone handle his work. But he wasn't ready yet. That was a matter for him and his doctor and would in no way be influenced by the impatience of Frau Vogel.

'I know that hard-headed woman from before!' Stefan concluded. 'Not that I didn't give her the run-around. She deserves something for the trouble I gave her.'

'I'll convey your message. It will please her that a connection has been re-established. I'll counsel her to be patient.'

'Thank you, Werner, I would be grateful. Tell her not to pester me, and all will be fine.'

Werner cleared his throat. 'Uh... meanwhile, Herr Lehmann, I have a favour to ask you...'

'Favour?'

'I need a verdict.'

'Now what can this be, Werner?' asked Stefan with a twinkle. Werner briefly explained.

'Our guest naturally wants your view of his work, Stefan,' said the dottoressa. 'We discussed the idolatry of art. It was an interesting talk.'

'Ah yes,' exclaimed Stefan. 'I broke with that! I'm no idolater. Down with the aesthetes and art worshippers! The devil take Flaubert, Gautier, Oscar Wilde and the rest. Living – that's the thing.' He chuckled. 'Nevertheless, somehow I'm still an artist. And if you're one of the cursed tribe too, Werner, of course you want to know if you're any good!'

'Yes, but...' began Clara.

Werner was impatient with the 'idolatry' debate which seemed more a bone of marital contention than anything to do with him.

Clara withdrew and Werner laid his work out on the table. With care Stefan began leafing through the pictures.

Dresden views in ink with a watercolour wash. Energy and

expression in the architectural detail, finials and balustrades taking centre-stage with the life below dashed in: a car, pedestrians, vendors, beggars. In chalk, careful portraits, scenes from everyday life – children in a park, a football match.

'Do you work with oils?'

'Yes, but obviously I couldn't bring them.'

'What kind of works?'

'The same subject-matter, but true to that medium.'

After a silence punctuated with humming, Stefan asked 'Have you read Kandinsky's *On the Problem of Form*?'

'Er… no.'

'I was reading it yesterday. It may have something to say to you. Where is it now?' He rummaged in the desk and took out a book. 'Ah, here it is. You see, Werner, Kandinsky argues that painters should not follow schools nowadays. They must be freed to become what they are.'

Werner pursed his lip anxiously as Stefan looked for the quote.

'Here we are. Kandinsky writes: "…it has no significance whether a real or abstract form is used by the artist… In principle, there is no question of form… Everything here depends upon the inner necessity which alone can make a form correct." You see. Inner necessity.'

'I understand. I agree for that matter.'

Stefan began looking through Werner's works again, more quickly this time, but with no less concentration.

'Werner,' he said at last, 'tell me.'

'Tell you what?'

'Where is *your* inner necessity? I understand you *feel* it. It's apparent in everything you say. You have come all the way to Venice out of this inner necessity, but somehow I don't see it in your work. It gets blocked somewhere between your brain and your hand.'

Werner's temple pulsed. 'Do you mind if I smoke?'

'Not at all.'

Werner lit up and drew in deeply. 'You don't like my work.'

'I didn't say that. I just...'

'You think I lack talent.'

'Well... talent...'

'Come now, Herr Lehmann.'

Stefan threw out his arms. 'What we want is boldness, simplicity, freedom! Let go of everything you grew up with.'

'You're saying my work is conventional.'

'It depicts the modern world, city life, ordinary people, that's good... Manet showed us...' Stefan's palms were sweating. He was finding it hard to look Werner in the eye. 'But that was two generations ago. Art now is... I too have had to force myself on. There's no guide any more. There are no rules. The situation is... The situation allows for purer expression.'

'Any fool can do it!'

'Not quite...'

'Chaos. Anything goes.'

Werner moved to the window and stared out across the lagoon. How it hurt. He couldn't keep up a pretence. Yet he must keep calm. The cigarette helped. But his angry back said everything.

'It's hard, Werner, I know, but all I am saying is find your own way.'

Busily stubbing out the cigarette, Werner turned. 'Your works, Herr Lehmann – the paintings I've seen today – inspire me, *would* inspire me if only... Somehow you have squared the circle. No wonder the German art world is awash with rumours about you. No wonder Frau Vogel longs to prise your paintings out of you. I would paint like you if I could.'

'That wouldn't do it,' countered Stefan. 'That's quite in opposition from what I have just said. Be *yourself*.'

Werner shook his head hopelessly.

'Look, my dear fellow,' said Stefan. 'I was once miserable and stuck. How to lose the past? How to go forward? I hid from the problem by various means. By that chance meeting with the man who was to become my doctor among the Tintorettos in the Scuola di San Rocco, I found my way. I came here. With that man I talked my way to root causes. I re-connected to my deeper self, hence to my creativity. Don't misunderstand me. Even now I suffer from depression and anxiety. I can still hallucinate and experience persecution mania. Nevertheless I work. I am disciplined. So far as my paintings – like my conversations with my doctor – have as their focus the products of my unconscious mind, they have been a key part of my recovery. That, together with meeting my wife and the prospect of becoming a father. But you, you will do what *you* have to do. '

Werner sensed an impending earthquake. Soon nothing would be the same. Meanwhile, it was a relief to revert to the previous subject.

'*Why* will you not exhibit?'

'It may change, but at the moment I would no more do that than publicise the contents of my talks with my doctor.'

'You painted that sublime portrait of my brother. I grew up with it at home. It was familiar, part of the furniture, then it was gone, you had taken it. Later, in Dresden, by a twist of fate, I encountered it again. It had less personal meaning for me now. Instead, it became an *aesthetic* yardstick to me. I love that picture. I contrived with Frau Vogel to go back and look at it again. Now what do I find? You have gone far beyond that masterpiece. I am disturbed, my world has turned upside down. You have aligned yourself with the moderns. I am lost. I give up.'

'Give up?'

'I have decided here and now: I'm giving up. I've learnt what I came here to learn. I have no real talent. Whether I am a modern or a reactionary, it makes no difference.'

'I did not say you had no talent!'

'Really, I'm giving up.'

'No, listen, Werner, my good fellow! That's too drastic. I think you have a talent… for architectural drawing at least. Perhaps you should re-direct your energies. Get a job in an architect's office, why not? See if that might be a way forward. Or what about magazine illustration? Meanwhile, live a little. Go to the cinema, stroll about, unwind, chase women, become … looser. Art will take care of itself. The muse will beckon – or she won't. Trust to fate.'

Werner stared bitterly at him. 'You have said enough, Herr Lehmann. I thank you for it. You cannot bring yourself to say it would be a loss to art if I stopped. If I had a vision that moved you, you would be mortified to think of my stopping.'

Werner turned back to the window. Stefan was looking again at his angry back, with Venice a blue line in the distance. He wanted to be helpful but more than that he wanted to be free of obligation to this distressed young man.

Werner was soon gone from San Lazarro, and left Venice the next day.

The locomotive chugged across the north Italian plain. Mist hung over the fields. There was a monotony in the endless farms and hamlets which chimed with his mood and almost comforted him.

Gradually the mist cleared. The sun brightened fields and red-roofed buildings. How fresh everything looked.

He was raw. As the train rumbled on and the world through the window was ever more radiant, a tear formed in the corner of his eye. It trickled to the top of his cheek where it evaporated in the warmth of the sun.

All beauty would from now on be a torture. He himself could never create it – neither beauty, nor meaning. He would be forever on the outside. Art, which he had revered since his first hesitant sketches in Jerusalem, belonged to others, infinitely to be envied.

The image came to him of a man standing alone on the quay while a ship carrying a band of travellers sets its course for a fabled city.

Still so near, rolling on the choppy seas, the ship turns, its sails fill.

How grandly the magnificent vessel rolls on the tide. The lucky ones are on the ship. They're leaving for ever. For some reason which he cannot understand the man on the quay has been left behind. His desolation is without limit.

'Architectural drawing! Magazine illustration! To think I saw myself as a budding Velasquez or Manet. Apparently I'm not even an artist. I'm a hack. Well, to hell with that. I'd rather go back to the kitchen and piss in the vichyssoise.'

Chapter 16

On the first Wednesday of the month Frau Vogel held a lavish party. The buffet was laid out in the dining room. There was dancing. In winter in the grand salon under the gaze of her modern masterpieces. In summer in a marquee.

By the end of a given year 'everyone' had come. The combinations were provocative. Frau Vogel had a genius for mixing new money, old money, Left and Right, artistic conservatives and the avant-garde.

'Plenty of young people and pretty girls!' was her motto. (Her husband Darius hated young people but had no difficulty with the pretty girls.) 'And artists, young artists,' she would add. 'We must encourage them, let them meet their future patrons.'

She pestered art teachers to give her the names of their better students. An embossed invitation would be sent. 'If you don't have a dinner jacket,' she would add in her own extravagant hand, 'don't worry, come as you are!' This made her seem unstuffy, she hoped. Once the party was underway, it helped her pick out the artists in the throng and bear down on them when the mood took her.

About young Werner Gustavus she felt vaguely guilty. She hadn't heard from him since he'd gone to Venice. Had he found Stefan Lehmann? She had paid him to do so. She would invite him and find out what had happened. Then the association could be wound up once and for all.

~

The man Miriam Fischer was to marry in a month's time, Herr Stauffer, was a little too taken up with a young woman. Miriam could see him from beside the Derain landscape she had been enjoying in spite of her dislike of its owner. To do him justice Herr Stauffer seemed as much mesmerised by the girl's waving ostrich feather as her person. Miriam had no doubt that she was talking the most superficial nonsense, larded with flapper slang that Herr Stauffer would be pretending to understand.

She turned back to the picture. She no longer saw Derain's red and purple trees. They were a screen on which she projected grim thoughts. How was it that older men went like moths to such a flame? They preferred an hour of giggles and boastful claptrap with a girl of twenty than decent talk with an intelligent woman their own age. The only thing to entice them away was another man! Business, politics, the world of men's affairs. It could be even harder to prise Herr Stauffer away from 'serious' discussion than from a pretty dunce like the one he was leering at now.

'No, it is we middle-aged women who suffer.'

In his own way Hugo had been as bad. 'Men ignore us. Other women, that's who's left for us. Men are a dead loss.' She watched them again. She wasn't jealous. It was closer to indignation and contempt.

And yet...

A stab. She looked at the floor. She must move away, sit down, find a quiet corner. If anyone saw her...

Hugo *had* been like that. It had gone on for years. It had had nothing to do with her being middle aged, she'd still been young. Then there had come a miracle ending all the pain and grief. Anton. She had known love at last. Then that too had died. By a painful paradox their love had become impossible the day Hugo had died.

Free to love elsewhere with her husband dead, she had only discovered an incompatibility with her lover, highlighted by the crisis they were all living through. In their desert captivity ties of kin and race asserted themselves. History locked Anton, Magda and Eva together; she, the Jewess, was the outsider. The illusion faded. She saw Anton as ruled by women, a maverick with unrealisable dreams. And yet even now she knew she still loved him. It didn't matter that the world could see he was no hero. He had saved her life.

'Anton, where are you now? I would forgive everything...'

She closed her eyes. Then – how unfortunate – the band, having played nothing but shimmy and New Orleans stomp, broke into a sad, sad song.

The song was new, it was everywhere, the cafes, the wireless. Anna kept playing it on the phonograph. And now here it was again. Tears on a clown's face. Death at night. Suicide. Oblivion. Miriam bit her mouth, humming inaudibly, her head lowered. She might choke. She steadied herself on a chair.

'Frau Fischer?'

Miriam was startled from her reverie. Werner Gustavus stood over her.

'It is Frau Fischer, isn't it? Are you feeling unwell?'

She grimaced.

'I congratulate you on your engagement.' He nodded in Herr Stauffer's direction. Miriam said nothing.

'Can you help me Frau Fischer. I have been looking for Anna.'

'She will be here soon.'

'I've been practising to do the Black Bottom with her.'

Miriam stood up, struggling to recover herself. 'She is coming soon with her...'

A shriek came from behind. 'Herr Gustavus. Just the person I'm looking for!' Frau Vogel burst between them. 'Do excuse me, dear Frau Fischer. There's a most important conversation going on over there and I demand that Herr Gustavus gives his opinion.' She laid her hand on Miriam's arm. 'We must find out what the young think, don't you agree,' she declared, leading Werner off and abandoning Miriam to her unpleasant thoughts.

'He'll find out soon enough, the sooner the better,' Miriam murmured to herself as she sat down again, waving her fan and trying not to look at Herr Stauffer with his flapper girl.

'And did you meet Herr Lehmann in Venice?' Frau Vogel asked Werner as they pressed through the throng.

'Yes. I was going to contact you and then the invitation came. I…'

'Tell me about it later.'

They had come to the fireplace. Grouped incongruously were a number of older people Werner recognised as Dresden art world figures: gallery owners, art teachers, critics. They shifted in their seats and hardly seemed to be enjoying themselves. Perhaps they were just shy, or the noise made it an uncongenial place to talk. If it had been an important conversation as Frau Vogel had claimed, it had petered out.

Frau Vogel gave the pot a good stir. 'Bettina, weren't you just saying…' She addressed the painter Bettina Feistl-Rohmeder of the German Art Society, enthroned on a high chair beside the crackling logs. '…that the moderns do nothing but distort and deform. I must say that with my Matisses and Kandinskys hanging all around us, I felt just a teeny bit attacked – though Bettina, you were as tactful as ever!'

'Here, young man, have a seat,' said one of the group.

'Yes, Herr Gustavus, take your place and tell us where *you* stand,' urged Frau Vogel.

Werner was still pondering his encounter with Miriam. He sensed that something was afoot in that quarter. But for now he must put that to one side. Perching on a stool he looked across at Bettina.

'Young man, have you read our magazine, the *Deutsche Kunstbericht?* We hope to persuade the young.'

'Er... yes, I... understand your desire to build the country back up.'

'Indeed. We want the removal of war blame, the revision of Versailles, a return to the borders of the Reich. We want…' She was probably going to say 'measures against the Jews' but checked herself, knowing there must be Jews in the circle. 'We want... a return to pride in German greatness.'

'Well, that bit I agree with,' nodded Werner.

'I am pleased to hear such healthy sentiments from a young artist. There are so many would-be Leon Trotskys among the city's intelligentsia.'

'I...'

Bettina raised both hands as if to say, hold on, wait to hear what I have so say.

'Art,' she declared, 'is the product of the soil, or if you like, the atmosphere of the time. How can a face with three eyes or childish blobs of colour reflect life today?'

Werner looked around at the circle to gauge the effect of what he was about to say.

'If... if I may say so...' he stuttered, 'b... better than Nordic imitations of Greek friezes.... or rustic scenes that would have pleased our grandparents.'

The circle stirred. Some nodded, others tutted and shook their heads.

'How little you understand us after all, young man!'

'Madam, if I may say so, your *volkisch* state will get nowhere if it loses itself in dreams of the past.'

'That's not it! We draw on the past to mould the present! The *volkisch* state will provide the right subjects – leaders, soldiers, workers, the heroic deeds that will accompany the birth of the new state. Who knows? New conquests surely.'

'That kind of art is *ersatz*, false.'

This was the signal for uproar.

'Nonsense!'

'Hear, hear!'

Everyone spoke at once. Arms were waved. Insults flew. The irony was not lost on Werner. He who had been so recently crushed by Stefan's critique of his conservatism was suddenly the champion of the avant-garde. The modernists grouped at the fire were now emboldened to fling curses at Bettina. From her throne she gave as good as she got.

Frau Vogel drifted away happy that things had 'taken off'. Bettina lectured. The modernists scoffed at her and congratulated one another.

But Werner's attention had shifted elsewhere.

He had seen Anna framed in the doorway. She stood still and was gazing intensely at something or someone out of view.

He had never seen her look so beautiful – so modern and fresh. He wanted to scream, to rage, to burst into tears. His Anna. What had happened to her? Who had done this?

She wore a tiara, diamond earrings and a necklace he had never seen before. Her golden hair had been cut to emphasise – surely it was the first time in her life – the sculptured beauty of her neck and shoulders. Her dress hung off her like the leaves of an exotic fruit. Its pale velvety green harmonised exquisitely with her natural colouring. The outfit was fabulous: treading a rare line between fashionable and original.

Suddenly – overnight – Anna had grown to the apex of her beauty.

He trembled. He must claim her, make love to this vision before she floated off to the heavens or into the arms of someone else – for surely, as she now appeared, no man would be able to resist her.

'Hey, Anna!' Leaving Bettina's circle, he tunnelled his way through the crowd. 'Anna.'

He was near but she didn't hear. Still she did not move. By now she was listening to a strikingly handsome young man of Jewish appearance. The conversation seemed intimate, familiar.

Who was this man? Why didn't Werner know about him?

There was a voice at his shoulder. 'Perhaps I should introduce you to Anna's cousin.'

Werner turned. Miriam, drawing on the cigarette in her mother-of-pearl holder, had regained her composure and had clearly marked him out.

'Why, yes.'

Still the cousins were talking. Neither of them had noticed they were the object of attention.

'However,' said Miriam, 'there is something you need to know.'

Werner was filled with foreboding.

'Frau Fischer, I know you have opposed my association with Anna. I don't altogether know why, as you yourself were willing enough to carry on with my father.'

Miriam blushed. 'Please do not mention your father any more. That is all in the past. Perhaps we could talk about you – your purposes. From now on you may need to be thinking afresh.'

'I have a purpose.' Even as he said this he knew that his purpose was about to be ripped from him. 'I have survived these difficult times. Anna and I have stood by each other. We will continue…'

'I am sorry to say nothing will continue.'

'What do you mean?'

She offered him a cigarette. He took it to steady his nerves.

'I do know,' said Miriam, 'that you and Anna love each other. However, I am afraid she has been deceiving herself believing that your love could win out – I don't think she was doing it deliberately by the way. Deep-down she always knew that she would have to make a suitable match. Ever since we came back here she has known that all roads were leading to David. He is wealthy, an already reputed leftist lawyer. He keeps agitators and trades unionists out of prison. Furthermore she likes him. She just didn't have the heart…'

Werner was dumbfounded. 'But we planned… We share everything. We look at things in the same way.'

'When she was younger, maybe, before she knew the world. Palestine and the war threw the most unlikely people together. Without that I don't suppose your father and I… But now that normality has at last returned... you and Anna are no longer suited.

David and Anna however... And she knows that...'

'Frau Fischer... I...' He was speechless. 'Please excuse me.'

He broke away from Miriam and hurried to Anna who now stood alone again in the doorway.

'Anna, what is this?'

She looked down. 'Werner, I can't talk about it now. My cousin's coming back soon with a drink for me.'

'You're going to marry him!'

She gazed at him imploringly. 'Werner, don't...'

'Don't what!'

'I was going to talk to you.'

'But last time...'

She shook her head. 'I wasn't ready to face it. My feelings for you were too strong. I didn't want it to spoil it.'

'Then it's true.'

Staring at the floor, wounded and guilt-ridden, she struggled to find words.

'However much I love you,' she said mournfully, 'we couldn't go on. Mama would never accept it. You have no money or prospects... You're not Jewish... I... didn't think... We would have had to...'

From the other side of the room, David was approaching with two filled glasses. Anna put her hand on Werner's arm and turning in towards him breathed a half-suppressed sob.

'Werner darling, you are my true love.... always...'

'Then come with me.'

'I can't.'

'This is your final revenge for the Valley of Rephaim!'

'No!'

David was upon them. Werner turned and stumbled away.

'I must get out of here,' he murmured, clutching the doorpost. 'I think I'm going to be ill.'

~

Later that evening he was due to meet his *Palästinadeutsche* cronies, Helmut Kappel and Emile. They'd come over from Munich partly to see him but also for political purposes.

The street was empty but for a receding line of lamps. Behind him were the lighted windows, the band, voices. Three figures, just shadows, loitered a little way off. He paused. They came nearer.

'Werner!'

'Oh Emile, Helmut. It's you. Hey, I thought we were meeting at the station later.'

'We got here early. We knew where you were so we thought we'd come and have a look.'

'It's some place, isn't it?'

'You're friends with the idle rich?'

This was the third man, a square-faced muscular boy in a shirt with rolled up sleeves though it was winter.

'This is Ernst. He's a Dresden comrade.'

'Comrade?'

'We're here to recruit,' Helmut explained. 'The NSDAP is galvanised. Adolf Hitler is on the way up. There's a big push on.'

Ernst whistled. 'Look at that.' He pointed up at a first floor window. A man and a woman in silhouette were kissing. 'Jews kissing. Disgusting! They're all Jews in there. Jews run this city – Jews and bolshevists.'

'I've just been in there. So what if there are Jews. They're not *all* Jews.'

'Ah, my friend, you obviously haven't seen the light. Don't you know how we all suffer at the hands of the Jews?'

Werner turned to Emile. 'I don't agree with you lot at all. If this is how far you've taken your ideas, Emile, why didn't you tell me? This might have to be the parting of the ways.'

The three young men looked at each other and shrugged.

'It's up to you.'

'I'm going home. Good-bye.'

'No, come on, stay. We'll all go and have a drink and talk about it. Maybe Ernst here overdoes it. It's not all about the Jews. There are lots of ways needed to restore the Fatherland.'

Werner hesitated. The others were moving away. He looked at the pavement, then closed his eyes.

'Anna, don't do it. Come back to me. I've done no wrong.'

His thoughts were shattered by breaking glass. Emile and Helmut were already halfway up the street. Ernst was picking up another stone. He hurled it at a second window. More glass broke, then Ernst too ran for it.

The band stopped playing. There were shouts and doors opening. The woman in the window was bent double, clutching her head.

Chapter 17

The bus driver grunted. Stefan, sweating in the midday heat, was using his best phrasebook Hebrew. Didn't the driver understand?

'Is this the bus for the German Colony?' he repeated.

The driver tutted and looked away.

'It's the next bus, behind,' said one of the passengers in German.

'Here it is,' called Clara.

And sure enough another bus drew up as the first left. They carried their flat package on to the bus and found a seat where they could lean it out of harm's way.

'We should have got a taxi.'

'I hate to do that when the bus goes straight there. It'll be all right,' Stefan added, patting the package. 'It's well-travelled!'

The foreign couple hardly attracted attention – for who wasn't 'foreign' here in Jewish west Jerusalem? – crop-haired Stefan in smock and cap, Clara in light, tailored cottons. Among the passengers were workers with open-necked blue shirts and bare-legged 'modern' women. Others were Jews in traditional garb.

The bus left the noise and dust of the terminal and started on its journey through a placid suburb. They cruised along boulevards lined with young trees, shops and flat-roofed villas. They strained up, crowned the curving hills, swooped down again into green valleys. There were plenty of stops. The bus became more crowded.

'I'm no Zionist,' murmured Stefan, 'but the one merit I saw in the Zionist experiment was its secular nature. However, I've seen more *shtetl* Jews in Palestine than anywhere else in my life.'

'There are plenty of modern people too. Look at these suburbs.'

Stefan was troubled. 'It all seems so fraught. There's an agitation in the air – and that's before you even notice the poor Arabs. It's their home. No wonder they're up in arms.'

'Time will tell.'

'I'm not optimistic.'

She grasped his hand. 'You're a wanderer, Stefan. You don't want anyone calling you home, telling you *this* is where you belong. Your politics comes from your psychology.'

'I'm not going to argue now – not in this heat, not in a crowded bus.'

'And not with your mission reaching its climax.'

The bus trundled on.

'German Colony,' shouted the driver in Hebrew and English.

They took their packet and clambered down. The bus roared away and they stood for a moment in the heat, gazing with momentary hesitation at the Colony entrance. Not a leaf moved. The cicadas rasped. The hills shimmered beyond.

'What a long time… '

Clara looked at him anxiously. 'Are you all right, Stefan?'

'I just hope we get a welcome. Magda never liked me. Anton may not have forgiven me.'

They entered the Colony and passed down the leafy street between the neatly laid out stone villas.

'The piety fills me with gloom,' said Stefan peering with distaste, as he had three decades before, at the scriptural mottos carved above the doors.

'You're gloomy anyway.'

'I'm nervous, Clara.'

'It will be fine. What you are doing, it's a good thing – for everybody.'

They found the Gustavus house and Stefan knocked on the door. A plumpish, good-looking middle-aged woman opened it.

Stefan removed his cap.

'I'm looking for Anton Gustavus. May I ask, are you Magda?'

The woman shook her head. 'No... Magda died.'

'Did she? Oh dear... I'm sorry... And Anton?'

'He's all right.'

'Oh, good.'

'I am Eva,' said the woman, to relieve the visitors of further awkwardness.

Stefan was taken aback. 'Eva… then we've met before – a long time ago to be sure. I'm Stefan Lehmann. Of course you cannot recognise me. Maybe you don't remember me. Why should you? And this is my wife Clara.'

'Hello Stefan, and hello Clara... Well, what a surprise, but do come in. Anton is out. He won't be long.'

Stefan did not hesitate once they were seated indoors.

'Eva… what happened?'

'Magda died of pneumonia in the winter of '21.'

'And you… patched things up with Anton?'

'I was back at the Colony after the war. I helped nurse Magda. Afterwards Anton and I were both alone, with no children. The Colony had forgiven me. The ones who remembered the "scarlet woman" were dying off. I teach the little ones. I am a pillar of virtue! Even Anton has mellowed.'

Clara caught for a moment the whiff of old passions.

'You've painted Anton a picture?' Eva asked brightly, glancing at the packet propped against the wall.

'I… would like to tell *him* about it.'

'Fine. And you, Frau Lehmann, how did you meet Stefan? But first let me get you something to drink. Mint tea?'

Tea was fetched and the story told briefly. Their little son was mentioned, Stefan's recent artistic success and Clara's job briefly described.

'Does Anton still do his carvings?'

'Not so much now. He's become interested in miniatures, engravings, things like that, and printing. The carving business was finally killed off by the war. We've made something of the garden too, in recent times. I'll show you.'

She led them out to the back. The garden was a mass of colours, of trailing plants, with rows of aubergine and tomato plants, palms and cactuses.

'An oasis in this heat,' breathed Clara.

'A vision of peace and plenty,' echoed Stefan.

There was a noise behind. In an instant the big man was there, filling the doorway, peering, disbelief spreading across his face.

'Stefan?'

They collided in a fervent embrace.

'My old friend, Anton!'

'I didn't recognise you with no hair. It's been too long.'

'It certainly has, you devil!'

'I'd given up hope of ever seeing you again.'

'I know, I know.'

'It was up to you, Stefan. I'm stuck here but you can move about a bit. Anyway now you're here. Do you have your toothbrush? Can you stay with us?'

'Not only my toothbrush, but my wife...'

'You're married? Then this must be the lucky woman…'

'Yes… And I'm a father. We have a little boy. We left him at home in good hands.'

After the introductions they went back inside. Eva brought more refreshment for the visitors and the conversation turned to politics. Anton's eye had fallen on the German language newspaper Stefan had put on the table. The headline included the name 'Jabotinsky'.

'What do you think of him?' asked Stefan warily.

'Well, Jews here may have to fight.'

'I thought you were a pacifist, Anton.'

'The world is not what it was before 1914, Stefan. New forces have been unleashed. Murder and fanaticism call for a different response. It's no longer nation against nation.'

'From what I've read Jabotinsky is a fanatic.'

'I don't think so. If you lived here... The Jews deserve a homeland.'

'Ach, it'll never work, Anton. It's all going on just as I said to Hugo it would in '98. Polarisation. Chaos. Tel Aviv for example. We've just come from there. A British soldier on every corner. In this kind of situation, men of goodwill are marginalised. Arab threats. Jewish threats. The extremists calling the tune, Jabotinsky for the Jews, the Mufti here in Jerusalem for the Arabs.'

'Now there's an extremist, Stefan! How should Jews counter that? You can't just lie down and wait to be annihilated. Men like the Mufti believe in murder pure and simple. The British are on the Arab side, what's more. The Arabs are innately servile, more ready than the Jews to bend the knee to a colonial power.'

'Nonsense. The British can see that the Arabs are the aggrieved party!'

'And you a Jew, Stefan!'

Anton cocked an ear. 'Ah, hear that?'

'Singing?'

The sound of male voices penetrated the little room.

'Beautiful,' murmured Clara. 'But eerie, not what I would expect.'

'They used to sing homely, harmless stuff,' said Anton, 'but not anymore. Listen carefully. You'll recognise it.' The song had a martial rhythm, rose to a height and ended with hoots and foot-stamping.

'Of course,' said Stefan. '*Morgenrot*.'

'That's it. Doesn't it take you back to 1914? Gone are the folk songs and hymns, it's all *Soldatenlieder* and *Deutschlandlieder*. Ridiculous when you remember that in 1914 thousands of raw recruits died with these songs on their lips. Pretty soon they had the sense to stop singing them on the Western Front. But years later the news hasn't reached the Jerusalem Germans. What do these idiots know? I have to close my ears once a week when they get together. But that's the German Colony – patriotic, and angry with our current overlords, the British.'

'The British seem to be making a hash of their Palestine Mandate.'

'That pleases the Colonists. But their main preoccupation is with Germany. After the war, returning soldiers infected them with *Freikorps* madness. They think they're in the back streets of Berlin fighting red revolution. They don't like Jews. They think the Jews here are all communists. They don't like Arabs much either but it's the Jews in particular.'

Eva suggested that Stefan might like to see Anton's workshop. The men left the women guardedly conversing in the parlour.

The desk and shelves in Anton's den were littered with artist's equipment: pens, pencils, brushes, paints, chalks, sponges, scalpels, ink pads, paper, engraving tools.

'Looks like you keep pretty busy. What's that?'

Stefan pointed to a bulky contraption with a handle. The floor underneath was stained.

'My printing press.'

'What do you print?'

'Posters, announcements of public meetings, political pamphlets in Yiddish, German, Hebrew – which I can speak a little now by the way. I give most of the profit back to the Colony. They bought me the press. It was my idea.'

Stefan's eye was caught by a photograph of a man pinned to a document.

'Ah, I should have hidden that,' Anton murmured.

'Why?'

Anton pointed to his easel. 'If you look over here... See?'

'The border pattern on the document. It's the same. You're copying it.'

'Correct. It's an identity document for a member of the Armenian church to present to the British authorities when he arrives in Palestine. In that drawer I've got a collection of similar documents bought or stolen. Jews have difficulty getting into this country in spite of Mr Balfour's "declaration". Forged documentation is extremely useful for the Zionists. I started this kind of thing before the war for a Zionist friend. He got hold of documents whenever he could and passed them on to me for copying. Then it was to get round the Turks. Now it's the British. It's all the same. No one really wants the Jews to have a homeland. So I help.'

'Anton, you *are* a fellow. What next?'

'It's what I do with my talents – rather than drown in a sea of idle fancies.'

'Rather than pursue art, you mean?'

'Of all the idolatries in the modern world, art's the worst. It's a bogus religion.'

'You're talking to an artist, old fellow. Careful what you say! However, I agree with you, as it happens. There is a lot of idolatry surrounding art. Clara is very hot on this.'

'Well, I have an added respect for your Clara. What is she, a psychiatrist, did she say?'

'That's right. She argues that whatever art itself expresses, the artist himself is rarely the ultimate source of wisdom. For that we look to the mystics, or perhaps to those who follow Freud and delve into the unconscious mind; maybe also to those ordinary people who through a capacity for love grasp the truth intuitively.' Stefan clasped his friend's arm. 'But Anton, old fellow, here you are, a paid-up gentile Zionist, a damn conspirator. You'd better watch out, hadn't you? Don't get arrested!'

Anton was looking at Stefan strangely.

'Anton?'

The big man turned away. Stefan looked down at the ink-stained floor.

'You're angry.'

When Stefan looked up, Anton was holding a piece of paper.

Stefan sighed. 'My letter.'

'You never followed it up, Stefan.'

Stefan shook his head slowly. 'No, to my undying shame.'

'You didn't go to Germany. I assumed not or you would surely have told me...'

'I...'

Colour rose to Anton's cheeks. He quivered with suppressed feeling. 'Couldn't you have let me know? Do you have any idea what it is like to have my hope re-kindled and then hear nothing? And now you turn up here and...'

'... expect a welcome. I have no excuse other than my illness. I was ill when I wrote to you. Crazed. Permanently drunk. My plan of visiting Germany to look for Johannes was totally unrealistic. I was going to write once I had recovered. Then over time I realised I could do better. I could visit you. Indeed I had to visit because there was something else I had to do. Wait.'

Calling to Eva and Clara, Stefan opened the cupboard where Eva had put his package. The two women came out. All three re-joined Anton. Stefan handed Anton the package.

'Unwrap it, old friend. It's for you. It comes with my profound apology for all my weaknesses and bad actions. It is rightfully yours.'

Taking a knife, Anton slit open the tough board which protected the precious object. He removed it slowly and placed it on his easel. He looked at it, unsmiling.

'I should never have taken it from you, Anton. I recently bought it back from Frau Vogel, the Dresden dealer I sold it to. Now it's come home. It's yours again.'

'It's... a fine likeness of poor Johannes,' stuttered Eva.

'It's a great work, Stefan,' added Clara. 'Though this way of painting isn't fashionable now, it's among your very best. A young life caught in time, yet timeless... moment and eternity. Like Vermeer, like Velasquez in *Las Meninas...*'

Anton had still said nothing. The others watched him nervously.

Out of his silence a howl, beginning as a low moan, gathered and slowly engulfed the room. The women put their hands to their ears.

Anton grabbed the portrait.

'Anton! No!'

'You're crazy!'

Lifting it so high that it brushed the ceiling, Anton smashed it down on to the hard iron of the printing press. The blows went on and on. The picture buckled and cracked apart. Pieces fell to the floor. The last bits of frame were flung onto the pile till Anton's hands were empty, shaking.

'You madman!' sobbed Eva. 'What have you done!'

Anton turned with blazing eyes to Stefan. 'I'm not sitting in this backwater for ever staring at a wretched portrait! If you, Stefan, with your art and your precious insights about yourself can't see what has to be done then *I* will.'

'Anton! Anton... Please...'

He gabbled on in a demented rush of words. '*I* will go to Germany... *I* will find my son Johannes... Listen, he was seen in Dresden in 1912 by the gallery owner... Stefan, your tourist in Venice met him at a recruiting office... He was a German prisoner-of-war, seen by Eva at the prison camp in Sinai... My God! So it goes on. The rumours never stop. The time has come. I'll leave here once and for all. I'll go through all the army records in Germany. After that I'll search, and I'll search. *That* will be my life. Eva, you can decide what to do, but *I* must go and find him!'

JOHANNES 5

After my escape from the POW camp I lived with the Bedouin. Their journeys trading goods across borders brought me back and forth between Transjordan and the Libyan Desert. It wasn't a bad life. I just had to be careful when I slept with their women. They were either virgins or wives. In either case it was a quick route to a slit throat. I began to get nervous.

One day I was selling goods in Khan el-Khalili, the Cairo *souk* which I had known as a boy. I asked after my old gang and drew a blank. Suddenly I caught sight of someone familiar, peering at a figurine in one of the antiquity shops. I made certain and tapped him on the shoulder.

'Do you remember me, Mr Rose?'

Older and frailer, the Englishman looked at me with dawning recognition.

'Ali,' he murmured with quivering lip, 'I would know you anywhere. What mischief have you been up to?'

We moved to a café and talked over coffee and a hookah.

He updated me on my old friends.

'All gone now. To the army, the police, married. *Respectable* at all events. Very disappointing. Your Christian Brothers, by the way, were interned when the war came. They were beastly Germans after all. They haven't been seen since, either. Rumour had it that you relieved them of funds.'

I blustered. 'Well… it all went to a good cause in the end.'

'I'm pleased to hear it, Ali. It was a long time ago and you were a mere child.' He looked at me with tears in his eye. 'You *were* a thief, you know. You stole my heart. I don't know if I ever recovered.' He pulled the mauve silk handkerchief from his breast pocket and dabbed his cheek.

'Well,' I said. 'I've had my heart stolen in turn.'

I told him about Zoraya and the still unthinkable fact that I had abandoned her in her hour of need. He was a good listener. We stayed on in the café and after went for a walk by the river. I realised that now I was grown up I quite liked Rose. By the end of our stroll we had come to an arrangement which suited us both and which set the course of my life for years to come.

Fearing for my safety among the Bedouin because of my womanising, I had been thinking of leaving them anyway. Pondering my options, I had wondered if I might enjoy work on a Nile steamer. My years at Aswan had given me a love of the river, its wildlife and the things that go on around a great waterway. I had thought it might be a good idea to find a base in Cairo, to improve my English – since so many Nile passengers spoke this language – and, so as to progress beyond mere deckhand or waiter, learn some mechanical and nautical skills. Talking to Rose I saw an opportunity to make a suggestion which I knew would make his eyes light up.

Shortly after I went back to the Bedouin encampment to say good-bye and then settled into Rose's flat. Over the coming months I learnt English from him in return for running errands, helping his research and teaching him German – he had always wanted to learn that language to read Winckelmann in the original. Apparently this great scholar fancied boys just like Rose, but he made it respectable by becoming an expert on Greek statues.

At the same time I studied nautical engineering from books in the library. When the time was ripe, I presented myself at one of the shipping companies as an Arabic-, German- and English-speaking ship's engineer.

Not surprisingly I was taken on, to do the long run to Luxor,

Aswan and the Cataracts, and back again.

This became my life. Rose was unhappy when I was away, which was most of the time, but I like to think I brightened his final years. He had cured himself of funny business with me. I put him off in any case by telling him about my affairs with female tourists and visits to my favourite Cairo brothel.

In all the years I passed through Aswan I never once crossed from the town to Elephantine Island. The past was the past. I didn't want to cry again. Assuming Massoud was still there – which I doubted as I never saw his balloon in the sky – it would be awkward and painful to see him without Zoraya.

Then poor Rose suddenly died of a stroke. I was away and never said good-bye to him. I was upset – more than I might have anticipated given that all the 'feeling' had been on his side.

Something changed. Bereft, I perhaps needed to replace Rose. Next time I was in Aswan I took the little ferry to the island and walked through the woods to Massoud's house.

I heard children playing behind the wall in the area where the balloon had once been berthed. I peeped over the wall and saw three children aged between about four and eleven. They were playing with makeshift wooden carts, pulling each other along, tumbling out, squabbling harmlessly.

I was just pondering the fact that the eldest boy looked uncannily like Massoud when the man himself appeared though a gate on the other side.

'Father!' the children called. Massoud bent to embrace them one by one. He looked older of course, more like a grandfather, but I saw how happy he was in the seconds before I ducked down behind the wall.

So Massoud was married and a father. That was a surprise. What was I to do? I felt shy, yet it would be absurd to walk away.

Rather than giving Massoud a shock by popping my head above the wall, I made for the front door and knocked.

A few minutes later I was ushered in to Massoud. It took him a moment but then he rushed to embrace me.

'Ali, my dear boy! You've come back at last. How you've changed. A handsome man in your prime. A little thin perhaps. You need feeding up. Stay with us, we can do that!' He turned to his offspring. 'Children, your mother will be most delighted to greet our guest.'

It was a normal enough thing to say but it puzzled me all the same as he called for drinks and I gave him an account of my life. He listened with rapt attention and kept calling to the children, 'Here, listen to this!'

'Why didn't you visit before, you devil? You must have been here a hundred times.'

I was wondering how to answer this when I heard a woman's voice behind me.

'Ah,' said Massoud beaming, 'here is my wife. Undoubtedly you will recognise her.'

I turned and found myself looking into eyes that had last viewed me helplessly from a snow-beaten window in Switzerland.

'Zoraya!'

She gasped. 'Why, Ali…'

'Yes,' said Massoud, refusing to see any awkwardness, 'our old friend Ali, a ship's engineeer on a flying visit.'

I could feel the blood draining from my face. My heart pounded. Was I going to faint?

'I thought…' I stuttered helplessly, 'you were… no longer with us.'

Zoraya had recovered enough to respond calmly, 'I got better quickly once I had the sense to leave the hospital and Europe.'

'And how… is your health now?'

'She's well,' interjected Massoud. 'Married life suits her almost as much as it suits me, doesn't it, my dear?'

He chuckled. Zoraya did not disagree.

Massoud touched me on the arm. 'We are second cousins,' he

said confidingly. 'The family tie is not so close. When she came back it seemed like the obvious thing. I'll tell you, we've never looked back. Once a year her father visits. We lead an excellent life here, well away from the world's travails. What about that Hitler in Germany? I'm worried about that devil. If war comes, he'll drive the English out of here once and for all. That would be no bad thing, except that he would be worse.'

As he spoke I was looking at Zoraya, desperately trying to gauge her state of mind.

'Children,' she announced, 'it's time for your tea. Are you staying, Ali? We will speak later.'

And with that she was gone.

We did speak, but only once during my few days' stay. Zoraya suggested a walk, I imagine with Massoud's approval. We went through the woods down to the water's edge.

As we sat watching the feluccas glide back and forth, she told me how happy she was with her life. I tried not to show I minded. I laughed and talked. We reminisced.

I reached for her hand. She let me hold it. When I began to stroke it, she withdrew. I had gone too far.

My mood changed.

'So where is *my* place in all this?'

'Your place?'

'Well...'

'Ali, you left me...'

'You said you loved that doctor.'

'What doctor? Oh Ali. I can't even remember his name. I waited for you. You never came. I got a bit better, still not completely recovered. Then the war ended and I left. It's all in the past now. Ali, now you are a family friend. Despite the passing of years you can see Massoud loves you as do I.'

I closed my eyes as waves of pain coursed through me. Then came the explosion.

'This is an outrage! You have betrayed me and our love!'

She started back in alarm. 'Ali! Calm down.'

'Why should I?'

'Are you still not over me?'

'I'm just getting used to what's happened – except that I can't. To think all these years I've been grieving for you…'

'Grieving for me? Ali, how often do I have to say it? You left me!'

I wouldn't hear it. '... And you were just getting on with pleasing yourself. You might have let me know.'

'And how was I to do that?'

It was a fair point. She'd had no idea where I was. She turned and faced me squarely.

'Ali, if you still have your feelings for me they don't belong in the real world. Find a wife, have children of your own. Children help us to put aside the selfish passions of youth. As for Massoud and me, come and stay with us whenever you are here. You will always be welcome.'

I leapt to my feet. 'To hell with this! You saved my life and I saved you! Have you forgotten? First you send me away when you've given up, practically at death's door…'

'I did not!'

'Then you marry an old man. What is it about me you are frightened of, Zoraya? Don't answer. I know what it is. You see in me a lost soul, and that's just what you are. We are the same now as we were in Omdurman, you and I. Lost souls only happy if we find someone who's suffered the same. I'm not fooled. You aren't happy. You've settled for a quiet life when the truth is you would like to come with me across the oceans and live the life of adventure. Come with me, Zoraya! We're twin souls, forever together, battling the devils inside and out. Everything else is a sham.'

She fell silent. The river rippled gently on. Egrets and cormorants winged back and forth. Children waved from a chugging launch. A lone swimmer passed in a bathing cap.

'Ali,' she said at last, 'perhaps I don't have the words to show you how wrong you are, but I will try. True, I bear sadness from my early years. True, you saved me when we were children. True, I fell in love with you as a young woman. But – perhaps through my illness, and maybe too because you disappeared when I needed you – I grew up. I am no longer that person. I am content with my life. I yearn for nothing – unless perhaps for this life I've found never to end. Perhaps that is indeed a definition of happiness though linked to sorrow since everything must end eventually. Certainly I am not longing – I hope you do not find this cruel – for some vagabondage with you across high seas and far continents. Leaving my husband aside, do you seriously think I could leave my children now? This dream of yours is no good for you, Ali. You must wake up to life. I fear for you otherwise.'

Now it was my turn to be silent. I sat down, lowered my head and stared between my knees at the dry earth.

'What happened to the balloon?' I asked after a few minutes.

'It burned.'

'Burned?'

'Spontaneously combusted. There was nothing left. Only cinders. It happened on the eve of our wedding. We were due to take guests up as part of the celebration.'

Her lovely dark eyes fixed on me with sadness and with knowing. We shared the same thought. The balloon had existed to nurture *us*. We had consummated our love in the skies. It would rather destroy itself than violate this sacred purpose.

The old sense of our souls' union flickered between us. Then each looked away.

Never again. Not after that. It was gone even by the time we stood up and returned back through the woods.

It was time for one of those revolutions by which my life has been punctuated. It seems I do not 'evolve'. I sit tight and then on a certain day everything changes. Perhaps in this way I re-live without knowing it the main event of my life, my kidnapping.

After saying good-bye to Massoud and Zoraya, I returned to Cairo and resigned from my job. I longed not for wife or family. Far from it. I just wanted to keep moving.

For a few years I became a wanderer. I have always had a knack for survival. I know how to thieve, to forage, to nose out work in return for board, to sleep out in comfort and safety. I will always take a lift from a passing truck. I know how to clamber on to a stationary goods train and travel hundreds of kilometres. I am good at crossing borders which from my point of view are a meaningless attempt to divide the natural world. What does a deer or fox know of lines on maps?

I travelled east. I was drawn to vast man-made things. Perhaps it began with the pyramids at Giza which I used to clamber up with the gang from the Cairo *souk*. At Hama in Syria I marvelled at the great wheels. At Gunbadh-I Quabus in Persia I stood beneath a huge tower, the mausoleum of a prince built a thousand years ago. I was staggered, struck dumb. After that, I went in search of similar monuments, half-ruined miracles of Islamic architecture, minarets or towers usually of coloured brickwork. As often as not there had once been a town around them but now they were surrounded by steppe or desert.

The lonelier these towers, the more marooned in a dry ocean, the more they appealed to me. I journeyed to the tomb tower at Radkan and further east, in Afghanistan, to the minarets at Jam and of Dawlatabad at Balkh. Coming back west I stood in Turkey high above Lake Van alongside the great Ulu tomb. I stole a camera and still have photographs of these edifices in a box, here where I write.

Eventually I became tired of the desert and longed for the green of temperate climes and for what lay to the west beyond that, the ocean.

Sooner than might seem possible I reached Brittany from Turkey. There I gloried in steep cliffs and dark rocks circled by Atlantic foam. Crewing fishing boats, I crossed to Cornwall where I slept in caves and awoke to see the seals bobbing on the grey waves. Still I was not satisfied. The west of Ireland beckoned. My journey ended in Connemara where I dug peat and returning to the flute after many years, made music at night with local fiddlers.

In the pub at Ballyconneely there was talk of approaching war. It was time to leave. I knew I must travel back far from there. War was one thing that might bar my way to Jerusalem.

Two months later I was at Haifa. I got off the boat on which I had stowed away at Athens. I walked into the city. I don't remember what happened exactly but it began with a woman eyeing me from a doorway. I thought it was Zoraya, so close was the resemblance, the dark eyes, olive skin and lithe figure.

'Are you...?' I stuttered. 'Do you...?' I couldn't think what question to ask that didn't sound crazy.

'You like me, eh?'

'I'm on my way to Jerusalem,' I said stiffly. 'I haven't time to stop.'

She pulled at my arm. 'Come on, let's climb to the temple, in the sunlight up there. Look! From there you can look down on the sea.'

She took me up to the Bahai temple and we looked down. The view across the town to the Mediterranean was superb. 'Here, sit down,' she said. 'Tell me about yourself.'

I told her my story.

She took my hand. 'Stay with me for a while. We can live off the fat of the land. You're a thief and I'm a professional woman. It'll work out.'

The bird called from beyond the shutters. Moonlight fell across her body. I moved my hand across to feel her smooth skin and sense her warmth. She stirred and went back to sleep. I couldn't settle. Zoraya, not Zoraya. I was in heaven and hell all at once. Finally I slept.

When I woke up to footsteps and the shouts of traders she was gone. Next day, and the days following, I climbed up and down looking for her in the streets. I thought I saw her sometimes for a second. Zoraya's face on a passing bus, her back view in the street.

Now I even doubt whether this really happened. My return to Palestine and an upsurge of grief had confused me.

I found my way to Jerusalem, entered the German Colony and enquired whether Anton and Magda were in residence.

'Who's asking?'

'I am Johannes, their son.'

The man I was speaking to stopped in his tracks and looked me up and down unpleasantly.

'Really. Well, if it's true I'm not sure you'll be welcome in these parts.'

'Why not?'

'They weren't popular, at least *he* wasn't. She died. He left for Germany with his fancy-woman.'

Thus began the strange months I spent at the Colony. Initially my arrival caused a stir, especially among the old timers who remembered me as a boy, but suspicion soon set in. Some Colonists took me for a liar and freeloader even though I worked hard for the Colony, others believed me but wanted me out anyway on account of their dislike of my father. No one had an address in Germany for my father and his second wife, Eva. They were history as far as the Colony was concerned. It was only known they had settled in Dresden because that was where they believed *I* was. The news of my brief presence in that city before the war must have reached them.

I stayed with an elderly, sick widow, Irene, who was kind to me. She remembered me as a small child. Apparently I was angelic! My disappearance devastated my parents and they never recovered. It was widely assumed in the Colony that I was dead but my father in particular would never accept that. Irene told me about my brother Werner, a clever boy apparently, a would-be artist, not much loved by his parents. 'They never got over you. They were so preoccupied with their grief there was not much space left for him.' Werner had left Jerusalem for Germany at the first opportunity.

Sadly Irene died while I was there. I became friendly with Maria, the romantic Catholic wife of one of the more ignorant Colonists. Childless and lonely, she walked with me over the Jerusalem hills. We talked a lot and became lovers briefly. After we had been found out I retreated down to the Dead Sea. The Colony was infected by Nazism by then. Maria's husband and some of his Nazi friends followed me down to En Gedi.

Just as I was refreshing myself in the cool waterfall that tumbles in a narrow torrent from the rock above, these brigands charged through the bushes, swastikas aloft, and beat me to a pulp, yelling at me that I was a communist and Jew-lover. The pool beneath that beautiful gush was reddened by my blood. Fortunately I dragged myself out before I drowned. My groans were heard by a good Samaritan, a passing goatherd. He lifted me up and tended my wounds.

I retreated to the caves of the Essenes at nearby Qumran.

What a struggle to limp through that stifling, unearthly landscape to get there. But I reached my goal in the end. I found a cave that was quiet, cool and neat.

Akira's spirit was with me. Under his guidance I sat facing the wall for many a day. I watched my hurt and my memories pass. What were they now? I could let them go.

When darkness fell, the heat of the day dropped, everything was silent apart from the call of night birds and I would sleep. During the night all my good work of the day was undone. I dreamt of Zoraya. She would come to me and wrap herself naked around me to form one body with mine. I would wake sobbing.

It was still dark. I looked out from the cave. I searched for an answer in the twinkling panoply of stars, all the while knowing I could not find one.

Immensity! Distance! How insignificant my sufferings yet still how piercing.

So it went on for weeks, but one morning I woke up and felt different. I was renewed and refreshed. I looked out at the moonscape, barren except for the scrawniest patches of vegetation. I heard the squawking birds. How beautiful was the world, even that arid corner of it. My spiritual practice had helped me after all.

'Enough, I am ready. I know where I have to go now.'

I was soon on the road again.

1934-39

Chapter 18

The evening before, Werner had suggested an outing, a stroll in the late spring sunshine, perhaps a beer or two – a change from their city life.

They took the train early. Werner was in unusually high spirits and only became irritable when little Erica played up, a mild embarrassment in the cramped compartment.

Angela, weary with a second pregnancy, gazed out at the countryside, relishing the hills bedazzled by morning sun. Hawthorn, white and pink, strewn like manna, was bright against dewy green.

Was her husband keeping something from her? She hoped he would relax. This outing had been his idea.

Thank God, twenty minutes out of Dresden they got off. Werner suggested a walk. He knew of a nice circle, not too strenuous. They strolled through the village. Swastika flags flew from the beer-house and all down the street. The Führer's picture was in every window. Villagers came out of manicured cottages and greeted the visitors heartily.

'If it weren't for the flags and the pictures of *him*,' Werner muttered as they left the village, 'it was like an operetta. A paradise of jolly yokels. I prefer country-folk surly and dung-covered. It's more natural.'

'That's the new Germany,' she replied with the irony that had become their stock-in-trade. 'We're all happy now.'

A little way out into the countryside they came to an iron gate. Beyond was a picture-book mansion with window boxes and timber balconies surrounded by a romantic but well-tended garden.

Angela sighed.

'You like it, dearest?'

She turned to him. Her fair hair, caught in the sunlight, framed her rueful smile.

'In a perfect world....' She bent down to Erica. 'What do *you* think of this house, darling?'

Erica gripped the bars of the gate with both hands, pushing her head through as if straining to get in.

'I think she likes it,' said Werner.

'Well, we all *like* it.'

'Shall we buy it?'

She was puzzled.

'I mean it!'

'And how could we afford it?'

'Money's been piling up. I've been embarrassed to tell you... And recently... with that Munich commission. I've brought you here specially, Angela.'

She drew back. 'You had a plan, Werner?'

'Yes.'

'That's why you've been odd.'

'Odd?'

'I don't like such tricks.'

Werner was thirty-six. He had filled out and was more solid, with his professorial spectacles and air of maturity. But sometimes he just seemed like a little boy.

'I hate to be in the dark even in small things. You ought to know that about me.'

'But if I had told you, you would have ruled it out! Especially with the baby on the way. You would have said you didn't want the upheaval. You had to *see* it.'

'Well, I've seen it. Now I understand why you've been strange.'

He recovered himself, reached into his pocket and held up a key.

'Werner!'

'The agent gave it to me.'

She shook her head irritably.

'Look, Angela, before we even step inside there are two things which greatly recommend this place to me. Both are a matter of urgency.'

'So what are your *two things*?'

'One is that last week I was offered a *Juden Wohnung*.'

'A house taken from Jews?'

'They are rewarding successful artists with these nowadays. I hummed and hawed and said I would consider it "in the light of my current domestic needs". We obviously cannot accept such a house.'

'No, of course not.'

'If I can say I've just found a place which is perfect for us my refusal will seem less suspicious to them.'

'I see. And your second thing?'

'Look, you know how impossibly cramped my current studio has become. Well, through this gate, the other side of the house, at the back, you will find...' – he threw out his arms – 'a studio! Large, purpose-built, facing north, with a skylight. It is *perfect.* It was added on by an artist before the war – he died a while ago.'

By the time they had emerged from their inspection and were heading back towards the beer-house in the midday heat, Angela had been persuaded. She could not but agree. It was a house to dream of, and apparently they could afford it.

They moved in without delay.

For a time their new home was to bring Werner and Angela the best that life could offer. Their second baby, Juliet, was born. Erica went to school with the village children. Such indoctrination as there was operated on a relatively harmless level and did not interfere with the basics of education. Angela made no friends among the unsophisticated village women but then she did not expect to, relying for her social life as she always had on infrequent meetings with a core of old Dresden friends. Werner had a telephone installed, which helped. Friends visited and marvelled. To avoid suspicion, meanwhile, she joined the Women's Labour League and occasionally took part in politically neutral activities such as visits to the elderly and cake-making.

Werner made full use of the studio, keeping regular hours. He was never idle and his paintings continued to sell.

~

How had Werner's artistic career taken off, given the debacle of his visit to the celebrated Stefan Lehmann in Venice?

It was certainly the opposite of what he had expected. Stefan had been polite but clear all those years ago: Werner had no special talent. Werner had responded in the moment by saying he would throw the towel in.

But it wasn't so simple. Drawing and painting had become a way of life. When Anna abandoned him, he had nothing else apart from his detested kitchen job. He continued with his art as a matter of habit and to comfort himself. The question of talent stopped bothering him so much. He was thinking about something else: a moral, or perhaps a political question.

He found satisfaction in depicting ordinary people, particularly the working class. He took his sketchbook to work and sketched the chefs and porters in his spare moments. He went to places where folk worked or played: factories and foundries, bus and train depots, road-works, beer-halls, sports-grounds, parks and municipal swimming baths.

He would take someone aside for a sketch which he would later build up in to a portrait, either by inviting the sitter to his room or from memory and imagination. (These works were in a freer, more 'modern' style.) In the library he studied the masters of dynamic group composition such as Tintoretto and Rubens. He himself began to depict large groups, always with a proletarian slant: the masses at work or enjoying themselves in their time off.

The point was not so much whether he was to be the Daumier of Dresden, but that he was devoting his time to a worthy subject: the people.

'This is a humanist enterprise and that's enough for me. To depict the lives of those who have no voice, who are poor and don't have much going for them even though we supposedly live in the era of the Common Man. Let others decide the artistic worth of what I do. I'm honouring the people. I respect myself for that.'

Perhaps he idealised his subjects. Maybe he told the truth about humdrum lives. Certainly there was something powerful previously missing. His palette tended to dark tones, his imagery towards starkness. As well as Daumier, the 'Potato Peelers' of Van Gogh was an influence he acknowledged.

He began to strike a chord. Just before he met Angela, he sold a painting. (This was probably what gave him the confidence to speak to the charming, well-educated girl, a stenographer on her lunch break, who sat near him in the library.)

The picture was the portrait of a beggar, a World War veteran he'd found in a Dresden street, with a stump and filthy bandages. More sales followed, then commissions. There was a small exhibition and favourable notices in the local press. By the time he was married he could afford a reasonable flat in the centre of town, with the hire of a studio nearby.

When the Nazis came to power, Hitler's predilections ruled in the visual arts as everywhere else. Werner was no man of the Right and certainly had no thought to express a Hitlerian ideology – rather the opposite if anything, in that he saw himself as a champion of the workers. But the Führer found in Werner's works (when they were pointed out to him) – and those of a few others to be sure – a template. Those German artists who were not depicting uplifting mythical or historical scenes, who preferred to depict modern life, should be expressing the essential 'nobility' of the 'racial community' undistorted by decadent, 'Jewish' experimentalism.

Werner, who never chose to be a Nazi artist, found he had been unwittingly painting in a style that accorded with Nazi taste.

When the first Nazi-organised 'Exhibition of German Art' was held Werner was a prominent exhibitor at the express request of the Führer. Unusually, but not uniquely, one of his freer pieces also found its way into the parallel exhibition of Decadent Art, confiscated works assembled by the Nazis for the purposes of informing the public what it should deride. Werner gathered that some of his works fitted Hitler's taste so exactly that he would be forgiven for previous lapses. The fact that his paintings, together with many others depicting toiling workers, would have sat just as comfortably in an exhibition of Soviet art of the time was an irony of which Werner was thoroughly conscious and secretly rather proud.

With his career taking off, the love of his wife and children, and with his new and perfect home, the pain of past rejections – of his parents, Anna and of Stefan Lehmann – could at last recede.

As he worked on his canvases in his fine studio, he heard the chattering of the birds, recalled the scuttling in the eaves that had wakened him that morning. He knew that through the door Angela was keeping everything in order, preparing their dinner, making-up and putting on a special frock before he emerged at 6 o'clock.

Once out of the studio he set aside thoughts of work. He would play games with the girls and bathe them. In the summer there would be early evening walks – everywhere as far as the eye could see, rolling hills catching the rays of the setting sun. Dinner with Angela over a bottle of wine was followed by an early night. Lying awake after their lovemaking he would ask himself what he had done, after a difficult start, to deserve such a good life.

As for politics, the excesses of the regime were a worry, but Werner and Angela hoped that once the government felt secure enough, it might relax its hold. Probably it would be better for Jews to find a home other than in Germany. It would cause an enormous upheaval and great distress but once it had happened, the new Germany – having rid itself of elements that it was not happy with – would find its feet. It might become less belligerent, both at home and abroad. Meanwhile this sense of unified purpose and respect for ordinary people shown by the regime – though vulgar in many manifestations – was something in principle Werner and Angela approved of.

In their rural isolation, it was easy for the couple to avoid evidence that might have led to deeper doubts.

~

At the opening of the 1938 Exhibition of German Art held in Dresden, Werner was approached by a Nazi emissary from Berlin.

A senior official in the Ministry of Propaganda, he had been holding court among statues of helmeted gods and bare-backed sons of toil for which he was himself partly responsible. With the lifeless forms towering over him, he caught sight of Werner and beckoned.

'Gustavus, there's something I need to discuss with you. Are you free this evening? It's Führer business.'

His ministry had lately been losing influence with Hitler so the Nazi was all the keener to push forward the Führer's pet projects.

'I... Well, yes.'

Within earshot were other Nazis, sceptics and secret oppositionists. It was suspected – some knew for a fact – Werner was no Nazi. Would he show himself up as careerist, a hypocrite?

'I... I can make myself free, Sir.'

'Good. I'll have a car come for you. We'll go to the Souterrain at Bläsewitz. I gather their *foie gras* is excellent.'

Those around turned away, murmuring.

'Gustavus?'

'I thought he was under suspicion.'

'That's a turn-up.'

'Must be a commission.'

The details of the evening's arrangement concluded, Werner looked for Angela. She was standing, loyally it felt to him, by one of his own pictures, some harvesters he had painted since moving to their new home. She wore navy, with a becoming white hat. With make-up and hair done that morning, she looked like Dietrich herself, far from the countrywoman of recent times.

'I wonder how she'll take this.'

She took it, when they spoke, as he took it – warily, yet with a tinge of excitement. Werner might get the chance to express something good and true, whatever was on offer. No question, he had to dine with the man from Berlin. What was more, it might have been dangerous to refuse.

At 8 o'clock he was peering into the dining area of the Souterrain. It was alien territory. There was unlikely to be anyone he knew among the uniformed SS and SA with their overdressed wives and girlfriends. But he could take it. Maybe he would confess over dinner that he knew all about fine restaurants from the other side of the food hatch.

'Can I take your coat, Sir?'

'Thank you.'

'You have a reservation?'

'I… think so.'

'Name of?'

He gave his host's name.

'Ah yes, we're expecting him,' the man said in a tone of disdain so subtle it might have been missed. 'Please wait here. Can I get you a drink?'

At that moment the Nazi from Berlin arrived with a flurry, briefcase in hand. Staff and guests parted as if by a law of nature as the two were shown to their table. They sat down surrounded by the civilized aromas and the tinkle of glass and cutlery.

Werner's host came straight to the point.

'The Führer wants a mural, and he wants you to paint it.'

Werner felt the man looking into the recess of his heart. Such men loved fear and doubt. That was what made people putty in their hands.

'I'm... honoured.'

The Nazi smiled. '*Of course* you are honoured.' He paused to taste the wine which had instantly appeared.

They both drank.

'He's noticed your work, as you know. In his generosity of spirit he forgives your aberrations. He likes your good stuff. He knows about your upbringing in Palestine. You live in the right part of the world, near enough to Dresden and to the site. In short, you're the man for the project.'

Werner took another sip of wine. 'And what is the project, Sir?'

'On the way out towards Heidenau, past the zoo, there is a modest neo-classical villa in large grounds. It was privately owned for three generations by wealthy Jews. It is now in our hands. Gauleiter Mutschmann showed the Führer on his last visit here. He was struck by the building and felt it should be put to good use. Speer and he had been thinking around that time about a German "Colonial College", part-college for those destined to serve in foreign parts, part-club for ex-pats, part-museum – to tell the truth the concept is a little vague. The Führer thought the villa – expanded, with Speer's help – would be ideal. When it was pointed out that Berlin was surely the place for such a building, he replied that Berlin shouldn't have everything. The rest of the country would be envious. It will also help tie Upper Saxony into the idea of the Greater Germany, a world-imperial nation. Furthermore, with Austria now in our hands a tilting of the centre of the gravity towards the south would be no bad thing. The institution will celebrate German colonial history in Africa. However, the Führer anticipates more colonies with his intended push to the east. There is no limit to what might be achieved through his diplomatic genius allied with the threat of force.'

Werner was flabbergasted. This was big. Could he take this on? What were the implications? He tried to keep calm enough to ask intelligent questions.

'Where do the murals come in, Sir?'

'They will decorate the main hall under the existing central rotunda and depict a recent episode at the Palestine German Colony in which you yourself grew up.'

'I left there years ago. I confess I don't know the recent history.'

Was this Werner's last bid to say: I don't know anything about this. Don't ask me. I'm not your man.

But if so, his host was too gripped by his theme to notice. 'We sent an agent to Jerusalem. We knew the German Colony was receptive, resentful as they have been of British Mandate rule in Palestine. His mission had to be discreet. The Führer insisted that the British in Palestine shouldn't feel threatened. He still hopes to keep them on our side or at least keep them neutral when we expand to the east in Europe. If we give the English a free hand in their colonies, so the argument goes, that will give him room for manoeuvre where he wants it. The agent held secret rallies in the meeting hall at the Jerusalem Colony. Plain-clothes supporters kept watch outside. Inside, Colonists put up the swastika flag and sang the Horst Wessel song. They sported our insignia and armbands. Speeches were made condemning the Jews. It was a little Nuremburg a stone's throw from Zion! Outside there were English soldiers everywhere. But the agent had the last laugh when he left bringing a group of recruits back to the Fatherland for training.'

Werner nodded cautiously.

'You'll enjoy this, Gustavus. They sailed from Haifa. They waited till the precise moment when they were outside the territorial waters of Palestine – outside British Mandate jurisdiction, that is. Then they donned uniforms and insignia and paraded on the deck, swastikas aloft. As the agent said, "You should have seen the looks the Zionists gave us from their deckchairs!"'

Werner smiled thinly.

'To the Führer this episode is emblematic. He has divided it into four "scenes" which I'll tell you about in a moment. If depicted with the right painterly skill, it will make a marvellous memorial of the heroic early period of our Reich. It will be there when we're all dead and gone centuries from now.' The Nazi looked at Werner keenly, daring him to share his delight in the idea of their both being dead. 'The title of the four pictures by the way is decided.'

'What is it?'

'"The Acceptance of the Führer-Principle by the German Colonists at Jerusalem."'

Werner gulped. This was a mouthful for sure.

The other reached for his briefcase and pulled out a large envelope. 'The Führer has done four sketches to illustrate his idea. Have a look.'

Werner leafed through the four drawings. They seemed hardly more than a muddle of figures with vaguely suggested backgrounds and a few props – a farmer's cart, flags, the deckchairs on the boat.

'The Führer will respect your artistic decisions. These are just suggestions, made by a fellow artist in a supportive spirit.'

'The titles are helpful,' said Werner gamely. He read them off. '"1. The toiling Colonists, noble but unenlightened." I see. They're hammering and sawing and going about their business. "2. The speech of the Führer's representative to the Colonists." That's in the meeting house, a rousing speech. "3. The newly inspired Colonists celebrate the Führer's birthday." Later on in the meeting house, presumably. Lots of flags. That'll be a challenge, to differentiate it sufficiently from the second one given that the setting is the same…'

'I am sure you can come up with something, Gustavus.'

'"4. The Colonists raise their insignia on the boat 12 miles from Haifa (outside territorial waters)." Ah, there are the deckchairs,' he murmured.

Werner paused, wanting to give every impression of a man who had given due weight to an important decision even though he knew he was acting blindly, recklessly and against his truer sense of self.

'Sir, I am immensely gratified to be offered this opportunity. I think I can rise to the challenge. The Führer's compositions offer an excellent basis. I see no reason to alter them in essence.'

'Don't you want to know if you're getting paid?'

'I... well...'

'You will be paid well, Gustavus. Furthermore, a trip back to Palestine to gather local detail is imperative. The Reich will bear that expense too. We want authenticity above all. These murals will receive maximum exposure. Photographs will appear in journals as far away as San Francisco and Tokyo. They must be perfect in every detail. However, that said, I have here in the envelope some useful photographs which our people in Jerusalem have sent us. We told them about the project and the Colonists gave them to us. Still, you will need to go there. All in good time. This is a long-term project. There is no rush, as such. Rome wasn't built in a day, eh? Nor the Sistine chapel daubed in a week, more to the point.'

'The comparison is daunting.'

'Nonsense, Gustavus. Reach for the stars. You can do it.'

At this point the *foie gras* arrived. The Nazi tucked in and wasn't to be interrupted.

Werner stared over his companion's shoulder. He ate, oblivious of the exquisite flavours passing by his palette.

They moved silently from the *foie gras* to the schnitzel.

'Sir, may I share a thought with you?'

'Please do.'

'In the "deckchair" mural – the Jews...'

'Yes?'

'There is an array of types in the Führer's sketch: banker with bowler hat and striped trousers, scruffy Orthodox, skull-capped hagglers. The face of each conforms to an unflattering stereotype...'

'Be careful where you are going with this, Gustavus.'

Werner pressed on. 'With regard to the Jews on the deckchairs in the final mural, I would like to say I am not a caricaturist. I would prefer to avoid that the mural would appear somewhat... propaganda-like if I might put it so.'

The deputy minister dropped his fork. 'Heaven forbid, Gustavus! Say no more, my good fellow. The Führer put those hooked noses in to show *you* they were Jews. He would be alarmed if this international-level masterwork ended up like a cartoon from *Der Stürmer.* No, a subtle portrayal of the racial type will do it absolutely. Have no fear.'

Later, after his agreement in principle to the commission, Werner made a request to his host. He had fortified himself and cleared his brain with black coffee.

'I wonder if I might ask a favour, Sir.'

'Ask away,' came the genial reply.

'It concerns a Jewish family.'

The Nazi official blinked. A half-smile formed on his thin lips. He sensed what was coming.

'Two women, a mother and daughter arrested recently with their husbands. They are innocent of any crime...'

Up went the hand. 'No more now, Gustavus. Petition my office with the details. Mark it for my attention. I will put the case forward for re-examination. I can't promise but I will be mindful of your work for us. Perhaps we can boot them out rather than lock them up.'

Later Werner understood that his companion at the Souterrain was as good as his word. Miriam, Anna and their husbands had apparently left the country. He believed they had ended up in Buenos Aires.

He pictured Anna with a flower stem in her mouth, dancing the tango, forgetful of their days and nights of love in Palestine and Dresden, unaware that it was he who had saved her.

Chapter 19

He stares at the brown envelope. He hasn't opened it since he arrived home from the Souterrain. It has lain on the kitchen table the whole of yesterday with the children buzzing round it. They could have spilt their milk on it. It could have fallen to the floor and been trodden on. Been swept up with books or newspapers when Angela was tidying and been lost.

He hasn't told Angela it contains drawings by that failed artist, the leader of their nation. He fears her reaction. She might say, 'Get them away. We're infected by them. What's more, I've been thinking about it. You can't take on this job after all. You have to find a way to refuse. It draws us in too far.'

This summer day, he is alone, she is out with the children. Heat gathers through the back door. Garden bees hum, grasshoppers chirp. Across the fields birds are swooping. They sing in the nearby trees. Innocent clouds sweep the summer sky.

He reaches for the envelope and pulls out the contents. He glances at the four inept sketches. How can something so timid stem from the hand that holds millions in its power?

'Timid.'

Calmly, defiantly almost, he lights a cigarette. Stefan Lehmann used that word of his own, Werner's work. Werner dare not think that he himself is some kind of Hitler, deep-down an artistic failure. He dare not think that he colludes with power out of this misery; annihilates himself as an artist by surrendering to a base aesthetic. Puffing on his cigarette, he manages to feel comfortable about everything.

He turns to the photographs. On the top of the little pile is a uniformed SS man. At the Souterrain his host explained that this was the agent who 'converted' the Colonists. 'He is not handsome, I'll grant that, but you can *make* him handsome, eh Gustavus, a veritable Siegfried. He was the hero of the whole thing after all.'

The other photos had been sent for authentic background and *dramatis personae.* 'We want verisimilitude with these murals. It's a prestigious project.'

Werner fetches beer from the larder, pours it into a stein, sits back down, takes a gulp and lights another cigarette. These photos show what used to be his home. What's it like now? Is he going to recognise people twenty years older?

The trees have all grown taller. The Colony is leafier and looks better established, more settled into the terrain. The views around show a land more built on, though the walled city in the distance is unchanged, likewise the grandly curved hills.

Group photos. They seem to have been taken on special occasions. Men, women and children dressed in their Sunday best and posing formally. One or two faces seem familiar but he can't be sure.

Finally, a clutch of studio portraits. These images are more 'modern', crisper. A professional photographer, for sure, although the sitters – all men – are dressed casually with open-necked shirts. The pictures are in the current photographic fashion, starkly lit monochrome, no clutter, each face plainly captured.

'Who did these? An artist for sure. Perhaps a Jewish refugee from Berlin or Vienna who has ended up with a studio on the Jaffa Road...'

He turns the first portrait over. As he anticipated, there is a studio stamp. The name is Jewish but the address is not the Jaffa Road but a street he doesn't recall. Also, someone has helpfully pencilled the name of the sitter.

'"Hermann B." No, I don't remember him... The next one – he's an interesting old bird. “Walter T.” Walter, yes, I remember him, he had a good singing voice. A fine singer but a bit of a bore.’

He looks at them one by one – some he knows, some not – until he comes to the last.

This one strikes him. A thin-faced, middle-aged man, chin on hand, looks straight into the camera lens. No bumpkin, he is cool but not cold; a man of intelligence.

‘Who is this?’

He turns the picture over.

His heart bangs against his ribs. He turns swiftly back to the image.

‘Well, I did not expect that.’

He stands up, steadies himself, walks around the table and out into the garden. He surveys the summer abundance of flowers, the reds, pinks and blues. A blur, a mere haze. He shuts his eyes.

‘Well… well… “Johannes G.” Is it you? Have you returned?’

Back indoors, he props the picture against the stein and gazes.

‘My brother... after all this time... so I’m going to meet you... and when I’ve done that... looked you over... heard the story... I’ll have to tell Father because I feel in my bones he doesn’t know...’

He finishes his cigarette, then gets through another, and another.

~

Ships sirens, mariners and dockers shouting. Creak of cranes and winches. Trucks stacked with crates rumbling along the quay. New arrivals calling for luggage and taxis.

As he tramped down the gangplank suitcase in hand, the heat and smells assaulted him. Ships oil and fish; floating into his nostrils too, market smells, of carcasses, vegetables and baking bread, spices, chicory, dung.

All parched and distilled by heat.

The East. His young life.

He was back where he came from.

He ambled from Haifa port towards the scruffy city. The contrast with the Aryan capsule that was Hitler's Germany dazed him. The shock to move among unharassed Jews – businessmen who in Weimar days would not have looked out of place on the Alexanderplatz, Zionist pioneers in shorts, blue-shirted workers, ringletted Hassidim. Outnumbering the Jews – for still, as he saw, Haifa was an Arab city – were their semitic brothers, from 'modern' Arabs to fellahin pushing barrows or crouched in shady corners. All kinds of women, from Hollywood girls to respectable matrons to Biblical carriers of clay pots. Who was Jew and who Arab? What a medley. Then the overlords, the gingery, pale-skinned British. Police on the beat, soldiers with fingers on triggers.

Deciding it was too late to travel on that day, he checked in at a down-at-heel pension where he was greeted by a striking receptionist, a mature woman with dark provocative eyes and gold earrings hanging down through thick black hair.

After a rest, he climbed up Mount Carmel. The dome of the Bahai temple gleamed in the late afternoon sun. In the gardens he watched the sun dropping out of a clear sky into the darkening Mediterranean. With the panorama before him he came up with an idea for the next two days. On a detour via Galilee he would re-visit places he had gone to long ago with Anna.

The receptionist – by now it was clear she was the owner – knocked on his door around midnight and asked him if he wanted anything.

'No… no thank you.'

He felt foolish in his dressing-gown, a stiff bourgeois. For a few minutes after he closed the door he rued the code of marital fidelity by which he lived.

In the morning, after they had indulged in small talk, she said, 'Tell me, do you think I am an Arab or Jewess?'

He had thought she was Jewish but he said he didn't know.

‘My father was a Jew from Sidon,’ she explained, ‘and my mother an Arab hotel owner here in Haifa. This hotel actually. My father was a guest. I was the result of a brief liaison.’

‘I see.’

As he looked away awkwardly, she challenged him. ‘You are haunted by Palestine. I can see it in your eyes. Whatever you have left behind at home, Palestine is your mistress, the one you love.’

‘I don’t know… I grew up in Jerusalem. Now… It’s complicated.’

‘It’s always complicated here in Palestine,’ she said, touching his arm. ‘I’m the proof!’

Fleeing what could indeed have turned into a ‘Palestine complication’, Werner took an ancient bus inland, up into the hills of Safed. The upland air invigorated him. Abundant olives, figs, pomegranates and vines stimulated nostalgic thoughts. After a night in this village of many ruins he descended to the Sea of Galilee. He recalled that beneath hovering storks he and Anna had once swum in the sticky waters near thickets of reeds and papyrus. Later they had kissed in the shade of oleanders.

Finding the spot, he remembered the bathe and the kiss. He was moved to sadness. What a lovely girl Anna had been. Sweet, vulnerable, bright and pretty. What a pair of innocents. How it had hurt him that she had left him for her cousin, a decision that even now seemed inexplicable, so out of character.

Was the Haifa woman right? Was he still caught up with Palestine? Was that all to do with Anna?

He moved on south, to lakeside Tiberius, into Samaria, past Nablus, to Ramallah. Bumping along and viewing the parched terrain through eyelashes dripping with sweat, a different feeling emerged. He was sick of the heat and dry earth, the monotony of grey eucalyptus, the interfering British, and the damned tense, Jew-Arab thing.

He missed Germany, not the fake, whipped-up Germany of the Nazis but the real Germany, its landscape, history and culture; a place epitomized by Dresden more than any other city, a country that would exist long after Hitler was dead and gone. He missed his work. He sorely missed Angela and his girls.

The reality of Palestine was finally providing an answer. His present life at home was what he wanted, what he missed. The past was the past.

The bus deposited him and his suitcase at the Damascus Gate. Tired of ruminating, he was ready for activity; eager for the long walk round the walls, past the Jaffa Gate and on to the German Colony. Over the next week or two he would sketch, take photos and, if he could face it, talk to Colonists about what had actually happened when the Nazi agent had come from Germany.

He was keen to get started, mainly so he could be home as soon as possible.

And of course – with his preoccupations this had become an afterthought – he would at last surely meet the brother he had never known.

~

She held a dagger with the words 'Blood and Honour' engraved on the handle.

'It's my husband's,' she said, fingering the blade with a mischievous half-smile. 'I drew the line at the swastikas on the wall. And the framed portrait of "the little corporal" as the English newspaper here calls him. But if he wants to leave a Nazi knife lying round the kitchen it's useful for carving up a water melon.'

She wore make-up unlike any Colonist he remembered. Her hair, fair and lustrous, was tied up in a fetching arrangement with Arab silk. No, she said, she was no real Colonist but she had married one. She'd been on a Holy Land pilgrimage from Germany and met him on a bus. 'I'm a Catholic. How did I end up here!'

'You have children?'

'No. To have children you have to... And we... don't...'

Werner was mildly embarrassed.

He had made no progress when he'd passed through the Colony gate half-an-hour before. People hadn't recognised him nor he them. The first settlers he'd met were too young. When he mentioned Johannes one said he didn't know him, another said he 'thought he'd gone'. A third was scratching his head when the woman stopped.

'You look like a tired traveller. Let me make you some tea.' She had led him off the main street. 'You can tell me what's going on in the big wide world. In return and I can tell *you* something.'

'About Johannes?'

'I'm your woman – unlucky that I am.'

'Can I meet him?'

'He went – just recently.'

Now, across the table, she watched him light a cigarette. Werner sensed a wish for intimacy. Her sights set on him. Sizing him up. If the business of smoking hadn't engaged him he'd have blushed.

'Let me look at you! I'm not going to eat you! I'm working something out.'

He blew the smoke out. 'What?'

She put her head to one side. 'Do I see something there?'

'What, madam?'

'Please call me Maria – named after the Magdalene herself.'

'Very well, Maria. What are you looking for? I'm Werner by the way.'

'I know. The famous brother.' Still she stared at him. 'Not sure... You're... heavier. I don't mean to be rude – you're a good-looking man. I mean more solid and... comfortable. I can see you're married. Happily, I would guess. He is lean. He is the leanest of the earth. One wanted to feed him up. I *did* feed him up...'

'You know him well?'

'He's a close friend. *My* friend. My husband hates him.'

'He's jealous?'

'Yes.'

Werner frowned. He needed the story. How long had Johannes been at the Colony? Why had he left? Where was he now?

'Clear daylight, please. Not a fog, Maria. What are the facts?'

'I wish I knew!'

'Oh, come on!' This was rude of him. But, as he reassured himself, if people are too open at the start that's a way it can quickly go.

'Very well, you poor man. You've come a long way. I'm not the factual type but I'll tell you all the facts as I know them.'

'I'd appreciate it even though I'm here for quite another reason...'

'Really, is that so? Do you want the facts or not?'

'Of course!'

It was even between them and it was thus that, having made them both tea, she told what she knew, while he listened, his eye fixed on the red melon pieces and the glinting Nazi blade.

'Very well... He was every bit the traveller, a man with hardened skin, worn boots and knapsack. He spoke to our hired workers in fluent Arabic but spoke German awkwardly, with an accent nobody had ever heard before. Soon it was known that Johannes Gustavus, the missing boy of 1898, had come back. He ended up in the house of an elderly widow called Irene. She was sick. He looked after her. I saw him about the place. He didn't say much. For a while he started to be accepted more. He was given work. Then the men started to mutter – he was at the women, it was said. They liked him too much. It was true that he was gentle and sad, and brought out a mothering instinct in us.

'The day came when I got to know him myself. I invited him in when he was passing and we started chatting. After that we became friends. Truly I was his *only* friend. He was reserved with me but less than with others. We felt close. I learned what there was to learn. He was a nomad, a wanderer over the face of the earth. He had been in Egypt, in Germany, in Asia and the far west. He had picked up an education, languages. He is very well-read. He has manual skills and knows how to find work. Over many hours – out walking on the hills or sitting here at this very table – he learned *my* story. I had lots to tell and no one to talk to since arriving here all those years ago.'

To Werner's surprise, Maria's eyes welled. 'He became my life.'

She wiped the tear from her cheek.

'So where is he now?'

Maria was still upset. 'At the Dead Sea,' she sniffed, 'but I'm coming to that. Things darkened. The Nazi influence grew. Intolerance was rife. It was always a tendency here anyway. People thought we were lovers. The men took him for a communist and Jew-lover, and he did nothing to protect himself. "All men are equal – and women as well," he said when put on the spot. "Jews are just people. Arabs too. It's your European white man who causes most of the trouble in the world, lording it over everybody." They started saying he was a fraud. "How come he knows nothing about Magda and Anton? He knew the story of the disappearance before he came here and pretended to be Johannes to be accepted, to get a roof over his head. He's a freeloader." A movement began to get him expelled. One night some of the men marched on Irene's house. He was living alone there as she had by then died. They lit torches and chanted. Communist, Jew-lover, queer – though how they squared that with the idea that he was sleeping with all their women, I don't know...'

Neither Maria nor Werner had heard Maria's husband come in. Peter stood behind the open kitchen door. His fists were clenched. He ground his teeth. It was his chance to find out the truth.

Maria continued, her voice loud from anguish, enough for Peter to hear every word.

'I heard a knock on my door. He was bleeding from blows to his head. I washed the blood away. He said he was going. He'd had enough of the world. He was going down to the waterfall at En Gedi by the Dead Sea. He'd done it before. The Dead Sea was his natural home, he said. He loved to walk along the shore and contemplate the "beautiful deadness". I begged him to stay. I seduced him into making love to me – in my marital bed. I don't care. I'm married to a brute. I was weeping. I loved him. It was his wound, a wound that was deep and cut him off… That made me love him… I couldn't bear to see him go.'

Behind the door Peter did not move.

'Either way he saved me. I will never forget him. And I know he'll never come back…'

Werner shook his head gravely. 'I'm sorry. You have suffered… As for me…'

'Look, you can always get down to En Gedi. He'll be there. Find him.'

Werner hesitated. 'I don't know… The Dead Sea. It's not a place to visit in summer. You can burn to death there.'

'I would go to him like a shot!' she exclaimed. 'I would come with you, so help me. But I can see…'

'What?'

She eyed him shrewdly. 'Something stops you. Perhaps you don't really want to meet your brother after all.'

Werner tapped the tip of the blade on the table. 'I'll see…'

By now Peter was through the half-open front door and heading for the beer-house muttering to himself. 'Jew-lover. In my bed with that Catholic whore. I'll get him.'

~

Coming down in the Ford truck, they rounded a bend and glimpsed the water, a vast bluish expanse lying between the mountains. Patterns spread across the surface, massive sinuous streaks of froth and ripple.

'*Ach*, the place is godforsaken,' muttered one of them. 'Look at it. I wouldn't want to shit there.'

'I've lived here all my life and never been down there,' said the cuckolded Peter, who was driving.

'It's another planet,' said the third. 'I've been but it was a waste of time apart from the waterfall which cools you down a treat. There's nothing there.'

At the bare north end, near where the waters of the Jordan empty and evaporate, the trunks and branches of palms and tamarisks, denuded of bark, encrusted with salt, lay like skeletons on the barren earth. Sulphur was strewn in layers or fragments on the gravel beaches. A deathly brown prevailed. Plants were faun or yellowish. Such wildlife as they saw – desert sand partridges, larks, darting hares, little porcupines, a slinking fox – were brownish too. Only the wheeling chats added the clearer distinction of black and white.

They left the plain and headed down the west side. On the left was the glossy water with the Mountains of Moab beyond. On the right the salt had escaped the waters and followed the rock up the valleys, impregnating the chalky marl and gypsum. Near the cliffs, fresh water running into the salt sea had created nooks of green.

Among these was En Gedi where they expected to find Johannes, lover of inferior races, fraud, homosexual, wife-stealer.

The one who'd been to the Dead Sea before knew where to stop. Peter switched off the engine. The air was insufferably hot and close. Apart from the bell-like song of grackles resounding from cliff to cliff above, there was silence.

'Now let's finish the job,' said the sweating Peter. 'Heil Hitler!'

They took the iron bars from their hiding-place under the seat. Tying on their swastika armbands, they marched in single file towards the cliffs. The bronze-winged grackles swooped and sang their bell-like song. Pulling aside fronds beneath the cliff, they saw the naked man cooling himself under the rushing torrent. His expression was blissful. He shouted with the joy of it.

They plunged in, dragged him from the waterfall and beat him till he fell in the pool. Around him the water reddened.

Pausing to shower themselves in the waterfall, they hurried back to the car and drove away, believing that if the blows hadn't killed him, he would die by drowning in the pool beneath the torrent.

Across the gluey waters of the Dead Sea the Mountains of Moab glowed red. The falling sun cast purple shadows in their deep ravines.

1945

Chapter 20

'Ah, Dresden!'

Anton Gustavus flung his arm out across the river towards the city, its broken skyline sharp against pale blue, a dome or glass roof catching in fierce points the rays of a low winter sun.

'The war has been on for more than five years, but somehow it's survived. A pearl in a blood-soaked abattoir, a jewel on the shit-house floor. I forget food queues, refugees, boy soldiers marching to a certain death. *This* keeps me alive. For a moment I can forget the stink in my nostrils.'

Eva had been listening to Anton's passionate opinions for half a century. She grimaced.

'People keep you alive, Anton, not a city however beautiful.'

'Yes, yes…'

'Me, for instance, and the handful of friends who can put up with you.'

The old man put his other arm round her. He rested his head on hers, feeling against his cheek the plain woollen hat which became her since she was the kind of fine-boned, clear-eyed woman who keeps her looks despite age and circumstances.

'I bow to your wisdom, dearest – as ever!'

'But you're right,' she conceded. 'It's the most beautiful city in the world. I've loved it since the moment I came here.'

Like everyone in January 1945, Anton and Eva Gustavus were hungry, but they never missed a daily walk. They strolled through the picturesque Altstadt, or headed to the turreted fairytale, the

Zwinger. A half-hour in the Frauenkirche or the Hofkirche, could bring calm especially if the organist was practising his Bach or Buxtehude. Then, on sunnier days there were the parks and the zoo.

It was true that recently the walks were more sobering than pleasant. The character of the city had been transformed by incomers. German refugees in their thousands arrived from the east on foot. Others emerged from trains and colonised the area around the station. Many in the streets were starved and frozen. Mothers and children with outstretched arms and haunted gazes, old people laden with bags, the luckier ones trundling pushcarts with kettles and pans dangling, young men with crutches, in bandages and tattered uniforms.

The refugees drifted in, an irregular flood. Like surf surging into inland gullies and receding, they moved up the street, and down again when some rumour of shelter had been confounded. Some gave up and stretched out with blankets in the doorways of empty shops. Many cried openly.

Today the elderly couple had crossed the wide Elbe just to get away a little. Distance returned the city to its natural glory. The view across the river was made more magical in winter stillness. Dresden seemed frozen in time.

~

They had arrived there nearly twenty years before. Anton's destruction of the portrait of Johannes, the shocking climax to Stefan Lehmann's visit to the German Colony, marked a turning point in Anton's life. He left Jerusalem for Dresden believing it was the best starting point for the search..

It hadn't been hard to persuade Eva to leave with him. Though the Colonists had warmed to her, she had little in common with them. Anton was now her life. The fact that Miriam Fischer was known to be in Dresden had not put her off. She had watched Anton and Miriam's passion wilt in the Sinai desert and knew it would not recover even supposing the two should ever run into each other.

Then there was Werner. His rumoured presence in Dresden had played some part too. However, they had no address for him and, mainly busy with the search for Johannes, they did not track him down.

'If we come across Werner, fine,' said Anton, 'but I can't go searching for another lost boy. I can't put you through it, Eva.' It was only much later, when Werner popped up in the newspapers as a local celebrity that they got to know anything about him at all.

As soon as they had arrived from Palestine they had both found work, Eva as infant teacher, Anton as carpenter. Spare time was taken up with detective work.

They did not have a great deal to go on. A 'possible Johannes' had talked to Frau Vogel, the art dealer, there before the Great War. Perhaps he was the same man that Stefan's Venice tourist had met later at the Munich recruiting office. Then there was the escaped prisoner, the 'Arab', glimpsed by Eva in Sinai.

Frau Vogel had died, so that led nowhere. They searched regimental lists, libraries, local government records, adoption files, national records in Berlin. They came up with nothing.

After a number of years Anton woke one morning with the certainty that the search for Johannes was over – from that day on.

He looked around him and found that he was living in the Nazi state. Everything he believed in was on a path to annihilation. With Eva he became an internal exile, numb, disbelieving, with nothing left in him to fight.

'If I were twenty years younger…' 'If my life hadn't been blighted…' Eva doubted he would have risked his life to oppose the regime. Few did. He was older now – as ever, more philosopher than man of action. That apart, he had improved with age. No longer a philanderer, he was loyal and hardworking.

They lived on a once infamous 'red' housing estate. In the

Weimar era it had housed the workers for nearby factories, bruisers who took on the NSDAP in the ferocious street battles of that time. Here was a reminder of the glory-days in the imposing main entrance to the estate, a pediment supported by a pair of proletarianised caryatids, now forlorn and soot-stained. In the wells and crannies of a buried socialism rats now skipped among excrement left by passing refugees.

Their flat was up some steps and along a windy walkway. Behind the plain front door lay Jerusalem. Anton had re-created his earlier life. Apart from their bedroom, which Eva insisted on keeping tidy, the flat was more workshop than home. Carvings ran along every shelf. Unfinished pictures leant this way and that. There was no spare space on the walls. As well as pots and pans the kitchen housed a lathe and printing equipment.

Arriving in Dresden all those years back, they soon learned that Miriam had re-married. She must have been living nearby. It had been strange to think of that, but something similar had happened before when old friends Anton and Hugo failed to meet in Jerusalem during the first war. It was as if the very thing that bound them separated them.

When Germany's nightmare had begun, Anton and Eva surmised that Miriam would have seen it coming and as a Jewess with funds and connections, have gone abroad. Out of touch with Werner, they neither knew that Miriam, Anna and their husbands had stayed and finally been arrested, nor that Werner had made a plea on their behalf.

Stefan Lehmann wrote a letter to Anton which arrived a few days before the second war broke out. He had moved to London, living in a house with a studio overlooking Hampstead Heath. His Italian wife worked at a famous psychological institute. He no longer drank. His letter breathed contentment, only shadowed by intimations of coming war and the prospect for both of them of internment as enemy aliens. Internment or no, it was hard for both Eva and Anton not to feel envy.

By the time the war came they had retired from work. Their life shrank and by 1945 was reduced drastically. Gossiping in small rooms over ersatz coffee with neighbours. Queuing for food. Radio. The daily walk. Chance conversations, rumours. 'I just met a fellow who says...'

But what did the future hold? Was there some iron in the German soul that meant Hitler's armies would never give in and would even turn it round? Or was it the opposite? A certain day, not far off, a push, a last straw and the edifice of evil would crumble in an instant to reveal its essential hollowness.

Realistically, defeat was coming, and the Americans or the Russians would march into Dresden. But how soon? And like everybody else they said, 'Let's hope it's the Americans.'

Occasionally Anton would ruefully mention Werner. 'I suppose he's sitting pretty somewhere round here, with plenty to eat and petrol for his official car.'

'Werner is not bad, he has just given in,' said Eva. 'I remember him, the poor boy. You weren't much of a father to him.'

'No, possibly not.'

Artistic friends who could stomach official exhibitions – which Anton could not – reported back about Werner's paintings. Evidently they were conventional rather than overtly propagandist. In '39 the local paper had covered the commission for murals in an expropriated neo-classical mansion.

Even if he had the energy to contact Werner, Anton could not face a son whom he now took for a Nazi sympathiser.

~

Stuck in the snow near the forest, Neumann, petty criminal, blackmailer and police informer dreams, but for how long? A minute? Hours?

Snow encasing him. Not cold. Numb. Sinking into a comfort that could soon end his life.

He sees at the edge of the forest a man in a thick coat, big boots and Russian army cap. This stranger wanders back and forth. He seems to be looking for something, but in a distracted way, breaking off to search the sky or scan the horizon.

Neumann sleeps again. In his dream this wanderer's eyes shine and grow huge. They become two lanterns suspended from the branches. The lanterns swing in the winter wind, crashing into each other wildly. The lights fall to the ground, go dark and roll away. The man stands at the edge of the forest with red sockets for eyes. He walks towards Neumann, blind, arms out-stretched. His steps are slow and carry the weight of the sad world.

'Stop, you madman!'

Woken by his own dream-shout, Neumann finds that the stranger remains where he was, some way off at the edge of the forest. He looks ordinary compared to the blinded horror of his dream. He stares. Neumann calls for help but the other doesn't move. He seems to be deciding what to do.

Neumann waves. 'Please...' He believes that his life depends on capturing the sympathy of the starer. 'Do you want me to die?' he calls hoarsely.

He bows his head and closes his eyes. Again sleep comes rolling toward him, a friend ready to embrace him and take away his cares for ever.

How Neumann recovered from this dire situation and made it to the road where he was able to pick up a lift into Dresden, remained a mystery to him.

It seemed the stranger had something to do with it. Did he come silently forward and scoop the snow away with his gloved hands? Did he bend down to revive Neumann's circulation, massaging limb by limb?

Surely Neumann did not dream the rescue, as he had earlier

dreamt the lanterns and the blood-filled eye sockets.

In time, Neumann staggered dazed and unaided to the road. He left the mystery-man just where he was, staring from the forest edge.

The only certain thing was: a man was there, a dweller in the forest who said, ‘I was born in Jerusalem.’

A truck carrying sandbags came. Neumann waved it down. Hunched next to the surly driver, confused by what had happened, distracted by the excruciating pain of frostbite, he nevertheless made a connection.

‘Could this be him? The son of that old Gustavus in my block, who came to Dresden looking for his lost son. How many Germans were “born in Jerusalem”? It must be him. I can turn this to my advantage. I might even hit the jackpot. I can also combine it with my other project.’

Chapter 21

In one of the many anomalies thrown up by a regime that subjected everything to the will of one man, Werner was still working on the Dresden mural commission as late as the winter of 1945. His local reputation was a factor. Dresden business leaders and senior Nazis had bought his works. His idealised depiction, *The Infantryman*, hung in the office of Gauleiter Mutschmann. The Gauleiter chose him for private portraits of his family. Werner had also exhibited in occupied Paris and in Budapest, and in the Great German Art Exhibitions in various provincial cities.

Surely there would now be no colonial college. As early as 1942 German reverses in North Africa must have persuaded Hitler that a German Middle Eastern Imperium was unlikely, never mind an empire spreading over the earth. However, the mural project was not cancelled. Werner drew his salary and had use of a car, the smart Benz.

True, once the war had begun, the building had been used to house foreign workers twenty to a room, fifty in the large room containing the murals, but he could still work there, as they were out during the day. He scarcely ever saw the exhausted and emaciated people that slept in the shadow of his creation.

Werner had first roughed out all four designs on the walls, in wash. He then worked almost exclusively on the first mural, depicting the 'noble but unenlightened' Colonists. He had brought this to its final form.

This huge picture had a special meaning for him. He emphasised the landscape: the trees and gardens of the Colony, the walled city in the distance, the curved hills; over all the pure blue sky. Figures – Colonists, locals – and terrain were swept into a vision: the Jerusalem of his youth. In this first picture there were no Swastikas.

Angela would come and read or knit while he worked. They would agree ruefully about the merits of the first mural and speculate about how it might be preserved till after the war.

'It's your masterpiece,' she had told him a few months before, squeezing his hand and looking with pride into his uncertain eyes – for still after all this time he carried the sting of Stefan Lehmann's rejection. 'It isn't Nazi. It shows Germans going about their business with the Arabs and Jews you've put in the near distance.'

'Well, that's it,' he agreed. 'I was aiming at a subtle universalism. It's a sort of paradise before the Fall.'

~

At dawn Werner woke up shivering. The tip of his nose was an icicle. Sleet peppered the window. He glanced at Angela, her fair strands mixed with grey falling across the bolster.

Pulling the blankets round him, he slid between sleeping and waking. Heaviness of heart merged with guilty dreams.

In a while he got up, put his dressing gown on and looked out at the bare garden. Snow from a week ago lay in grubby patches. The field beyond the gate was as cold and shrivelled as a corpse, the sky its grey shroud. Nothing moved in the black trees and spiky hedgerows. Surely the birds had been spirited away, the rabbits and squirrels swallowed by the cadaver earth.

'What a change...'

Domestically things had indeed altered beyond recognition. Last week he had presented Angela with two Baltic turbot and a pair of nylons, the last bounty that privilege (which had once brought rare vintages, sides of beef, and French perfume) was likely to secure him. She thanked him, but nowadays was tense and wary.

Their daughters were fractious. They no longer rushed breathless and full of stories as he emerged from the studio or returned from a work trip. They sidled round the doorpost and stole suspicious glances.

As Germany was assailed by its enemies sweeping in from east and west, roads in this part of the country were choked with refugees heading westward: Germans who till recently had lived in lands to the east, and Jews being marched back into Germany from extermination camps abandoned to the Russians. By this frozen January morning the Red Army was so close that if the wind was in the right direction their artillery could be heard.

At night the Flying Fortress planes streamed – a long sinister rumble – to their targets, Leipzig, Halle, Leune, Chemnitz. Thud, thud. Thud. Werner felt it in his stomach even when he covered his ears with a pillow or fists. They were all frozen cold. There was no coal, only coal dust. Everyone – refugees, villagers, foreign workers – was starving. The family were living on scones baked from scraps, and potato soup.

The population didn't hide their sullen stares. The sleek Benz made them believe that he was one of the authors of their destruction.

'We can't move for people tramping through the village,' Erica moaned. 'They steal everything and keep knocking on the door – as if we had anything to give away.'

Next week the thirteen-year-old was to report for duty as an auxiliary with the flak artillery.

'I heard people saying bad things about the Führer on the bus,' said Werner's favourite, Juliet, screwing up her face in a shrewish expression that was new and disagreeable to him.

'And they write on walls,' added Erica.

'It's to be expected,' said Werner, ever the calm explicator.

Explaining the nightmare had become second nature. Thus he avoided knowing it properly, feeling it.

He had survived and prospered. Prosperity must surely end but there was still survival. He narrowed his eyes at the bleak landscape. Detachment was essential – and must continue.

'Now for the Twilight of the Gods – and whatever lies beyond.'

~

He was calling on a friend in Neustadt, next to the street where the Fischers had lived. Emerging from the visit, he felt a pang of nostalgia. Should he turn the corner and walk past the Fischer house? It might sadden him but there would be reward in it: a richer sense of the past, a sharper perception, perhaps, of his own merit in standing out against dangerous times and saving Miriam, Anna and their husbands through his risky appeal to the Berlin high-up over dinner at the Souterrain.

He took the turning and strolled towards the house, recalling various episodes from two decades before: his confrontation with Miriam in the grand hallway; hiding in the bushes in the days before he met Anna; midnight kisses behind the big lime trees. Hadn't they carved their names? Perhaps he would have a look if he could remember which tree.

He stopped in front of the house itself. Like the others he had passed it had fallen on hard times. Chunks of plaster had gone, paint was peeling. The front gate was hanging off the hinge, the garden a wasteland.

'Used to belong to Jews,' came a voice from behind. He had not noticed a woman wrapped in winter scarves come out of the next-door house.

He turned.

'Yes... I knew them.'

She pulled her fingertip across her scarf-enfolded throat. They were dead, she was saying.

'No, I don't think so. They went away. I.. .' He thought better of saying more.

The woman checked to right and left.

'Theresienstadt,' she whispered.

'What?'

'Martha over the road was friendly with the Mrs. She got a card from her from Theresienstadt. She and the daughter were there. They'd already been separated from their husbands. Then who knows what? She heard nothing more.'

Werner shook his head. 'No. They got to South America – Argentina in fact.'

'South America? No, no. They were in the east. Probably worked to death. Pity. I can say it to you. They were good people, cultured, you know what I mean?'

A chasm opened up in front of Werner. He stared at the cracked pavement.

'Well, let's hope... These things are always uncertain...'

The woman walked off. Now his thoughts were racing. Angela had found out – he had tried to forget it but now it was close to home – that Theresienstadt, a so-called model colony with shops, and even an orchestra, was a hideous lie. The Nazis had made a propaganda film about it. It was all fake. Only last year the Red Cross had issued a positive report, but they had been tricked. Everybody knew it. Those Jews who weren't worked to death there were sent east for liquidation. Either way Theresienstadt meant certain death. Angela herself had it on authority. And if this Martha had had a card from there...

His heart beat hard. His head swam, he was about to faint. Leaning biliously against the front wall of the dilapidated Fischer mansion, he knew. His 'good deed' was a fiction. Like the Red Cross he had been hoodwinked. Anna, Miriam and their menfolk were dead.

And how did they die? Miriam, the man she married, Anna's decent-looking husband, the cousin... And Anna herself – Anna who sang and danced and filled his Jerusalem days, who rescued him in Dresden only to fall away from him with a sigh. How?

Worked to death? Starved, bundles of bones? Machine gunned, buried in a mass grave somewhere in the eternal plains of Poland? Gassed, fighting for air? There had been rumours of gas, of incineration, of industrial-scale murder. What was true? That tender girl, her body, her eyes and lips, her very brain. Am I responsible in some way?

I never wanted any of it. I saw nothing special in Jews either good or bad. I knew the 'Protocols' were a fiction when I read them in the caves of Aceldama with Emile. I loved a Jewish girl. She was just a girl. She hurt me in the end. So what? I found Angela. I love her now. How did this madness ever take hold? Perhaps if I'd grown up here rather than in Palestine I'd understand it.

He steadied himself against the crumbling masonry. All his life he had been trapped in a glass tank like the scorpions he had collected as a boy. From his birth he had been encased by his parents' grief. With Johannes ruling everything, the world was never truly within Werner's reach, rather it sat beyond, a thing of wonder.

Yes, the world was wondrous. It held Anna, Angela, his daughters, that precious jewel Dresden itself, the Saxon landscape, clouds on a summer's day, pictures, sublime Venice, Jerusalem hillsides in spring.

'Now I see it,' he murmured. His life as an artist was a forlorn attempt to assuage his separation from the world. Pitifully he represented the wondrous world – from the other side of something, his prison wall, his glass cage.

This was the lifelessness of his work. Finally he had only been admired by Nazis: themselves on the other side of life, fuelling hatred and destruction from the void.

It all added up.

'But there's still the mural – and maybe that is something different. Surely that *lives*. Angela believes in it. She's usually right about the important things. I have a chance yet.'

He turned and walked quickly to his car, dreaming of getting back to his work.

~

A knock. Eva jumped. Like anyone nowadays she could never rule out the possibility that a rap on the door would change everything in a moment. Her heart beat faster as she went forward.

'Frau Gustavus?'

Neumann, in winter coat and cap, stood shivering on the mat. He smiled, but with his shifty look and bandaged hands, he disconcerted Eva.

'Yes?'

'May I come in?' Neumann gave a false name, Braun. 'I have something I have to tell your husband. Is he in?'

Wrapping her shawl around her to keep out the cold, she had an instinct to stall him. 'Yes, but he's resting at the moment.'

'Can I wait in here till he surfaces?'

She paused. 'Very well, Herr Braun.'

She showed him to the cluttered living-room and offered him a seat.

'Tell him it's a personal matter, nothing to be alarmed about, the opposite in fact. Incidentally,' Neumann added breezily, 'I'm wearing these bandages because I'm suffering from frostbite. God, it was painful. I was near the forest and the blizzard got me. Luckily I got out and a doctor here in Dresden wrapped my arms up for me.' He waved his bandaged hands. 'Anyway, that's not what brings me here. You go and fetch him, Frau Gustavus.'

She returned with a bleary and irritable Anton.

'Ah, Herr Gustavus.'

'What can I do for you?' queried Anton, sitting down while Eva hovered. Neumann's false bonhomie struck him. Eva had already whispered that the visitor was a 'phony'.

'I'll come to the point, Herr Gustavus.' Neumann's gruesome smile had gone. 'I know your history. The stuff that's nearly got you locked up, your opinions. I know where you were born – I can still hear that Württemberg accent. I know you made a life in Palestine where you fell in love with our friends, the Jews. Then I know why you came back to the Fatherland. The son you've spent your whole life looking for, the other one you don't want to know even though he's rich and famous.'

Anton narrowed his eyes. 'How do you know all this?'

'An old friend mentioned it.'

'Who?'

Neumann seemed to be debating whether to let on.

'Block warden, Andreas Schmidt,' he admitted finally.

Anton sniffed derisively. 'I knew block wardens were Nazi informers. I didn't know they snitched to petty crooks.'

'Come off it, Herr Gustavus. Andreas and I gossip now and again. It's as well for you. A fortunate coincidence has occurred.'

'Coincidence?' Anton was keeping his calm. Despite his distaste he wanted to know what the visitor had to say. Eva was watching intently.

'To put it simply, I've run into your son, Johannes.'

Anton looked up sharply. 'Well?' he said after a pause.

'He's living in the forest.'

'Forest? Which forest? Where, for God's sake?'

Rubbing his bandaged hands together, he said, 'Ah, well, you see, that's for me to know and you to find out.'

Eva and Anton stared at each other.

'What do you mean, Herr Braun?' asked Eva, sitting down to calm herself. She could see Anton raging and didn't want him to throttle the man or drive him away before everything had become clear.

'I have a proposition. I will take you to him but it's a big risk for me and it's time-consuming. In short I need payment.'

'Payment?'

'How much?' asked Eva.

He named a large sum.

'What! You...' Anton hoisted himself from his chair.

'Anton!' said Eva grabbing his arm. 'Sit. Wait.'

'What do you mean wait! Where in a million years do we get that sort of money from?'

'Let's hear more from Herr Braun.'

'A very sensible attitude if I may say so, Frau Gustavus.'

'Anyway,' said Anton, 'How do we know if the man you have met is my son?'

Neumann told an embroidered story of his meeting in the forest. What hadn't this stranger said or implied! Neumann was a master. He knew how to edge his victims into the palm of his hand by playing on their vulnerabilities.

Despite suspicion and boiling indignation at being asked for money, Anton was desperate to believe him.

'He is an outlaw. He would contact you eventually no doubt, but he's waiting until... things change. You could wait for this, but on the other hand when will "things change"? The war is not over yet. It might take months. I can lead you to him straight away.'

Anton sat back and shook his head. 'I'll have to wait. I have no money.'

'I know that Herr Gustavus! Do you think I don't know that? Of course I do, but Braun is clever, Braun has thought it through. *You* don't have any money...'

'Yes?'

'But your other son Werner does. The whole world knows that. That bit I didn't need to research. He has shares, he has savings, he has property, he even has – I've heard – dollars under the bed.'

Eva and Anton looked at each other. It dawned on them before Neumann said more.

‘I thought you might… tap him, so to speak. Then we’ll all be happy. Me, Herr Gustavus, Frau Gustavus, even your other son will be happy to meet his elder brother – he’ll think it money well spent. And then of course Johannes himself…’

Neumann’s grin returned. He knew victory when he saw it. The old man was trying to hide his emotion. He had no choice but to fall into line.

Chapter 22

On her way back to the car from her work at the Women's Labour League, Angela bumped into Pastor Johst. She offered him a lift back to the village.

Johst's presence irritated Angela. The pale light exposed the yellow teeth and sagging skin of the testy cleric.

'Look at that,' he whined as they approached the village. Berlin evacuees were shivering by the roadside. They scowled at the car.

'What a blight! Stealing, getting the girls pregnant. You used to be able to keep your door unlocked. Now, with things going the way they are, they've got bolder. They curse everybody – the "nobs" (that's you and me!), even the Führer if they think nobody's listening.'

Angela agreed about the evacuees but was in no mood to have it spelled out. She felt guilty that she'd used their position with the Gauleiter to make sure no one was billeted on her. Instead this starved and unruly mob were crammed into the villagers' cottages.

The pastor hadn't finished with his misery. As she dropped him off at the rectory he confided in her that defeat was imminent, a certainty.

'The wireless tells us that we can crush the enemy once and for all now that they're on our soil. Who do they think believes that? It's a calamity, the end.'

Angela was surprised at his frankness. You could be shot for saying things like that. Slowing to turn into their drive she noticed two men standing at the front door, one of them tall, bearded and leaning on a stick.

She knew instantly it was Werner's father though she had never met him.

~

Werner slid into first gear and drove out through the gate. Beside him, Anton rested his weathered hands on his stick. After the negotiation back in the house, father and son, who had not spoken for twenty-seven years, continued their silence as the Benz left the narrow lanes and hit the deserted main road.

From the back Neumann kept up a continuous chat.

'You like the car, Herr Gustavus? Lovely walnut dashboard...'

'I like it well enough.'

'It's everything, you see, Herr Gustavus. The purring engine, the suspension, dials, polished wood, leather. It's like a holiday from real life to ride in these. Our German workmanship beats all rivals.'

'Doubtless.'

Anton broke his silence with a derisive snort. Werner hadn't heard this noise for a long time. How well he knew it all the same. He blushed, then shame turned to anger. He gripped the steering wheel and stared at the road as if in eating the tarmac up he could consume his father away also.

Anton: threadbare and grizzled but sure of himself as ever. 'My son,' he had said confidently on arrival, 'I have a proposal that might interest you...'

Werner hated the old man next to him now, hated his smell, his breathing, his yellow teeth, the old self-centredness.

Hated too what he was getting Werner into. Wasn't life hard enough? Angela had thought her husband was crazy; that was without Werner telling her about the money he had paid over to the garrulous little crook now lounging in the back as if he owned the car and Werner were the chauffeur.

How horrible it had been to have the two of them under his roof, brief though the visit had been; his home – refuge from all that was invidious in past and present – violated.

Neumann talked on. 'I have a business arrangement involving certain young people. I need to settle them, then we'll head for the forest. It'll be dark by then. We'll take torches – you brought torches didn't you, Herr Gustavus? I did mention it, I said it will be dark and by God it will be. Except nowadays with the bombing, the whole sky's lit up even when the bombs are falling miles away. I was forgetting that. Still, it'll be dark enough in the forest. Yes, we'll certainly need torches. Not that I don't remember exactly where we're heading. I know where I got stuck in the snow that day. Your Johannes will be around there.'

They drove on under darkening skies between spiky hedgerows and half snow-covered fields. The Erzgebirge mountains to the south were dull white in the distance.

'Not a car in sight, is there, Herr Gustavus? No one has petrol, except for people of your importance of course...'

'Importance...' Anton growled.

Werner, driving on with pursed lips, expected more in this vein from the old man but Anton was silent.

'He's depending on me now. He's obviously thought better of provoking me.'

On the contrary, Anton had been preparing an indictment. He spoke above the rumble of the wheels with a hoarse intensity.

'How did you get yourself into this position, Werner, that's what I'd like to know. Back in Jerusalem, you were a serious boy. You had education. You had morality. Your politics were sound. You believed in the rights of all peoples, particularly the rights of Jews. Your first love was a Jewish girl. You were a budding artist. An artist can only concern himself with truth. Lies are anathema. How did this all come about?'

The atmosphere was tightening. Neumann pricked up his ears.

'Ambition? Love of privilege? A colonial's sense of inferiority? A sudden conversion perhaps. Or maybe you were just frightened to say no. Now you're in deep and it's too late. Up to your neck in a criminal regime hell-bent before everything else on killing all Jews.'

Werner gritted his teeth. 'Father, how do you know the regime is killing every single Jew?'

'Then what happened to those who were sent east? Where are they?'

'If they were killing all Jews why are those we see on the roads being marched back into Germany?'

'That's a good point, Herr Gustavus,' came from the back. 'I say the same thing to people who say the Jews have all been murdered in the east. What do people know?'

'How trusting you both are!'

Something in Werner broke. Hurt found words. Harsh, loud words. He wrenched the car over on to a verge and switched the engine off. In the silence of a winter landscape a beast was born.

'Father! Enough!'

'Oh, for goodness sake...'

'How long do you think I will put up with this? I put my hand in my pocket. I produce a great deal of money. All I am met with is your contempt. You've lived a short distance from me for twenty years and made no effort to contact me. I have a wife, you couldn't be less interested. Worse, you have grand-children, you don't want to know them. Just like all those years ago, hurting my mother with your womanising, selfishness and vanity.'

Werner was spitting back in one outburst every drop of rejection his father, through indifference, had ever fed him. Anton was shaking his head in wonderment.

'You spooned with every woman you could lay your hands on, German, Jewish, Arab, Turk, Armenian and Coptic for all I know. Watch out, you daughters of Zion! Here comes Anton, big goat! Mooning about with Miriam while her husband pays for his honour with his life. Taking up with Eva again since she was fool enough to take you back even though you'd once broken her heart. Devoting your life to a boy who was gone, gone, gone and abandoning your other son.' Werner's voice dropped. He turned to his father, quivering. 'A son who was before your very eyes, longing for your attention. Not even saying good-bye when I left home.'

'I recall that you left without saying good-bye to *me*.'

Now Werner yelled, louder still. 'That child was me! Me! *Me* guilty? What about you! You smug, selfish, vain old man. I've half a mind to turf you out of the car with this petty gangster in the back and let you both die of cold.' Werner grabbed the door handle. 'Go on, get out, get out both of you! Go and find Johannes in the forest by yourselves. I've done my bit. Keep the money. I've plenty where that came from. I've earned it in sweat and troubled conscience.'

At last it was over. He withdrew his hand. His head sank on to the steering wheel.

The snow fields lay quiet. Nothing moved. They sat on in silence, Anton staring ahead, eyes narrow.

'Werner,' he said calmly at last, 'you've done well for yourself by going along with things. What you said about me might be true, I wish it weren't. It makes no difference. There is no redemption for you, and you know it.'

Neumann sighed impatiently. 'I've got an appointment to keep, Herr Gustavus.'

Werner switched on the engine and pulled out into the road. He had had his say but his father was right, as always.

~

Red discs stood out in the monochrome landscape.

'Military police. What do they want?' Werner came to a halt, showed his pass and drove on. 'Trekkers.'

He pressed forward then stopped. A stream of refugees was

hobbling towards a village in the half-distance. The road narrowed. Trucks and horse-drawn carts queued up behind. Werner had no choice but to wait.

'We're hemmed in now,' said Neumann. 'Damn. I've got a schedule to keep. These people are a disaster. Why do they come flooding from the east? Why haven't they hurled themselves against the Russian tanks? I need a cigarette for my nerves. Have you got one, Herr Gustavus?'

Werner and Neumann lit up. The smoke drifted to a crack in the window.

Anton stared at the refugees. 'The shattered dream of *Lebensraum.* Hitler encouraged ordinary Germans to colonise the east. Now the east is coming to them.'

A short gap opened up. Werner pressed his foot down, deftly overtook those in front and pulled up just behind the marchers.

A villager tapped on Werner's window. Werner lowered it.

'That was neatly done, Sir.' The villager pointed ahead. 'Look, we have an SS corporal in the rear. We have marchers with that look peculiar to the race. You are being delayed by a herd of God's Chosen on their way from one of the eastern Lagers. Don't mistake them for German folk.'

Werner said nothing and closed the window. They edged alongside the column. Women and children in the last stages of fatigue and emaciation shuffled forward.

Villagers peered from their doorsteps. Children ran around and shouted. 'Who are you! Where are you going! Did you see the Russians!'

Someone fell. The guards rushed forward. The front part of the column carried on and became separated.

'Look at that lot wandering off ahead,' Neumann muttered.

The Benz moved forward just behind the separated group. From a doorway a woman emerged with a large loaf. The stragglers surged towards her, arms outstretched. She broke the loaf up and handed the pieces out.

'Someone needs to tell that woman to stop feeding Jews,' said Neumann.

'They need food like anyone else,' said Werner.

A neighbour remonstrated with the woman who straight away obediently turned and went back inside. The village children meanwhile turned their questions into stones, hurling them with vicious accuracy at the women and children's heads.

Anton leaped out of the car, waving his stick. 'Hey, you kids. Stop that! These marchers are on the way to factories. They need to eat so they can work for the Reich. Leave them be.'

He pulled some of the children away. Others backed off. The remainder of the column was catching up. Anton got back in. Werner revved and moved smoothly away.

His father's act of minor heroism perturbed him further. He too had had a thought to prevent the children but had delayed. He paid for this with further private mortification.

~

It was already late enough in the day for headlights. They lit up the signpost half-buried in a drift remaining from recent snow. Werner swung the car into the turning. It was hard to hold to the track, pock-marked and beaded with trails of mammals and birds. Branches bent and brushed the car roof.

After a few minutes, above the engine's low rumble, a noise rose out of the forest. Neumann shot his head round. 'What's that?'

'It's behind.'

There was a bump on Werner's side, followed by a sharp rap on her window as he stopped the car.

'Braun! *Möchst du tanzen gehen?* Where did you get your fine motor?'

Neumann wound down the window, letting in a blast of winter

air. 'Hello Jens.'

'Who are your friends?'

'This is Herr Gustavus and his father, also Herr Gustavus.'

Werner nodded. Anton stared, ignoring everybody and everything.

'Hey, Herr Gustavuses, do you dig Jitterbug? Glenn Miller?'

'Sure,' said Werner, 'but Paul Whiteman's better.'

'Ah, so you know your stuff, Herr Gustavus. Are we nearly there, Braun?'

'A few bends.'

'We came by a back way. But Dobbin here nearly rammed you.'

'Dobbin?'

A horse-drawn covered wagon could just be made out in the dark.

'That's a nice horse,' said Neumann. 'But first things first. Have you got the dough?'

'Dough for Braun everybody!' shouted Jens. Emerging from the car Neumann waved his torch at the horse and wagon. Thirty or so kids shivered in the dark: boys with check shirts and quiffs over their eyes; girls heavily made up wearing low-cut blouses. While the money was being collected, Neumann stroked the horse's nose.

'Hi boys and girls. I'm Braun.'

'Hi Braun.'

Neumann stuffed the money, a mixture of coins and notes, into his pockets.

'It's all ready for you,' he said. 'I just have to get the generator going, then the music can start. There's a radiogram and a pile of records.'

'Good,' said Jens, swinging onto the wagon and grabbing the reins. 'We've got to watch it, though. The Heidenau gang are out to get us. They might come and have a crack at us. We're prepared, don't think we aren't. Bastards. Anyway, we'll see you soon. You'll beat us to it in that smart motor, Braun.'

'*Bis bald.*'

'Bis bald.'

Neumann got back in. Werner moved off.

'They're harmless enough,' said Neumann. 'And if we must have a few "disaffected young" I prefer these "Swing-Heini" types to the middle-class rolled-umbrella fops with their pro-English ideas. These kids worship America. Our enemies! The world's gone mad.'

Anton exploded. 'Braun! What the hell's going on!'

'Have patience, Herr Gustavus. I have a little diversion to attend to. We'll be away from here in a matter of minutes and then we can turn our attention to your business. It's hand to mouth these days. I have to earn a crust where I can.'

They emerged out of the forest, drove up across an open field and arrived at the barn. Werner parked the car at the back and switched off.

'Come on out to stretch your legs,' said Neumann.

'I'll stay here,' said Anton.

Werner and Neumann got out. The sky to the north was filled with flashes and low rumbling.

'Magdeburg,' Neumann said as they walked round to the front of the barn. 'Could even be Berlin. It's a long way off. Dresden's turn soon.'

'It isn't strategic enough, Braun. Some of the factories have already been bombed. There's not much else for them to go for in Dresden.'

'Children, women, the old, their own prisoners. Why not? Maybe they'll go for the station. It'll be full of refugees arriving from the east. Roosevelt is a mass murderer.' Neumann stopped and touched Werner's arm. 'Listen to those bombs. So many booms they blur into one long rumble. Herr Gustavus, every second we stroll here in the quiet of the country, thousands die from the bombs. The lucky ones die in a second. The Americans are doing it. And now to make a living I've got to dance to Glenn Miller. The world's gone mad, like I said.'

~

A bulb hung with coloured paper gave off a rancid light. Equipment and straw bales were stacked to the side. The makeshift dancehall thundered to the blare of brass from a mahogany radiogram.

The kids formed a jitterbugging mass.

'"In the Mood", boys and girls!' shouted Neumann. 'Hot off the press.'

Neumann took off his jacket. 'I might have a dance myself,' he murmured conspiratorially to Werner. 'I got the record from a Swedish guy. Mind you, I expect this radiogram is used to civilized sounds, not to this mayhem. I'm worried the speaker will give out. Listen to this racket! I'm a sensitive man. This stuff is a mixture of Jewish sentimentality and negro lust. Whine, whine, whine, blare, blare, blare. Dreamt up in hell – or America. It's like a disease, it's all about sex.'

More, more cried the boys and girls.

'In the Mood' started again, the shouting brass, that single drum-tap that set the tune off, the drum tap the Swing-Heinis – the whole world, in January 1945 – loved. And when the number finished the kids had to have it a third time.

A girl came towards Werner and held out her hand. 'Come on. You oldies can be "in the mood" too.'

'Thank you,' said Werner politely, 'but I'm sitting it out. I'll stay here. I'm learning a lot.'

She wandered off and Werner lost sight of her. Neumann too had disappeared. Werner debated with himself whether to ask another of the spare girls for a dance after all and, deciding against, also went outside. He needed to check his father was all right in the car and press Neumann to get on with the business in hand.

First, he would collect himself with a cigarette. He leant against the wall, collar up, smoking, listening mournfully to the bombs.

Flashes from the sky flickered on the fields.

Suddenly headlights gleamed between the trees, then vanished, shone again. A vehicle emerged and headed up the track towards the farm.

Werner watched intently as the truck came nearer. Young men in bandanas and American flying jackets with wool collars clung to the roof and running board.

'They're here!' shouted the Swing-Heinis who had taken a break from the dancing and were hanging about outside. 'Those Heidenau pricks. Bolt the door!'

They vanished back inside. The door was shut. Everything went quiet. Werner secluded himself behind a tree.

Slowing first, the truck shot through the farm gate, finally screeched to a halt. The boys leapt off, waving their clubs.

'Come out, you nancy-boys! Yellow creeps. You're fucked.'

They banged their clubs against the door and threw their bodies against it. It would not give way.

The invaders fell to discussing what to do. A log was trundled forward. A group of them took hold of it on either side. They held it steadily, ready to drive forward and crash the door to pieces.

'*Ein, zwei, drei...*'

At that moment the door flew open from the inside. The Swing-Heinis poured out. The attackers dropped the log and the two groups set upon each other with fists and clubs. The Swing-Heini girls huddled at the door shouting their boys on.

Amid shouting and screams the fight continued. Some of the kids were running round the barn, chasing and beating each other.

Still Werner watched. Unlike the kids, he noticed another set of headlights approaching at speed. Finally the brawlers froze, caught in the glare. Girls backed away into the barn. Uniformed Gestapo jumped down and raced forwards with crunching boots. Shouting and lashing out, the men herded the nearest boys and girls into the lorry. Others ran off to round up the rest.

A lieutenant was directing operations from the truck. Suddenly, seeing a man run off, he whipped out his Luger and fired. The fugitive, silhouetted against the stars, a poor soul, stopped as if incredulous, flung out his arms and fell with slow-motion acrobatic elegance.

The lieutenant approached the body.

'Yes, that's Neumann,' he said to one of his men. 'That's who we're after. Bundle him up and stick him in the truck. The ground's too hard to bury him. Be quick about it. We want to get out of here.'

'*Scheisse*, it's Braun,' murmured Werner. 'Now what do we do?' Keeping to the shadows he shot round to the back of the barn. The Benz lay gleaming under the stars, with his father inside. He tapped on the window.

'Father,' he hissed, 'we have to hide. There's mayhem here. Gestapo.'

Werner started off for a clump of evergreens where they could be well hidden and observe what was going on. He looked back to see his father still in the car with the door half open, struggling with his stick to lift himself out.

'He needs my help.'

He dashed back and helped the old man out. Panting, Anton hobbled after him.

While the Gestapo went about their business, father and son after all these years were crouched in the bushes like schoolboys playing hide-and-seek.

Werner felt a hand on his sleeve. His father needed to hold on to him to keep him upright.

He brushed his father's hand with his own, an attempt at reassurance. It was an awkward gesture but a sign that something in Werner was opening out. His bitterness at the powerful father who had denied him was about to dissolve in an awareness of his age and infirmity.

Momentarily rapt, oblivious of the external drama, he thought of time passing, of impermanence. The bombs fell, the regime would die. In the eye of time, his father's death – his own too perhaps – was only a step away. Look at Braun, one moment a performer, the next a body falling.

'Father,' he murmured. 'Something happened in '39 you ought to know about.'

'What's that, boy? I can't hear.'

Werner dared to speak up. They were far enough away. There was no risk of being heard. 'I went back to the Germany Colony...'

The story was quickly told. Anton, peering anxiously through the leaves at the truck and the hurrying men, stayed silent. Was he even listening?

'So you see, Father,' Werner concluded, 'the man Maria loved was clearly Johannes, and there's no reason to think he wouldn't have found his way back here. He was here before and he's a traveller, for goodness sake. He told Braun. He gets around. And he's a survivor. That was how Maria described him.'

Still Anton said nothing. Outside, things were on the move. The lieutenant detailed two men to take the horse and wagon and another pair to take the truck from Heidenau. He swung himself up into the cabin. The sergeant gave a shout and the convoy moved off down the lane towards the forest. The receding engine sounds were smothered by the bombs thudding to the north. The lights twinkled to nothing in the frozen night.

The two men emerged from their hiding place.

'We can't waste any time,' said Werner. 'We need to start looking in the forest.'

'But the forest is huge.'

'Father, this is no time for a faint heart. We can make a start. If we don't find him tonight, we'll come back. It's Johannes. I know it. I'm not going to back away a second time. Braun was scum – his real name was Neumann by the way – but I'm sure that what he had for sale was the genuine article.'

Werner made to move off but Anton stayed where he was.

‘Father?’

Anton fixed him with a level gaze. ‘Why didn’t you tell me about your Palestine trip?’ He seemed more sad than angry.

Werner was at a loss. He shrugged and shook his head in an acknowledgment of failure even if his words implied a defence. ‘I... I felt there was nothing certain. Nothing to be done, certainly not once war broke out.’

Anton looked away. The air remained full of ominous rumbles. The old man seemed to be discovering in himself a desire to rescue Werner, to make amends.

‘It’s not your fault,’ he said at last as Werner came towards him. ‘I am to blame. I was not the father to you I should have been.’

Werner lifted his gloved hand to touch Anton’s arm. Under a canopy of stars and dim flashes from far-off mayhem, they fell upon each other’s shoulders.

They became close over the days which followed. The forest was a tough adversary, overgrown and with tracks hidden. The only sound when they rested from beating the paths and calling Johannes’s name, was the scuttle of squirrels and melancholy squawk of birds. The air was dank and cold, smelling of earth and sodden wood.

Nevertheless they went to it with a will and returned to a new section each day. Anton felt respect for the effort Werner was putting in on behalf of a brother he had never met, and who had blighted his life. Werner sensed his father’s acknowledgment and found himself reciprocating. With dawning affection he remembered the twinkling eye he’d loved as a little boy.

JOHANNES 6

My hideaway is a hollowed-out mound concealed in the densest part of the forest. The path through the surrounding undergrowth is all but invisible should anyone trouble to come this far.

As you come through the doorway you enter a chamber which I constructed myself out of tarpaulin and local timber.

Just room to stand. A skylight. Bottle of schnapps and an oil lamp on a table. Sink, shelves. Above a grate, a flue extending up through the ceiling. One corner is stacked with chopped firewood. I only burn the fire at night as the smoke might give me away even though I am deep in the forest.

A stream trickles nearby. Without a water source this life would not have been possible.

Who owns this part of the forest? No one knows, it's been disputed for a generation. The case continues in spite of the war. That's why the Forestry Service never comes. I have never seen a soul round here.

I am unknown – non-citizen, non-combatant, no number, no file. It has to stay that way until the end of this war, which must surely be near.

I was careless a few weeks ago. I rescued a man who was stuck in the snow a little way off from here. I warmed him up with schnapps. He clearly guessed I was holed up in the forest.

He was intrigued by my accent, which he could not place. Off my guard, I told him I was born in Jerusalem. He seemed pre-occupied as he left me. He even forgot to thank me for saving his life. Perhaps he thought I was a fugitive Jew and was pondering whether to turn me in.

I doubt anybody can take time off from defending the Fatherland to come and look for me in this wilderness.

I had another conversation lately, with a wanderer who had lost his mind. He grabbed me and looked me hard in the eye. His garbled sentences have stayed with me.

'Listen. My roots were buried in the railway platform... A tree in deepest winter with no leaf or bud, an old ash... Millions passed that way... "That tree will soon be firewood," said the station master.'

'What are you saying?' I stuttered.

'Millions...' he croaked. 'Millions... I've watched the flaying of large gentle animals, and a queue of women and children snaking in the snow towards a shed.'

What an odd thing to say. He let go of me and stumbled on. You hear terrible rumours. I never saw him again anyway.

I live on nuts, grains, fruits, roots. Tulip roots are good. I know how to make a good soup out of nettles. I forage for mushrooms and trap the occasional rabbit or squirrel. Sometimes – very cautiously – I steal when the chance comes.

I haven't written the story of how I came here from Palestine. After leaving Qumran it was the usual tale of living by the seat of my pants, begging and thieving, stowing away, jumping on trains, finding leaks in borders. Too familiar to bear repeating.

I was set up here within a year of the war starting. My old reluctance to contact my family, even though that is in theory the plan, continued. I felt sure my father and possibly my brother were somewhere near. However, it was only recently, after a delay of some four years that I walked by night and by roundabout ways into the city which I had last visited in 1913. Dresden had gone downhill. It was a mess, full of starving refugees and boy soldiers.

I didn't know where to start. Obviously I had to avoid contact with officials. There could be no access to whatever lists the state keeps of its citizens. Telephone directories yielded nothing. It was a long shot but I moved from one housing estate to another asking caretakers or anyone I ran into if they knew the name.

I was disappointed yet relieved. Soon I could give up and go home to the forest. When the Nazis were gone, *then* it would be possible because I would come out of hiding. Probably I would find some reason not to do it even then.

On the point of leaving I found myself walking past an elegant domed mansion standing back from the road. Lots of people were milling about. It was clearly being used as a refugee centre. Maybe I could pass as a refugee and get a night's sleep and a bowl of soup there.

I walked up the steps into the main entrance hall. Across the hall people in uniform sat behind a trestle table. I pondered whether to fake an identity and concluded that it was an unnecessary risk. I was turning to go when the walls caught my attention.

Three of these expanses were covered with unfinished sketches for a mural. The fourth wall displayed the finished product, a vast painting, a landscape with a city. The flat-roofed buildings, towers, domes, bare rounded hills, blue sky above and exotic costumes were instantly recognisable: the city of my birth, Jerusalem.

I went towards it open-mouthed. What was going on? Here in this beautiful city of Dresden, was a huge depiction of another city far older, yet more fantastic. What's more, this city was longed for by the regime's most reviled enemies, the Jews. How was this to be explained?

One thing was certain. The artist had gone to a lot of trouble. There was so much detail. He must have used photographs. I'm no art critic but I was impressed.

I caught sight of a middle-aged man in a smock with paintbrush in hand, climbing down from a wheeled platform.

'Ah, there's the artist. I'll ask him what it's all about.'

I watched him as he bent over a tray of paints and brushes, clearly in the act of packing up for the day. He wore wire-rimmed glasses like Himmler's. In fact he looked like Himmler but taller. Bald, serious, the clever type.

Every so often he looked up at his work, narrowed his eyes and pursed his lips. He glanced at his watch.

'Damn, I'm late,' I heard him mutter as I came near.

'Excuse me,' I said politely.

He turned and frowned.

'I wondered…'

'Look I'm sorry,' he stuttered. 'I've been completely caught up here today. I'm in a terrible rush. Can it wait?'

'I just was interested in your mural. It's Jerusalem, isn't it?'

'Yes... Look…' He studied his watch again. He was already moving away. 'It's a reception. I'm late. They'll… kill me. Well, they won't, but you know… Look, I'm here on Friday if you want to continue the discussion.'

He was gone.

A few days passed. Enough time for me to put two and two together and reach a very respectable four.

Jerusalem… artist… the right age… a 'serious' fellow. If that painter wasn't my brother Werner, I'd be amazed.

I couldn't wait till Friday. I had to get back. But I now had something to go on. At last I found I was truly ready. No more of the hanging back. Sooner rather than later I would return and meet the artist again. Surely that would also lead to my father.

I set out again towards the city. It took me longer than before. Recent falls of snow and an icy wind held me back. As light faded there was no sign of the city on the horizon.

I trudged on in the dark. It was taking me hours. It was then that I heard the rumble of aircraft. Lights appeared in the sky above the city and fell slowly. I stopped and leant on a gate, watching with dread. Sure enough, the rumble in the sky became a roar. Then came the booms and crashes. I watched horrified as they came without end, one upon another. The sky was constantly lit with flashes. Not just yellow and orange but weird new colours – greens, blues and purples. Before long the sky above the city began to turn red. This hellish glow grew and grew till it reached to the heavens. Never have I seen anything so beautiful or so monstrous.

I cried aloud and turned on my heel.

Since then I have buried myself in my lair. This is my comfort as I think about what happened, nothing but a huge and pointless catastrophe.

Today I climbed to a vantage point. Everything was quiet in the skies but a vast column of smoke reaches from the city high into the sky.

If there was ever father or brother in that city of fire, neither is likely to have survived.

I am alone as always. Perhaps I want to be.

I've recorded my story up to this day. There's nothing more to say and who am I writing it for now anyway? I was going to give it to my father.

1945-46

Chapter 23

On Shrove Tuesday, after their latest outing to the forest, Werner parked the car near the Grosser Garten. It was Anton's idea. Eva was visiting a neighbour. He had no wish to go back to an empty flat just yet, particularly as everybody was out celebrating. There was entertainment in just watching people out with their children, some dressed in ridiculous costumes, some tipsy, all in a festive spasm that belonged to earlier times.

But there was more to it. He had arranged to meet a woman.

'A woman, Father?' Remembering Anton's womanising of old, Werner had feared the worst.

'I've received a letter from a woman here in Dresden who says that she once knew Johannes well and would like to find out where he is now. Here, you can read it if you want.'

Anton halted his stroll and pulled the letter from his pocket. Werner took it from its envelope, unfolded it and read by the light of his torch – there was no street-lighting in these blackout days.

Dear Herr Gustavus
Forgive me approaching you but I have heard of you through a mutual friend, Frau Eberl. She was talking to me one day and mentioned that a friend of hers, Herr Gustavus, had once lived in Jerusalem, and furthermore that his son had been kidnapped there and never found.

Herr Gustavus, I have reason to believe that a friend of mine from long ago, whom I knew as Ali, was indeed your son.

I have not seen Ali for many years. Frau Eberl told me that you had come to Dresden believing that this was where he might be living. I assume you have not found him, or Frau Eberl would have known about this, but I feel it would be useful – if also painful – for both of us to meet and exchange what we know.

I hope you agree and look forward to your reply.

Sincerely

Zoraya Schmidt-Orabi

'Why have you only just mentioned this?' asked Werner, both in shock and a little peeved.

'I only received the letter a few days ago. Remember, you waited long enough before telling me you'd heard about Johannes's stay in the Colony. I've been pondering it. I've learnt the hard way to be cautious. I keep believing but always I say to myself, "It may not be." Besides which, Sophie Eberl is a rumour-monger and it's hard to credit anything that comes from that quarter.'

'So what did you do?'

'I wrote back suggesting a meeting here. I indicated the very bench.'

Father and son strolled along, momentarily distracted from the imminent encounter by the lakes, the little castles, the shadows moving under the trees.

'A good idea to come here, Werner. Darkness and romance. It reminds me of my youth. Let's sit. This is the bench. She isn't here yet. It's a bit earlier than I said.' He lowered himself and stuck out his legs and stick.

'As far as I can see from our map,' Werner said, changing the subject, 'there is just one more section of the forest we need to cover. I'm glad we're coming to the end. On the other hand, it's dispiriting we haven't found him. He must be there.'

'In spite of myself, my deep caution, and even though Braun was a villain, I agree with you. I just feel he might be there. I seemed to *sense* him in the forest.'

The two men lapsed into their separate thoughts. The garden was quiet under the stars. Loving couples kissed. Tired children leant against their mothers.

'Herr Gustavus?'

A heavily coated and booted, elegant middle-aged woman held out her hand. It was hard to tell in the dark but she seemed of middle-eastern appearance.

Both men rose to their feet, shook hands and made a space for her between them on the bench. Anton explained that Werner was the brother of Johannes.

'Thank you for agreeing to see me, Herr Gustavus, and it is an unexpected pleasure to meet his brother.' The woman spoke with a foreign accent.

All three settled themselves on the bench.

'We are intrigued,' said Anton, 'to know more about your connection with my son. Despite people saying they have seen him, in my darkest moments I have feared he died within a few days of his kidnapping. We have had no proof otherwise, only hearsay – even to this very day. Now we are looking for him in the forest. The latest information is he's there.'

'Well, let me tell you what I knew of your son and then I can hear from you. It's a great misfortune to me that I ever came back to Germany but perhaps at last through meeting you both some good can come of it.'

'What misfortune, Madam? You mean the war?'

'Of course. I came in '39 to visit my dying father who lived here in Dresden. My husband had died, my children were grown up. I thought I would be here a month or two. I've been marooned here ever since, trying to survive like everybody else.'

'So how *did* you know Johannes?'

Zoraya smiled sadly, then stood up. 'Look, I'm rather cold just sitting here. Shall we walk a little? I'll tell you as we go.'

The three started off and Zoraya began. Anton and Werner were so gripped by her words that when something unexpected happened they hardly noticed. A siren had begun to wail. The two men, shocked and distracted by stories of Omdurman and Aswan, were determined to hear Zoraya out. More sirens started off, near and far. Shouts and hurrying footsteps came from all around. It didn't enter the men's heads to panic.

At last they decided to head together for the garden gates. There was a crush. Everyone was shouting at once.

'What's that light, Mummy?'

'Light?'

'Right up there. Look, a green light.'

'A star?'

'You're not looking in the right place, Mummy. Over there.'

'Oh God. Christmas trees.'

'Christmas trees, Mummy? We've had Christmas.'

'They light up the city. So they know where to drop their bombs. Now will you hold my hand and do what you're told!'

The crowd fanned out from the gates into the streets. The green lights floated down. Mysterious, deeply ominous. The Christmas trees Miriam Fischer had foreseen – above the Striezel market the last Christmas before the Great War.

Panting, limping along, Anton was pulled into the reality of the moment and the fact that Dresden was about to be bombed.

'Werner, I must get back to Eva. She should be in the shelter. What about you? Will you come with me? And you, Madam? Will you come too, or do you live nearby?'

'I... I'll stay with you for the moment if I may...'

Now the sirens were wailing from every corner of the city. The streets were filled with cries and the clatter of feet.

'Werner, answer me...'

A frozen figure in a wave of panic, Werner was staring at the ground. 'Father... you go on. I'll see you back at your flat... I... must go somewhere.'

'Where in heaven's name?'

'It doesn't matter... It's connected to my work... It's not far... Look, I have to go. We'll meet up soon. Good-bye, Madam – and thank you.'

They moved in opposite directions, Anton and their companion towards Eva and home, Werner to the villa and his mural.

~

'Pray God it'll soon be over!'

'We'll be buried alive.'

'Pray to God.'

'I don't want to die.'

About a dozen crouched in a cellar, sharing the space with two mattresses, a small cupboard and a bucket with a lid. The bombs whistled and crashed, sometimes so near that Werner could believe they had landed on the house above.

Werner had had no hope of getting to his destination before it began. Two minutes from the Grosser Garten a frantic warden had ushered him down into the cellar of a house.

The ground shook again as if pounded by giant mallets. With every explosion it seemed as if the walls would cave in.

'God...'

'When will it end?'

'Bloody American swine.'

'Don't blame the Americans. Blame the maniac who got us into this.'

'Quiet.'

'I'll speak my mind. We're all going to die anyway.'

'Sh...This is a small space. We mustn't talk. It uses up oxygen.'

Another crash came from nearby, and another. Werner bowed his head. The pressure on his ears was unbearable. It was like being trapped in a box in deepest ocean. Immeasurable force surrounded them. It could inundate and obliterate them.

All went quiet. They held their breaths. They switched on their torches and exchanged glances. For several minutes no one spoke.

And there it was at last: a distant wail.

'All clear. Thank God.'

Should they leave or stay put? Some said that they should wait till a warden let them know it was safe to leave. Others wanted to get out and make up their own minds about what to do.

'There might be an incendiary in the house above.'

'Then we can leave from next door by going through the Breakthrough.'

'It's true, we have two possible ways of getting out.'

As was customary there was indeed a Breakthrough, an escape to the basement of the next house, which was unaccountably empty.

'I have to get there,' Werner said to nobody in particular.

Most were now gathering themselves to leave. A few opted for staying.

In his eagerness Werner led the way, clambering up the rickety ladder to the cellar exit. He touched the door which was heavy and made of metal. He drew back sharply. The handle had burnt his hand. With his handkerchief he gripped the handle again and edged the door open. His lips and nose were singed. All he had seen was dust and flickering light. He slammed the door shut.

'My God! The heat.'

'Try next door.'

Already the leavers were clambering through the Breakthrough and making for the next door steps. The door was quickly opened. From the bottom of the steps, with the others filing up the steps in front, Werner could see smoke billowing in the hallway. The flames danced across the floor licking their way up to the ceiling.

'The rest of you who want to stay – you can't! You have to get out. Both houses above are burning. Don't wait. Fire will spread down. It will burn everything including people and air.'

The ground shook. Plaster fell from the cellar ceiling.

'Hell!'

'Another raid!'

'What happened to the sirens?'

'It could be just a stray bomb.'

'The sirens were probably knocked out in the first raid.'

In an instant there was chaos. A mass of people, having charged from outside through the front door of the second house, tumbled down the steps to the basement.

'Hey! We're trying to get out!'

'You can't! The whole street's on fire and now they're bombing again.'

A woman warden was at the top of the stairs vainly trying to keep control. Within a minute both cellars were packed. Children clung to mothers. More explosions, tumbling plaster, shaking ground.

Werner was in despair. He was convinced the fires would spread down and engulf them all even if they were not first obliterated by a direct hit. There remained the slim hope that the fire in the first house was not as bad as he had assumed when he opened the metal door.

He edged his way past the huddled mass, towards the Breakthrough.

'Excuse me. I'm sorry. I must get through.'

It was slow going but as it turned out this saved his life. He stood at the Breakthrough. His feet were planted in the second cellar. He was peering through at the steps up to the metal door wondering how to get there. In an instant a blast flung the metal door down the stairs. The door ripped through the people in its path. There were screams followed by a roar of flame. Those in the main path burnt instantly. For a second he saw them. Then… they were gone. The whole of the first cellar was ablaze.

'Oh no.'

Thinking faster than the dazed and desperate people round him, he climbed back up the cellar steps of the second house, opened the door and threw himself forward. A door close to the exit led as he expected to a small water closet. He took his handkerchief and a filthy hand towel lying on the floor, plunged them into the grimy water in the lavatory bowl and thrust them dripping into his coat pocket.

Leaving behind the moans and shrieks below, others were now pouring out of the house into the street. Flames licking at his feet, he offered the towel to a stricken woman. 'Take it. You'll need it.'

She nodded to him in mute thanks, shoved the towel in her mouth and was gone. Pondering which route to take, Werner put the handkerchief in his mouth, shielded his face with his arms and set off.

He made little progress. Fire rained from the night sky on to fleeing silhouettes. Some didn't make it more than a few paces before waving their arms and collapsing from lack of oxygen, dead before the pursuing flames claimed them. The air was full of whirling objects. Sparks like orange snowflakes, bits of glass, hot metal, curtains with flame wings, flying planks.

All around, from the houses, from cellars, from along the street, cries of the dying. Already it was no street, just a mass of craters. Familiar objects lay strewn in the rubble. Who – just today – had boiled a kettle on that stove, leant unthinkingly against that mantelpiece?

Some got through, he could see. It was a matter of where the pockets of unburned oxygen remained, where the flames held back, where missiles flew wide – a mixture of luck and judgment.

Sucking on his handkerchief and covering his face he joined the procession to the corner. But people were coming back.

'You can't go that way! We've come from there. Everything's burning.'

But he must, he would.

It was clear. The second wave of bombing still hadn't finished. Between gaps in the flames the Christmas trees still hovered. There was a flash in the near-distance. This was followed by many more. The explosions came nearer.

A whine, a pause. The ground rocked. Werner fell against the wall. A rat tumbled from a window and darted past his feet. The flash and enveloping thunder joined as if to end the world once and for all. All was gathered into a continuous roar. Water tanks and a balcony fell into the fire.

The ground burned the soles of his feet. He used the dead as stepping stones. He was nowhere near his destination.

Somewhere between Striesen and the villa, perhaps around four o'clock in the morning, a dying fire-fighter handed him a damp cloth.

'Go, friend, go, you must.' As he fell his buckle scalded Werner's outstretched hand. He probably saved Werner's life.

The streets which were no longer streets were filled with shadows crying for loved ones. Fleeing bats crackled as they burned. Rats careered through the flames and darkness.

It only needed someone to breathe a solution – the Waldpark, the bridges, the meadows, the heath, the Grosser Garten – for the cry to be taken up. A crowd would set off, trampling those in its path, until hopelessness or asphyxia struck, and it would falter and fall. A few pressed on, muttering the word of salvation.

An inferno – a firestorm – stood between Werner and where he wanted to go.

'The river!' someone shouted. 'Make for the river.'

'It makes sense. Pray God.'

As he headed that way his view opened out and he could see some parts of the city. Beyond the roaring yellow, red and gold, buildings stood untouched. But how easily the fires spread. Flames leapt from building to building, seeming to burn out at first on a balcony or ledge, then establishing themselves with the aid of the wind. These flames licked the side of the building. Soon the building was another pillar of fire etching the night. Those containing chemicals jagged the night with plumes of apple green and aquamarine.

At last he reached the Elbe. But hope that it was the safest place was mistaken. Here the wind was at its fiercest. The firestorm drew air from outside the city to replace what had been burned. The river was the natural conduit. Wind sucked the flames and projectiles along the riverside paths.

People plummeted off bridges and paths, but it was too cold to stay in and they soon scrambled out. A ledge under one of the bridges was a better bet but people were fighting each other for the good places.

Bodies floated past, some with staring eyes.

~

Dawn came darkly. A cloud of smoke, a column miles wide rising into the sky above the smouldering city, blocked out the sun.

Anton and Zoraya had survived but never reached Anton's home. Leaning on one another, at the extremes of fatigue, they came to the Elbe meadows, a mass camp, crowded out.

'Here, you two,' someone called in the half-light, 'squeeze in here. You're all in.'

Warmed by the surrounding bodies, Anton and Zoraya lay down and slept for a couple of hours. Anton woke up to the taste of bitter charcoal, and the sweet smell of corpses.

He nudged Zoraya. 'I must get back to Eva.'

'Wait, they'll bring food here eventually. It must be a designated place of refuge.'

'No, I can't. I have to find my wife.'

'I'll come with you, Herr Gustavus. You can't go alone.'

Away from the meadow and back in the city proper they were part of a multitude that passed this way and that through rubble and burned corpses.

Torn up tramlines in the air. Carbonised bodies shrunk to half size. Bus passengers still sitting in rows as if they had just fallen asleep, but all charred. Others, dead but not burned; killed, they guessed, by a blast some way off, spleen or kidney ruptured. More, tailors dummies, white, with their clothes blown off. By the women's clinic, blackened women with bellies blasted open, their babies hanging half out. Some who had clawed themselves on to a fence to escape. Charred, still hanging there. From near and far came the crash of collapsing buildings.

To avoid catching fire themselves they dodged the sparks darting among the clouds of smoke and plunged their coats into water between blackened, floating bodies. Near the paint factory the smell of sulphur was thick and poisonous. They reeled away.

Zoraya glimpsed a giraffe.

'Am I dreaming?'

'No, I saw it too.'

'The army pioneers told us to watch out,' said somebody nearby. 'There could be snakes, even tigers.'

'In Dresden?'

'They hit the zoo,' said the stranger. 'The animals that didn't die, got out. Look, there's a monkey.'

A corpse swung from a lamppost across the road, the flames licking his feet.

'The Kripos aren't wasting time. If you're caught looting, they'll string you up straight away.'

The drone of aircraft had alerted their companion.

'Now what's this?'

'They're coming back!'

Enemy planes packed in formation were circling nearby, flying low, their machine-guns shooting at defenceless people.

'Down on your faces! Split up! Scatter!'

They clambered together behind a broken wall. Others flung

themselves down and prayed out loud to God.

The planes circled again, machine-gunning the people.

~

The villa was a blackened ruin. The dome had gone and three of the supporting walls. Such fierce flames burned near that it could only be a matter of time before nothing was left.

Miracle. The first mural wall still stood.

Werner approached.

There! How it gleamed in the flickering light. A mighty jewel. Only as he drew nearer still did this grand pattern became a representation – of buildings and trees, of toiling men and women, of the fabled city Jerusalem: its domes, towers, mighty walls, encompassing hills.

A wonderful illumination, as large and upstanding as a stage backdrop, made all the more dramatic and imposing by the surrounding ruination and light from the flames dancing nearer by the second.

Above the mural, where the dome had joined the wall, squatted a monkey. The animal watched Werner tiptoe forward, take his hat off and rest it against his breast in a gesture which maybe even a monkey could discern was one of love and awe.

'Did I do *that*? Surely I *am* an artist!'

The monkey put a hand down onto the top of the wall, lowered himself and dropped down the paint surface as if it were a jungle cliff. Once on the ground he turned and looked at the painting, nodded his head a few times, then just as quickly shimmied back up and returned to his perch.

Burnt timber crackled, sparks flew through doors and windows, patches of flame licked the charcoal floor.

'Soon the flames will get it. All that labour, all that determination. I proved something at last but now no one will know.'

He briefly shook his head in despair, then returned to gazing.

So rapt was Werner, he did not hear the drone of approaching fighters, or the rat-a-tat of machine guns.

He glanced up at the little mammal perched on his creation. Its tail curled down over the pure blue Jerusalem sky. Every few seconds it leant down and, at an awkward angle, peered downwards across the painting.

'At least *he* likes it...'

It was Werner's last thought before a bullet from the sky tore through his body with horrific finality.

Chapter 24

Anton's home was gone. The block was black rubble. He stood in disbelief. The entrance to the block shelter was covered with collapsed masonry.

'She could be buried in there.'

A woman poking about in the rubble recognised him as a neighbour.

'My wife… Do you know… I was somewhere else in the city…'

'Me too… I was out visiting my mother… I wonder what happened to everybody in the block… There's a medical post down that way, on the junction with the main road. Just a few medics doing what they can. You could try.'

Anton had a moment of wild hope. Zoraya held his arm as he stumbled to the junction. A queue of the burned and injured waited silently. He saw immediately that Eva was not among them.

Several stretchers were on the ground with bodies lying on them. Anton peered at them one by one. If they were not dead they were in the final stages, fearfully burned, eyes haunted or blank.

She was there.

'Eva!'

Her eyes were closed. Cheek white, lips deadly blue. He leant down and touched her forehead. Thank God, it was not cold.

'Eva. It's me. I'm alive. I've found you.'

Her eyes stayed closed.

'You should leave her, old man,' a medic called.

'How is she? Is she going to be all right?'

The man shook his head. 'It's possible but she must be kept quiet and still.'

'Can I sit with her and hold her hand?'

'Just don't talk to her. She needs all her energy.'

Anton reached beneath the blanket for Eva's hand, holding it between the thighs which were so familiar to him. He held it gently. She did not respond.

His eye wandered to a patch of ground that seemed to have been dug since the bombing. 'They've already started digging the graves.'

He prayed, repeating the words under his breath, over and over again. He forgot where he was, forgot too about Zoraya, who respectfully stood a little way off.

He felt a minute squeeze.

'Eva!'

He bent his ear to her mouth. She wanted to speak. 'Johannes…' Her voice was faint.

'What, dearest?'

'Have you found him?'

'Not yet. He's there. I know it. I'll go back.'

'Go… you must…'

Soon he doubted she was breathing. As the minutes passed he felt the warmth drain from her hand and from her thighs. He turned to Zoraya. 'She's gone.'

~

That same day, Zoraya helped him see to Eva's burial. There was no point in staying around. They headed back towards the meadow.

Anton's grief was mirrored in their companions of the road. They shared their stories of horror and loss. 'Have you seen a man… I'm looking for a little girl… I've lost my wife… My house used to be here. My family are all buried underneath… Help me… The authorities are no use. They can't cope with a situation like this…'

'I've just buried my wife,' Anton said. 'Now we have to get somewhere. Do you know where the nearest Red Cross soup kitchen is? We must have something before we set out or we'll never get there.'

Everywhere carbonised bodies were strewn on the road, hanging from windows. Where army pioneers had managed to get to work, the bodies were arranged in tidy piles five metres high. Shadows fled past. Cries and curses. Flying sparks. The crash of collapsing masonry. A crowd staring up at a bombed out building.

'What's that?'

'The Kripos have strung up more looters. Why stop and stare? There are enough corpses.'

After another night in the meadow they walked at first light. On and on they walked, out into the country, one foot before the other, the stick to help Anton. Sometimes Zoraya began to tell him something about Johannes as she had known him, but he was too depleted to ask more and she gave up. His one thought was to find his son before his strength gave out.

A pale sun rose through ebony branches. Occasionally a clearing revealed the dense column of smoke still rising from the city. All around there was only silence, that stillness of frozen field and forest, of wintered ash and elm, leafless hedgerows, quiet of creeping fox and hibernating badger.

A farmer in a truck stopped and asked if they wanted a lift. They climbed on.

'You've come from the city, my friend?'

'I lost my wife.'

'I'm sorry. We live in the worst of times.'

The farmer drove on. Eventually he said, 'What did we do to deserve this?'

'Everything. We deserved it all right.'

The farmer wasn't sure about that and glanced suspiciously at Zoraya. It was only then that he seemed to notice her foreign appearance. He clammed up.

Anton told him where they were heading.

'There's nobody there, in that part of the forest. It's completely untended, a wilderness. I'll take you near, then you'll be on your own.'

The truck bumped down the frozen track. Snow lay in patches where clumps of withered grass and brambles had shaded the ground from the sun of recent days. The forest thickened as they pressed on.

At last they stopped.

'I'll drop you here. This track is unpassable by vehicle, blocked by fallen trees. But if you can follow it eventually you'll come out on the other side of the forest.'

They started out. It was more dank and overgrown here than in the parts Anton had traversed with Werner. He still had his torch but the battery was running low. They stumbled about in the murk, Anton beating the undergrowth with his stick. The trees echoed with his hoarse cry.

'Johannes! Johannes! We're here. Where are you?'

Zoraya too called out, 'Ali, I'm here. It's me, Zoraya. Come out.'

In time they lost the track altogether. The day was ending. They still had a few scraps of food left.

'Johannes! Come! You're there. I know it.'

'Ali! Ali!'

In the deep twilight something moved a little way off. Twigs cracked and branches creaked but it was hard to say where.

Then they heard it.

'Hello...'

'What?'

A man's voice, mysteriously enclosing them, echoing between the trees. It could have come from anywhere. Anton straightened himself and careered forward, stick raised.

'Wait,' called Zoraya. 'Where are you going? We don't know where...'

But Anton was sure, and determined. 'Hey! Hey! Stop!'

He beat his way through, sending dead leaves flying.

'Wait, for God's sake! Johannes!'

Again, only the silence and deepening dark of the forest.

'We're being watched,' whispered Zoraya. 'I'm certain.'

'Where?'

'There! Through there.'

Anton lunged forward again. Coming to a clearing he started to run.

Crash! He tripped on a root. The world turned upside-down in an instant. He was flat on the ground. Had his head hit a stone? It hurt enough.

'Dear God, what now?' He closed his eyes. Zoraya ran towards him and bent down.

'Oh, in the name of Allah. Here, let me help you.'

She was felt his forehead, loosened his top button.

Branches parting. A cough.

Zoraya looked up. A shadow loomed near. Grabbing Anton's torch, she shone the beam into the face.

Her heart stopped. She could not speak.

'Ali,' she said at last.

'Zoraya,' he breathed, his hand reaching forward.

'Yes, it's me, Ali.' She collected herself quickly. 'But this is no time for a touching reunion. Help me attend to your father.'

Johannes bent down. 'Father,' he whispered. 'I'm here. It's me, Johannes.'

The old man was breathing hard. He struggled to speak, tried and gave up several times.

'I have missed you,' he murmured at last. 'Sweet boy. You can never know.'

'We've found each other at last, Father.'

Johannes turned to Zoraya. 'We must get him to my place. It's near.'

‘How can we move him?’

‘We must try.’

They half-dragged, half-carried the old man. It was a big effort for both of them, especially getting him through the tiny door of Johannes’s bunker. Once inside they made him warm and comfortable, but his heart and lungs were fatally weakened. He was fading.

The hours passed and the old man slipped in and out of consciousness. Awkwardness vanished and Johannes and Zoraya started to talk in low voices. In time, breaking off, they gazed into each other’s eyes, stroked each other, finally leant forward and kissed.

‘Life is full of ironies,’ said Zoraya. ‘If I hadn’t come back here to see a dying father who hardly deserved such loyalty, I would never have seen you again. But here I am in this strange place of safety.’ She looked round the cramped space.

‘How did you create this, Ali?’ she whispered with the fading old man lying near. ‘I must say, it sums you up.’

‘What do you mean?’

‘You’re a survivor. When humanity has destroyed itself, there’ll just be you left in a hole in the ground.’

‘At Omdurman you and the flute were my lifesavers. The flute has gone – though I did pick one up to play folk music in Ireland a few years ago. You were gone. Then I really was on my own.’

Anton opened his eyes. ‘Johannes... you’re still here...’

‘Yes Father, I’m here.’

The old man spoke with great effort. ‘I waited... Johannes... I looked… I went everywhere…’

‘I know, Father.’

There was a long pause.

‘When you were a boy... I can see you now… fair boy… scamp… in the railway carriage… sitting for Stefan’s portrait… asleep on the cart while we… were… full of ourselves… So clever, we knew nothing…you stepped down to the tunnel… never saw you again… Is it you?'

Johannes returned Anton's searching look. Hearts beating, eye and eye together. Knowledge, wonder, incomprehension.

'Yes, it's me.'

Johannes told him in brief some of his story. Since he had written it down lately it came easily to him – the orphanage, Cairo, Aswan, life on the Nile, his wandering years, return to the Colony. Lastly this, his home in the forest. Zoraya was the thread.

'And now you have brought her back to me, Father. I lost her, just as earlier I lost you and Mother.'

Zoraya tenderly watched father and son.

'My poor boy,' whispered Anton.

'Poor you and Mother.'

'Come closer, my boy…'

Johannes took the big man in his arms. It was awkward but he managed to find a comfortable position.

'Tell me more stories, son.'

'Very well, Father. I went to lots of places. You could say I've seen the world. I can tell you about the great wheels of Hama… the Mausoleum of a prince in Persia… all the coloured brick towers of Persia, Afghanistan. Then over the other side there's the Atlantic crashing on to the dark rocks of the west, Camelot and Lyonesse, the twelve peaks of Connemara.'

'The wheels... my boy…Were you there? At Hama? I saw a picture once. I always wanted…'

He smiled and closed his eyes.

'He can go now, Ali,' Zoraya murmured at length. 'All is well with him.'

A little later Anton breathed his last. They crossed his arms over his chest and sat in silence. Zoraya took Johannes's hand and looked into his eyes.

'Dear man… Now you've found your father, you've lost him.'

'Yes.'

They held each other. Just then it was too sad for further words.

The next day, in weak winter sunshine, they dug a grave in a glade a little way off. It took a couple of hours, the earth was so hard. Dragging the large body down into the hole, they arranged it tidily and covered it over.

In the weeks to come Johannes and Zoraya settled into a new life together. It was one of great hardship – Zoraya hated having no change of clothes – but they were full of hope. When spring came, they strolled hand-in-hand in the forest. The sun shone strongly. Trees burst into leaf. The forest was filled with song. They made love in the cramped bunker, or more often lying on a bed of old leaves on the forest floor.

Often they sat by the grave. They made a memorial of stones and logs, and replenished the flowers from spring abundance, primroses, violets, daffodils and fruit blossoms.

Sometimes on warm nights, unable to sleep from excitement and wonder, Johannes left Zoraya. With the moon above, he crouched down over the man buried in the earth now moist from spring rains. 'Father,' he whispered, 'you hadn't changed, you know. I did remember you... Are you at peace now? Where are you?'

He would think about his brother too. Zoraya had given him an impression of Werner from her brief meeting the night the bombs fell. 'He seemed a nervous person,' she had said. 'not at ease with himself.' Johannes added this to his own impression. He pondered the memory of the artist narrowing his eyes at his mural, then rushing to get away. He grieved for the wasted opportunity.

'He was agitated – just fixed on his mural and then thinking about not being late for some Nazi cocktail party. If only he had stopped…'

Johannes accepted that Werner had died in the firestorm, certain he would have come looking for him if it were not so. Mentally he buried his brother with his father in the forest grave.

At last Johannes and Zoraya saw soldiers in unfamiliar uniforms on the roads and knew that it was over.

Passing refugees glimpsed Johannes crouched over the grave, whispering, silvered by the light of the moon. They peered through the trees. Were they imagining him? Was he a ghost?

~

Johannes Gustavus, also known as Ali, has been a ghost to many for most of his life. But now he lives in the love of a woman, the widow Zoraya, his childhood sweetheart miraculously returned to him.

As resourceful as when they fled Omdurman with a flute and little else, Ali and Zoraya plan their route back to Aswan. They hope to find their way south through Austria to the Adriatic and ply the waters with the wind of freedom in their hair. The blue Mediterranean, then the mighty Nile.

'We will arrive at Elephantine Island by felucca from Luxor,' says Zoraya. 'No other way is possible.'

They picture the greetings of her children and grandchildren. They hope the spirit of Massoud will bless them.

'He was as much a father to me as a husband,' says Zoraya. 'If I believed in the afterlife I would say he is looking down and smiling on my happiness. He was not a jealous man.'

At midsummer they leave the forest. They head first for the charred wilderness that was once Dresden. Zoraya finds the block where she lived. It is blackened rubble.

Town by town they meet further devastation. They pick their way through to the American sector and learn where to find the soup kitchens and temporary camps. Over the border in Austria they look for work. Progress is slow but by the following spring they are ready to head on further south.

As they descend from the Tyrol, the Adriatic lies brilliant in the blinding southern sun. They seek the shade. Zoraya pulls a fig from a tree and offers it to Johannes before taking another for herself.

‘Do you ever feel that our adventure is only just beginning?’ says Johannes. ‘For instance we could just stay here for a while.’

‘It’s a lovely spot and I love figs but I must get back to my children.’

He doesn’t protest. Compared with where he’s been he’s close to heaven anyway.

‘Right, let’s keep on then.’

They come to a road. ‘We can turn left for Trieste or right for Venice. Surely we can get a boat from either. Do you have a preference?’

‘I’ve always wanted to see Venice.’

‘Me too.’

~

A gondola slips under the Bridge of Sighs and heads out across the Basin of St Mark’s towards the asylum island where some years before, Stefan Lehmann, painter of Johannes’s boyhood portrait, perfected his art. The portrait is no more, smashed to pieces by the late Anton Gustavus.

Johannes and Zoraya know nothing of the connection. They have asked the gondolier to take them to the asylum island on a whim.

They start out in sunshine but as they approach the island, a mist descends. The island seems deserted. There is no sign of life in the buildings, the grounds are deserted. A bell tolls.

‘Where are the mad people?’

‘I can’t see anyone.’

‘They must be there. Listen to the bell. Who would ring a bell for no one?’

Rocked by the pull of the gondolier’s oar, they peer through the mist at the lines of blank windows. Johannes imagines the inmates trapped in the dormitories, sedated or gagged. The gondola comes to rest, swaying gently, the wavelets clicking against the hull.

Johannes has no words for what he feels. It is as if his past life lies behind the window panes.

'No, no one is there. They've closed it, you can tell.'

A little boy wanders from room to deserted room. The bell-rope hangs from the ceiling. He tugs at it again and again. The gong booms across the dark sea. No one hears. No one comes.

A single tear forms in the watching man's eye. Slowly it dries on his cheek. The gondola rocks. The wavelets knock the sides.

Zoraya touches his arm. They exchange a glance and he turns to the gondolier. 'It's enough. Take us home now, please.'

The black craft bears them silently away.

Acknowledgements

My heartfelt thanks go to all who have helped me with this book. They notably include Fay Bartram, Jacob Bartram, Pamela Bartram, Peter Bartram, Tracy Chevalier, Tessa Dalley, Ora Dresner, James Greene, Nina Killham, Arran Olivares Whitaker, Dale Reynolds, Angela Royston, Robert Royston and Wendy Toole.

I would also like to thank everyone at, or connected with Alliance Publishing Press for their enthusiasm and efficiency in bringing the book to publication.

Lightning Source UK Ltd.
Milton Keynes UK
UKOW06f2341210116

266844UK00012B/110/P